Augustine David Crake

Edwy the fair or the first chronicle of Æscendune

A tale of the days of Saint Dunstan

Augustine David Crake

Edwy the fair or the first chronicle of Æscendune
A tale of the days of Saint Dunstan

ISBN/EAN: 9783742856661

Manufactured in Europe, USA, Canada, Australia, Japa

Cover: Foto ©Andreas Hilbeck / pixelio.de

Manufactured and distributed by brebook publishing software
(www.brebook.com)

Augustine David Crake

Edwy the fair or the first chronicle of Æscendune

EDWY THE FAIR

OR THE

FIRST CHRONICLE OF ÆSCENDUNE

A Tale of the Days of Saint Dunstan

BY THE REV.

A. D. CRAKE, B.A.

AUTHOR OF 'HISTORY OF THE CHURCH UNDER THE ROMAN EMPIRE,'
'ALFGAR THE DANE,' ETC

"Facilis descensus Averno;
Noctes atque dies patet atri ianua Ditis;
Sed revocare gradum superasque evadere ad auras,
Hoc opus, hic labor est."—VIRGIL, *Æneid*, vi. 126.

SECOND EDITION

RIVINGTONS

London, Oxford, and Cambridge

MDCCCLXXX

PREFACE.

It has been the aim of the Author, in a series of
original tales told to the senior boys of a large school,
to illustrate interesting or difficult passages of Church
History by the aid of fiction. Two of these tales—
" Æmilius," a tale of the Decian and Valerian perse-
cutions; and " Evanus," a tale of the days of Constantine—he has already published, and desires gratefully
to acknowledge the kindness with which they have
been received.

He is thus encouraged to submit another attempt
to the public, having its scene of action in our own
land, although in times very dissimilar to our own;
and for its object, the illustration of the struggle between the regal and ecclesiastical powers in the days
of the ill-fated and ill-advised King Edwy.

Scarcely can one find a schoolboy who has not read
the touching legend of Edwy and Elgiva—for it is
little more than a legend in most of its details; and
which of these youthful readers has not execrated the
cruelty of the Churchmen who separated those unhappy lovers? while the tragical story of the fate of
the hapless Elgiva has been the theme of many a poet
and even historian, who has accepted the tale as if it

were of as undoubted authenticity as the Reform
Bill.

The writer can well remember the impression the
tale made upon his youthful imagination, and the dis-
like, to use a mild word, with which he ever viewed
the character of the great statesman and ecclesiastic of
the tenth century, Dunstan, until a wider knowledge
of history and a more accurate judgment came with
maturer years; and testimonies to the ability and
genius of that monk, who had been the moving spirit
of his age, began to force themselves upon him.

Lord Macaulay has well summed up the relative
positions of Church and State in that age in the following words: " It is true that the Church had been
deeply corrupted by superstition, yet she retained
enough of the sublime theology and benevolent morality of her early days to elevate many intellects, and
to purify many hearts.   That the sacerdotal order
should encroach on the functions of the chief magistrate, would in our time be a great evil.   But that
which in an age of good government is an evil, may
in an age of grossly bad government be a blessing.
It is better that men should be governed by priest-
craft than by brute violence; *by such a prelate as
Dunstan*, than by such a warrior as Penda."

The Church was indeed the salt of the earth, even
if the salt had somewhat lost its savour; it was the
only power which could step in between the tyrant
and his victim, which could teach the irresponsible
great—irresponsible to man—their responsibility to the
great and awful Being whose creatures they were;
And again, it was then the only home of civilisation

and learning. It has been well said that for the learning of this age to vilify the monks and monasteries of the mediæval period, is for the oak to revile the acorn from which it sprang.

The overwhelming realisation of these facts, the determination to set up the dominion of truth and justice which they held to be identical with that of the Church, as *that* was identical with the kingdom of God, supplies the key to the lives and characters of such men as Ambrose, Cyril, Dunstan, and Becket. They each came in collision with the civil power; but Ambrose against Justina or even Theodosius, Cyril against Orestes, Dunstan against Edwy, Becket against Henry Plantagenet — each represented, in a greater or less degree, the cause of religion, nay of humanity, against its worst foes, tyranny or moral corruption.

Yet not one of these great men was without his faults; this is only to say he was human; but more may be admitted—personal motives *would* mix themselves with nobler emotions. Self *would* assert her fatal claims, and great mistakes were sometimes made by those who would have forfeited their lives rather than have committed them, had they known what they were doing. Yet, on the whole, their cause was that of God and man, and they fought nobly. Shall we asperse their memories because they " had this treasure in earthen vessels "?

The tale itself is intended to depict what the writer believes to be the true relative positions of Edwy and the great ecclesiastic; therefore he will not attempt to deal with the subject here. It will be noticed, however, that he has shorn the narrative of the dread catastrophe with which it terminated in all the histories of our childhood. Scarcely any writer has made such wise research into the history of this period as Mr. E. A. Freeman, and the author has adopted his conclusions upon this point. With him he has therefore admitted the marriage of Edwy with Elgiva, although it was an uncanonical marriage beyond all doubt, and has given her the title of queen, which she bore in a document preserved by Lappenburg. But, in agreement with the same authority, the writer feels most happy to be able to reject the story of Elgiva's supposed tragical death. All sorts of stories are told by later writers, utterly contradictory and confused, of a woman killed by the Mercians in their revolt. This could not be Elgiva, for she was not divorced till the rebellion was over; and even the sad tale that she was seized by the officers of Odo, and branded to disfigure her beauty, rests on no good authority. In spite of the reluctance with which men relinquish a touching tragedy, the calumny should be banished from the pages of historians; and it is painful to see it repeated, as if of undoubted authenticity, in a recent popular history for children by one of the greatest of modern novelists.

Edwy's character has cost the writer much thought. He has endeavoured to paint him faithfully—not so bad as all the monastic writers of the succeeding period (the only writers with few exceptions) describe him; but still such a youth as the circumstances under which he became placed would probably have made him :—capable of sincere attachment, brave, and devoted to his friends, yet careless of all religious obligations; bitterly hostile to the Church, that is to Christianity, for the terms were then synonymous; and reckless of obligations, or of the sanctity of truth and justice.

His measures against S. Dunstan, as they are related in the tale, have the authority of history; although it is needless to say that the agents are in part fictitious characters. The writer's object has been to subordinate fiction to history, and never to contradict historic fact; if he has failed in this intention, it has been his misfortune rather than his fault; for he has had recourse to all such authorities as lay in his reach.[*] Especially, he is glad to find that the character he had conceived as Edwy's perfectly coincides with the description given by Palgrave in his valuable History of the Anglo-Saxons:—" Edwy was a youth of singular beauty, but vain, rash, petulant, profligate, and surrounded by a host of young courtiers, all bent on encouraging and emulating the vices of their master."

Another object of the tale has been to depict the trials and temptations, the fall and the recovery, of a lad fresh from a home full of religious influences, when thrown amidst the snares which abounded then as now. The motto, " Facilis descensus Averno," etc., epitomises the whole story.

In relating a tale of the days of S. Dunstan, the author has felt bound to give the religious colouring which actually prevailed in that day. He has found much authority and information in Johnson's Anglo-

---

[*] For authorities for his various statements the Author must beg to refer his readers to the notes at the end of the volume.

Saxon Canons, especially those of Elfric, probably contemporaneous with the tale. He has written in no controversial spirit, but with an honest desire to set forth the truth.

It may be objected that he has made all his characters speak in very modern English, and has not affected the archaisms commonly found in tales of the time. To this he would reply, that if the genuine language were preserved, it would be utterly unintelligible to modern Englishmen, and therefore he has thought it preferable to translate into the vernacular of to-day. The English which men spoke then was no more stilted or formal to them than ours is to us.

Although he has followed Mr. Freeman in the use of the terms English and Welsh, as far less likely to mislead than the terms Saxons and Britons, and far truer to history, yet he has not thought proper to follow the obsolete spelling of proper names; he has not, *e.g.*, spelt Edwy, Eadwig — or Elgiva, Ælfgifu. Custom has Latinised the appellations, and as he has rejected obsolete terms in conversation, he has felt it more consistent to reject these *more correct*, but less familiar, orthographies.

The title, "First Chronicle of Æscendune," has been adopted, because the tale here given is but the first of a series of tales which have been told, but not yet written, attaching themselves to the same family and locality at intervals of generations. Thus, the second illustrates the struggle between Edmund Ironside and Canute; the third, the Norman Conquest; etc. Their appearance in print must depend upon the indulgence extended to the present volume.

In conclusion, the writer dedicates this book with great respect to Mrs. Trevelyan, authoress of "Lectures upon the History of England;" whose first volume, years ago, first taught him to appreciate, in some degree, the character of S. Dunstan.

ALL SAINTS' SCHOOL, BLOXHAM,
Easter 1874.

CONTENTS.

CONTENTS.

CONTENTS. XV

CHAPTER I.

" THIS IS THE FOREST PRIMEVAL."

IT was a lovely eventide of the sunny month of May, and
the declining rays of the sun penetrated the thick foliage
of an old English forest, lighting up in chequered pattern
the velvet sward thick with moss, and casting uncertain
rays as the wind shook the boughs. Every bush seemed
instinct with life, for April showers and May sun had
united to force each leaf and spray into its fairest development, and the drowsy hum of countless insects told, as it
saluted the ears, the tale of approaching summer.

Two boys reclined upon the mossy bank beneath an
aged oak ; their dress, no less than their general demeanour,
denoted them to be the sons of some substantial thane.
They were clad in hunting costume : leggings of skin
over boots of untanned leather protected their limbs from
thorn or brier, and over their under garments they wore
tunics of a dull green hue, edged at the collar and cuffs
with brown fur, and fastened by richly ornamented belts :
their bows lay by their sides, while quivers of arrows
were suspended to their girdles, and two spears, such
as were used in the chase of the wild boar, lay by them on
the grass. They had the same fair hair, which, untouched
by the shears, hung negligently around neck and shoulder ;
the same blue eyes added an indescribable softness to the
features ; they had the same well-knit frames and agile
movements, but yet there was a difference. The elder
seemed possessed of greater vivacity of expression ; but
although each well-strung muscle indicated physical prowess,
there was an uncertain expression in his glance and in the

play of his features, which suggested a yielding and somewhat vacillating character; while the younger lacking the full physical development, and somewhat of the engaging expression of his brother, had that calm and steady bearing which indicated present and future government of the passions.

"By Thor and Woden, Alfred, we shall be here all night. At what hour did that stupid churl Oscar say that the deer trooped down to drink?"

"Not till sunset, Elfric; and it wants half-an-hour yet; see, the sun is still high."

"I do think it is never going to set; here we have been hunting, hunting all the day, and got nothing for our pains."

"You forget the hare and the rabbit here."

"Toss them to the dogs. Here, Bran, you brute, take this hare your masters have been hunting all day, for your dinner;" and as he spoke he tossed the solitary victim of his own prowess in the chase to the huge wolf-hound, which made a speedy meal upon the hare, while Alfred threw the rabbit to the other of their two canine companions.

"I would almost as soon have lost this holiday, and spent the time with Father Cuthbert, to be bored by his everlasting talk about our duties, and forced to repeat 'hic, hæc, hoc,' till my head ached. What a long homily he preached us this morning—and then that long story about the saint." *

"You are out of spirits. Father Cuthbert's tales are not so bad after all: you seemed to like the legend he told us the other night."

"Yes, about our ancestor Sebbald and his glorious death; there was something in that tale worth hearing; it stirred the blood—none of your moping saints that Sebbald."

"I once heard another legend from Father Cuthbert, about the burning of Croyland Abbey, and how the abbot

* See Note A.—Homilies in the Anglo-Saxon Church.

stood, saying mass at the altar, without flinching or even turning his head, when the Danes, having fired the place, broke into the chapel.　Do you not think it wanted more bravery to do that in cold blood than to stand firm in all the excitement of a battle?"

"You are made to be a monk, Alfred, and I daresay, if you get the chance, will be a martyr, and get put in the calendar by-and-by.　I suppose they will keep your relics here in the priory church, and you will be S. Alfred of Æscendune; for me, I would sooner die as the old sea-kings loved to die, surrounded by heaps of slain, with my sword broken in my hand."

It was at this moment that their conversation was suddenly interrupted by a loud crashing of boughs in the adjacent underwood, a rush as of some wild beast, a loud cry in boyish tones—

"Help! help! the wolf! the wolf!"

Elfric jumped up in an instant, and rushed forward heedless of danger, followed closely by his younger brother, who was scarcely less eager to render immediate assistance.

The cries for help became more and more piercing, as if some pressing danger menaced the utterer.　Elfric, who, in spite of his flippant speech, was by no means destitute of keen sympathies and self-devotion, hurried forward, fearless of danger, bounding through thicket and underwood, until, arriving upon a small clearing, the whole scene flashed upon him.

A huge grey wolf, wounded and bleeding, was about to rush for the second time upon a youth in hunting costume, whose broken spear, broken in the first encounter with the beast he had disturbed, seemed to deprive him of all chance of success in the desperate encounter evidently impending.　His trembling limbs showed his extreme apprehension, and the sweat stood in huge drops on his forehead; his eyes were fixed upon the beast as if he were fascinated, while the shaft of his spear, presented feebly against the coming onslaught, showed that he had lost his self-possession, for he neglected the bow and arrows which were slung at his side—if indeed there was time to use them.

The beast sprang, but as he did so another spear was stoutly presented to meet him, and he literally impaled himself in his eager spring on the weapon of Elfric.

Still, such was his weight that the boy fell backward beneath the mighty rush, and such the tenacity of life that, though desperately wounded, even to death, the beast sought the prostrate lad with teeth and claws, in frantic fury, until a blow from the hunting-knife, which Elfric well knew how to use, laid the wolf lifeless at his side.

Breathless, but not severely injured, he rose from the ground covered with blood ; his garments torn, his face reddened by exertion, and paused a moment, while he seemed to strive to repress the wild beatings of his heart, which bounded as if it would burst its prison.

But far more exhausted was the other combatant, yet scarcely so much by exertion as by fear, of which he still bore the evident traces. After a few moments he broke the silence, and his words seemed incoherent.

" Where is my horse ? the beast threw me—I wish the wolves may get *him*—I fear you are hurt ; not much, I hope ; where can those serfs be ? *Fine* vassals, to desert their master in peril. I'll have them hung. But, by S. Cuthbert, you are all covered with blood."

" 'Tis that of the wolf, then, for I have scarcely a scratch : one of the beast's claws ripped up my sleeve, and the skin with it ; that was all he could do before he felt the cold steel between his ribs."

" Not a moment too soon, or he would have killed you before we could interfere ; why, as you rolled together, I I could hardly see which was boy and which was wolf. But where's my horse ? did you see a white horse rush past you ?"

" We heard a rush as of some wild animal."

" Wild enough. I was riding through the glade, and my attendants were on in front, when we stumbled on this wolf, crouched under that thicket. The horse started so violently that it threw me almost upon the monster you have killed."

Here the speaker paused, and blew impatient blasts upon a horn which had been slung round his neck. They were soon answered, and some attendants, dressed in semi-hunting costume, made their appearance with haste and confusion, which showed their apprehensions.

"Guthred! Eadmer! Why did you get so far away from me? I might have been killed. Look at this monstrous wolf; why, its teeth are dreadful. It broke my spear; and would have had me down, but for *this*—this youth. I forgot, I haven't asked to whom I am indebted? Aren't you two brothers?"

"Our father is the Thane of Æscendune. His hall is not far from here. Will you not go home with us? we have plenty of room for you and yours."

"To be sure I will. Æscendune? I have heard the name: I can't remember where. Have you horses?"

"No; we were hunting on foot, and expecting to let fly our shafts at some deer. May I ask, in return, the name of our guest?"

Before the youth could answer, one of the attendants strode forward, and with an air of importance replied, "You are about to receive the honour of a visit from the future lord of Britain, Prince Edwy."

"Keep your lips closed till I give you leave to open them, Guthred. You may leave me to announce myself. I shall be only too glad to go with you both; and these two huntsmen deserve to be left in the forest to the mercy of your wolves."

Somewhat startled to find that they had saved the future Basileus or King of Britain—the hope of the royal line of Cerdic—the brothers led their guest through the darkening forest until the distant light of a clearing appeared in the west, and they emerged from the shadow of the trees upon the brow of a gentle hill.

Below them lay the castle (if such it should be called) of their father the Thane of Æscendune. Utterly unlike the castellated buildings which, at a later period, formed the dwellings of the proud Norman nobility, it was a low irregular building, the lower parts of which were of stone, and the upper portions, when there was a second story, of thick timber from the forest.

A river, from which the evening mist was slowly rising, lay beyond, and supplied water to a moat which surrounded the edifice, for in those troublous times few country dwellings lacked such necessary protection. The memory of the Danish invasions was too recent; the marauders of either nation still lurked in the far recesses of the forest, and plundered the Saxon inhabitant or the Danish settler indiscriminately, as occasion served.

On the inner side of the moat a strong palisade of timber completed the defence. One portal, opening upon a drawbridge, formed the sole apparent means of ingress or egress.

Passing the drawbridge unquestioned, the boys entered the courtyard, around which the chief apartments were grouped. Before them a flight of stone steps led to the great hall where all the members of the community took their meals in common, and where, around the great fire, they wiled away the slow hours of a winter evening.

On each side of the great hall stood the bowers, as the small dormitories were called, furnished very simply for the use of the higher domestics with small round tables, common stools, and beds in recesses like boxes or cupboards. Such were commonly the only sleeping chambers, but at Æscendune, as generally in the halls of the rich, a wide staircase conducted to a gallery above, from each side of which opened sleeping and sitting apartments allotted to the use of the family. It was only in the houses of the wealthy that such an upper floor was found.

On the right hand, as they entered the courtyard, stood the private chapel of the household, where mass was said by the chaplain, to whom allusion has been already made, as the first duty of the day, and where each night generally saw the household again assembled for compline or evening prayers.*   On the left hand were domestic offices.

Upon the steps of his hall stood Ella, the Thane of Æscendune, the representative of a long line of warlike ancestors, who had occupied the soil since the Saxon conquest of Mercia.

He was clad in a woollen tunic reaching to the knee, over which a cloak fastened by a clasp of gold was loosely thrown; and his feet were clad in black pointed boots, while strips of painted leather were wound over red stockings from the knee to the ankle.

"You are late, my sons," he said, "and I perceive you have brought us a visitor.   He is welcome."

"Father," said Elfric, in a voice somewhat expressive of awe, "it is Prince Edwy!"

The thane had in his earlier days been at court, and had known the murdered Edmund, the royal father of his guest, intimately.   It was not without emotion, therefore, that he welcomed the son to his home, and saluted him with that manly yet reverential homage their relative positions required of him.

"Welcome, thrice welcome, my prince," he said, "to these humble halls."   He added, with some emotion, "I could think the royal Edmund stood before me, as I knew him while yet myself a youth."

The domestics, who had assembled, gazed upon their visitor with country curiosity, yet were not wanting in rude but expressive courtesy; and soon he was conducted to the best chamber the house afforded, where change of raiment and every comfort within the reach of his host was provided, while the cooks were charged to make sumptuous additions to the approaching supper.

* See Note B.—Services of the Church.

CHAPTER II.

THE earlier fortunes of the house of Æscendune must here obtrude themselves upon the notice of the reader, in order that he may more easily comprehend the subsequent pages of our veritable history.

Sebbald, the remote ancestor of the family, was amongst the earliest Saxon conquerors of Mercia. He fell in battle with the Britons, or Welshmen as our ancestors called them, leaving sons valiant as their sire, to whom were given the fertile lands lying between the river Avon and the mighty midland forests, to which they gave the name " Æscendune."

They had held their own for three hundred years with varying fortunes ; once or twice home and hearth were desolated by the fierce tide of Danish invasion, but the wars subsided, and the old family resumed its position, amidst the joy of their dependants and serfs, to whom they were endeared by a thousand memories of past benefits.

But a generation only had passed since the shadow of a great woe fell on the family of Æscendune.

Offa, who was then the thane, had two sons, Oswald the elder, and Ella the younger, with whom our readers are already acquainted.

The elder possessed few of the family virtues save brute courage. He was ever rebellious, even in boyhood, and arrived at man's estate in the midst of unsettled times of war and tumult. Weary of the restraints of home, he joined a band of Danish marauders, and shared their victories, enriching himself with the spoils of his own countrymen.   Thus he remained an outlaw, for his father disowned him in consequence of his crime, until, fighting against his own people in the great battle of Brunanburgh,[*] where Athelstane so gloriously conquered the allied Danes, Scots, and Welsh, he was taken prisoner.

The victor king sat in judgment upon the recreant, surrounded by his chief nobility and vassal kings.   The guilt of the prisoner was evident, nay undenied, and the respect in which his sire was held alone delayed the doom of a cruel death from being pronounced upon him.

While the council yet deliberated, Offa appeared amongst them, and, like a second Brutus, took his place amongst his peers.   Disclaiming all personal interest in the matter, he sternly proposed that the claims of justice should be satisfied.

Yet they hesitated to shed Oswald's blood: the alternative they adopted was perhaps not more merciful—although a common doom in those times.   They selected a crazy worm-eaten boat, and sent the criminal to sea, without sail, oar, or rudder, with a loaf of bread and cruse of water, the wind blowing freshly from off the land.

Oswald was never heard of again; but after his supposed death, information was brought to his father that the outlaw had been married to a Danish woman, and had left a son—an orphan—for the mother died in childbirth.

Offa resolved to seek the boy, and to adopt him, as if in reparation for the past.   The effort he had made had cost him a bitter pang, and the father's heart was well-nigh broken.   For a time the inquiries were unsuccessful.   It was discovered that the mother was dead, that she had died before the tragedy, but not a word could be learned respecting the boy, and many had begun to doubt his existence, when, after years had elapsed, one of the executioners of the cruel doom deposed on his deathbed that a boy of some ten summers had appeared on the beach, had called the victim "father," and had so persistently

[*] See Note C.—Battle of Brunanburgh.

entreated to share his doom, that they had allowed him to do so, but had concealed the fact, rightly fearing blame, if not punishment. The priest who had attended his dying bed, and heard his last confession, bore the tidings to Offa at the penitent's desire. The old thane never seemed to lift up his head again : the sacrifice his sense of duty had exacted from him had been too great for a heart naturally full of domestic affection, and he sank and died after a few months in the arms of his younger and beloved son Ella.

The foundation of the neighbouring priory and church of S. Wilfred had been the consolation of his later years, but the work was only half completed at his death. It was carried on with equal zeal by Ella, now the Thane of Æscendune.

He married Edith, the daughter of a rich thane of Wessex, and the marriage proved a most happy one.

Sincerely religious, after the fashion of their day, they honoured God with their substance, enriched the church of S. Wilfred, where the dust of the aged Offa awaited the resurrection of the just, and continued the labour of building the priory. Day after day they were constant in their attendance at mass and evensong, and strove to live as foster-parents to their dependants and serfs.

The chief man in his hundred, Ella acted as reeve or magistrate, holding his court for the administration of justice each month, and giving such just judgment as became one who had the fear of God before him. No appeal was ever made from him to the ealdorman (earl) or scir-gerefa (sheriff) ; and the wisdom and mercy of his rule were universally renowned.

His land was partly cultivated by his own theows, who were in those days slaves attached to the soil, and partly let out to free husbandmen (or ceorls) who owed their lord rent in kind or in money, and paid him, as " his men," feudal service.

Around his hospitable board the poor of the district found sustenance, while work was made for all in draining meres, mending roads, building the priory, or in the various agricultural labours of the year.

In the first year of King Edmund the lady Edith presented her lord with his first-born son, to whom in baptism they gave the name Elfric, and a year later Alfred was born, and named after the great king. One daughter, named Edgitha, completed the fruits of their happy union, and in their simple fashion they strove to train their children in the fear of the Lord.

We will now resume the thread of our story.

It was now the hour of eventide, and the time for "laying the board" drew near. From forest and field came in ceorl and theow, hanging up their weapons or agricultural implements around the lower end of the hall. Meanwhile the domestics brought in large tressels, and then huge heavy boards, which they arranged so as to form the dining-table, shaped like the letter T, the upper portion being furnished with the richest dainties for the family and their guest, the lower with simpler fare for the dependants.

A wild boar caught in the forest formed the chief dish, and was placed at the upper end, while mutton and beef, dressed in various ways, flanked it on either side.

The thane, Ella, occupied the central seat at the high table: his chair, rudely carved, had borne the weight of his ancestors before him; on his left hand was seated the once lovely Edith. Age had deprived her of her youthful beauty, but not of the sweet expression which told of her gentleness and purity of heart; they had left their impress on each line of her speaking countenance; and few left her presence unimpressed with respect and esteem.

On his right hand sat Prince Edwy, "Edwy the fair" men called him, and right well he deserved the name. His face was one which inspired interest at a glance: his large blue eyes, his golden hair which floated over his shoulders, his sweet voice, his graceful bearing, all united to impress the beholders.

Elfric, Alfred, and their sister Edgitha, completed the company at the high table.

The hungry crowd of ceorls and serfs, who were, as we have said, fresh from field or forest, sat at the lower table, which was spread with huge joints of roasted meat, loaves of bread, wedges of cheese, piles of cabbage or other vegetables, rolls or coils of broiled eels, and huge pieces of boiled pork or bacon.

Around the table sat the hounds and other dogs, open-jawed, waiting such good luck as they might hope to receive at the hands of their masters, while many "loaf-eaters," as the serfs were called who fed at their master's table, stood with the dogs, or sat on the rush-strewn floor, for want of room at the board.

It was marvellous to see how the food disappeared, as hand after hand was stretched out to the dishes, in the absence of forks—a modern invention—and huge horns of ale helped the meat downwards.

Game, steaks of beef and venison on spits, were handed round. The choicer joints were indeed reserved for the upper board, but profusion was the rule everywhere throughout the hall, and there was probably not a serf, nay, not even a dog, whose appetite was not fully satisfied before the end of the feast.

The prince seemed thoroughly to have recovered his spirits, somewhat damped perhaps before by his adventure with the wolf, and exerted his talents to make himself agreeable. He had seen life on an extended scale, young as he was, and his anecdotes of London and the court, if a little wild, were still interesting. Elfric and Alfred listened to his somewhat random talk, with that respect boys ever pay to those who have seen more of the wide world than themselves — a respect perhaps heightened by the high rank of their princely guest, who was, however, only a month or two older than Elfric.

As they heard of the marvels of London, and of the court, home and its attractions seemed to become dim by comparison, and Elfric especially longed to share such happiness.

Their father seemed to wish to change the conversation, as he asked the prince whether he had been long in Mercia. Edwy replied, "Nay, my host; this is almost my first day of perfect freedom, and I only left London, and my uncle the king, a few days back. Dunstan has gone down to Glastonbury, for which the Saints be thanked, and I am released for a few days from poring over the musty old manuscripts to which he dooms me."

"It is well, my prince, that you should have a preceptor so well qualified to instruct you in the arts your great ancestor King Alfred so nobly adorned."

"Ah yes, Alfred," said Edwy, yawning; "but you know we can't all be saints or heroes like him: for my part, I sometimes wish he had never lived."

The astonished looks of the company seemed to demand further explanation.

"Because it is always, 'Alfred did this,' and 'Alfred did that.' If I am tired of 'hic, hæc, hoc,' I am told Alfred was never weary; if I complain of a headache, Dunstan says Alfred never complained of pain or illness, but bore all with heroic fortitude, and all the rest of it. If I want a better dinner than my respected uncle gives us on fast-days in the palace, I am told Alfred never ate anything beyond a handful of parched corn on such days; if I lose my temper, I am told Alfred never lost his; and so on, till I get sick of his name; and here it greets me in the woods of Mercia."

"I crave pardon, my liege," said Ella, who hardly knew whether to smile or frown at the sarcastic petulance of his guest, who went on with a sly smile—

"And now old Dunstan does not know where I am. He left me with a huge pile of books in musty Latin, or crabbed English, and I had to read *this* and to write *that*, as if I were no prince, but a scrivener, and had to get my living by my pen; but as soon as he was gone I had a *headache*, and persuaded my venerable uncle the king, through the physician, that I needed change of air."

"But what will Dunstan say?"

"Oh, he must fight it out with Sigebert the leech, and Sigebert knows which side his bread is buttered."

The whole tone of Edwy indicated plainly that the headache was but a pretence, but he spoke with such sly simplicity that the boys could not help joining in his contagious laughter; sympathising, doubtless, in his love of a holiday in the woods.

"Your headache is not gone yet, I trust, my prince," said Elfric.

"Why?" said Edwy, turning his eyes upon him with a smile.

"Because we have splendid woods near here for hunting, and I must have (he whispered these words into Edwy's ear) a headache too."

Edwy quite understood the request conveyed in these words, and turning to the old thane requested him to allow his boys to join the sport on the morrow as a kind of bodyguard, adding some very complimentary words on the subject of Elfric's courage shown in the rescue that afternoon.

"Why, yes," said the old thane, "I have always tried to bring up the boys so as to fear neither man nor beast, and Elfric did indifferently well in the tussle. So he has earned a holiday for himself and brother, with Father Cuthbert's leave," and Ella turned to the ecclesiastic.

"They are good boys," said the priest, "only, my lord, Elfric is somewhat behind in his studies."

Elfric's looks expressed his contempt of the "studies," but he dared not express the feeling before his father.

"But I trust, my prince," said Ella, "that we shall not keep you from your duties at court. Dunstan is a severe, although a holy man."

"Oh, he is gone to have another encounter with the Evil One at Glastonbury, and is fashioning a pair of tongs for the purpose," said Edwy, alluding to the legend already current amongst the credulous populace ; " and I wish," he muttered, " the Evil One would get the best of it and fly away with him. But (in a louder tone) he cannot return for a month, which means a month's holiday for me."

Ella could interpose no further objection, although scarcely satisfied with the programme.

The conversation here became general. It turned upon the subject of hunting and war, and the enthusiasm of young Edwy quite captivated the thane, who seemed to see Edmund, the father of the young prince, before his eyes, as he had known him in his own impetuous youth. Dear, indeed, had that prince been to Ella, both before and after his elevation to the throne, and as he heard the sweet boyish voice of Edwy, his thoughts were guided by memory to that ill-omened feast at Pucklechurch, where the vindictive outlaw Leolf had murdered his king! The sword of Ella had been amongst those which avenged the crime on the murderer, but they could not call back the vital spark which had fled. " Edmund the Magnificent," as they loved to call him, was dead.*

So, as Ella listened, he could hardly help condoning the wild speeches of the young prince in deference to the memory of the past.

And now they removed the festive board from the hall, while kneeling serfs offered basin and towel to the thane and his guest to wash their hands. Wine began to circulate freely in goblets of wood inlaid with gold or silver ; the clinking of cups, the drinking of healths and pledges opened the revel, cupbearers poured out the wine. The *glee-wood* (harp) was introduced, while pipes, flutes, and soft horns accompanied its strains. So they sang—

> How Æthelstane king,
> Of earls the lord,

---

* See Note D.—Murder of Edmund.

> To warriors the ring-giver
> Glory world-long
> Had won in the strife,
> By edge of the sword,
> At Brunanburgh.

And Ella—who had stood by his father's side in that dread field where Danes, Scots, and Welshmen, fled before the English sword—listened with enthusiasm, till he thought of his brother Oswald, when tears, unobserved, rolled down his cheeks. Not so with the boys. They had no secret sorrow to hide, and they listened like those whose young blood boils at the thought of mighty deeds, and longed to imitate them. And when the gleeman finished his lengthy flight of music and poesy, they applauded him till the roof rang again.

Song followed song, legend legend, the revelry grew louder, while the lady Edith, with her daughter, retired to their bower, where they employed their needles on delicate embroidery. A representation in bright colours of the consecration of the church of S. Wilfred occupied the hands of the little Edgitha, while her mother wove sacred pictures to serve as hangings for the sanctuary of the priory church.

But soon the tolling of the bell announced that it was the compline hour, nine o'clock, and that hour was never allowed to pass unobserved at Æscendune, but formed the termination of the labour or the feast, after which it was customary for the whole household to retire, as well they might who rose with the early dawn.

Neither was it passed by on this occasion, although the boys looked very disappointed, for they would fain have listened to song or legend till midnight, if not later.

"Come, my children," said the thane; "we must rise early, so let us all commit ourselves to the keeping of God and His holy angels, and seek our pillows."

So the whole party repaired to the chapel, where the

chaplain said the compline office or nightsong, after which Ella saluted his royal guest with reverent affection, and bestowed his paternal benediction upon his children. Then the whole party separated for the night.

The household was speedily buried in sleep, save the solitary sentinel who paced around the building. Not that danger was apprehended from any source, but precaution had become habitual in those days of turmoil. Occasionally the howl of the wolf was heard from the woods, and the sleepers half awoke, then dreamt of the chase as the night flew by.

CHAPTER III.

LEAVING HOME.

THE sun arose in a bright and cloudless sky on the follow-ing morning, and his first beams aroused every sleeper in the hall of Æscendune from his couch of straw, for softer material was seldom or never used for repose. Even the chamber in which the prince slept could not be called luxurious: the bed was in a box-like recess; its coverlets, worked richly by the fair hands of the ladies, who had little other occupation, covered a mattress which even modern school-boys would call rough and uncomfortable.

The wind played with the tapestry which represented the history of Joseph and his brethren, as it found its way in through crevices in the ill-built walls. There were two or three stools over which the thane's care for his guest had caused coverlets to be thrown; a round table of rough construction stood like a tripod on three legs, upon which stood the unwonted luxury of ewer and basin, for most people had to perform their ablutions at the nearest con-venient well or spring.

Leaving this chamber in good time, Prince Edwy acom-panied his new friends to the priory church, where they heard mass before the sun was high in the heavens, after which they returned to the hall to take a light breakfast before they sought the attractions of the chase in the forest. Full of life they mounted their horses, and galloped in the wild exuberance of animal spirits with their dogs through the leafy arches of the forest, startling the red deer, the

wolf, or the wild boar. Soon they roused a mighty individual of the latter tribe, who turned to bay, when the
boys dismounted and finished the affair with their boar-
spears, not without some personal danger, and the loss of a
couple of dogs. Onward again they swept, past leafy
glades of beech-trees, where the swineherd drove his half
tame charges, or where the woodcutters plied their toil, and
loaded their rude carts or hand-barrows with fuel for the
kitchen of the hall; past rookeries, where the birds made
the air lively by their noise; over brook, through the half-
dry marsh, until they came upon an old wolf, whom they
followed and slew for want of better game, not without a
desperate struggle, in which Elfric, ever the foremost, got
a much worse scratch than on the preceding day.

But how enjoyable the sport was, how sweet to breathe
the bright pure air of that May day; how grand to out-
strip the wind over the yielding turf, and at last to carry
home the trophies of their prowess, the scalp of the wolf,
the tusks of the boar, leaving the serfs to bring in the suc-
culent flesh of the latter, while the hawks and crows fed
upon the former. And then with what appetite they sat
down to their "noon-meat," taken, however, at the late
hour of three, after which they wandered down to the river
and angled for the trout which abounded in the clear stream.

The youthful reader will not wonder that such attractions sufficed to detain Edwy several days, during which he
was continually hunting in the adjacent forests, always
attended by Elfric, and sometimes by Alfred. To the elder
brother he seemed to have conceived a real liking, and
expressed great reluctance to part with him.

"Could you not return with me to court," he said,
"and relieve the tedium of old Dunstan's society? You cannot think what pleasures London affords; it *is* life there
indeed—it is true there are no forests like these, but then,
in the winter, when the country is so dreary, the town is
the place."

"My father will never consent to my leaving home,"

returned Elfric, who inwardly felt his heart was with the prince.

"We might overcome that. I am to have a page. You might be nominally my page, really my companion; and should I ever be king, you would find you had not served me in vain."

The idea had got such strong possession of the mind of Edwy, that he ventilated it the same night at the supper-table, but met with scant encouragement. Still he did not despair; for, as he told Elfric, the influence of his royal uncle, King Edred, might be hopefully exerted on their joint behalf.

"I mean to get you to town," he said. "I shall persuade my old uncle, who is more a monk than a king, that you are dreadfully pious, attached to monkish Latin, and all that sort of thing, so that he will long to get you to town, if it is only to set an example to me."

"But if he does not find that I answer his expectations?"

"Oh, it will be too late to alter then; you will be comfortably installed in the palace; and, between you and me, he is but old and feeble, and has always had a disease of some kind. I expect he will soon die, and then who will be king save Edwy, and who in England shall be higher than his friend Elfric?"

It was a brilliant prospect, as it seemed to boys of fifteen, for such was the mature age of the speakers.

Shortly after the last conversation, an express came from the court to seek the young prince—the messenger had been long delayed from ignorance of the present abode of Edwy, who had carefully concealed the secret until he felt he could tarry no longer, fearing the wrath not only of the king, but of Dunstan, whom he dreaded yet more than his uncle.

So he and his attendants, who had, like him, found pleasant entertainment at Æscendune, bade farewell to the home where he had been so hospitably entertained; and so ended a visit, pregnant with the most important results, then utterly unforeseen and unintended, to the family he had honoured by his presence.

Some few weeks passed, and under the tuition of their chaplain, who was charged with their education, Elfric and Alfred had returned to their usual course of life.

It would seem somewhat a hard one to a lover of modern ease. They rose early, as we have already seen, and before breaking their fast went with their father and most of the household to the early mass at the monastery of S. Wilfred, returned to an early meal, and then worked hard, on ordinary occasions at their Latin, and such other studies as were pursued in that primitive age of England. The mid-day meal was succeeded by somewhat severe bodily exercise, generally hunting the boar or wolf which still abounded in the forests, an excitement not unattended by danger, which, however, their father would never permit them to shun. He knew full well the importance of personal courage at an age when the dangers of hunting were only initiatory to the stern duties of war, and no Englishman could shun the latter when his country called upon him to take up arms. Nor were martial exercises unknown to the boys; the bow, it is true, was somewhat neglected then in England, but the use of sword, shield, and battle-axe was daily inculcated. "Si vis pacem," Father Cuthbert said on such occasions, "para arma."

Wearied by their exertions, whether at home or abroad, the brothers welcomed the evening social meal, and the rest which followed, when old Saxon legend or the harp of the gleeman enlivened the household fire, till compline sweetly closed the day.

Swiftly and pleasantly were passing the weeks succeeding the visit of the prince, when a royal messenger appeared, bearing a letter sealed with the king's signet. The old thane, who had passed his youth in more troublous times, and could scarcely read the Anglo-Saxon version of the Gospels, then extant, could not construe the monkish

Latin in which it was King Edred's good pleasure to write.

So the chaplain, Cuthbert, read him the letter, in which the king greeted his loyal and well-beloved subject, Ella of Æscendune, and begged of him, as a great favour, that he would send his eldest boy to court, to be the companion of the young prince, who had (the king said) conceived a great affection for Elfric.

"I hear," added Edred, "that your boy is a boy after his father's heart, full of love for the saints, diligent in his studies, and I trust well qualified to amend by example the somewhat giddy ways of my nephew."

Ella felt that this latter commendation might be better bestowed upon Alfred, who, although far less full of boyish spirit and energy than his brother, was far more attached to his religious duties, as also far more attentive to the wishes of his parents ; but his love for Elfric blinded him to more serious defects in the character of his son, or he might have feared their development in a congenial soil.

So the father saw his boy alone, and communicated the contents of the letter. The news was indeed welcome to Elfric, who panted for travel and adventure, and the freedom he fancied he should get in Edwy's society. But Ella hardly perceived this, and enlarged upon the dangers to which his son would be exposed, and tried to put before the boy all the "pros " and "cons " of the question faithfully. "He would not keep him back," he said, "if he desired to leave home," but as he uttered the words he felt his heart very heavy, for Æscendune would lose half its brightness in losing Elfric.

But Elfric's choice was already made, and he only succeeded in repressing his delight with great difficulty, in deference to the serious aspect and words of his revered sire. But his decision, for it was left to him, was unchanged, and he stammered forth his desire to be a man, and to see the world, in words mingled with expressions of his deep love for his parents, which he was sure nothing could ever change. Strange to say, now that the parental consent was gained, and no obstacle lay between him and the accomplishment of his ardent wish, he did not feel half so happy as he had expected to feel. Home affections seemed to increase as the hours rushed by which were to be his last in the bosom of his family; every familiar object became precious as the thought arose that it might be seen for the last time; favourites, both men and animals, had to be bidden farewell. There was the old forester, the gleeman, the warder, the gardener, the chamberlain, the cellarius, the cook (not an unimportant personage in Saxon households), the foster-mother, his old nurse, and many a friend in the village. Then there were his favourite dogs, his pony, some pigeons he had reared; and all had some claim on his affection, home-nurtured as he had been in a most kindly household.

But the appointed day came, the horse which was to bear him away stood at the door, another horse loaded with his personal effects stood near, for carriages were then unknown, neither would the roads have permitted their use, so changed were the times since the Roman period.

His father and mother, his brother and sister, stood without the drawbridge, where the last good-bye took place; tears started unbidden to his eyes—he was only fifteen—as he heard the parting blessing, and as his mother pressed him to her bosom. Alfred and his sister Edith seemed almost broken-hearted at the parting. But Elfric tried to bear up, and the end came. The little cavalcade left the castle, two attendants, well armed and mounted, being his body-guard.

Again and again he looked back; and when, after a journey of two miles, the envious woods closed in, and hid the dear familiar home from his sight, a strange sense of desolation rushed upon him, as if he were alone in the world.

The route taken by the cavalcade led them in the

first place to Warwick, even then a flourishing Saxon town : this was the limit of Elfric's previous wanderings, and when they left it for the south, the whole country was strange to him.

The royal messenger had business at the cathedral city of Dorchester, at the junction of the Tame and Isis, and they did not take the more direct route by the Watling Street, the most perfect Roman road remaining. The land was but thinly peopled, forests covered the greater portion, and desolate marshes much of the remainder; thus, through alternate forest and marsh, the travellers advanced along the ruinous remains of an old Roman cross road, which had once afforded good accommodation to travellers, but had been suffered to fall into utter ruin and decay by the neglect of their successors, our own barbarous ancestors. Originally it had been paved with stone, and causeways had been formed over marsh and mere, but the stones had been taken away, for the road formed the most accessible quarry in the neighbourhood. Here and there, however, it was still good, surviving the wear of centuries, and even the old mile-posts of iron were still existing covered with rust, with the letters denoting so many Roman miles,—or thousands of paces,—still legible.

A few hours' riding from Warwick brought them at the close of the day in sight of Beranbyrig (Banbury), where three centuries earlier a bloody battle had been fought,* wherein success—almost for the last time—visited the British arms, and saved the Celtic race from expulsion for twenty years.

The spot was very interesting to Elfric, for here his ancestor Sebbald had fought by the side of the invading king, Cynric, the son of Cerdic, and had fallen "gloriously" on the field.

"Look," said Anlaf, the guide, "at that sloping ground which rises to the north-west. There the Welsh (Britons) stood, formed in nine strong battalions. In that hollow

* A.D. 556—Anglo-Saxon Chronicle.

they placed their archers, and here their javelin-men and cavalry were arranged after the old Roman fashion. Our Englishmen were all in one battalion, and charged them fiercely, when they were thrown into confusion by the cunning tricks of the Welsh, who made up in craft what they wanted in manly courage. Look at this brook which flows to the river, it was running with blood that evening, and our men lay piled in huge heaps where they tried to scale the hill which you see yonder."

"And did the Welsh gain the day so easily?" said Elfric, sorrowfully.

"I don't wonder; they were fighting for their lives, and even a rat will fight if you get him into a corner; besides, they had all their best men here."

"Do you know where Sebbald fell?" said Elfric, referring to his own ancestor.

"Just under this hillock, close by King Cynric, who fought like a lion to save the body, but was unable to do so. The Welsh were then gaining the day. Still, even his foes respected his valour, and gave your forefather a fair and honourable burial."

Leaving the battlefield, they entered the Saxon town, which was defended on one side by the Cherwell, on the other by a mound and palisade, with an outer ditch supplied by the river. Here they found hospitable entertainment, and left on the morrow for the town of Kirtlington.

They left Beranbyrig early, and reached the village of Sutthun (King's Sutton), where they perceived a great multitude of people collected around a well at the outskirts of the village.

"What are these people doing?" asked Elfric.

"Oh, do you not know?" replied Anlaf. "This is S. Rumbald's well," and he crossed himself piously.

"Who was S. Rumbald?" asked Elfric innocently.

"Oh, he was son of the king of Northumbria, and of his queen, the daughter of the old king Penda of Mercia,

and the strange thing is that he is a saint although he only
lived three days."

" How could that be ? "

" Why it was a miracle, you see.   On the day after his
birth he was taken to Braceleam (Brackley), where he was
baptized, and after his baptism he actually preached an
eloquent sermon to the people.   They brought him back to
Sutthun next day, where he died, having first blessed this
well, so that many precious gifts of healing are shown
thereat.   His relics were removed first to Braceleam, then to
Buccingaham (Buckingham), where his shrine is venerated by
the faithful   But come, you must drink of the holy water."

So they approached the spot, and, after much labour to
get at the well, drank of the water, which had a brackish
taste, and proceeded on their journey southward through
Kirtlington, then a considerable city, although now a small
village.   It was their intention to pass by the cathedral
city of Dorchester, where Wulfstan was then bishop, where
they arrived on the second night of their journey.

It was the largest city Elfric had as yet seen, possessing
several churches, of which only one now remains. The hand
of the ruthless Danes had not yet been laid heavily upon it,
and the magnificence of the sacred fanes, built by cunning
architects from abroad, amazed the Mercian boy.

There was the tomb of the great Birinus, the apostle of
Mercia, who had founded the see in the year 630 A.D., and
to whose shrine multitudes of pilgrims flocked each year.
But the remains of Roman greatness most astonished Elfric.
The ruins of the amphitheatre situate near the river Tame
were grand even in their decay, and all the imaginative
faculties of the boy were aroused, as one of the most learned
inhabitants described the scenes of former days, of which
tradition had been preserved, the gladiatorial combats, the
wild beast fights.

The heir of Æscendune found hospitality at the episcopal palace, where Wulfstan,* once the turbulent Archbishop

* See Note E.—Wulfstan, and the See of Dorchester.

of York, held his court. The prelate seemed favourably impressed with his youthful guest, whom he dismissed with a warm commendation to Dunstan.

They left the city early in the morning, and passed through Bænesington (Benson), which having been originally taken from the Welsh by the Saxon chieftain Cuthulf, in the year 571, became the scene of the great victory of Offa, the Mercian king, over Cynewulf of Wessex in the year 777. One of Elfric's ancestors had fought on the side of Offa, and the exploits of this doughty warrior had formed the subject of a ballad often sung in the winter evenings at Æscendune, so that Elfric explored the scene with great curiosity. Inferior to Dorchester, it was still a considerable town.

Late at night they reached Reading, where they slept, and started early on the morrow for London, where they arrived on the evening of the fourth day.

CHAPTER IV.

LONDON, in the days of King Edred, differed widely from the stately and populous city we know in these days, and almost as widely from the elegant " Colonia Augusta," or Londinium, of the Roman period. Narrow, crooked, and unpaved lanes wound between houses, or rather lowly cottages, built of timber, and roofed with thatch, so that it is not wonderful that a conflagration was an event to be dreaded.

Evidence met the eye on every side how utterly the first Englishmen had failed to preserve the cities they had conquered, and how far inferior they were in cultivation, or rather civilisation, to the softer race they had so ruthlessly expelled ; for on every side broken pedestal and shattered column appeared clumsily imbedded in the rude domestic architecture of our forefathers.

St. Paul's Cathedral rose on the hill once sacred to Diana, but was wholly built within the ruins of the vast temple which had once occupied the site, and which, magnificent in decay, still surrounded it like an outwork. Further on were the wrecks of the citadel, where once the stern legionary had watched by day and night, and where Roman discipline and order had held sway, while the wall raised by Constantine, broken and imperfect, still rose on the banks of the river. Near the Ludgate was the palace of the Saxon king, and the ruins of an aqueduct overshadowed its humbler portal, while without the walls the river Fleet rolled, amidst vineyards and pleasant meadows dotted with houses, to join the mighty Thames.

Edred, the reigning king of England, was the brother of the murdered Edmund, and, in accordance with the custom of the day, had ascended the throne on the death of his brother, seeing that the two infant sons of the late king, Edwy and Edgar, were too young to reign, and the idea of hereditary right was not sufficiently developed in the minds of our forefathers to suggest the notion of a regency. It must also be remembered that, within certain limits, there was an elective power in the Witenagemot or Parliament, although generally limited in its scope to members of the royal family.

Edred was of very delicate constitution, and suffered from an inward disease which seldom allowed him an interval of rest and ease. Like so many sufferers he had found his consolation in religion, and the only crime ever laid to his charge (if it were a crime) was that he loved the Church too much. Still he had repeatedly proved that he was strong in purpose and will, and the insurgent Danes who had settled in Northumbria had owned his prowess. In the internal affairs of his kingdom he was chiefly governed by the advice of the great ecclesiastic and statesman, with whose name our readers will shortly become familiar.

Upon the morning after the arrival of Elfric in London, Edwy, the young prince, and his new companion, sat in a room on the upper floor of the palace, which had but two floors, and would have been considered in these days very deficient in architectural beauty.

The window of the room opened upon the river, and commanded a pleasant view of the woods and meadows on the Surrey side, then almost uninhabited, being completely unprotected in case of invasion, a contingency never long absent from the mind in the days of the sea kings.

A table covered with manuscripts, both in Latin and Anglo-Saxon, occupied the centre of the room, and there Elfric was seated, looking somewhat aimlessly at a Latin vocabulary, while Edwy was standing listlessly at the window. The " library," if it deserved the name, was very unlike a modern library; books were few, and yet very expensive, so that perhaps there was no fuller collection in any layman's house in the kingdom. There were Alfred's translations into Anglo-Saxon, the " Chronicle of Orosius," or the History of the World; the " History of the Venerable Bede," both in his original Latin and in English; Boethius on the " Consolations of Philosophy;" narratives from ancient mythology; extracts from the works of S. Augustine and S. Gregory; and the Apologues or Fables from Æsop.*

"Oh, put those stupid books aside," exclaimed the prince; " this is your first day in town, and I mean to take a holiday; that surly old Dunstan should have left word to that effect last night."

" Will he not be here soon ?"

" Yes, he is coming this morning, the old bear, to superintend my progress, and I wish him joy thereof."

" What has he given you to do ?" inquired Elfric.

" Why, a wretched exercise to write out. There, you see it before you; isn't it a nuisance ?"

" It is not very hard, is it ?"

" Don't *you* think it hard ? See whether you can do it ?"

Elfric smiled, and wrote out the simple Latin with ease, for he had been well instructed by Father Cuthbert at Æscendune.

He had scarcely finished when a firm step was heard upon the stairs.

" Hush," said Edwy; " here comes Dunstan. Be sure you look solemn enough," and he composed his own countenance into an expression of preternatural gravity.

The door opened, and an ecclesiastic in the prime of life entered the room, one whose mien impressed the beholder with an indefinable awe.

He was dressed in the Benedictine habit, just then becoming common in England, and his features were those of a

* See Note F.—Anglo-Saxon Literature.

man formed by nature to command, while they reconciled the beholder to the admission of the fact by the sad yet sweet smile which frequently played on the shapely countenance. He was now in the thirtieth year of his age, having been born in the first year of King Athelstane, and had been abbot of Glastonbury for several years, although his services as counsellor to King Edred had led him to spend much of his time in town, and he had therefore accepted the general direction of the education of the heir to the throne. Such was Dunstan.

He seemed but little welcome to Edwy, and the benediction with which he greeted his pupil was. but coldly received. Not appearing to notice this, he mildly said, " You must introduce your young companion to me, my prince. Am I not right in concluding that I see before me Elfric, heir to the lands of Æscendune ?"

Elfric blushed as he bent the knee to the great churchman to receive the priestly benediction with which he was greeted, but remained silent. " Father Cuthbert, whom I knew well years agone, has told me about you, and your brother Alfred ; is not that his name ?"

" He is so named, my father."

" I am glad to perceive that my royal pupil has chosen so meet a companion, for Father Cuthbert speaks well of your learning. You write the Latin tongue, he tells me, with some little facility."

Elfric feared his powers had been overrated. " I trust you have resumed your studies after your long holiday," continued Dunstan. " Youth is the season for sowing, age for reaping."

" I have had a very bad headache," said Edwy, " and have only been able to write a page of Latin. Here it is, father."

And he extended the exercise Elfric had written to the abbot, who looked at the writing for one moment, and then glanced severely at the prince. The character was very like his own, but there was a difference.

" Is this your handwriting, Prince Edwy ?" he asked.

"Of course. Elfric saw me write it, did you not?" Elfric was not used to falsehood; he could not frame his lips to say "Yes." Dunstan observed his confusion, and he turned to the prince with a look in which contempt seemed to struggle with passive self-possession.

"I trust, Edwy," he said, "you will remember that the word of a king is said to be his bond, and so should the word of a prince be if he ever hopes to reign. I shall give Father Benedict charge to superintend your studies as usual."

He wished them a grave good morning, and left the room. As soon as the last sound of his steps had ceased, Edwy turned sharply to Elfric—

"Why did you not say yes at once? Surely you have a tongue?"

"It has never learnt to lie."

"Pooh! What is the harm of such a white lie as that would have been? If you cannot give the credit of a Latin exercise, which you happen to have written, to your future king, you must be selfish; it is my writing, if you give it me, isn't it?"

Elfric did not quite see the matter in that light, yet did not care to dispute the point; but his conscience was ill at ease, and he was glad to change the subject.

"When can we go out?" he said, for he was anxious to see the city.

"Oh, not till after the midday meal, and you must see the palace first; come now."

So they descended and traversed the various courts of the building, the dormitories, the great dining-hall, the audience chambers where Edred was then receiving his subjects, who waited in the anteroom, which alone the two boys ventured to enter. Finally, after traversing several courts and passages, they reached the guard-room.

Three or four of the "hus-carles" or household guards were here on duty. But in the embrasure of the window, poring over a map, sat one of very different mien from the common soldiers, and whose air and manner, no less than his dress, proclaimed the officer.

"Redwald," said the prince, advancing to the window, "let me make you acquainted with my friend and companion, Elfric of Æscendune."

The officer started, as if with some sudden surprise, but it passed away so quickly that the beholder might fancy the start had only existed in imagination, as perhaps it did.

"This gallant warrior," said Edwy to Elfric, "is my friend and counsellor in many ways; and if he lives there shall not be a thane in England who shall stand above him. You will soon find out his value, Elfric."

"My prince is pleased to flatter his humble servant," said Redwald.

But Elfric was gazing upon the soldier with feelings he could scarcely analyse. There was something in his look and the tone of his voice which struck a hidden chord, and awoke recollections as if of a previous existence.

"Redwald," as Edwy named him, was tall and dark, with many of the characteristics of the Danish race about him. His nose was slightly aquiline, his eyes hid beneath bushy eyebrows, while his massive jaw denoted energy of character—energy which one instinctively felt was quite as likely to be exerted for evil as for good.

He was captain of the hus-carles, and had but recently entered the royal service. Few knew his lineage. He spoke the Anglo-Saxon tongue with great fluency, and bore testimonials certifying his valour and faithfulness from the court of Normandy, where the Northmen under Rollo had some half-century earlier founded a flourishing state, then ruled over by the noble Duke "Richard the Fearless."

Edwy seemed to be on intimate terms with this soldier of fortune; in fact, with all his proud anticipation of his future greatness, he was never haughty to his inferiors, perhaps we should say *seldom*, for we shall hereafter note exceptions to this rule. It would be a great mistake to suppose that the pomp and ceremony of our Norman kings was shared by their English predecessors: the manners and customs of the court of Edred were simplicity itself.

After a few moments of private conversation with Redwald, the boys returned to their chamber to prepare for dinner.

"You noted that man," said Edwy; "well, I don't know how I should live without him."

Elfric's looks expressed surprise.

" You will find out by and by ; you have little idea how strictly we are kept here, and how much one is indebted to one's servants for the gift of liberty, especially in Lent and on fast days, when one does not get half enough to eat, and must sometimes escape the gloom and starvation of the palace."

" Starvation ?"

"What else do you call it, when you get nothing but fish, fish, fish, and bread and water to help it down. My uncle is awfully religious.   I can hardly stand it sometimes. He would like to spend half the day in chapel, but, happily for all the rest of us, the affairs of state are too urgent for that, so we do get a *little* breathing time, or else I should have to twist my mouth all of one side singing dolorous chants and tunes which are worse than a Danish war-whoop, for he likes, he says, to hear the service hearty."

" But it helps you on with your Latin."

"Not much of that, for I sing anything that comes into my head ; the singing men make such a noise, they can hear no one else, and I fancy they don't know what a word of the Latin prayers means."

" But isn't it irreverent—*too* irreverent, I mean ; Father Cuthbert made me afraid to mock God, he told such stories about judgment."

" All fudge and nonsense—oh, I beg your pardon, it is all very godly and pious, and really I expect to be greatly edified by your piety in chapel. Pray, when shall you be canonised ?"

Elfric could not bear ridicule, and blushed for the

second time that morning. Just then the bell rang for dinner, or rather was struck with a mallet by the master of the ceremonies.

King Edred dined that day, as one might say, in the bosom of his family; only Dunstan was present, besides the boys Edwy, Edgar his younger brother, and Elfric. It was then that Elfric first saw the younger prince, a pale studious-looking boy of twelve, but with a very firm and intellectual expression of countenance. He was a great favourite with Dunstan, whom the boy, unlike his brother, regarded with the greatest respect and reverence.

The conversation was somewhat stiff; Edred spoke a few kind words to the young stranger, and then conversed in an under tone with Dunstan, the whole dinner time; the princes themselves were awed by the presence of their uncle and his spiritual guide.

But at last, like all other things, it was over, and with feelings of joy the boys broke forth from the restraint. The whole afternoon was spent in seeing the sights of London, and they all three, for Edgar accompanied them, returned to the evening meal, fatigued in body, but in high spirits. Compline in the royal chapel terminated the day, as mass had begun it.

CHAPTER V.

TEMPTATION.

BUT a few days had passed before Elfric learned the secret of Redwald's influence over the young prince.

The household of Edred was conducted with the strictest propriety.*　All rose with the lark, and the first duty was to attend at the early mass in the royal chapel.　Breakfast followed, and then the king on ordinary days gave the whole forenoon to business of state, and he thought it his duty to see that each member of the royal household had some definite employment, knowing that idleness was the mother of many evils.　So the young princes had their tasks assigned them by their tutor, as we have already seen, and the spare hours which were saved from their studies were given to such practice in the use of the national weapons as seemed necessary to those who might hereafter lead armies, or to gymnastic exercises which strengthened nerve and muscle for a time of need.

In the afternoon they might ride or walk abroad, but a strict interdict was placed upon certain haunts where temptation might perchance be found, and they had to return by evensong, which the king generally attended in person when at home.　Then, in winter, indoor recreations till compline, for it was a strict rule of the king that his nephews should not leave the palace after sundown.

He further caused their tutor, who directed their education under the supervision of Dunstan—Father Benedict—whom we have already introduced, to see that they properly discharged all the duties of public and private devotion.

* See Note G.—The Court of Edred.

But he did not see, in the excess of his zeal, that he was really destroying the prospects which were nearest his heart, and that there can be no more fatal mistake than to compel the performance of religious duties which exceed the measure of the youthful capacity or endurance.

With Edgar, who was naturally pious, the system produced no evil result; but with Edwy the effect was most sad. He had become, as we have seen, deceitful; and a character, naturally fair, was undermined to an extent which neither the king nor Dunstan suspected.

The reader may naturally ask how could Dunstan, so astute as he was, make this mistake, or at least suffer Edred to make it?

The fact was that Dunstan understood the affairs of state better than those of the heart, and although well fitted for a guide to men of sincere piety, and capable of opposing to the wicked an iron will and inflexible resolution, he did not understand the young, and seemed to have forgotten his own youth. Sincerely truthful and straightforward, he hardly knew whether to feel more disgust or surprise at Edwy's evident unfaithfulness. He little knew that *unfaithfulness* was only one of his failings, and not the worst.

A few nights after Elfric's arrival, when the palace gates had been shut for the night, the compline service said, the household guard posted, and the boys had retired to their sleeping apartments, he heard a low knock at his door. He opened it, and Edwy entered.

"Are you disposed for a pleasant evening, Elfric?"

"Such pleasure as there is in sleep."

"No, I do not mean *that*. We cannot sleep, like bears in winter, during all the hours which should be given to mirth. I am going out this evening, and I want you to go with me."

"Going out?"

"Yes. Don't stand staring there, as if I was talking Latin or something harder; but get your shoes on again.

No; you had better come down *without* shoes; it will make less noise."

"But how can we get out? I have not the least idea where you are going?"

"All in good time. We shall get out easily enough. Are you coming?"

Half fearful, yet not liking to resist the prince, and his curiosity pressing him to solve the secret, Elfric followed Edwy down the stairs to the lower hall, where Redwald was on guard. He seemed to await the lads, for he bowed at once to the prince and proceeded to the outer door, where, at an imperious signal from him, the warder threw the little inner portal open, and the three passed out.

"Is the boat ready?" said Edwy.

"It is; and trusty rowers await you."

Redwald led the way to the river's brink, and there pointed out a skiff lying at a short distance from the shore. At a signal, the men who manned it pulled in and received the two youths on board, then pulled at once out into the stream.

"How do you like an evening on the river?" said Edwy.

"It is very beautiful, and the stars are very bright to-night; but where are we going?"

"You will soon find out."

Finding his royal companion so uncommunicative, Elfric remained silent, trusting that a few minutes would unravel the mystery.

But an hour had passed, during which the boat steadily progressed up stream, before the watermen pulled in for the shore, and a dark building loomed before them in dim shadow.

"Here is the place," said Edwy. "Be ready, my men, to take us back about midnight, or a little later;" and he threw some pieces of money amongst them. Passing through a large garden, they arrived at a porch before a stout door garnished with knobs of iron, which might bid defiance to thief or burglar.

" Whose house is this ?" asked Elfric.

" Wait ; you shall soon see."

The loud knocking Edwy made at the door soon brought some domestics, who, opening a small wicket, discovered the identity of their principal visitor, and immediately threw open the door.

" Thanks," said Edwy ; " we were almost frozen."

Passing through a kind of atrium—for the old Roman fashion was still sometimes followed in this particular—the domestics ushered the visitors into a room brilliantly lighted by torches stuck in cressets projecting from the walls, and by huge wax candles upon a table spread for a feast. The light revealed a small but apparently select party, who seemed to await the prince : a lady, who appeared to be the mistress of the mansion ; a young girl apparently about the age of Edwy, who, calling her his fair cousin, saluted her fondly ; and two or three youths, whose gaudy dress and affected manners were strongly in contrast with the stern simplicity of the times.

After saluting each person with the greatest freedom, Edwy introduced his companion.

" Here is a young novice I have brought to learn the noble art of merry-making, of wine and wassail. We have both been literally starved at the palace—I should say monastery—of Monk Edred to-day. It is Friday, and we have been splendidly dining upon salt fish served up on golden salvers. My goodness ! the flavour of that precious cod is yet in my mouth. Food for cats, I do assure you, and served up to kings. What did you think of it, Elfric ?"

Elfric was ashamed to say that it had not been so very bad after all. Truth to say his conscience was uneasy, for he had been brought up to respect the fasts of the Church, and he saw a trial awaiting him in the luscious dishes before him.

" What does it matter ?" the reader may exclaim ; " it is not that which goeth into the mouth which defileth a man," etc.

True, most wise critic, but it *is* that which goeth out; and if disobedience be not amongst the evils which defile, then Adam did not fall in Paradise when he ate the forbidden fruit.

Elfric could not touch flesh on fast days without the instinctive feeling that he was doing wrong, and no one can sin against the conviction of the heart without danger.

The party now seated themselves, and without any grace or further preface the feast began. Servants appeared and served up the most exquisite dishes, of a delicacy almost unknown in England at that day, and poured rich wines into silver goblets. It was evident that wealth abounded in the family they were visiting, and that they had expended it freely for the gratification of Edwy.

Ethelgiva, the lady of the house, was of noble presence, which almost seemed to justify the claim of royal blood which was made for her. Tall and commanding, age had not bent her form, although her locks were already white. Her beauty, which must have been marvellous in her younger days, had attracted the attention of a younger son of the reigning house, and they were married at an early age, secretly, without the sanction of the king.

The fruit of their union was Elgiva, a name destined to fill a place in a sad and painful tragedy; but we are anticipating, and must crave the reader's pardon.

Bright and cheerful indeed was the fair Elgiva at this moment. Her beauty was remarkable even in a land so famed for the beauty of its daughters; and the ill-advised Edwy may be pitied, if not altogether pardoned, for his infatuation, for infatuation it was in a day when the near tie of blood between them precluded the possibility of lawful matrimony, save at the expense of a dispensation never likely to be conceded, since the temperament of men like Odo, the Archbishop of Canterbury, and of Dunstan, was opposed to any relaxation of the law in the case of the great when such relaxation was unattainable by the poor and lowly.

To return to our subject.—The feast proceeded with great animation. At first Elfric hesitated when the meat was placed before him, but he withered, in his weakness, before the mocking smile of Edwy, and the sarcasm which played upon the lips of the rest of the company, who perceived his hesitation. So he yielded, and, shaking off all restraint, ate heartily.

Dish followed dish, and the wine-cup circulated with great freedom. Excited as he was, Elfric could but remark the loose tone of the conversation. Subjects were freely discussed which had never found admittance either in the palace of King Edred or at Æscendune, and which, indeed, caused him to look up with surprise, remembering in whose presence he sat.

But, as is often the case in an age where opinion is severely repressed in its outward expression, and amongst those compelled against their will to observe silence on such subjects on ordinary occasions, all restraint seemed abandoned at the table of Ethelgiva. It was not that the language was *coarse*, but whether the conversation turned upon the restraints of the clergy, or the court, or upon the fashionable frivolities of the day—for there were frivolities and fashions even in that primitive age—there was a freedom of expression bordering upon profanity or licentiousness.

Edred was mocked as an old babbler; Dunstan was sometimes a fool, sometimes a hypocrite, sometimes even a sorcerer, although this was said sneeringly; the clergy were divided into fools and knaves; the claims of the Church—that is of Christianity—derided, and the principle freely avowed—"Enjoy life while you can, for you know not what may come after."

Excited by the wine he had drunk, Elfric became as wild in his talk as the other young men, and as the intoxicating drink mounted to his brain, seemed to think that he had just learnt how to enjoy life. The ladies retired at last, and Edwy followed them. Elfric was on the point of rising too, but a hint from his companions restrained him. The wine-cup still circulated, the conversation, now unrestrained, initiated the boy into many an evil secret he had never known earlier; and so the hours passed on, till Edwy, himself much flushed, came in and said that it was time to depart, for midnight had long been tolled from the distant towers of London.

He smiled as he saw by Elfric's bloodshot eyes and unsteady gait, as he rose, upsetting his seat, that his companion was something less master of himself than usual; he felt, it need hardly be said, no remorse, but rather regarded the whole thing as what might now be termed "a jolly lark."

"Shall you require bearers, or can you walk to the boat? I do not wonder you are ill, you have eaten too much fish to-day; it is a shame to make the knees weak through fasting in this style."

"I—I—am all right now."

"You will be better in the air."

So, bidding a farewell of somewhat doubtful character to his entertainers, Elfric was assisted to the boat. The air did not revive him, he felt wretchedly feverish and giddy, and could hardly tell how he reached the river.

Reach it, however, he did, and the strong arms of the watermen impelled the boat rapidly down the tide, until it reached the stairs near the palace.

Here Redwald was in waiting, and assisted them to land.

"You are very late, or rather early," he said.

"Yes," said Edwy, "but it has been a jolly evening, only poor Elfric has been ill, having of course weakened himself by fasting."

Redwald smiled such a scornful smile, and muttered some words to himself. Yet it did not seem as if he were altogether displeased at the state in which he saw Elfric. It may be added that Edwy was but little better.

"You must keep silent," said Redwald; "I believe the king and Dunstan are hearing matins in the chapel: it is the festival of some saint or other, who went to the grid-iron in olden days."

The outer gate of the palace was cautiously opened, and, taking off their shoes, the youths ascended the stairs which led to their apartments as lightly as possible.

" Send the leech Sigebert to us in the morning ; he must report Elfric unwell—for he will hardly get up to hear Dunstan mumble mass."

" Perhaps your royal highness had better rest also."

" And bring suspicion upon us both ? No," said Edwy, " one will be enough to report ill at once ; Dunstan is an old fox."

Poor Elfric could hardly get to bed, and, almost for the first time since infancy, he laid himself down without one prayer. Edwy left him in the dark, and there he lay, his head throbbing, and a burning thirst seeming to consume him.

Long before morning he was very sick, and when the bell was sounded for the early mass it need hardly be said that *he* was unable to rise.

Sigebert, the physician, who, like Redwald, was in the confidence of the *future* king, Edwy, came in to see him, and asked what was the matter."

" I am very sick and ill," gasped Elfric.

I suppose you have taken something that disagreed with you—too much fish perhaps " (with a smile).

" No—no—I do not "——

" I understand," said the leech ; " you will soon be better ; meanwhile, I will account for your absence at chapel. Here, take this medicine ; you will find it relieve you."

And he gave Elfric a mixture which assuaged his burning thirst, and bathed his forehead with some powerful essence which refreshed him greatly, whereupon the leech departed.

Only an hour later, and Edred, hearing from the physician of Elfric's sudden illness, came in to see the boy, whose bright cheerful face and merry disposition had greatly attracted him. This was hardest of all for Elfric to bear ; he had to evade the kind questions of the king, and to hear expressions of sympathy which he felt he did not deserve.

More than once he felt inclined to tell all, but the fear of the prince restrained him, and also a sense of what he thought honour, for he would not betray his companion, and he could not confess his own guilt without implicating Edwy.

Poor boy! it would have been far better for him had he done so: he had taken his first step downward.

CHAPTER VI.

IT becomes our painful duty to record that from the date of the feast, described in our last chapter, the character of poor Elfric underwent rapid deterioration. In the first place, the fact of his having yielded to the forbidden indulgence, and—as he felt—disgraced himself, gave Edwy, as the master of the secret, great power over him, and he never failed to use this power whenever he saw any inclination on the part of his vassal to throw off the servitude. It was not that he deliberately intended to injure Elfric, but he had come to regard virtue as either weakness or hypocrisy, at least such virtues as temperance, purity, or self-restraint.

The great change which was creeping over Elfric became visible to others: he seemed to lose his bright smile; the look of boyish innocence faded from his countenance, and gave place to an expression of sullen reserve; he showed less ardour in all his sports and pastimes, became subject to fits of melancholy, and often seemed lost in thought, anxious thought, in the midst of his studies.

He seldom had the power, even if the will, to communicate with home. Mercia was in many respects an independent state, subject to the same king, but governed by a code of laws differing from those of Wessex; and it was only when a royal messenger or some chance traveller left court for the banks of the Midland Avon, that Elfric could use the art of writing, a knowledge he was singular in possessing, thanks to the wisdom of his sire.

So the home authorities knew little of the absent one, for whom they offered up many a fervent prayer, and of whom they constantly spoke and thought. And yet, so mysterious are the ways of Providence, it seemed as if these prayers were unanswered—*seemed* indeed, yet they were not forgotten before God.

Seemed forgotten; for Elfric was rapidly becoming reckless. Many subsequent scenes of indulgence had followed the first one, and other haunts, residences of licentious young nobles, or taverns, had been sought out by the youths, and always by Redwald's connivance.

He was Edwy's evil genius, and always seemed at hand whensoever the prince sought occasion to sin. Still, he was not at all suspected by Edred, before whom he kept up an appearance of the strictest morality—always punctual in his attendance at mass, matins, and evensong, and with a various stock of phrases of pious import ready at tongue in case of need or opportunity of using them to advantage. ·

To Elfric, his behaviour was always reserved, yet he seemed even more ready to lend him a helping hand downward than did the prince.

So time passed on; weeks became months; and Christmas with all its hallowed associations had passed; it had been Elfric's first Christmas away from home, and he was sad at heart, in spite of the boisterous merriment of his companions. The spring of the year 955 came on, and Lent drew near, a season to which Edwy looked forward with great dread, for, as he said, there would be nothing in the whole palace to eat until Easter, and he could not even hope to bribe the cook.

The canons of the church required all persons to make confession, and so enter upon the fast-tide, having "thus purified their minds;"* it may, alas! be easily guessed how the guilty lads performed this duty, how enforced confession only led to their adding the sin of further deceit, and that of a deadly kind.

* See Note H.—Confession in the Anglo-Saxon Church.

Thus they entered upon Lent: their abstinence was entirely compulsory, not voluntary; and although they made up for it in some degree when they could get away from the palace, yet even this was difficult, for it was positively unlawful for butchers to sell or for people to buy meat at the prohibited seasons, and the law was not easily evaded. But it was a prayerless Lent also to Elfric, for he had, alas! even discontinued his habit of daily prayer, a habit he had hitherto maintained from childhood, a habit first learned at his mother's knee.

Holy Week came, and was spent with great strictness; the king seemed to divide his whole time between the business of state and the duties of religion.

Dunstan was absent at Glastonbury, but other ecclesiastics thronged the palace, and there were few, save the guilty boys and Redwald, who seemed uninfluenced by the solemn commemoration.

But it must not be supposed that Elfric was wholly uninfluenced: after the preaching of the Passion by a poor simple monk on Good Friday, he retired to his own little room, where he wept as if his heart would break. Had Dunstan been then in town, the whole story would have been told, and much misery saved, for Elfric felt he could trust him if he could trust anybody; but unhappily Dunstan was, as we have seen, keeping Passion-tide at his abbey.

Still, Elfric felt he must tell all, and submit to the advice and penance which might be imposed; and as he sat weeping over his sin that Good Friday night, with the thought that he might find pardon and peace through the Great Sacrifice so touchingly pleaded that day, he felt that the first step to amendment must lie in a full and frank confession of all; he knew he should grievously offend Edwy, and that he should lose the favour of his future king, but he could not help it.

"Why, oh why did I leave Æscendune, dear Æscendune?—fool that I was—I will go back."

And a sweet desire of home and kindred rose up before him—of his father's loving welcome, his fond mother's chaste kiss, and of the dear old woods and waters—the hallowed associations of his home life. He rose up to seek Father Benedict, determined to enter upon the path of peace at any cost, when Edwy entered.

He did not see in the gathering darkness the traces of emotion visible on poor Elfric's countenance, and he began in his usual careless way—

"How are you, Elfric, my boy; glad Lent is nearly over ? What a dismal time that wretched monk preached this morning !"

"Edwy, I am utterly miserable: I must tell all; I cannot live like this any longer."

"What a burst of penitence ! go to confession ; to be sure it *looks* well, and if one can only manage to get out a few tears they account him a saint ; tell me the receipt."

"But, Edwy, I must tell all."

"Not if you are wise."

"Why not ? it is all in secrecy."

"No it is *not ;* you will be required as a penance to go and tell the king all that we have done ; you may do so, and I will manage to represent matters so as to throw the whole blame on you ; you will be sent home in disgrace."

Poor Elfric hung down his head ; the thought of his disgrace reaching home had not occurred to him.

"Come," said Edwy, "I don't want to be hard upon you. Cheer up, my man. What have you done amiss ? Only enjoyed yourself as nature has guided you. Why should you think God meant us to pass through life like those miserable shavelings Edred delights to honour ? Cheer up, Elfric ; your bright face was never meant for that of a hypocrite. If you are so dreadfully bad, you are in a pretty numerous company ; and I don't think the shavelings believe their own tales about fire and torment hereafter. They are merry enough, considering."

In short, poor Elfric's short-lived penitence was given

to the winds. Edwy went alone to be shriven on the morrow.

On Easter-day they both received the Holy Communion in the royal chapel.

From that time remorse ceased to visit the heir of Æscendune, as if he had at last quenched the Spirit, and he became so utterly wild and reckless, that at last Dunstan thought it necessary to speak to him privately on the subject. It was nearly six months after Easter.

The boy entered the study set apart for the use of the great monk and statesman with a palpitating heart, but he managed to repress its beatings, and put on a perfectly unconcerned expression of countenance. He had gained in self-control if in nothing else.

"I wished to speak with you, Elfric," said the abbot, "upon a very serious matter. When you first came here, I was delighted to have you as a companion to the prince. You were evidently well brought up, and bore an excellent character; but, I grieve to say, you have greatly changed for the worse. Are you not aware of it?"

"No, father. What have I done?"

Dunstan sighed at the tone of the reply, and continued—

"It is not any particular action of which I wish to accuse you, but of the general tenor of your conduct. I do not speak harshly, my boy; but if truth be told, you are as idle as you were once diligent, as sullen and reserved as once candid and open: and, my son, your face tells a tale of even worse things, and, but that I am puzzled to know where you could obtain the means of self-indulgence, I should attribute more serious vices to you."

"Who has accused me, father?"

"Yourself—that is, your own face and manner. Did you ever contemplate yourself in a mirror when at home? there is a steel one against that wall, go and look at yourself now."

Elfric blushed deeply.

"My face is still the same," he said.

"It is the same, and yet *not* the same.   Innocence once took her place at its portals, and had sealed it as her own; the expression is all changed ; my boy, I am absolutely certain that all is not well with you.   For your own sake, delay no longer to avoid the danger of losing your salvation, for the habits you form now will perhaps cling to you through life.   Turn now to your own self; confess your sin, and be at peace."

"I came to confession at Shrove-tide ; I am not required to come now, am I ?"

"Required ! No, my boy, it is your own sense of guilt, alone, which should draw you.   The Church, since there has been no public scandal, leaves you to your own judgment at such a time as this.   Have you never felt such remorse of conscience as would tell you your duty ?"

"Never."   He thought of Good Friday, and blushed.

"Your tone and words belie each other, my boy.   God grant you repentance ; you will not accept my help now, but the time may come when you will seek help in vain."

Elfric bowed, without reply, and at a sign left the chamber.

. A few weeks later, at the beginning of November, Edred left London for a tour in the west, and quitted his nephews with more than his usual affection, although his good-bye to Elfric was more constrained, for the good old king, not knowing the whole truth, was beginning to fear that Elfric was a dangerous companion.   He little thought that he was rather sinned against than sinning.

Dunstan was to follow him in a week, and only remained behind to discharge necessary business.

The heart of the amorous Edwy beat with delight as he saw his uncle depart, and he made arrangements at once to spend the night after Dunstan's departure in mirth and jollity at the house of Ethelgiva and her fair daughter.

He came back after an interview with Redwald on the subject, and found Elfric in their common study.   There

was an alcove in the room, and it was covered by a
curtain.

"O Elfric," said the prince, "is it not delightful?
The two tyrants, the king and the monk, will soon be gone.
I wish the Evil One would fly off with them both, and
when the cat is away will not the mice play? I have
made all the arrangements; we shall have such a night at
the lady Ethelgiva's."

"How is the fair Elgiva?"

It was now Edwy's turn to blush and look confused.

"I wish I had the power of teasing you, Elfric. But
if you have a secret you keep it close. Remember old
Dunstan vanishes on the fifteenth, and the same evening,
oh, won't it be joyful? But I am tired of work. Come
and let us take some fresh air."

They left the room, when the curtain parted, and the
astonished countenance of Father Benedict, who had been
quietly reading in the deep embrasure of the window, presently appeared. He looked like a man at whose feet a
thunderbolt had fallen, and hastily left the room.

The week passed rapidly away, and at its close Dunstan
took his departure. A train of horses awaited him, and
he bade the young princes Edwy and Edgar farewell, with
the usual charge to work diligently and obey Father
Benedict.

That same night, after the clerks had sung compline in
the chapel, and the chamberlain had seen to the safety of
the palace, Edwy came quietly to the room of his page,
and the two left as on the first occasion. Redwald attended them, and just before the boat left the bank he
spoke a word of caution.

"I fear," he said, in a low tone, "that all is not quite
right. That old fox Dunstan is up to some trick; he has
not really left town."

"Perhaps he has a *similar* appointment to-night," said
Edwy, sarcastically. "I should keep mine though he and
all his monks from Glastonbury barred the way."

They reached the castellated mansion of Ethelgiva in due course, and the programme of the former evening was repeated, save that, if there was any change, the conversation was more licentious, and the wine-cup passed more freely.

It was midnight, and one of the company was favouring them with a song of questionable propriety, when a heavy knock was heard at the door.

The servants went to answer it, and all the company awaited the issue in suspense.

One of the principal domestics returned with haste, and whispered some words into the ear of Ethelgiva which seemed to discompose her.

"What can this mean?" she said. "A guard of soldiers demand admittance in the king's name!"

A louder knocking attested the fact.

"You *must* admit them, or they will batter the door down. Edwy, Elfric! here, hide yourselves behind that curtain, it veils a deep recess."

They had scarcely concealed themselves when Dunstan entered, attended by a guard of the royal hus-carles.

"What means this insolence?" said Ethelgiva.

"No insolence is intended, royal lady, nor could be offered to the widow of the Etheling, by me," replied Dunstan, "but I seek to discharge a sacred trust committed to me. Where are my pupils, the Prince Edwy and his companion?"

"In their beds, at the palace, I should suppose."

"Nay, be not so perfidious; they are here, lady, and probably within hearing; they must come forth, or I must order the guard to search the house, which I should regret."

"By whose authority?"

"By that of the king, whose signet is on my hand."

"They are not here; they left half-an-hour ago."

"Pardon me, madam, if I observe that we have watched the house for an hour. Had not this scene better terminate?" he added, with icy coldness.

At this moment a favourite dog, which Edwy had often

petted, and which had entered with the guard, found him out behind the curtain, and in its vociferous joy betrayed the whole secret.

Confusion or smiles sat on every face save that of the imperturbable Dunstan.

"Your dog, madam, is more truthful than its mistress," he said, bluntly yet quietly; and then, advancing to the recess, he drew aside the curtain and gazed upon the discovered couple. "Will you kindly return to the palace with me ?"

"How dare you, insolent monk, intrude upon the pleasures of your future king ?"

"I dare by the orders of the *present* king, your royal uncle, who has committed the whole matter into my hands; and, Prince Edwy, in the discharge of my duty 'dare' is a superfluous word. Will you, as I said before, both follow me, if you are sufficiently masters of yourselves to do so ?"

The import of all this was seen at a glance, but there was no course but submission, and Edwy well knew how utterly indefensible his conduct was; so, with crestfallen gait, he and Elfric followed their captor to the river, where was another large boat by the side of their own. They entered it, and returned to the palace stairs much more sober than on previous occasions.

CHAPTER VII.

"THE KING IS DEAD !—LONG LIVE THE KING !"

THE unhappy Elfric passed the night in a most unenviable frame of mind. He felt distinctly how utterly he was in the power of Dunstan, and that he could only expect to return home in disgrace ; yet there was no real repentance in all this : he had sinned and suffered, but although he dreaded punishment he no longer hated sin.

He scarcely slept at all, and early in the morning he rose to seek an interview with Edwy, when he found that he was a prisoner. One of the hus-carles posted at his door forbade all communication.

Early in the morning the bell sounded for the early service, still he was not released, and later his breakfast was brought to him, after which he heard a heavy step approaching, and Dunstan appeared at the door of the sleeping-chamber.

He entered, and gazed at Elfric for a moment without speaking, as if he would read his very heart by his face; it was hardly comfortable.

"Elfric," he said at last, "do you remember the warning I gave you six months ago ?"

"No," said Elfric, determined, in desperation, to deny everything.

"I fear you are hardly telling me the truth ; you *must* remember it, unhappy boy ! Why were you not warned in time ? why did you refuse the advice which might have saved you from all this ?"

"Because it was my fate, I suppose."

"Men make their own fates, and as they make their beds so must they lie upon them ; however, I have not come here to reproach you, but to bid you prepare to return home."

"Home !—so soon ?" said Elfric.

"Yes, you must leave to-morrow, when a messenger will be prepared to accompany you, and to explain the cause of your dismissal from court to your father, whom I most sincerely pity ; and let me hope that you will find leisure to repent of your grievous sin in the solitude of your native home."

"Must my father be told everything ?"

"I fear he must : you have left us no choice ; and it is the better thing, both for him and for you ; he will understand better what steps are necessary for your reformation— a reformation, I trust, which will be accomplished in good time, whereat no one will rejoice more than I."

A pert answer rose to Elfric's lips, but he dared not give utterance to it ; the speaker was too great in his wrath to be defied with impunity.

"Farewell," said Dunstan, "would that I could say the word with brighter hopes ; but should you ever repent of your sin, as I trust you may, it will gladden me to hear of it. I fear you may have done great harm to England in the person of her future king, but God forgive you in that case ! "

Elfric felt the injustice of the last accusation ; he coloured, and an indignant denial had almost risen to his lips, but he repressed it for Edwy's sake—faithful, even in his vice, to his friend.

"Am I to consider myself a prisoner ? you have posted a sentinel, as if I were a criminal."

"You must be confined to your apartment, but you may have books and anything else you desire. The prince is forbidden to see you again. Your confinement will only be for one day ; to-morrow you will be free enough ; let me beg you to use the occasion for calm reflection, and, I hope, penitence."

Dunstan left the room, and Elfric heard his retreating steps go heavily down the stairs, when a sudden and almost unaccountable feeling came over him—a feeling that he had thrown himself away, and that he was committed to evil, perhaps never to be able to retrace his course, never to all eternity; the retreating steps sounded as if his sentence were passed and the door of mercy shut. He shook off the strange feeling; yet, could he have seen the future which lay undiscovered before him, and which must intervene before he should see that face again, or hear those steps, he might have been unable thus to shake off the nameless dread.

The day wore away, night drew on; he laid himself down and tried to sleep, when he heard voices conversing outside, and recognised Edwy's tones; immediately after the prince entered.

"What a shame, Elfric," he said, "to make you a prisoner like this, and to send you away—for they say you are to go to-morrow—you shall not be forgotten if ever I become king, and I don't think it will be long first. The first thing I shall do will be to send for you; you will come, won't you?"

"I will be yours for life or death."

"I knew it, and this is the faithful friend from whom they would separate me; well, we will have this last evening together in peace; old Dunstan has gone out, and Redwald has put a man as your guard who never sees anything he is not wanted to see."

"What a convenient thing!"

"But you seem very dull; is anything on your mind which I do not know? What did Dunstan say to you?"

"He is going to write home to my father all particulars. It will make home miserable."

"Perhaps we may find a remedy for that," said Edwy, and left the room hastily.

Shortly he returned in company with Redwald.

"Come with us, Elfric," said the prince; "there is no one in the palace to interfere with us. Old Dunstan received a sudden message, and has gone out hastily; we will go and see what he has written."

Somewhat startled at the audacity of the proposal, Elfric followed the prince, and Redwald accompanied them. After passing through a few passages, they arrived at the cell, or rather study, usually occupied by Dunstan when at court, and entered it, not without a slight feeling of dread, or rather of reluctance.

"Here it is," said Edwy, and held up a parchment, folded, sealed, and directed to "Ella, Thane of Æscendune."

"I should like to know what he has written," said the prince. "Redwald, you understand these things; can you open the letter without breaking the seal?"

"There is no need of that," replied the captain of the hus-carles, "I can easily seal it again; see, there is the signet, and here the wax."

So he broke the letter open and extended it to the prince, whose liberal education had given him the faculty of reading the monkish Latin, in which Dunstan wrote, at a glance, and he read aloud—

"To my Brother in Christ,

"Ella, Thane of Æscendune—

"It grieveth me much, most beloved brother, to be under the necessity of sending your son Elfric home in some little disgrace; but it is, alas! a necessity that I should do so, in virtue of the authority our good lord and king, Edred, hath entrusted to me. The lad was bright, and, I think, innocent of aught like deadly sin, when he came to this huge Babel, where the devil seems to lead men even as he will, and he hath fallen here into evil company—nay, into the very company most evil of all in this wicked world, that of designing and shameless women, albeit of noble birth. It hath been made apparent to me that there is great danger to both the prince and your son in any further connection, therefore I return Elfric to your care, sincerely hoping that, by God's help, you will be enabled to take such measures as will lead to his speedy reformation, for which I devoutly pray. The bearer will give such further in-

"Wishing you health, and an abiding-place in the favour of God and His saints—Your brother in the faith of Christ,

"DUNSTAN, O.S.B."

Edwy read the letter aloud with many a vindictive comment, and then said to Redwald—

"What can be done? *must* this letter go?"

"Does your father know the Saint's handwriting, Elfric?"

"He never heard from him before, I believe."

"Well, then, I will venture to enclose a different message," and he sat down at the table, and wrote—

"To MY BROTHER IN CHRIST,

"ELLA, THANE OF ÆSCENDUNE—

"It rejoiceth me much, most beloved brother, to send you good tidings of the good behaviour and growth in grace of your son, whom the king hath concluded to send home for the benefit of his health, since London hath in some degree destroyed the ruddy hue of his countenance, and he needeth a change, as his paleness sufficiently declareth.

"The king hath bidden me express his great satisfaction with the lad's conduct, and the prince mourneth his enforced departure. Wishing you health and an abiding-place in the favour of God and His saints—Your brother in the faith of Christ,　　　　　　　　　　　　　"DUNSTAN, O.S.B."

The boys laughed aloud as they read the forgery.

"But about the messenger—will he not tell the truth?"

"Oh, I will see to him, he is not above a bribe, and knows it is his interest to serve his future king, although Dunstan thinks him so trusty."

All at once the booming of a heavy bell smote their ears.

"It is the bell of S. Paul's, it tolls for the death of some noble," said Redwald; "what can it mean? has any member of the royal family been ill?"

They listened to the solemn dirge-like sound as it floated through the air, calling upon all good Christians to pray for the repose of the departed or departing soul. No prayer rose to their lips, and they soon returned to the subject in hand.

"When is the letter to be despatched?"

"Early in the morning the messenger will await you; and now, I should recommend some sleep to prepare for a fatiguing journey."

Elfric and the prince returned to their chamber, but they did not take Redwald's hint, and remained talking till just before daybreak, when they were aroused by the hasty step of an armed heel, and Redwald stood before them. His demeanour was very strange; he bent down on one knee, took the hand of Edwy, who resigned it passively to him, kissed it and cried aloud—

"God save the king!"

"What can you mean, Redwald?" exclaimed both the youths.

"Heard you not the passing bell last night? Edred sleeps with his fathers; he died at Frome on S. Clement's day."

For a moment they were both silent.

"And Edwy, the great grandson of Alfred, is king of England."

At first the young prince was deeply shocked at the sudden news of the death of his uncle, to whom, in spite of appearances, he was somewhat attached. He turned pale, and was again silent for some minutes; at last, he gulped down a cup of water, and asked—

"But how did Dunstan know?"

"Why, it is a strange tale. Three days ago, at the very hour the king must have died, he says that he saw a bright light, and beheld a vision of angels, who said, 'Edred hath died in the Lord,' but he treated it as a dream, and last night a messenger came with the news of the sudden illness of the king, bidding Dunstan hasten to his side. He left everything, and started immediately, but in a few miles met another messenger, bearing the news of the death. He has gone on, but sent the messenger forward to the Bishop of London, who caused the great bell to be tolled.

"We must all die some day," said Edwy, musingly; "but it is very very sudden."

"And I trust he has obtained a better kingdom," added Redwald; "he must, you know, if the monks tell the truth, so why should we weep for him?"

"At least," said Edwy, looking up, "Elfric need not go home now."

"No, certainly not, but he had better disappear from court for a time. The lady Ethelgiva might afford him hospitality, or he might stay at the royal palace at Kingston. I will tell the messenger to keep out of the way, and Dunstan may suppose that his orders have been obeyed to the letter."

"Why should we trouble what he may think or say?"

"Because the Witan has not yet met, and until it has gone through the form, the mere *form*, of recognising your title, you are not actually king. Dunstan has some influence. Suppose he should use it for Edgar?"

"Edgar, the palefaced little priestling!"

"All the better for that in Dunstan's eyes. Nay, be advised, my king; keep all things quiet until the coronation is over, then let Dunstan know who you are and who he is."

"Indeed I will. He shall have cause to rue his insolent behaviour the other night."

"Bide your time, my liege; and now the great officers of state require your presence below."

A few days later a sorrowful procession entered the old city of Winchester, the capital of Wessex, and once a favourite residence of Edred, now to be his last earthly resting-place. Much had the citizens loved him; and as the long train defiled into the open space around the old minster—old, even then—the vast assemblage, grouped beneath the trees around the sacred precincts, lifted up their voices and joined in the funeral hymn, while many wept tears of genuine sorrow. It was awe-inspiring, that burst of tuneful wailing, as the monks entered the sacred pile, and it made men's hearts thrill with the sense of the unseen world into which their king had entered, and where, as they believed, their supplications might yet follow him.

There were the chief mourners—Edwy and Edgar—and they followed the royal corpse, the latter greatly afflicted, and shedding genuine tears of sorrow—and the royal household. All the nobility of Wessex, and many of the nobles from Mercia and other provinces, were gathered together, and amidst the solemn silence of the vast crowd, Dunstan performed the last sad and solemn rites with a broken voice; while the archbishop—Odo the Good, as he was frequently called—assisted in the dread solemnity.

It was over; the coffin was lowered to the royal vaults to repose in peace, the incense* had ceased to float dreamily beneath the lofty roof, the various lights which had borne part in the ceremony were extinguished, the choral anthem had ceased, for Edred slept with his fathers.

And outside, the future king was welcomed with loud cries of "God save King Edwy, and make him *just* as Alfred, *pious* as Edred, and *warlike* as Athelstane!" "Long live the heir of Cerdic's ancient line !" Thus their cries anticipated the decision of the Witan, and without all was noise and clamour; while within the sacred fane the ashes of him who had so lately ruled England rested in peace by the side of his royal father Edward, the son of Alfred, three of whose sons—Athelstane, Edmund, Edred—had now reigned in succession.

It must not be supposed that Edwy was as yet king by the law of the land. The early English writers all speak of their kings as elected; it was not until the Witan had recognised them, that they were crowned and assumed

* See Note I.—Incense in the Anglo-Saxon Church.

the royal prerogatives. Edwy had followed Redwald's advice: he had kept Elfric out of the way, and meant to do so until his coronation day. And meanwhile he condescended to disguise his real feelings, and to affect sorrow for his past failings when in the presence of Dunstan.

Yet he took advantage of the greater liberty he now enjoyed to renew his visits to the mansion up the Thames, and to spend whole days in the society of Elgiva. In their simplicity and deep love they thought all the obstacles to their happy union now removed. Alas! ill-fated pair!

CHAPTER VIII.

NOTHING could exceed in solemnity the "hallowing of the king," as the coronation ceremony was termed in Anglo-Saxon times. It was looked upon as an event of both civil and ecclesiastical importance, and therefore nothing was omitted which could lend dignity to the occasion.

The Witan, or parliament, had already met and given its consent to the coronation of Edwy. It was not, as we have already remarked, a mere matter of course that the direct heir should occupy the throne. Edred had already ascended, while Edwy, the son of his elder brother, was an infant, not as regent, but as king; and in any case of un-fitness on the part of the heir-apparent, it was in the power of the Witan to pass him over, and to choose for the public good some other member of the royal house. The same Witan conferred upon Edgar the title of sub-king of Mercia under his brother. Solemn and imposing was the meeting of the Witenagemot, or "assembly of the wise." It was divided into three estates. *The first* consisted of the only class who, as a rule, had any learning in those days—the clergy, represented by the bishop, abbot, and their principal officials : *the second* consisted of the vassal kings of Scotland, Cumbria, Wales, Mona, the Hebrides, and other dependent states, the great earls, as of Mercia or East Anglia, and other mighty magnates : *the third*, of the lesser thanes, who were the especial vassals of the king, or the great land-holders, for the possession of *land* was an essential part of a title to nobility.

Amongst these sat Ella of Æscendune, who, in spite of his age, had come to the metropolis to testify his loyalty and fealty to the son of the murdered Edmund, his old friend and companion in arms, and to behold his own eldest son once more.

It was the morning of a beautiful day in early spring, one of those days of which the poet has written—

> "Sweet day, so calm, so pure, so bright,
> The bridal of the earth and sky "—

when winter seems to have loosed its stern hold upon the frozen earth, and the songs of countless birds welcome the bright sunlight, the harbinger of approaching summer.

The roads leading to Kingston - on - Thames were thronged with travellers of every degree—the ealdorman or earl with his numerous attendants, the bishop with rude ecclesiastical pomp, the peasant in his rough jerkin—all hastening to the approaching ceremony, which, as it had been definitely fixed, was to take place at that royal city.

There Athelstane had been crowned with great pomp and splendour, for it was peculiarly " *Cynges tun* " or the King's Town, and after the coronation it was customary for the newly-crowned monarch to take formal possession of his kingdom by standing on a great stone in the churchyard.

The previous night, Archbishop Odo had arrived from Canterbury, and his bosom friend and brother, Dunstan, from Glastonbury, as also Cynesige, Bishop of Lichfield, a man in every way like-minded with them ; while nearly all the other prelates, abbots, and nobles, arrived in the early morn of the eventful day.

The solemn service of the coronation mass was about to commence, and the people were assembling in the great church of St. Mary, filling every inch of available room. Every figure was bent forward in earnest gaze, and every heart seemed to beat more quickly, as the faint and distant sound of deep solemn music, the monastic choirs chanting the processional psalms, drew near.

Suddenly the jubilant strains filled the whole church, as the white-robed train entered the sacred building while they sang—

"Quoniam prævenisti eum in benedictionibus dulcedinis, posuisti in capiti ejus coronam de lapide pretioso."*

Incense ascended in clouds to the lofty roof, torches were uplifted, banners floated in the air, every eye was now strained to catch a glimpse of the youthful monarch.

He came at last. Oh, how lovely the ill-fated boy looked that day! His beauty was of a somewhat fragile character, his complexion almost too fair, his hair shone around his shoulders in waves of gold, for men then wore their hair long, his eyes blue as the azure vault on that sweet spring morning: alas, that his spiritual being should not have been equally fair!

Elfric stood by his father, amidst the crowd of thanes, near the rood-screen, for he had spent the last few days at Kingston, and there his father had found him, and had embraced him with joy, little dreaming of the change which had come over his darling boy.

"Look, father, is he not every inch a king?" Elfric could not help exclaiming, forgetting the place and the occasion in his pride in his king and his friend.

He would have been one of the four boys who bore the royal train, but it had not seemed advisable on such a day to offend Dunstan too seriously.

The mass proceeded after the royal party had all taken their places, and the coronation service was incorporated into the rite, following the Nicene Creed and preceding the canon.

Kneeling before the altar, the young prince might well tremble with emotion. Before him stood the archbishop, clad in full pontifical vestments; around were the most noted prelates and wisest abbots of England; behind him

* Psalm xxi. 3.

the nobility, gentry, and commonalty of the whole country—all gazing upon him, as the archbishop dictated the solemn words of the oath, which Edwy repeated with trembling voice after him.

"In the name of the ever-blessed Trinity, I promise three things to the Christian people, my subjects :

"*First*, that the Church of God within my realm shall enjoy peace, free from any molestation."

"*Secondly*, that I will prevent, to the utmost of my power, theft and every fraud in all ranks of men."

"*Thirdly*, that I will preserve and maintain justice and mercy in all judicial proceedings, so that the good and merciful God may, according to His mercy, forgive us all our sins, Who liveth and reigneth for ever and ever.   Amen."*

Then followed a most solemn charge from "Odo the Good," setting forth all the deep responsibilities of the oath Edwy had taken, and of the awful account to be rendered to God of the flock committed to his youthful charge, at the great and awful day of judgment.

Then the holy oil was solemnly poured upon the head of the kneeling boy, after which he made the usual offertory of " gold, frankincense, and myrrh," at the altar, emblematical of the visit of the three kings of old, who from Sheba bore their gold and incense to the Lord.

Then was the sacred bracelet put upon his arm, the crown on his head, the sceptre in his hand, after which the mass proceeded.

It is touching to recall the worship of those far-off days, when all the surrounding circumstances differed so widely from those of the present hour ; yet the Church, in her holy conservatism, has kept intact and almost changeless all that is hers ; that day the " Nicene Creed," " Sanctus," " Agnus Dei," " Gloria in Excelsis," rolled as now in strains of melody towards heaven, and the " Te Deum " which concluded the jubilant service is our Te Deum still, albeit in the vulgar tongue.

* From an Anglo-Saxon MS.

The sacred rites concluded, the royal procession left the church and proceeded to the churchyard, when Edwy took formal possession of Wessex, by the ceremony of standing upon a large rock called the King's Stone, whence the town derived its name.

The feast was spread in the palace hard by, and all the nobles and thanes (if the words are not synonymous) flocked thither, while the multitude had their liberal feast spread at various tables throughout the town, at the royal expense.

Elfric followed his father to the palace, and was about to take his place at the board, when a page appeared and summoned him to the presence of Edwy.

"I shall keep a vacant place for you by my side," said Ella, "so that we may feast together, my son, when the king releases you; it is a great honour that he should think of you now."

Elfric followed the messenger, who led him into the interior of the palace, where he found Edwy impatiently awaiting him in the royal dressing-chamber.

Elfric had expected to find the newly-crowned king deeply impressed, but if such had been the case, at the moment it had passed away.

"Thanks to all the saints, including S. George, and especially the dragon, that I can look into your jolly face again, Elfric; it is a relief after all the grim-beards who have surrounded me to-day. I shudder when I think of them."

Elfric had been about to kneel and kiss the royal hand, in token of homage, but Edwy saw the intention and prohibited him.

"No more of that an thou lovest me, Elfric; my poor hand is almost worn out already."

"The day must have tired you, the scene was so exciting."

Edwy yawned as he replied, "Thank God it is over; I thought Odo was going to preach to me all day, and the incense almost stifled me; the one good thing is that it is done now, and all England—Kent, Sussex, Wessex, Essex, Northumbria, East Anglia, and Mercia—have all acknowledged me as their liege lord, the Basileus of Britain. What is done can't be undone, and Dunstan may eat his leek now, and go to fight Satan again."

Elfric looked up in some surprise.

" What do you think, my friend ; who do you suppose is here in the palace, in the royal apartments ? "

" Who ? "

" Elgiva, the fair Elgiva, the lovely Elgiva, dear Elgiva, and her mother. Oh, but I shall love to look upon her face when the feast is done, and the grim-beards have gone ! "

" But Dunstan ? "

" Dunstan may go and hang himself ; he can't scrape off the consecrated oil, or carry away crown, bracelet, and sceptre, to hide with the other royal treasures at Glastonbury ; but the feast is beginning, and you must come and sit on my right hand."

" No, no," said Elfric, who saw at once what an impropriety this would be, " not yet ; besides, my old father is here, and has kept a seat beside himself for me."

" Well, good-bye for the present ; I shall expect you after the feast. Elgiva will be glad to see you."

Elfric returned to his father, but a feeling of sadness had taken possession of him, an apprehension of coming evil.

The feast began ; the clergy and the nobility of the land were assembled in the great hall of the palace, and there was that profusion of good cheer which befitted the day, for the English were, like their German ancestors, in the habit of considering the feast an essential part of any solemnity.

How much was eaten and drunk upon the occasion it would be dangerous to say, for it would probably exceed all modern experience, but it seemed to the impatient Edwy that the feast and the subsequent drinking of pledges and healths would never end, and he was impatient the whole time to get away and be in the company of the charmer.

An opportunity seemed at last to offer itself to his immature judgment. Gleemen had sung, harpers had harped, but the excitement culminated when Siward, a Northumbrian noble, who was a great musician, and skilful in improvisation, did not disdain, like the royal Alfred, to take the harp and pour forth an extemporary ode of great beauty, whereupon the whole multitude rose to their feet and waved their wine-cups in the air, in ardent appreciation of the patriotic sentiments he had uttered, and the beauty of the music and poetry.

During the full din of their heated applause, when all eyes were fixed upon the accomplished musician, Edwy rose softly from his chair; a door was just behind him, and he took advantage of it to leave the hall and thread the passages quickly, till he came to the room where he had left Elgiva, when he threw aside his royal mantle and all his restraint at the same time.

It was not for a few moments that the company in the hall discovered the absence of their king, but when they did there was a sudden hush, and men looked at each other in mute astonishment; it appeared to all, with scarce an exception, a gross insult to the assembled majesty of the nation.*

Poor Edwy, in his thoughtlessness and want of proper feeling, little knew the deep anger such a proceeding would cause; in his lack of a reverential spirit he was constantly, as we have seen, offending against the respect due to the Church, the State, or himself—first as heir-presumptive, then as king.

Men stood mute, as we have said, then murmurs of indignation at the slight arose, and all looked at Dunstan.

He beckoned to Cynesige of Lichfield, who came to his side. "We must bring this thoughtless boy back," he said, " or great harm will be done."

"But how ?"

* "All were indignant at the shameless deed, and murmured amongst themselves."—*William of Malmesbury.*

" By persuasion, *if possible.*   Follow me."

The two prelates entered the interior of the palace, and sought the king's private chamber.

As they drew near they heard the sound of merry laughter, and each of them frowned as men might do who were little accustomed to condone the weakness of human flesh.   Entering the chamber very unceremoniously, they paused, as if aghast, when they beheld the king in the company of Elgiva, his royal diadem cast upon the ground.

He started in surprise, and for a moment in fear ; then, remembering who he was, he exclaimed, angrily—" How dare you, sir monk, intrude upon the privacy of your king, unbidden ? "

" We do so as the ambassadors of the King of kings."

It is out of our power to describe the scene which followed, the fiery words of Edwy, the stern yet quiet rejoinders of the churchmen, the tears of the mother and daughter ; but it is well known how the scene ended.   Edwy absolutely refused to return to the assembled guests, saying he would forfeit his kingdom first ; and Dunstan replied that for his (Edwy's) own sake he should then be compelled to use force, and suiting the action to the word, he and Cynesige took each an arm of the youthful king, and led him back by compulsion to the assembled nobles and clergy.

Before condemning Dunstan, we must remember that Elgiva could not stand in the relation of the affianced bride of the king ; that Edwy really seemed to set the laws of both Church and State at defiance, those very laws which but that day he had sworn solemnly to maintain ; and that but recently he had stood in the relation of pupil to Dunstan, so that in his zeal for Church and State, the abbot forgot the respect due to the king.   He saw only the *boy,* and forgot the sovereign.

The guests assembled in the banqueting-hall had seen the desertion of their royal master with murmurs both loud and deep ; but when they saw him return escorted by

Dunstan and Cynesige, their unanimous approval showed that in their eyes the churchmen had taken a proper step.

Yet, although Edwy tried to make a show of having returned of his own free will, an innocent device at which his captors connived when they entered the hall with him, the bitterest passions were rankling in his heart, and he determined to take a terrible revenge, should it ever be in his power, upon Dunstan.

There was comparatively little show of merriment during the rest of the feast, and the noble company separated earlier than was usual on such occasions.

"If this be the way King Edwy treats his guests," said the Earl of Mercia, "he will find scant loyalty north of the Thames."

"Nor in East Anglia," said another.

"There is another of the line of Cerdic living."

"Yes, Edgar, his brother."

"Dunstan and Cynesige brought him back with some difficulty, I'll be bound."

"Yes; although he tried to smile, I saw the black frown hidden beneath."

"He will take revenge for all this."

"Upon whom?"

"Why, upon Dunstan to be sure."

"But how can he? Dunstan is too powerful for that."

"Wait and see."

Such was the general tone of the conversation, from which the sentiments of the community might be inferred.

Elfric went, as he had been bidden to do, at the conclusion of the feast, to seek Edwy, and found him, it is needless to state, in a towering rage.

"Elfric," he said, "am I a king? or did I dream I was crowned to-day?"

"You certainly were."

"And yet these insolent monks have dared to force me from the company of Elgiva to return to that sottish feast, and what is worse, I find they have dared to send her and her mother home under an escort, so that I cannot even apologise to them. As I live, if I am a king I will have revenge."

"I trust so, indeed," said Elfric, "they deserve death."

"I would it were in my power to inflict it; but this accursed monk — I go mad when I mention his name — is all too powerful. I believe Satan helps him."

"Still there may be ways, if you only wait till you can look around you."

"There may indeed."

"Only have patience; all will be in your hands some day."

"And if it be in my power I will restore the worship of Woden and Thor, and burn every monk's nest in the land."

"*They* were at least the gods of warriors."

"Elfric, you will stand by me, will you not?"

"With my life."

"Come to the window, now; see the old sots departing. There a priest, there a thane, there an earl—all drunk, I do believe; don't you think so?"

"Yes, yes," said Elfric, disregarding the testimony of both his eyes that they were all perfectly sober. Just then his eye caught a very disagreeable object, and he turned somewhat pale.

"What are you looking at?" said Edwy.

"There is that old fox, Dunstan, talking with my father; he will learn that I am here."

"What does it matter?"

"Only that he will easily persuade my father to take me home."

"Then the commands of a king must outweigh those of a father. I have heard Dunstan say a king is the father of *all* his people, and I command you to stay."

"I want to stay with all my heart."

"Then you *shall*, even if I have to make a pretence of detaining you by force."

The anticipations of Elfric were not far wrong. Dunstan had found out the truth. He had sought out the old thane to condole with him upon the pain he supposed he must recently have inflicted by his letter.

"I cannot express to you, my old friend and brother," he said, "the great pain with which I sent your poor boy Elfric home, but it was a necessity."

"Sent him home?" said Ella.

"Yes, at the time our lamented Edred died." .

"Sent him home!" repeated Ella, in such undisguised amazement that Dunstan soon perceived something was amiss, and in a few short minutes became possessed of the whole facts, while Ella learnt his son's disgrace.

They conferred long and earnestly. The father's heart was sorely wounded, but he could not think that Elfric would resist his commands, and he promised to take him back at once to Æscendune, where he hoped all would soon be well—"soon, very soon," he said falteringly.

So the old thane went to his lodgings, hard by the palace, where he awaited his son.

Late in the evening Elfric arrived, his countenance flushed with wine : he had been seeking courage for the part he had to play in the wine-cup.

Long and painful, most painful, was the interview that followed. Hardened in his rebellion, the unhappy Elfric defied his father's authority and justified his sin, flatly refusing to return home, in which he pretended to be justified by "the duty a subject owed to his sovereign."

Thus roused to energy, Ella solemnly adjured his boy to remember the story of his uncle Oswald, and the sad fate *he* had met with. It was very seldom indeed that Ella alluded to his unhappy brother, the story was too painful ; but now that Elfric seemed to be commencing a similar course of disobedience, the example of the miserable outlaw came too forcibly to his mind to be altogether suppressed.

"Beware, my son," added Ella, "lest the curse which

fell upon Oswald fall upon you, and your younger brother succeed to your inheritance."

"It is not a large one," said Elfric, "and in that case, the king whom I serve will find me a better one."

"Is it not written, 'Put not your trust in princes?' O my son, my son; you will bring my grey hairs with sorrow to the grave!"

It was of no avail. The old thane arose in the morning with the intention of taking Elfric home even by force, such force as Dunstan had used, if necessary, but found that the youth had disappeared in the night; neither could he learn what had become of him, but he shrewdly guessed that the young king could have told him.

Broken-hearted by his son's cruel desertion, the thane of Æscendune returned home alone.

CHAPTER IX.

RICH in historical associations and reputed sanctity, the abbey of Glastonbury was the ecclesiastical centre of western England. Here grew the holy thorn which Joseph of Arimathea had planted when, fatigued with travel, he had struck his staff into the ground, and lo! a goodly tree; here was the holy well of which he had drunk, and where he baptized his converts, so that its waters became possessed of miraculous power to heal diseases.

Here again were memorials, dear to the vanquished Welsh; for did not Arthur, the *great* King Arthur, the hero of a thousand fights, the subject of gleeman's melody and of the minstrel's praise, lie buried here? if indeed he *were* dead, and not spirited away by magic power.

A Welsh population still existed around the abbey, for it was near the borders of *West* Wales, as a large portion of Devon and Cornwall was then called, and Exeter had not long become an English town.* The legends of Glastonbury were nearly all of that distant day when the Saxons and Angles had not yet discovered Britain, and she reposed safe under the protection of mighty Rome; hence, it was the object of pilgrimage and of deep veneration to all those of Celtic blood, while the English were unwilling to be behind in their veneration.

Here, in the first year of the great English king Athelstane, Dunstan was born, the son of Herstan and Kynedred,

* The Welsh were driven from Exeter by King Athelstane; before that time, Englishmen and Welsh had inhabited it with equal rights.

both persons of rank—a man destined to influence the Anglo-Saxon race first in person and then in spirit for generations—the greatest man of his time, whether, as his contemporaries thought, mighty for good, or, as men of narrower minds have thought, mighty for evil.

In his early youth, Glastonbury lay, as it lies now, in ruin and decay ; the Danes had ravaged it, and its holy walls were no longer eloquent with prayer and praise. Yet the old inhabitants still talked with regret of the departed glories of the fane ; the pilgrim and the stranger still visited the consecrated well, hoping to gain strength from its healing wave, for the soil had been hallowed by the blood of martyrs and the holy lives of saints ; here kings and nobles, laying aside their greatness, had retired to prepare for the long and endless home, and in the calm seclusion of the cloister had found peace.

Here the mind of the young Dunstan was moulded for his future work ; here, weak in body, but precocious in intellect, he drew in, as if with his vital breath, legend and tradition ; here, from a body of Scottish missionaries, or, as we should now call them, Irish,* he learned with rapidity all that a boy could acquire of civil or ecclesiastical lore, and both in Latin and in theology his progress amazed his tutors.

Up to this time the world had held possession of his heart, and, balancing the advantages of a religious and a secular life, he chose, as most young people would choose, the attractions of court, to which his parents' rank entitled him, and leaving Glastonbury he repaired to the court of Edmund.

There his extraordinary talents excited envy, and he was accused of magical arts : his harp had been heard to pour forth strains of ravishing beauty when no human hand was near, and other like prodigies, savouring of the black art, were said to attend him, so that he fled the court, and took refuge with his uncle, Elphege, the Bishop of Winchester.

A long illness followed, during which the youth, dis-

* The earliest inhabitants of Ireland were called Scots.

gusted with the world, and startled by his narrow escape
from death, reversed the choice he had previously made,
and renounced the world and its pleasures.

Ordained priest at Winchester, he was sent back with
a monk's attire to Glastonbury, where he gave himself up
to austerities, such as, in a greater or less degree, always
accompanied a conversion in those days; here miracles
were reported to attend him, and stories of his personal
conflicts with the Evil One were handed from mouth to
mouth, until his fame had filled the country round.*

The influence he rapidly acquired enabled him to
commence the great work of rebuilding Glastonbury, in
which he was only interrupted by the frequent calls which
he had to court, to become the adviser of King Edmund;
where indeed he was often in the discharge of the office of
prime minister of the kingdom, and showed as much
aptitude in civil as in ecclesiastical affairs.

Glastonbury being rebuilt, the Benedictine† rule was
introduced, and Dunstan himself became abbot. It was
far the noblest and best monastic code of the day, being
peculiarly adapted to prevent the cloister from becoming
the abode of either idleness or profligacy.

But this was not done without much opposition; the
secular priests—as the married clergy and those who lived
amongst their flocks (as English clergy do now) were called
—opposed the introduction of the Benedictine rule with
all their might, and were always thorns in Dunstan's side.

The unfortunate Edmund, after the sad event at Pucklechurch, on the feast of S. Augustine, was buried at Glastonbury by the abbot, and his two sons, Edwy and Edgar,
were put under Dunstan's especial care by the new king
Edred. The rest of the story is tolerably well known to
our readers.

The first steps of Edwy's reign were all taken with a

* See Note J.—Legends about S. Dunstan.
† See Note K.—The Benedictine rule.

view to one great end—to revenge himself and to destroy Dunstan, who, aware of the royal enmity, and of his inability to restrain the sovereign, withdrew himself quietly to Glastonbury, and confined himself to the discharge of his duties as its abbot.

But this did not satisfy Edwy, who, panting for the ruin of the monk he hated, sought occasion for a quarrel, and soon found it. Dunstan had been the royal almoner, and had had the disposal of large sums of money, for purposes connected with the Church, on which they had been strictly expended. Now Edwy required a strict account of all these disbursements, which Dunstan refused to give, saying it had already been given to Edred, and that no person had any right to investigate the charities of the departed king.

His stout resistance gained the day in the first instance, but Edwy never felt at rest while Dunstan lived at peace in the land, and Ethelgiva and her fair daughter were ever inciting him to fresh acts of hostility, little as he needed such incitement.

The first measures were of a very dishonourable kind. Evil reports were spread abroad to destroy the character of the great abbot, and prepare people's minds for his disgrace; then disaffection was stirred up amongst the secular clergy surrounding Glastonbury—a very easy thing; and attempts were made in vain to create a faction against him in his own abbey; then at last the neighbouring thanes, many of Danish extraction and scarcely Christian, were stirred up to invade the territory of the abbey, and were promised immunity and secure possession of their plunder. They liked the pleasant excitement of galloping over Dunstan's ecclesiastical patrimony, of plundering the farms and driving away the cattle, and there was scarcely a night in which some fresh outrage was not committed. At this point the action of our tale recommences.

It will be remembered that the father of Ella had found relief from his grief, after the death of his unhappy son

Oswald, in building and endowing the monastery of S. Wilfred, situate on the river's bank, at a short distance from the hall.

The completion of the work had, however, been reserved for his son, and, everything being now done, it became the earnest desire of Ella, with the consent of the brethren who had been gathered into the incomplete building, to place it under the Benedictine rule.

For this end he determined to send a messenger to negotiate with Dunstan at Glastonbury, and, yielding to Alfred's most earnest request, he consented to send him, in company with Father Cuthbert, who was to be the future prior, upon the mission.

Since the desertion of Elfric, his brother Alfred had been as a ministering angel to his father, so tender had been his affection, yet so manly and pure. He was by nature gifted with great talents, and his progress in ecclesiastical lore, almost the only lore of the day, would have well fitted him for the Church ; but if this idea had ever been in the mind of the thane, he put it aside after the departure of Elfric.

But it must not be supposed that the *only* literature of the period was in Latin. Alfred, the great King Alfred, skilful in learning as in war, had translated into English (as we have mentioned earlier in our tale) the *History of the World*, by Orosius, and other works, which formed a part of the royal library in the palace of Edred. All these works were known to his young namesake, Alfred, far better than they had been either to Edwy or Elfric, in their idleness, and he was well informed beyond the average scope of his time. But his imagination had long been fired by the accounts he had received of Glastonbury and its sanctuary, so that he eagerly besought his father to allow him to go thither.

But the poor old thane felt much like Jacob when he was begged to send Benjamin into Egypt. Elfric was not, so far as home ties were concerned, they had never heard of him since the coronation-day, and now they would take Alfred from him. It may seem strange to our readers that Ella should regard a journey from the Midlands to Glastonbury in so serious a light; but Wessex and Mercia had long been independent states, communication infrequent, and it would certainly be many weeks before Alfred could return; while inexperience magnified the actual dangers of the way.

Coaches and carriages were not in use, neither would the state of the roads have rendered such use practicable. All travellers were forced to journey on horseback, and, like Elfric when he departed from home, to carry all their baggage in a similar manner.

The navigation of the Avon, which would have opened the readiest road to the south-west, was impeded by sandbanks and rapids; there were as yet no locks, no canals.

Once the Romans had made matchless roads, as in other parts of their empire, but not a stone had been laid thereon since the days of Hengist and Horsa, and many a stone had been taken away for building purposes, or to pave the courtyards of Saxon homes.*

Still the ancient Foss-way, which once extended from Lincolnshire to Devonshire, formed the best route, and it was decided to travel by it, making a brief detour, so as to enable the party to pass the first night at the residence of an old friend of the family who dwelt on the high borderland which separates the counties of Oxford and Warwick, in old times the frontier between the two Celtic tribes, the Dobuni and the Carnabii.

So Father Cuthbert and Alfred, with three attendant serfs, left Æscendune early on a fine summer morning, and followed a bye-road through the forest, until, after a few difficulties, arising from entanglement in copse or swamp, they reached the Foss-way. Wide and spacious, this grand old road ran through the dense forest in an almost unbroken line; huge trees overshadowed it on either side, and the growth of underwood was so dense that no one could penetrate it without difficulty. Sometimes the scene changed, and a

* See Note I.—The Roman roads.

dense swamp, amidst which the timber of former generations rotted away, succeeded, but the grand old road still offered, even in its decay, a firm and sure footing. Built with consummate skill, the lower strata of which it was composed remained so firm and unyielding, that, could the Romans but have returned for a few years, they might have restored it to its ancient perfection, when the traveller might post rapidly upon it from Lincoln even to Totness in Devonshire.

Little, however, did our travellers think of the grand men of old, who had built this mighty causeway six or seven centuries earlier. Their chief feeling, when they reached it, was one of relief; the change was so acceptable from the tangled and miry bypath through the forest.

"Holy S. Wilfred," exclaimed Father Cuthbert, "but my steed hath wallowed like a hog. I have sunk in the deep mire where was no footing."

"A little grooming will soon make him clean again, father."

"But verily we have passed through a slough and a wilderness, and my inner man needeth refreshment; let us even partake of the savoury pies wherewith the provident care of thy father hath provided us."

The suggestion was by no means a bad one, and the party sat down on a green and sloping bank, overshadowed by a mighty oak which grew by the wayside. It was noontide, and the shelter from the heat was not at all unpleasant. Their wallets were overhauled, and choice provision found against famine by the road. There were few, very few inns where travellers could obtain decent accommodation, and every preparation had been made for a camp out when necessary.

So they ate their midday meal with thankfulness of heart, and reclined awhile ere courting more fatigue. The day was lovely, and the silence of the woods almost oppressive; nought save the hum of insects broke its tranquillity.

Fatigued by the exertions of the morning, the whole party fell asleep; the gentle breeze, the quiet rustling of the leaves, all combined to lull the senses. While they thus slept, the day wore on, and the sun was declining when they awoke and wondered that they had wasted their time for so long a period.

Starting again with renewed energy, they travelled onward through the mighty forest till sunset, when they approached the high ground which now runs along the northern boundary of Oxfordshire, and of which Edgehill forms a portion. Their progress had been slow, for the road, although secure, was yet in so neglected a state as to form an obstacle to rapid travelling, and they had met no fellow-travellers. Leaving the Foss-way, which followed the valley, and slowly ascending the hill by a well-marked track, they looked back from its summit upon a glorious view. Far as the eye could reach stretched the forest to the northward, one huge unbroken expanse, save where the thin wreaths of smoke showed some village or homestead, where English farmers already wrestled with the obstacles nature had formed. But westward the view was more home-like; the setting sun was sinking behind the huge heights now known as the Malvern Hills, which reared their forms proudly in the distant horizon.

The western sky was rich in the hues of the departing sun, which cast its declining beams upon village and homestead, thinly scattered in the fertile vale through which the Foss-way pursued its course.

But our travellers did not stay long to contemplate the beauty of the scene; they were yet ten miles from the hospitable roof where they had purposed spending the night, and they had overslept themselves so long at their noontide halt, that they found darkness growing apace, while their weary animals could scarcely advance farther.

"Is there no inn, no Christian dwelling near, where we may repose? Verily my limbs bend beneath me with fatigue," said Father Cuthbert.

"There is no dwelling of Christian man nearer than

the halls of the Thane of Rollrich, and we shall scarcely reach them for a couple of hours," said Oswy, the serf.

" Thou art a Job's comforter. What sayest thou, Anlac ?"

" There are the remains of an old temple of heathen times not far from here, a little on the right hand of the road, but they say the place is haunted."

" Has it a roof to shelter us ?"

" Part of the ruins are well covered."

" Then thither we will go. Peradventure it will prove a safe abiding-place against wolves or evil men, and if there be demons we must even exorcise them."

When they had emerged from the forest, they had, as we have seen, ascended the high table-land which formed the northern frontier of the territory of the Dobuni—passing over the very ground where, seven hundred years later, the troops of the King and the Parliament were arrayed against each other in deadly combat for the first time.

But at this remote period the country where the Celts had once lived, and whence their civilised descendants had been driven by the English, had become a barren moorland. Scarce a tree grew on the heights, but a wild common, with valley and hill alternating, much as on Dartmoor at the present day, stretched before the travellers, and was traversed by the old Roman trackway. Dreary indeed it looked in the darkening twilight; here and there some huge crag overtopped the road, and then the track lay along a flat surface. It was after passing some huge misshapen stones, which spoke of early Celtic worship, that suddenly, in the distance on the right, the ruined temple lay before them.

Pillars of beautiful workmanship, evidently reared by Roman skill, surrounded a paved quadrangle raised upon a terrace approached on all sides by steps. These steps and the pavement were alike of stone, but where weeds *could* grow they *had* grown, and the footing was damp and slippery with rank vegetation and fungus growth.

At the extremity of the quadrangle the roof still partly covered the adytum or shrine from the sky, the platform reared itself upon its flight of massive steps where early British Christianity had demolished the idol, and beneath were chambers once appropriated to the use of the priests, which, by the aid of fire, could shortly be made habitable.

There was plenty of brushwood and underwood near, and our travellers speedily made a large fire, which expelled the damp from the place, albeit, as the smoke could only escape by an aperture in the roof, which, it is needless to say, was not embraced in the original design of the architect, it was not till the blaze had subsided and the glowing embers alone warmed the chamber, that mortal lungs could bear the stifling atmosphere, so charged had it been with smoke.

Still it was very acceptable shelter to the travellers, who must otherwise have camped out on the exposed moorland, and they made a hearty and comfortable meal, which being concluded, Father Cuthbert made a very brief address.

" My brethren," he said, " we have travelled, like Abraham from Ur of the Chaldees, not ' sine numine,' that is not without God's protection ; and as we are about to sleep in a place where devils once deluded Christian people, it will not be amiss to say the nightsong, and commend ourselves ' in manus Altissimi,' that is to say, to God's care."

The compline service was familiar to each one present, and Father Cuthbert intoned it in a stentorian voice, particularly those portions of the 91st Psalm which seemed to defy the Evil One, and he recited just as if he were sure Satan was listening—" Thou shalt go upon the lion and the adder ; the young lion and the *dragon* shalt thou tread under thy feet."

All the company seemed to feel comfort in the words, and, first posting a sentinel, to be relieved every three hours, they commended themselves to sleep.

Alfred found his couch very pleasant at first, but before he had been long asleep his rest became disturbed by singular dreams.

He thought he was standing within a grassy glade in a deep forest; it was darkening twilight, and he felt anxious to find his way from the spot, when his guardian angel appeared to him, and pointed out a narrow track between two huge rocks. He followed until he heard many voices, and saw a strange light reflected on the tree tops, as if from beneath, when amidst the din of voices he recognised Elfric's tones. "Wouldst thou save thy brother, then proceed," his guardian angel seemed to whisper.

He strove, in his dream, to proceed, when he awoke so vividly impressed that he felt convinced coming events were casting their shadows before. He could not drive the thought of Elfric from his mind; he slept, but again in wild dreams his brother seemed to appear; once he seemed to oppose Elfric's passage over a plank which crossed a roaring torrent; then he seemed as if he were falling, falling, amidst rushing waters, when he awoke.

"I can sleep no longer. I will look out at the night," he said.

A faint moon had arisen, and lent an uncertain light to the outlines of hill, crag, and moorland, while it gilded the cornice above, where the wind seemed to linger and moan over departed greatness. The Druidical worship of olden days, the deluded worshippers now turned into dust, and the cruel rites of their bloodstained worship, older even than those of the ruined temple, rose before his imagination, until fancy seemed to people the silent wastes before him with those who had once crowded round that circle of misshapen stones which stood out vividly on the verge of the plain.

He felt that nameless fear which such thoughts excite so strongly, that he sought the company of the sentinel whom they had posted to guard their slumbers, and found not one but two at the post.

"Oswy and Anlac! both watching?"

"It was too lonesome for one," said Oswy.

"Have you seen or heard aught amiss?"

"Yes. About an hour ago, there were cries such as men make when they die in torture, smothered by other sounds like the beating of drums, blowing of horns, and I know not what."

" You were surely dreaming ?"

" No ; it came from yonder circle of stones, and a light like that of a great fire seemed to shine around."

Alfred made no reply ; but he remembered that they had talked of the Druidical rites the night before, and thought that the idea had taken such hold upon the minds of his followers as to suggest the sounds to their fancy. Still he watched with them till the first red streak of day appeared in the east.

CHAPTER X.

EARLY in the morning our travellers arose and took their way through an open country which abounded with British and Roman remains, no fewer than three entrenched camps, once fortifying the frontier of the Dobuni, lying within sight or hard by the road, which, skirting the summit of the watershed between the Thames and the Avon, afforded magnificent views.

About an hour after starting they came upon a singular monument of Druidical times, consisting of sixty huge stones arranged in a circular form, with an entrance at the north-east, while a single rock or large stone, the largest of all, stood apart from the circle, as if looking down into the valley beneath.*

"What can be the origin of this circle?" said Alfred.

"It belongs to the old days of heathenesse; before the Welsh were conquered by the Romans, perhaps before our Blessed Lord came into the world, these stones were placed as you now see them," replied Father Cuthbert.

"What purpose could they serve?"

"For their devil worship, I suppose; you see those five stones which stand at some little distance?"

"They are the Five Whispering Knights," said Oswy.

"They are the remains of a cromlech or altar whereon they offered their sons and daughters unto devils, and shed innocent blood, wherefore the Lord brought the Romans upon them."

* See Note M.—The Rollright Stones.

" But the Romans were idolatrous too."

" Yet their religion was milder than the one it superseded. Jupiter required no human sacrifices ; and even otherwise, God has said that the wicked man is often His sword to avenge Him of His adversaries."

" Oswy looks as if he had a tale to tell."

" Speak out, Oswy, and let us all hear," said the good father.

" Well, then," said Oswy, " these were not once stones at all, but living men—a king, five knights, and sixty soldiers—who came to take Long Compton, the town down there, in the valley ; but it so happened that a great enchanter dwelt there, and being out that morning he saw them coming, muttered his spells, and while the king— that stone yonder—was in front looking down on his prey, the five knights all whispering together, and the sixty soldiers behind in a circle, they were all suddenly changed into stone."

They all laughed heartily at this, and leaving the Rholdrwyg Stones, turned aside to the hospitable hall where they ought to have spent the previous night. So delighted was the Thane of Rholdrwyg or Rollrich to receive his guests that he detained them almost by force all that day, and it was only on the morrow that he permitted them to continue their journey.

They joined the Foss-way again after a few miles at Stow on the Wold ; the road was so good that they succeeded in reaching Cirencester, the ancient Corinium, that night, a distance of nearly thirty miles. Here they found a considerable population, for the town had been one of great importance, and was still one of the chief cities of southern Mercia, full of the remains of her departed Roman greatness, with shattered column and shapely arch yet diversifying the thatched hovels of the Mercians.

Two more days brought them to Bath, but the old Roman city had been utterly destroyed, and long subsequently the English town had been founded upon its site, so that there seemed no identity between Bath and Aquæ Solis, such as prevailed between Cirencester and Corinium.

One day's journey from Bath brought them at eventide within an easy day of Glastonbury, so that they paused in their journey for the last time at a well-known hostelry, chiefly occupied by pilgrims bound for Glastonbury, for the morrow was a high festival, or rather the commencement of one, and Dunstan was expected to conduct the ceremonies in person.

So crowded was the hostelry that Alfred and his revered tutor could only obtain a small chamber for their private accommodation, while their servants were forced to content themselves with such share of the straw of the outbuildings as they could obtain, in company with many others.

It was still early when they stopped at the inn, for one of their horses, which they had purchased by the way, had broken down so completely that they could not well proceed, and they were about to enter a dark and dangerous forest, full of ravenous bears and wolves, which had already cast its shade upon their path.

But this was not an uncommon feature in English travelling of that century, when there were no horses to be hired at the inns, and travellers could only *purchase* the animals they needed (if there were any to be sold); the forest, too, was reported to be the haunt of freebooters, and men dared to affirm that they were encouraged by the king to prey upon the fraternity at Glastonbury.

Still the dangers of the forest did not deter Alfred, who dearly loved woodland scenery and sport, from strolling therein when their hasty meal had been despatched, weary of the continuous objurgations and small-talk of the crowded inn.

He had wandered some distance, lost in thought, when all at once he started in some surprise, for the spot on which he was seemed familiar to him, although he had never been in Wessex before.

Yes, he certainly knew the glade, with the fine beech

trees surrounding it : where could he have seen it before ?
All at once he remembered his dream in the ruined temple,
and started to discover the secret foreknowledge he had thus
possessed.

He wandered up and down the glade till it became
dusk, and then shook off the thoughts to which he had been
a prey, and started to return to the inn, when, to his dismay,
he found he had forgotten in which direction it lay.

While seeking to find the path by which he had entered
the glade, he suddenly noticed a beaten track between two
huge rocks, which seemed to point in the direction he had
come, and yet which he recognised as the path he had been
bidden to follow in his dream. He hesitated not, but committed himself to it, while darkness seemed to increase each
moment. He was beginning to fear the dangers of a night
in the woods, when he was startled by a sound as of many
low voices, and at the same moment became conscious that
a light was tinging with red the upper branches of the trees
at no little distance, as if proceeding from some fire, hidden
by the formation of the ground.

At first he thought that he was in the neighbourhood of
outlaws, and tried to retire, but, as in his dream, he felt so
strong an impulse to discover the party whom the woods
concealed that he persevered.

Suddenly he stopped short, for he had come to the edge
of a kind of natural amphitheatre, a deep hollow in the
earth, the sides of which were covered with bushes and
trees, while the area at the bottom might perhaps have
covered a hundred square yards, and was clothed with
verdant turf. Not one, but several fires were burning,
and around them were reclining small groups of armed
men, while some were walking about chatting with each
other.

Alfred gazed in much surprise, for the party did not at
all realise his conception of a body of freebooters or robbers;
they all seemed to wear the same uniform, and to resemble
each other in their accoutrements and characteristics ; they

rather resembled, in short, a detachment of regular forces than a body of men whom chance might have thrown together, or the fortune of predatory war.

While he gazed upon them, two of their number, whose attire was rich and costly, and who seemed to be of higher rank than the rest, perhaps their officers, attracted his attention as they walked near the spot where, clinging to a tree, he overlooked the encampment from above.

One of them was a tall, dark warrior, whose whole demeanour was that of the professional soldier, whose dress was plain yet rich, and who might easily be guessed to be the commander of the party. He was talking earnestly, but in a subdued tone, to his younger companion, whom he seemed to be labouring to convince of the propriety of some course of action.

Alfred watched them eagerly ; the form of the younger —for so he appeared by his slender frame—seemed familiar to him, and when at last they turned their faces and walked towards him, the light of a neighbouring fire showed him the face of his brother Elfric.

" My dream ! " he mentally exclaimed.

They were evidently talking about some very important subject, and it was also evident that the objections of the younger, whatever they might be, were becoming rapidly over-ruled, when, as chance, if it were chance, would have it, they paused in their circuit of the little camp just beneath the tree where Alfred was posted.

" You see," said the elder, " that our course is clear, so definitely clear that we have but to do our duty to the king, while we avenge a thousand little insults we have ourselves received from this insolent monk—such insults as warriors wash out with blood."

" Yet he is a churchman, and it would be called utter sacrilege."

" Sacrilege ! is a churchman's blood redder than that of a layman, and is he not doomed as a traitor by a judgment as righteous as ever English law pronounced ? did he not keep Edwy from his throne during the lifetime of the usurper Edred ? "

"That was the sentence of the Witan, and *you* served Edred."

"I did not owe the allegiance of an Englishman to either, being of foreign birth, and so was no traitor ; as for the Witan, it is well known Dunstan influenced their decision at the death of the royal Edmund."

"I never heard the assertion before."

"You have many things still to learn ; you are but young as yet. But let it pass. Does not his conduct to Queen Elgiva merit death ? "

"I think it does. But still not without sentence of law."

"That sentence has been in fact pronounced, for in such cases as these, where the subject is too powerful for the direct action of the law to reach him, the decision of the king and council must pass for law, and *they* have decided that Dunstan must die, and have left the execution of the sentence to us."

He did not add that the council in question consisted of the giddy young nobles who had surrounded Edwy from the first, aided by a few hoary sinners whose lives of plunder and rapine had given them a personal hatred of the Church.

Elfric heaved a sigh, and said—"If so, I suppose I must obey ; but I wish I had not been sent on the expedition."

"It is to test your loyalty."

"Then it shall be proved. I have no personal motives of gratitude towards Dunstan."

"Rather the contrary."

"Rather the contrary, as you say. But what sound was that ? Surely something stirred the bush ? "

"A rabbit or a hare. You are becoming fanciful and timid. Well, you will remember that to-morrow there must be *no* timidity, *no* yielding to what some would call conscience, but wise men the scruples of superstition. We shall not reach the monastery till dark, most of the visitors will then have quitted it, and we shall take the old fox in a trap."

" You will not slay him in cold blood ? "

" No. I shall bid him follow me to the king, and if he and his resist, as probably they will, then their blood be on their own heads. But surely "——

At that moment a large stone, which Alfred had most inopportunely dislodged, rolled down the bank, and made Elfric, who was in its path, leap aside. Alfred, whose foot had rested upon it, slipped, and for a moment seemed in danger of following the stone, but he had happily time to grasp the tree securely, and by its aid he drew himself back and darted into the wood.

Luckily there was moonlight enough to guide him by the track he had hitherto followed, and he ran forward, dreading nothing so much as to fall into the hands of the friends of his brother, and trusting that he might prevent the execution of the foul deed he had heard meditated. He ran for a long distance before he paused, when he became aware that pursuers were on his track. Luckily his life had been spent so much in the open air that he was capable of great exertion, and could run well. So he resumed his course, although he knew not where it would lead him, and soon had the pleasure of feeling that he was distancing his pursuers. Yet every time he ran over a piece of smooth turf he fancied he could hear them in his rear, and it was with the greatest feeling of relief that he suddenly emerged from the wood upon the Foss-way, and saw the lights of the hostelry at no great distance below him.

His pursuers did not follow him farther, probably unwilling to betray their presence to the neighbourhood, and perhaps utterly unconscious that the intruder upon their peace was possessed of any dangerous secrets, or other than some rustic woodman belated on his homeward way, who would be unable in any degree to interfere with them or to guess their designs.

But it was not till the ardour of his flight had abated, that Alfred could fully realise that his unhappy brother was committed to a deed of scandalous atrocity, and the discovery was hard for him to bear. The strong impression which his dream had made upon him—an impression that he was to be the means of saving his brother from some great sin—came upon him now with greater force than ever, and was of great comfort. The identity of the scenery he had seen in dreamland with the actual scenery he had gone through, made him feel that he was under the special guidance of Providence.

Returning to the inn he sought Father Cuthbert, and found him somewhat uneasy at his long absence, and to him he communicated all that he had seen and heard.

The good father was a man of sound sense but of much affection, and at first he could not credit that the boy he had loved so well, Elfric of Æscendune, should have grown to be the associate of murderers, for such only could either he or Alfred style the agents of Edwy's wrath.

But, once fully convinced, he was equal to the emergency. "We will not start at once; we should but break down on the road, and defeat our own object. We must rest quietly, and sleep soundly if possible, and start with the earliest dawn. We shall reach Glastonbury by midday, and be able to warn the holy abbot of his danger in good time."

So Alfred was forced to curb his impatience and to try to sleep soundly. Father Cuthbert soon gave good assurance that *he* was asleep; but the noisy manner in which the assurance was given banished sleep from the eyelids of his anxious pupil. At length he yielded to weariness both of mind and body, and the overwrought brain was still.

He was but little refreshed when he heard Father Cuthbert's morning salutation, "Benedicamus Domino," and could hardly stammer out the customary reply, "Deo gratias."

Every one rose early in those days, and the timely departure of the party from Æscendune excited no special comment. Hundreds of pilgrims were on the road, and Alfred expressed his conviction that there would be force enough at Glastonbury to protect Dunstan, to which Father Cuthbert replied—"If he would accept *such protection.*"

On former days their journey had been frequently impeded by broken bridges and dangerous fords; but as they drew near Glastonbury the presence of a mighty civilising power became manifest. The fields were well tilled, for the possessions for miles around the abbey were let to tenant farmers by the monks, who had first reclaimed them from the wilderness. The farm-houses and the abodes of the poor were better constructed, and the streams were all bridged over, while the old Roman road was kept in tolerable repair.

A short distance before they reached the city, the pilgrims, who were a space in advance of the party, came in sight of the towers of the monastery, whereupon they all paused for one moment, and raised the solemn strain then but recently composed—

I.

Founded on the Rock of Ages,
  Salem, city of the blest,
Built of living stones most precious,
  Vision of eternal rest,
Angel hands, in love attending,
  Thee in bridal robes invest.

II.

Down from God all new descending
  Thee our joyful eyes behold,
Like a bride adorned for spousals,
  Decked with radiant wealth untold;
All thy streets and walls are fashioned,
  All are bright with purest gold !

III.

Gates of pearl, for ever open,
　Welcome there the loved, the lost ;
Ransomed by their Saviour's merits ;
　This the price their freedom cost :
City of eternal refuge,
　Haven of the tempest-tost.

IV.

Fierce the blow, and firm the pressure,
　Which hath polished thus each stone :
Well the Master-mind hath fitted
　To his chosen place each one.
When the Architect takes reck'ning,
　He will count the work His Own.

V.

Glory be to God, the Father ;
　Glory to th' Eternal Son ;
Glory to the Blessed Spirit :
　One in Three, and Three in One.
Glory, honour, might, dominion,
　While eternal ages run.　Amen.*

The grand strains seemed to bring assurance of Divine aid to Alfred, and he could but imitate Father Cuthbert, who lifted up his stentorian voice and thundered out in chorus, as they drew near the pilgrims.

Here they left the Foss-way for the side road leading to the monastery, now only a short distance from them.

* For this new translation of Urbs beata the author is indebted to his friend the Rev. Gerald Moultrie.

CHAPTER XI.

THE FLIGHT OF DUNSTAN.

IT was the day of S. Alban, the protomartyr of England, and the saint was greatly honoured at Glastonbury, where, as we have seen, Dunstan was in residence, and, as a natural consequence, every department of the monastic life was quickened by his presence. The abbey was full of monks who had professed the Benedictine rule, and having but recently been rebuilt, it possessed many improvements hardly yet introduced into English architecture in general. The greater part of the building was of stone, and it was not, in its general features, unlike some of the older colleges at Oxford or Cambridge, although the order of the architecture was, of course, exclusively that of the Saxon period, characterised by the heavy and massive, yet imposing, circular arch.

But upon the church or abbey chapel all the skill of the architect had been concentrated, and it seemed worthy alike of its founder and of its object. Seen upon the morning in question, when the bright summer sun filled every corner with gladsome light, just as the long procession of white-robed priests, and monks in their sombre garb, with their hoods thrown back, were entering for high mass, and the choral psalm arose, it was peculiarly imposing.

The procession had not long entered the church, when the party of pilgrims we have described, closely followed by our friends from Æscendune, entered the quadrangle, and crossed it to the great porch of the church. It was with the greatest difficulty they could enter, for the whole floor of the huge building was crowded with kneeling worshippers. The portion of Scripture appointed for the epistle was being chanted, and the words struck Alfred's ears as he entered—

"He pleased God, and was beloved of Him, so that, living among sinners, he was translated." *

The words seemed to come upon him with special application to the danger the great abbot was in, and the thought that the martyr's day might be stained by a deed of blood, or, as some might say, hallowed by another martyrdom, added to his agitation.

And now he had gained a position where the high altar was in full view, illuminated by its countless tapers, and fragrant with aromatic odours. *There,* in the centre of the altar, his face turned to the people as the sequence was ended, and the chanting of the gospel from the rood-loft began, stood the celebrant, and Alfred gazed for the first time upon the face of Dunstan, brought out in strong relief by the glare of the artificial light.

He strove earnestly to concentrate his thoughts upon the sacred words. They were from the sixteenth of S. Matthew, beginning at the words—

"Then said Jesus unto His disciples, If any man will come after Me, let him deny himself, and take up his cross, and follow Me."

"For whosoever will save his life, shall lose it; and whosoever will lose his life for My sake, shall find it."

He could not but feel the strange coincidence that words such as these should come to strengthen him, when he felt he had most need to shelter himself under the shadow of the Cross. The service proceeded, the creed, sanctus, and other choral portions being sung by the whole monastic body in sonorous strains; and for a time Alfred was able to make a virtue of necessity, and to give himself wholly to the solemnity; but when it was over, and the procession left the church, he sought an immediate interview with the abbot, in company with Father Cuthbert.

* Wisdom iv. 10.

Dunstan had removed his sacerdotal garments, and had returned to his own cell, which only differed in size from the cells of his brethren. The furniture was studiously plain : hard wooden chairs ; an unvarnished table ; a wooden bedstead, with no bed, and only a loose coverlet of sackcloth ; the walls uncovered by tapestry, the floor unfurnished with rushes ;—such was the chamber of the man who had ruled England, and still exercised the most unbounded spiritual influence in the land.

There was no ostentation in this ; every monk in the monastery lived in similar simplicity. Precious books and manuscripts, deeply laden with gold and colours, were deposited on coarse wooden shelves, while the Benedictine Breviary lay on the table, written by some learned and painstaking scribe, skilful in illumination.

The appearance of the abbot was little changed since we last beheld him ; perhaps care had traced a few more lines in his countenance, and his general manner was more prompt and decided, now that danger menaced him, for menace him he knew it did, although he hardly knew from what quarter the bolt would fall.

A lay brother brought him some slight refreshment, the first he had taken during the day.

The humility inculcated by each precept of the order forbade the brother in question to speak, until his superior gave him leave to do so ; but Dunstan read at once the desire of his subordinate, and said—

" What hast thou to tell me, Brother Osgood ?"

" Many people are without, seeking speech of thee."

" This is the case each day ; are there any whose business appears pressing ?"

" A company has arrived from Æscendune, or some such place in Mercia, and two of the party—a priest and a young layman—seek an immediate interview, saying their business is of life and death."

" Æscendune !—admit them first."

The brother left the cell at once, and soon returned,

ushering in Father Cuthbert and Alfred, who saluted the great churchman with all due humility, and waited for him to speak, not without much evident uneasiness; perhaps some little impatience was also manifest.

"Are you of the house of Æscendune, my son?" enquired Dunstan of Alfred. "Methinks I know you by your likeness to your brother Elfric."

"I am the son of Ella, father; we have been sent on pressing business, which is notified by this parchment" (presenting the formal request on the part of the brethren of Æscendune, which was the original cause of their journey); "but we have yet a more pressing matter to bring before you: wicked men seek your life, my father."

"I am well aware of that; surely you do not dream, my son, that my eyes are closed to a fact known throughout unhappy England."

"But, my father, I speak of immediate danger, which God in His great mercy enabled me to discover but last night; this very night the abbey will be attacked, and your life or liberty in danger."

"This night?" said Dunstan, in surprise; "and how have you discovered this? Do not hesitate, my son; tell me all."

Thus adjured, Alfred repeated the whole story of his discovery of the concealed expedition.

"You saw the leaders closely then?" said Dunstan, when he had finished; "describe the elder one to me."

"A tall dark man, like a foreign soldier, in plain but rich apparel, a scar on the right cheek."

"Stay, my son, I know him; his name is Redwald, and he is the captain of the king's body-guard. Now describe the other with whom he held converse."

"Father, I cannot."

"My son "——but Dunstan paused, for he saw that poor Alfred had covered his face with his hands, and he at once divined the truth, with full conviction, at the same time, of the truth and earnestness of Alfred's statement.

"My son, God can dispose and turn the hearts of all

men as seemeth best to His wisdom; and I doubt not, in answer to our fervent prayers, He will turn the heart of your poor brother. Meanwhile, we ourselves will take such precautions as shall spare him the guilt of sacrilege. Brother Osgood, summon the prior to my presence, and cause the brethren to assemble, one and all, in the chapter-house: we have need of instant deliberation."

The lay brother departed, and Dunstan, whose cheerfulness did not desert him for one moment, chatted familiarly with Father Cuthbert, or perused the parchment the good father had just presented through Alfred.

"It is a great and pleasing thing," he said, "to behold how our Order is spreading through this benighted land, and how spiritual children arise everywhere to our holy father Benedict; surely the time is near at hand when the wilderness shall blossom as the rose."

The prior, Father Guthlac, entered at this moment, and Dunstan talked apart with him for some moments with extreme earnestness, but only the last words which passed between them were audible.

"Yes, my brother, you have the words of Scripture," said Dunstan, "to support your proposal: 'When they persecute you in one city, flee ye unto another.'"

"Yet it is hard to leave a spot one has reared with such tender care."

"There was One Who left more for us; and I do not think they will destroy the place, or even *attempt* to destroy it: they will fill it with those 'slow bellies, those evil beasts,' the secular clergy, with their wives."

"Fitter it should be a stye for hogs." *

"Nay, they are men after all; yet there is some reason to fear that, like hogs, they wallow in the mire of sensuality; but their day will be but a short one."

"My father!"

"But a short one; it hath been foreshown me in visions

---

* The reader will remember the strong feeling of animosity then existing between seculars and regulars.

of the night that the Evil One will triumph indeed, but that his triumph will be very short; and, alas! a green tree which standeth in the pride of its youth and might must, ere the close of that triumph, be hewn down."

"By our hands, father?"

"God forbid! by the Hand of God; I speak but as it has been revealed to me."

It was a well-known fact that Dunstan either was subject to marvellous hallucinations, and was a monomaniac on that one point, while so wise in all other matters, or that he was the object of special revelations, and was favoured with spiritual visions, as well as temptations, which do not ordinarily fall within the observation or experience of men.

So Father Guthlac and the rest of the company listened with the greatest reverence to his declaration, as to the words of an inspired oracle.

"But let us go to our brethren; they await us," said Dunstan, speaking to the prior. "Brother Osgood, take these our guests to the refectorarius, and ask him to see that they and all their company taste our bounty at least this day; to-morrow we may have nought to offer them."

In the famous chapter of the whole house of Glastonbury which followed, and which became historical, prompt resolution was taken on Dunstan's report, which did honour to the brotherhood, as evincing both their resignation and their trust in God, Who they believed would, to use the touching phrase of the Psalmist, "turn their captivity as the rivers in the south;" so that they "who went forth weeping, bearing good seed, should come again with joy, and bring their sheaves with them."

So it was at once agreed that the whole community should break up immediately; that within the next hour all the monks should depart for the various monasteries of the Benedictine order; and that Dunstan himself, with but two companions, should take refuge across the sea, sailing from the nearest port on the Somersetshire coast.

A dozen of the brethren were to return with Father Cuthbert and Alfred to Æscendune at once, and to bear with them all the necessary powers for the accomplishment of the good thane's wishes in regard to the monastery of S. Wilfred, while Father Cuthbert was then and there admitted by Dunstan to the order of S. Benedict—the necessity of the case justifying some departure from the customary formalities.

All being completely ordered and arranged, the chapter broke up, and within an hour the monks were leaving as rapidly as boys leave school when breaking-up day comes, but not quite so joyously. They strove to attract as little attention as possible, and, in most cases, travelled in the ordinary dress of the country.

Father Cuthbert and the Benedictines who were to accompany him on his return—so much more speedy than had been anticipated—were already prepared to start, when, to their surprise, Alfred could not be found.

Alfred was at that moment in the cell of Dunstan, with whom he had obtained, not without great trouble, another brief interview.

"God bless you, my son," said Dunstan, "and render unto you according to all you have done for His glory this day, and restore you your brother safe in body and soul!"

But it was not merely for a blessing that Alfred had sought the abbot.

"Father," he said, "if I have happily been of service to you, I ask but one favour in return; one brother has sought your life, let the other remain with you as a body-guard."

"But your father?"

"I am satisfied that I am but speaking as he would have me speak."

"But you will become an exile."

"Gladly, if I can but serve you, father."

"But, my child, I have no means of support for *you* abroad; as monks we shall find hospitality in every Benedictine house, but you are only a layman."

"Then, father, I but ask you to allow me to accompany you to the coast."

"I grant it, my son, for I believe God inspires the wish. Be it as you desire, but one of your serfs must accompany you ; it would not be safe to travel home alone."

So Father Cuthbert and the Benedictines started back to Æscendune without Alfred, bearing Dunstan's explanation of the matter to the half-bereaved father, whose faith, they feared, would be sorely tried, and leaving Oswy to be his companion.

It was now drawing near nightfall, and the abbey was almost deserted ; all the pilgrims had left with the monks, although many of them would willingly have put their trust in the arm of flesh and remained to fight for Dunstan against his temporal foes, even as he — so they piously believed — routed their spiritual enemies. In that vast abbey there were now but six persons—Dunstan, Guthlac, Alfred, the lay brother Osgood, Oswy, and a guide who knew all the by-paths of the country.

Desolate and solitary indeed seemed the huge pile of untenanted buildings as the evening breeze swept through them. The last straggler had gone ; Dunstan was still in his cell arranging or destroying certain papers : the guide and lay brothers held six strong and serviceable horses in the courtyard below, near the open gate, impatient to start, and blaming secretly the dilatoriness of their great chieftain. They watched the sun as he sank lower and lower in the western sky, and thought of the woods and forests they must traverse, frequented by wolves, and sometimes by outlaws whom they dreaded far more. Still Dunstan did not appear.

Alfred and Guthlac, on a watch-tower above, gazed on the plain stretched before them. Mile after mile it extended towards that forest where the enemy was now known to lurk, and they watched each road, nay, each copse and field, with jealous eye, lest it should conceal an enemy. Ofttimes the shadow of some passing cloud, as it swept over moor or mere, was taken for an armed host; ofttimes the wind, as it sighed amongst the trees and blew the dried leaves hither and thither, seemed to carry the warning " An enemy is near."

At length danger seemed to show itself plainly: just as the sun set, a dark shadow moved from a distant angle of the forest on the plain beneath, and the words "The enemy!" escaped simultaneously from Alfred and Guthlac as the setting sun seemed reflected upon spear and sword, flashing in a hundred points as they caught the reflection of the departing luminary.

Alfred, at the prior's desire, hurried to the chamber of Dunstan.

"Father," he said, "the enemy are near. They have left the forest."

"That is four miles in distance: there will be time for me to finish this letter to my brother of Abingdon."

"But, father, their horses may be fleeter than ours."

"We are under God's protection: I am sure we shall not be overtaken; be at peace, my son."

Poor Alfred felt as if his faith were very sorely tried indeed, but he strove to acquiesce.

It was now quite dark, and the ears of the would-be fugitives were strained to catch the sounds which should warn them of approaching danger.

At length they fancied they heard sounds arise from the plain before them: suppressed noises, such as must unavoidably be made by a force on its passage; and Alfred again sought the cell of Dunstan, yet dared not enter, urgent though the emergency seemed.

At this moment he was startled by a demoniacal burst of laughter, which seemed to fill the corridor in which he waited with exultant joy.

What could it be? he felt as if he had never heard such laughter before—so terrible, yet so boisterous.

A moment of dread silence, and then it began again, and filled each corridor and chamber.

At that moment Dunstan came forth, and saw the pale face of Alfred.

"It is only the devil," he said ; "we are not ignorant of his devices.   O Satan ! thou that wert once an angel in heaven, art thou reduced to bray like a jackass ?" *

Again the exultant peal resounded.

"Be at peace," said the abbot ; "thou rejoicest at my departure ; I shall soon return to defy thee and thy allies."

And the laughter ceased.

"We must lose no time," he said ; "the moment is at hand."

Locking each door behind him, he reached the party in the courtyard, and each person mounted in a moment ; then they passed under the great archway. Osgood remained behind one moment to lock the great gates, and then they all rode forth boldly into the darkness.

They passed rapidly in a direction at right angles to that in which their pursuers were approaching, and at the distance of a mile they halted for one moment to ascertain the cause of a great uproar which suddenly arose.

It was not difficult to divine its cause : it was the beating of axes and hammers on the great outer door of the monastery.

"It will occupy them nearly an hour," said Dunstan, " and we shall be far far away before they have succeeded in effecting an entrance."

So they rode on rapidly into the night. Before them lay the Foss-way, the road was good and well known to them, the moon was shining brightly, and their spirits rose with the excitement and the exertion.   Onward ! onward !

* This demoniacal laughter is one of the many legends about S. Dunstan.

CHAPTER XII.

THE unhappy Elfric had indeed fallen from his former self before he reached the depth at which our readers have just seen him, joining with Redwald in the unhallowed enterprise so happily frustrated, if indeed it were yet frustrated, by his own brother.

But when his father had returned to Æscendune alone, Elfric felt that home-ties were shattered, and that he had nothing but the royal favour to depend upon, so he yielded to the wishes of King Edwy in all points.

Immediately after his coronation, the reckless and ill-advised Edwy had married Elgiva,* in defiance of the ban of the Church, and then had abandoned himself to the riotous society and foolish counsels of young nobles vainer than those who cost Rehoboam so large a portion of his kingdom. Amongst these Elfric was soon conspicuous and soon a leader. His spirit and physical courage, far beyond his years, excited their admiration, and in return they taught him all the mysteries of evil which were yet unknown to him.

Under such influences both the king and his favourite threw off all outward semblance even of religion, and only sought the means of enjoyment. Redwald ministered without reserve or restraint to all their pleasures, and under his evil influence Edwy even found occasion to rob and plunder his own grandmother, a venerable Saxon princess, in order that he might waste the ill-gotten substance in riotous living.

* See Preface, page viii.

Yet there was a refinement in his vice; he did not care for coarse sensual indulgence to any great extent; his wickedness was that of a sensitive cultivated intellect, of a highly-wrought nervous temperament.

Unscrupulous — careless of truth — contemptuous of religion — yet he had all that attraction in his person which first endeared him to Elfric, whom he really loved. Alas! his love was deadly as the breath of the upas tree to his friend and victim. When the first measures of vengeance were taken against Dunstan, with the concurrence of wicked but able ministers of state, Redwald was selected as the agent who should bribe the thanes, and begin the course of conduct which should eventually lead to the destruction of the enemy of the king. He had only waited till the temper of the times seemed turned against Dunstan (he judged it wrongly); and the king seemed secure against every foe ere he planned the expedition we have introduced to our readers.

We will now resume the thread of our narrative.

When the band of soldiers, headed by Redwald, had gained the gates of the monastery, they found them, as we have seen, firmly locked and barred.

"Blow your horns; rouse up these sleepy monks to some purpose," said Redwald. "Why, they have not a light about the place."

A loud and vigorous blast of horns was blown, while the greater part of the troop dismounted and paused impatiently for an answer from within.

"Two or three of you step forward with your axes," exclaimed Redwald.

They did so, and thundered on the gate without any success, so stoutly was it made.

"What can it mean?" said Redwald. "All is silent as the grave."

"No; there is some one laughing at us," said Elfric.

A peal of merry laughter was heard within.

Redwald was thoroughly enraged, and seizing an axe

with his own hand, he set the example of applying it to the gate, but without any result save to split a few planks, while the iron framework, designed by Dunstan himself, who was clever at such arts, held as firmly as ever.

Unprovided with other means of forcing it, the besiegers had recourse to fire, and gathering fuel with some difficulty, they piled it against the gate. Shortly the woodwork caught, and the whole gate presently yielded to the action of the fire; the iron bars, loosened by the destruction of the woodwork, gave way, and the besiegers rushed into the quadrangle. Here, all was dark and silent, not a sound to be heard or a light seen.

"What can it mean? Have they fled? You all heard the laughter?"

"There it is again."

The boisterous and untimely mirth had begun just within the abbot's lodgings, and the doorway at the foot was immediately attacked.

It presently yielded, and Redwald, who had obtained a good notion of the place, rushed with his chief villains to the chamber he knew to be Dunstan's; yet he began to fear failure, for the absence of all the inmates was disheartening. No, not all, for there was the loud laughter within the very chamber of the abbot.

The door was fastened securely, and while the axes were doing their destructive work upon it, the mocking laughter was again heard. Redwald had become so enraged that he mentally vowed the direst vengeance upon the untimely jester, when the door burst open and he rushed in.

"Where is he? Surely there was some one here?"

"Who could it be? We all heard the laughter."

But victim there was none; and searching all the place in vain, they had to satiate their vengeance by destroying the humble furniture of the abbot.

What to do next they knew not, and Redwald, deeply mystified, was reluctantly forced to own his discomfiture, and to prepare to pass the night in the abbey. Accordingly, his men dispersed in search of food and wine. Some found their way to the buttery ; it was but poorly supplied, all the provisions in the place having been given to the poorer pilgrims by the departing monks. The cellar was not so easily emptied, and such wine as had been stored up for future use was at once appropriated.

Redwald and Elfric, having shared the common meal gloomily, were seated in the abbot's chamber—little did Elfric dream that his brother had so recently been in the same room—when one of the guards entered, bringing with him a stranger. He turned out to be a neighbouring thane, one of those bitter enemies to Dunstan whom Edwy had planted round the monastery, and he came to give information that he had seen Dunstan with five companions escaping by the Foss-way.

Redwald jumped up eagerly. "How long since?" he asked.

"About two hours, and ten miles off. I was returning home from a distant farm of mine."

"Why did you not stop them ?"

"I was too weak for that ; they were six to one. I heard you had been seen coming here by a cowherd, and came to warn you. If you ride fast you may catch the holy fox yet before he runs to earth ; but you must be very quick."

"What pace were they riding ?"

"Slowly at that moment ; it was up a hill."

Redwald rushed from the room, crying, "To horse, to horse !" but found only a portion of his men awake ; the others were mainly drunk and sleeping it off on the floor.

Cursing their untimely indulgence, he got about a dozen men rapidly mounted on the fleetest horses, taking care Elfric should be one, and dashed off in pursuit of the fugitives.

Dunstan and his party had ridden some four or five hours, when the moon became overcast, and low peals of distant thunder were heard. The atmosphere was so intensely hot, and the silence of nature so oppressive, that it was evident some convulsion was at hand.

" Is there any shelter near ? "

" Only a ruined city* in the wood on the left hand; but it is a dangerous place to approach after nightfall. They say evil spirits lurk there."

" They tell that story of every ruined place, be it city, temple, or house ; and even if it be, we have more cause to dread evil men than evil spirits."

The guide hesitated no longer, and struck into a by-path, which penetrated the depth of the woody marsh through which the Foss-way then had its course. After a minute or two it became evident, from the footing, that they were upon the paved work of a causeway overgrown with weeds and rank herbage; huge mounds showed where fortifications had once existed, and shortly, broken pillars and ruined walls appeared at irregular intervals.

They had little time to look around them, for the storm had come rapidly up, and the glare of the lightning was incessant, while the rain poured down in absolute torrents. Before them rose a huge ruin covered with ivy, and with the roof partly protecting the interior, it was so large that they were able to lead their horses within its protection and wait the cessation of the rain.

Between the flashes the sky was intensely dark, but they were almost incessant, and revealed the city of the dead in which they had found refuge. It was an ancient Welsh town, and in the latter years of the deadly struggle with the English, had been taken after a protracted resistance. Tradition had not even preserved its name, and only stated that every living soul had perished in the massacre when the outer walls were at length stormed and the town given to fire and sword. The victors, as was frequently the case, had avoided the spot, preferring to build else-

* See Note N.—Ruined British cities.

where, and, like Silchester or Anderida, it had fallen into desolation such as befel mighty Babylon.

And now the ignorant rustic peopled its buildings with the imaginary forms of doleful creatures, and shunned the fatal precincts where once family love and social affections had flourished; where hearts, long mouldered to dust, had beaten with tender affection; where all the little circumstances which make up life—the trivial round, the common task—had gone on beneath the summer's sun or winter's storm, till the great convulsion which ended the existence of the whole community.

Dunstan noticed that his whole party crowded closely together, and when the lightning illuminated each face saw that fear had left its visible mark.

The continuous roar of thunder, the hissing of the descending rain, the wind which blew in angry gusts, prevented all conversation until nearly an hour had elapsed, when the strife began to diminish. It was a sad and mournful sight to gaze upon the remains of departed greatness when thus illuminated by the electric flash, and easily might the fancy, deceived by the transient glimpses of things, people the ruins with the shades of their departed inhabitants.

"Father," said Alfred, at length, "who *were* they who lived here ?   Do you know aught about them ?"

"The men whom our ancestors subdued—the Welsh, or British—an unhappy race."

"Were they heathen ?"

"At one time, but they were converted by the missions from Rome and the East, of which the earliest was that of S. Joseph of Arimathea to our own Glastonbury ; he may have preached to the very people who lived here, nay, in this very basilica, which, I think, may have been converted into a church."

It was indeed the ruin of a basilica wherein they stood, but no trace survived to show whether Dunstan's conjecture was correct.

" It seems strange that God should have permitted them to fall before the sword of our *heathen* ancestors."

" Their own historian Gildas, who lies buried at Glastonbury, explains it. He tells us that such was the corruption of faith and of morals towards the close of their brief day, that had not the Saxon sword interposed, plague, pestilence, or famine, or some similar calamity, must have done the fatal work. God grant that *we*, now that in turn we have received the message of the Gospel, may be more faithful servants, or similar ruin may, at no distant period, await the Englishman also, as it did the Welshman."

He sighed deeply, and Alfred echoed the sigh in his heart ; he read the abbot's thoughts.

" Do you believe," said he, after a pause, " that their spirits ever revisit the earth ? "

" I know not ; many wise men have thought it possible, and that they may haunt the places where they sinned, ever bearing their condemnation within them, even while they clothe themselves in semblance of the mortal flesh they once wore."

The whole party shuddered, and Father Guthlac said, deprecatingly—

" My father, let us not talk of this now ; we are too weak to bear it, and the place is so awful."

By this time the wind had made a huge rent in the black clouds overhead, and the moon came suddenly in sight, sailing tranquilly in the azure void above, and casting her beams on the ruins, as she had once cast them on the beauteous city, its basilicas, palaces, and temples yet standing.

At this moment their guide came hastily to them. " We are in some danger, father. Horsemen, twelve of them, are galloping along the Foss-way in spite of the storm.

Dunstan left the shelter which was no longer needed, the rain having ceased, and followed the guide to the summit of the huge mound which marked the fall of some

giant bastion of early days.   From that position they could
see the Foss-way, now about half-a-mile distant, in the
bright moonlight, and Dunstan's eye at once caught twelve
figures—horsemen—sweeping down it like the wind, which
brought the sound of their passage faintly to the ear.

"Wait," he said, "and see whether they pass the by-
path; in that case we are safe."

The whole party was now on the mound, their persons
carefully concealed from the view of the horsemen, while
they watched their passage with intense anxiety.   The
enemy reached the by-path; eleven of them passed over it,
but the twelfth reined his horse suddenly, almost upon its
haunches, and pointed to the ground.   He had evidently
seen the tracks of the fugitives upon the soft turf.

The next moment they all turned their horses into the
by-path.

"Follow," said the guide; and they all rushed eagerly
down the mound and mounted at once.

"Follow me closely; I think I can save you from them;
only lose not a moment."

The guide led them by a wandering path amongst the
ruins, where their tracks would leave the least trace, until
he passed through a gap in the external fortifications on
the opposite side.   Then he rode rapidly along a descending path in the woods, until the sound of rushing water
greeted their ears, and they arrived on the brink of a small
river which was swollen by the violent rain, and which
dashed along an irregular and stony bed with fearful impe-
tuosity.   There was but one mode of crossing it: a bridge
constructed of planks was thrown over, which *one* horseman
might pass at a time.   The whole party rode over in safety,
although the crazy old bridge bent terribly beneath the
weight of each rider.

But when all were over, the guide motioned to Alfred
and Oswy to remain behind for one moment, while the
monks proceeded.   He threw himself from his horse, and
taking the axe which he had slung behind him, commenced

hacking away at the bridge. But although the bridge was old, yet it was tough ; and although Alfred, and Oswy who was armed with a small battle-axe, assisted with all their might, the work seemed long.

Before it was completed, they heard the voices of their pursuers calling to each other amongst the ruins. They had evidently lost the track, and were separating to find it.

Crash went one huge plank into the rolling torrent, then a second, and but *one* beam remained, when a horseman emerged from the trees opposite, and by the light of the moon Alfred recognised his brother.

Desperate in the excitement of the chase, Elfric leapt from his horse, and drawing his sword rushed upon the bridge. Alfred, who felt it tremble, cried—" Back, Elfric ! back if you value your life ! " while at the same moment, true to his duty, without raising his axe or any other attempt at offence, he opposed his own body in passive resistance to Elfric's passage over the beam.

Elfric knew the voice, and drew back in utter amazement. He had already stepped from the half-severed beam, when he saw it bend, break, and roll, with Alfred, who had advanced to the middle of the bridge, into the torrent beneath, which swept both beam and man away with resistless force.

CHAPTER XIII.

THE reader is, we trust, somewhat impatient to learn the fate of Alfred of Æscendune, whom we left in so critical a position.

The fall of the bridge was so sudden and unexpected, that he scarcely knew where he was, till he found himself sucked rapidly down stream by the raging waters, when he struck out like a man, and battled for dear life. But the only result seemed to be that he was bruised and battered against the rocks and stones, until, exhausted, he was on the point of succumbing to his fate, as the current bore him into a calm deep pool, where he sank helplessly, his strength gone. But the guide, and his companion Oswy, had succeeded in reaching the spot, which was inaccessible from the other side, and plunging at once into the waters, the latter succeeded in bringing the dying youth to land. Dunstan and the other members of the party were soon on the spot; the lay brother was skilled in the art of restoring suspended animation, and they soon had the happiness of beholding Alfred return to consciousness; he raised his head, and gazed about him like one in a dream, not able to realise his position.

"Where am I? what have I been doing?" he exclaimed.

"You are safe, my dear son, and in the hands of friends," replied Dunstan, "although you have had a narrow, narrow escape; we are secure for the *present* from our foes."

They consulted together in low tones as to their future movements, and the abbot inquired particularly of the guide concerning the fords and bridges.

"There is a ford only a mile or two away, but I expect they will find they cannot cross it."

"Is there no place of refuge near? he is unable to sit his horse."

"There is a cottage close by, kept by a cowherd, who is a good and true man."

"Then lead us to it at once," replied Dunstan.

Alfred had by this time recognised his position, and he implored Dunstan not to endanger his own safety for *his* sake; but the abbot paid no attention. They reached the cottage just as the day was dawning, and the east was bright with rosy light. It was such a place as the great king, after whom Alfred was named, had found refuge in when pressed by the Danes. It was poor, but neat and clean beyond the usual degree; and when the wants of their early visitors were known, and Dunstan was recognised, the utmost zeal was displayed in his cause.

All that could be done for Alfred was done at once; but he was manifestly too shaken and bruised to be able to travel; and, giving him his fatherly blessing, Dunstan was compelled by the guide to hurry on, leaving him in the care of Oswy.

They had not, however, great fear of their pursuers, for their own horses were comparatively fresh after the rest in the ruined city, and those of their foes would be necessarily fatigued, after the rapid ride along the Foss-way, and their exertions to pass the stream.

So it was not with great uneasiness, well mounted as they were, that, gaining the road, they beheld their pursuers in the distance, who, on their part, beholding their intended victims afar off, hastened to spur their horses on.

It was useless: the pursued had the advantage, and after the gallop of a mile or two, it became evident they were in no especial danger, although it must be remembered that a false step or slip, or any accident, would have been fatal.

"I should not mind racing them down the Foss to the Sea Town,"* said the guide; "but if the abbot has no objection, I should prefer leaving them to pursue the road, while we take a cross-country route, which I have often travelled; it is a very good one."

"By all means," said Dunstan, "and then we may slacken this furious pace."   They were quite out of sight of their pursuers when, coming upon a track of dry stony ground, they suddenly left the road, and crossing a wild heath, put a copse between them and the enemy, who did not this time discover for miles the absence of the footprints, for the soil was very dry and hard, the storm not having passed that way, and the foe were intent upon hard riding.

So they gained a long start, and eventually reached a hill, from which they obtained their first view of the sea. It was eventide, and the western sun, sinking towards the promontories beyond the distant Exe, reddened the waters with his glowing light.   Dunstan and his brethren thanked God.   "We have come to the setting sun," said they, "and at eventide have seen light; let us thank Him Who hath preserved us."

But the guide, who knew what relentless pursuers were yet behind, would allow them no rest.   In another hour they reached a small fishing village on the coast, where a solitary bark was kept.   The owner was just about to put out for an evening's fishing, but at the earnest request of his visitors, backed by much gold, he consented to take them over to the opposite coast.

"The weather promises to be very clear and fine," he said; "and we may sail across without any danger."

It was indeed a lovely night; they stepped on board, the anchor was loosed, the sail set, and with the wind behind, they stood rapidly out to sea.   They were quite silent, each immersed in his own thoughts.   At last they

* Seaton in Devonshire.

heard the sound of horsemen galloping on the fast-receding shore, and looking back, they saw twelve riders reach the beach, and pause, looking wistfully out to sea.

"Our soul is escaped, even as a bird out of the snare of the fowler; the snare is broken, and we are delivered," said Dunstan.

"Our help standeth in the name of the Lord, Who hath made heaven and earth," replied Father Guthlac.

Meanwhile, Alfred rapidly gained strength. Happily no bones were broken, he was only sadly bruised; the next day he expressed his earnest wish to return home, but his host would not permit him, saying he should have to answer to Dunstan some day for his guest.

The time passed monotonously enough that second day, yet not unpleasantly: there were a thousand things to observe in the woods and marshes around, full of animal life.

Early in the morning, a sweet fresh morning, the cowherd drove his cattle forth to graze, where he knew the pastures were sweetest, and Alfred would willingly have gone too, but they told him he must rest. So he took his breakfast of hot milk and bread, with oat cakes baked on the hearth, and waited patiently till the warmth of the day tempted him out, under the care of Oswy, to watch the distant herd, to drink of the clear spring, or recline under some huge spreading beech, while the breeze made sweet melodies in his ears, and lulled him pleasantly to sleep.

At midday they returned to the customary dinner, which was not of such inferior quality as one would now expect to find in such a place, contrasting strongly with the fare on the tables of the rich: *then* there was far more equality in the food of rich and poor, and Alfred had no cause to complain of the cowherd's table.

Then he sauntered forth again with Oswy, and strove to amuse himself with the book of nature; till just at even-

tide, as he was longing earnestly that he could know the
fate of his fugitive friends, they heard the sound of a
horse at full trot, and soon the guide appeared in sight.

Alfred rose up eagerly.

" Are they safe ?" he cried.

" Yes, quite safe ; they had got a mile out to sea when
their pursuers got to the beach ; I saw it all, hidden in a
woody hill above."

" Did they try to follow ?"

" They could not ; there was no boat : I never saw men
in such a rage."

Alfred felt as if a weight were removed from his heart ;
then he looked up in the face of the guide.   " Will you guide
us home ?" he said.

" Yes," was the reply ; " the holy abbot particularly desired me to return to his son Alfred, and to take care of
him on his journey home ; and if you will have me as
your guide, I will warrant you a safe journey to Æscendune, for we are not worth following."

" Then let us start to-morrow morning," said Alfred,
longing to be once more in his old father's presence, and
to cheer his mother's heart.

They returned together to the cowherd's cottage, and
slept peacefully that night.   Early in the morning they
retook the path to the Foss-way, crossing the stream at a
ford higher up.   Their horses being well rested and full
of spirit for the journey, they passed Glastonbury, still
empty and desolate, in the middle of the day, and retraced
by easy stages the whole of Alfred's previous route from
home.

After a week's easy travelling, by the blessing of
Providence, they reached the neighbourhood of Æscendune :
it had never looked so lovely, so home-like to Alfred
as then.   He felt as if every spot were full of joy ; and as
he was recognised by person after person, by his favourite
dogs as they bounded forth, and finally fell into his
mother's arms at the gate of the hall, he experienced

feelings which in these days, when we are all so familiar with the thought of travel, can seldom be realised.

Then he had to recount his adventures that night, after supper, to an admiring audience, who listened enraptured to his account of the holiness of Dunstan and the cruelty of his foes. But it will easily be imagined that he made no allusion to his rencontre with Elfric ; and Oswy, instructed by his young master, was equally silent.

He had quite made up his mind to persevere in this course : it could do no good to tell father or mother how grievously Elfric had fallen, and how nearly he had been the involuntary instrument of his brother's death.

"God can change his heart," said Alfred to himself, "and bring him home like the prodigal son about whom Father Cuthbert talks so often."

So he prayed earnestly every day for his brother, and many a supplication on his behalf arose from the altar of S. Wilfred : time will show whether they were lost.

CHAPTER XIV.

EDWY AND ELGIVA.

EDWY, King of England, and Elgiva, his queen, gave a
great feast at their royal palace in London, a month after
the events recorded in our last chapter; and a numerous
company had assembled to do honour to their hospitality.
Yet the company was very different from that which had
assembled round the same hospitable board in the days of
King Edred. *First,* the Churchmen were conspicuous by their
absence; and secondly, all the old grey-headed counsellors
who had been the pride and ornament of the reigns of
Edmund and Edred, were not seen; for, after the rumour of
their marriage had reached Odo, he had pronounced the sentence of the lesser excommunication upon them, severing
them from the sacraments; and this was felt by the old
counsellors of Edred to be a most serious stigma, yet one
which they could not call undeserved: hence they deserted
the court.

In their place were the young and giddy, the headstrong
sons of wiser fathers, the spendthrifts, the young fops of
the period, those who went in for a fast life, to use a modern
phrase—who spent the night, if not the day, over the wine-
cup, and consumed their substance in riotous living;—such
were they who gathered around Edwy the Fair and the yet
fairer Elgiva.

And truly king and queen more beautiful in person had
never sat upon a throne; and it was difficult to look upon
them and feel aught but admiration, save when one knew all
their history, and then pity and sorrow might supply the
place of admiration, at least with the sober-minded.

Fish, flesh, and fowl; nought was wanting. The earth, the air, and the water, all yielded their tribute; for was it not the anniversary of the marriage—the uncanonical marriage, alas!—of the royal pair, if marriage it had truly been?

Eels of enormous size, fine as the Roman lamprey, pike roasted with puddings in their bellies, tench and carp stewed; while the sea yielded its skate, its sturgeon, and its porpoise, which the skill of the cook had so curiously dressed with fragrant spices that it won him great renown. The very smell, said a young gourmand, was a dinner in itself; and the wild buck supplied its haunch, and the boar its head, while fowl of all kinds were handed round on spits.

The drinking was of like sumptuous character, and Rhenish wine contended with the wines of sunny France for precedence, as they were passed round in silver cups and gold-mounted horns; for glass was seldom, if ever, used for such purposes then.

The floor was strewed with the sweetest summer flowers, and exhaled an odour balmy as the breath of eastern climes, where the breeze plays with the orange blossoms. The tapestry was beautifully woven by foreign artists, and represented the loves of the gods; while there was nothing in keeping with the olden style throughout the whole apartment.

But *one* seat was vacant near the king's throne, and every now and then Edwy seemed to cast a wistful eye upon it, as if he would fain see its ordinary occupant there.

The gleemen rose and sang, the harpers harped, but something was wanting; they brought tears to the eyes of the fair queen by their plaintive songs of hapless lovers, which had superseded alike the war-songs of Athelstane and the monkish odes of Edred.

"Where is Elfric? he promised to be back by our wedding-day; why does he delay, my Edwy?" asked Elgiva.

"It is little less than treason to the queen of youth and

beauty to be thus absent, my Elgiva; but remember he has been unwell, and Redwald told me that for prudential reasons they delayed his return to court."

"And your brother Edgar"——

"Is somewhere in Mercia: the churlish boy has declined our invitation to honour our feast with his presence. We do not want his serious face at the board; I am sure he would preach on the duty of fasting."

"He has but seldom been our visitor."

"No; he is afraid, perhaps, to trust his cold heart within the magic of my Elgiva's sunshine, lest the ice should be melted."

These had been asides, while all the company were listening to the gleeman; but now Edwy threw himself heart and soul into the current conversation, and all went merry as a marriage-peal, until the ceremoniarius —for Edwy loved formality in some things—threw open the folding-doors and announced the captain of the hus-carles, and Elfric of Æscendune.

The whole company rose to receive them, and Elfric in particular received a warm welcome; but it was at once seen that there was a marked constraint upon him: his eye was restless and uneasy, and he seemed like one carrying a load at his breast.

In truth, since that fatal night when, as he believed, he had witnessed the death of his brother, he had striven in vain to drown care and to banish remorse; the thought of his aged father deprived of both his sons—the one by death, the other by desertion—*would* force its way unbidden to his mind. Still, he had determined to throw aside reserve in honour of the occasion, and he made heroic efforts to appear happy and gay.

Redwald was at his ease, as usual in all company, and seemed to cause prodigious laughter as he told his adventures to the younger folk at the bottom of the board. Dark and malign as his demeanour usually was, yet he could affect a light and airy character at times.

" Redwald, my trusty champion," said Edwy, " this is the first campaign thou hast ever returned from unsuccessful. Tell us, how did Dunstan outwit you ? "

" By the aid of the devil, my liege."

" Doubtless ; but we had all hoped for a different result, and that thou wouldst either have left the traitor no eyes in his head, or no head on his shoulders. Said I not rightly, my Elgiva ? "

The eyes of the fair enemy of the abbot flashed fire, and she exchanged some very significant words with her mother, Ethelgiva, who occupied the next chair.

" Come, my fairy-given* one, you must not be too hard on Redwald, who doubtless did his best : how was it, Elfric ? "

" The devil was certainly on Dunstan's side : he and no other could have betrayed our coming, for betrayed it was."

" How long had he left when you reached the abbey ? "

" Only an hour or two ; but there was a sound of mocking laughter, doubtless caused by his incantations, which kept us for some hours forcing doors and the like."

" And you could discover no cause ? "

" None whatever ; however, we found he had taken the Foss-way for the coast, and followed, and nearly caught him."

" What prevented you ? "

Elfric turned pale as if with great mental emotion, and tried to proceed in vain.

" You are not well," said Elgiva, anxiously.

" Not quite," he said ; and then, overcoming his feelings by a vigorous effort, while no one save Redwald suspected the true cause, he continued—

" There had been a great storm, and they had broken down the only bridge which existed for miles over a swollen river : we lost hours."

" And yet, as your messengers told us, you arrived in time to see him leave the coast."

* Elgiva or Ælfgifu, signifies fairy gift.

"The vessel which bore him was still distinctly in sight when we stood on the sands."

"But had you no means of following?"

"None: it was a lonely fishing village with a small harbour, and his bark was a mere fishing smack, the only one of the place."

"I trust the sea has swallowed him," said the king; "but there is a rumour to-day that he is playing the saint in Flanders with great pomp. Well, only let him show his face in England again, and the devil may pinch my nose with his tongs if I leave him a head on his shoulders: he shall be a sacrifice to your outraged dignity, my Elgiva."

"And yours, my Edwy."

Husband and wife were quite agreed on this subject: they had never forgiven Dunstan in the least degree, and, identifying him with religion, had well-nigh abjured it altogether.

The ordinary dishes being now removed, the guests all partook lavishly of wine, and, their heads already heated, yielded entirely to the excitement of the moment. Toast after toast was drunk to the king: he was compared to Apollo for his beauty, and Elgiva to Venus; while the old northern mythology was ransacked also for appellations in honour of the youthful pair.

Adjoining, in the outer hall, the higher domestics had their music and dancing, and the king and queen came to honour the entertainment by their presence. So the happy hours wore away, and at length the company were on the eve of departure, for fatigue was making itself felt, when an ominous blowing of a horn was heard at the outer gate.

A pause, during which the company looked at each other, so strangely had the sound struck them, and yet they knew not why, save that it was an unlikely hour for such an occurrence.

There was one only who knew what the message would

probably be—Redwald; and he had kept the secret purposely from the king.

The doors opened, and an usher brought in a messenger, who had only been allowed a moment to change a dusty dress, ere he broke into the presence of royalty.

"Speak," said Edwy, as the messenger bowed before him, and kissed his hand.

"My lord and king;"—and the messenger glanced at Elgiva.

"Let him speak, Edwy, my lord. Are we not one? What you can bear, your wife must bear also."

Thus adjured, the messenger spoke his news.

"Mercia has revolted, and proclaimed Edgar king."

"The cause alleged?"

"I know not, my lord."

"I can tell you," said Redwald; "the banishment of the holy fox, Dunstan, and very shame prevents my adding that "——

"No more," said Edwy; "I can guess the rest." He wished to spare Elgiva.

He walked up and down the hall several times. His festive air had gone. "And on my wedding-day too," he said. "Redwald, you knew this."

"Yes, my lord, but I wished to spare my king upon his wedding-day, still I have not spared myself. The necessary steps are taken, your immediate vassals are summoned, and my own men are ready to march; we will sweep these rebels off the field."

"Elfric," said the king, "you must be my right hand in the field: you will be ready to invade your native Mercia to-morrow. Think you your own friends are firm."

"My father, although he has disowned me, would never disown his lawful king; the duty and love he bore to your murdered father would forbid."

"Well, Redwald, have you known this many hours?"

"I heard it at the frontier town of Mercia, Reading, last night, and took all my measures immediately."

"Then, can we really depend upon Wessex?"

"I trust so indeed, my lord, else we should be in a very bad way indeed."

"Well, we *must* rest now. Elgiva, darling, this is a cold termination to our first anniversary, but your husband's love shall ever protect you until he be cold in death. Good-night, Elfric, be ready for the morrow. Good-night, Redwald, trustiest warrior who ever served a grateful lord. Good-night, gentlemen all."

And thus the royal party broke up, and thus ended the first anniversary of the ill-starred union.

On the morrow all was haste and confusion in the royal palace. Elgiva departed early for Winchester, which, being farther removed from the frontier, was safer than London from any sudden excursion on the part of the Mercians, and the city was also devoted to the royal family. The citizens of London were directed to provide for the defence of their city, while the royal guards, attended by the immediate vassals of the crown, prepared to march into the heart of the rebellious district.

It is too often supposed that the feudal system was of Norman importation, whereas its very foundation—the act of homage, or of "becoming your man,"—was brought by the Saxons and Angles from their German home. The lord was the protector of the vassal, but the vassal was bound to attend his feudal superior both in peace and war. So imperative was this obligation, that a vassal who abandoned his lord in the field of battle was liable to the death of a traitor.

Therefore Edwy soon found himself at the head of a compact body of ten thousand men, all bound to stand by him to death. But there was one very disheartening circumstance, which attracted notice. No volunteers joined the little army, although a royal proclamation had promised lands from the territories of the rebels to each successful combatant in the cause of Edwy and Elgiva.

The fear of the Church hung on all; the conviction that the law of both Church and State had been broken by the young king; the universal belief in the sanctity of Dunstan, and in the true patriotism of Odo, whom they called "the good;" the thoughtless misgovernment since the wiser counsellors had dispersed;—all these things weakened the hearts of the followers of Edwy.

There was therefore but little enthusiasm when the inhabitants saw the soldiers of the king march out by the Watling Street, and the soldiers themselves looked dispirited.

It was early dawn on the second day from the feast that the departure took place. Cynewulf, a valiant Earl of Wessex, was the real commander; nominally, Edwy commanded in person, and Elfric rode out of London by his side. Redwald's rank would not have entitled him to the chief command.

Passing through the environs of the city, they gained the open country, and marched steadily along the causeway the Romans had so firmly laid, until they reached Verulam or S. Alban's, where they passed the night. It excited great discontent amongst the inhabitants that Edwy did not visit the shrine of the saint, the glory of their town; and his departure again took place amidst gloomy silence.

They were now about to cross the frontier and enter Mercia, then in many respects an independent state, governed, it might be, by the same monarch and Witan as Wessex, even as Scotland and England are governed by the same sovereign and Parliament, yet retaining like them its own peculiar code of laws in many respects.

And now Mercia had sternly refused to be governed any longer by the "enemy of the Church," and chose the Etheling, Edgar, to be its king.

Acting with the sanction of Odo, whom he deeply revered, the young Edgar, then only in his fifteenth year, accepted the offer, and the whole force of Mercia was gathering to support him when Edwy crossed the border.

It must not be supposed that either Cynewulf or Redwald expected to conquer the Mercians with ten thousand men. No; their design was simpler: they had learned where Edgar was residing, and that the forces around him were small. One bold stroke might secure his person, and then Edwy might make his own terms. This was the secret of the advice they both gave to the young king.

Redwald had, as we shall see, deep designs of his own to serve also, but they had been locked for years in his own breast, and no servant could seem more trusty and faithful than he did, or act with more energy in his master's cause.

The forces of Edwy, as we have related, left S. Alban's on the second morning, and travelled, horse and foot, very rapidly all that day.

Crossing the Icknield Street at Dunstable, where the remains of a huge temple, once sacred to Diana, were visible, they entered Mercia, and soon' reached Towcester, a town which had been walled round by King Athelstane; here they found no force prepared to receive them, and the town opened its gates at once.

They tarried here for a day, while they sent scouts and spies in all directions, many of whom never returned. The troops were quartered freely upon the inhabitants, who were evidently very hostile; and, in return, the soldiers of Edwy insulted the women and bullied the men. Every hour some quarrel arose, and generally ended in bloodshed; the citizens being commonly the victims.

Late at night messengers arrived at the royal quarters, bringing information that Edgar was at Alcester, the ancient Alauna, beyond the Avon, and that Osric, the great Earl of Mercia, was with him collecting troops.

A council was held at once, and it was decided to leave the Watling Street and to march for the Avon by cross-

country routes. They rested that night amidst the ruins of
the ancient Brinavæ, and here another council was held,
to deliberate on their future movements, and it was decided to march westward at once, for tidings came that
Edgar's forces were rapidly increasing, and prudence suggested prompt measures. Edwy was becoming very anxious.

The route for the next day was then made out; and,
with beating heart, Elfric learned that they purposed crossing
the river not far from Æscendune.

"Elfric, my friend," said Edwy, "there will be a chance
for you to visit Æscendune, and to obtain the old man's
forgiveness." He said this with a slight sneer.

"I cannot go there; I would die first."

Edwy started at the tone of deep feeling with which
the words were said; he knew nothing of the rencontre
of Elfric with his brother.

"Still I think that *I* must spend this coming night
there, and I will try and act the Christian for the occasion;
perhaps I may do you a good turn, while I renew my
acquaintance with your people."

In his very heart Elfric wished that Edwy might never
arrive there, yet he knew not what to say.

"Well," said the prince, observing his hesitation, "you
may go on with Cynewulf and the main body of the army,
which will cross the Avon higher up, and I will make excuse
that your duties detain you. I *must* go—I have special
reasons, I wish at least to secure the fidelity of the few—and
Redwald will accompany me; we join the army on the
morrow, without losing any time by the move."

And so the matter was settled.

CHAPTER XV.

THE ROYAL GUEST.

It was the morning of the first of August, and the sun, dispersing the early mists, gave promise of a bright summer day.

The inhabitants of Æscendune, lord and vassals alike, were astir from the early daybreak; for that day the harvest was to be commenced, and the crops were heavier than had been known for many a year. A good harvest meant peace and prosperity in those times, a bad harvest famine, and perhaps rebellion; for if the home crop failed, commerce did not, as now, supply the deficiency.

So it was with joy and gladness that the people went forth that day to reap with their sharp sickles in their hands, while the freshness of the early morn filled each heart insensibly with energy and life. The corn fell on the upland before their sharp strokes, while behind each reaper the younger labourers gathered it into sheaves.

Old Ella stood in their midst looking on the familiar scene, while his pious heart returned many a fervent thanksgiving to the Giver of all good. Under the shade of some spreading beeches, which bordered the field, the domestics from the manor-house were spreading the banquet for the reapers—mead and ale, corn puddings prepared in various modes with milk, huge joints of cold roast beef—for the hour when toil should have sharpened the appetite of the whole party.

By the side of his father stood young Alfred, administering with filial affection to all his wants, as if he felt constrained to supply a double service in his own person now that Elfric was no more, or, at least, dead to home ties.

Thicker and thicker fell the wheat, and they thought surely such heavy sheaves had never fallen to their lot before.

At last the blowing of a horn summoned all the reapers to their dinner, and when Father Cuthbert had said grace, the whole party fell to—the thane at the head of them; and when the desire of eating and drinking was appeased, the labourers lay on the grass, in the cool shade, to pass away the hour of noontide heat, before resuming their toil.

"Father," said Alfred, "a horseman is coming."

"My old eyes are somewhat dim; I do not see any one approaching."

"Nor I, as yet, but I hear him; listen, he is just crossing the brook; I can hear the splashing."

"Some royal messenger, perhaps, from Edgar or from Edwy, my son. I fear such may be the case; yet I wish I could be left in peace, afar from the strife which must convulse the land, if the ill-advised brothers cannot agree to reign—the one over Mercia, the other over Wessex."

"We have repeatedly said that we should be quite neutral, father."

"And yet, my son, we offend both parties, and, I fear me, we shall be forced to defend ourselves in the end. But God is our refuge and strength, a very present help in trouble. And now that I am old I can lean more and more upon Him. He will be a father to you, my Alfred, when these hoary hairs are hidden in the grave."

It was seldom that the old thane expressed his devotion in this strain; it seemed to Alfred as if there were a foreboding of coming trial in it, and he felt as when a cloud veils the face of the sun in early spring.

The messenger now came in sight—a tall, resolute looking man, well armed and well mounted, and evidently bound for the hall. But when he saw the party beneath

the trees he bent his course aside, and saluting the thane
with all deference, inquired if he spoke to Ella of Æscendune.

"I am he," replied Ella. "I trust you are not the
bearer of other than good tidings ; but will you first refresh
yourself, since it is ill talking between the full and the
fasting ?"

"With gladness do I accept your bounty ; for I have
ridden since early dawn, and rider and horse are both
exhausted."

"There is corn for your horse, and food and wine for
his master. Uhred, take charge of the steed. Alfred, my
son, place that best joint of beef before the stranger, and
those wheaten cakes. I drink to you, fair sir."

The messenger seemed in no hurry to open his tale
until he had eaten and drunk, and it was with the greatest
patience that the thane, who was one of nature's gentlemen,
awaited his leisure.

At length the messenger looked up, and pushed his
wooden platter aside.

"I have come to be the bearer of good tidings to you,
noble thane. Edwy, your king, with a small troop of
horse, his royal retinue, proposes honouring your roof with
his presence, and asks bed and board of his loyal subject,
Ella of Æscendune."

"The king's will is my law ; and since it pleases the son
of my late beloved master, King Edmund, to visit me, he
shall find no lack of hospitality. But may I ask what sudden event has brought him into the heart of our country ?"

"He comes to chastise rebellion. A large force of
several thousand men crosses the river a few miles higher
this evening, and, not to incommode you with numbers, King
Edwy comes apart from his followers."

Although he foresaw grave inconvenience, and even
danger, in the proposal, yet Ella could not appear churlish
and inhospitable; therefore, learning from the messenger
that the king might be expected before sunset, he returned

home to make such preparations as should suggest themselves for the entertainment of his royal master, for so he still would have styled Edwy, deeply as he felt he had been wronged by him.

"Father," said Alfred, as he walked homeward by his side, "think you Elfric will be in his train ? I wish he may be."

"Alas, my son! I fear I shall never see poor Elfric again. My mind always seems to misgive me when I think of him ; and I have so strong a foreboding that he has received my last blessing, that I cannot overcome it. No, Alfred, I fear we shall *not* see Elfric to-night."

No more was said upon the subject ; they reached the hall in good time, and startled the lady Edith by their tidings.

Instantly all was in preparation : the best casks of wine were broached, fowls and wild birds alike had cause to lament that their lives were shortened, chamberlain and cook were busy, clean rushes were brought in to adorn the floor of the hall, sweet flowers and aromatic grass for that of the royal bedchamber ; and it was not till a flourish of trumpets announced the approach of the cavalcade that all was ready, and the maidens and men-servants, arrayed in their best holiday attire, stood grouped without the gate to receive their king.

At last the glitter of the departing ray upon pointed lances announced the approach, and soon the whole party might be seen—a hundred horse accompanying the king's person, and one or two nobles of distinction, including Redwald, riding by his side.

When the train first reached the spot from which the castle was visible, a strange thing occurred. The king's eyes were fixed upon Redwald, and, to the royal astonishment, the whole frame of that worthy seemed shaken by a sudden emotion. His countenance became pale, his lips were compressed, and his eyes seemed to dart fire.

"What is the matter, my Redwald ?" asked the king.

"Oh, nothing, my lord!" said he, resuming his wonted aspect with difficulty, but at last becoming calm as a lake when the wind has died away; "only a sudden spasm."

"I hope you are not ill?"

"No, my lord; you need not really feel anxious concerning me.   The hall of Æscendune appears a pleasant place for a summer residence," he added.

"I have been there before," said the king.   "Spent some weeks there.   Yes; I thought it a great change for the better *then*, after the musty odour of sanctity which reigned in the palace of my uncle the monk, but all things go by comparison.   I might not relish a month there *now*."

"Yet it looks like a place formidable for its kind, and it might not be amiss to persuade the worthy old thane to receive a garrison there, so that if the worst came to the worst we might have a place of refuge, otherwise the Mercians would soon have possession of it."

"Ella is one of themselves."

"But the rebel Edgar may not forgive him for entertaining us?"

"He can hardly help himself.   Still, the smoke of those fires, which, I trust, betokens good cheer, and the peaceful aspect of that party coming out to meet us, in the midst of whom I recognise old Ella and his son Alfred, Elfric's brother, does not look much like compulsion."

"Making the best of a bad bargain, perhaps."

"I prefer to think otherwise."

At this moment the two parties met, and Edwy at once dismounted from his courser with that bewitching and kingly grace which became "Edwy the Fair."   He advanced gracefully to the old thane, and, preventing the customary mark of homage, embraced him as a son might embrace a father—"For," said he, "Elfric has taught me to revere you as a father, even if Æscendune had not taught me before then.   I robbed you of your son, now I offer you *two* sons, Elfric and my-self."

The tears stood in the old man's eyes at this reception, and the mention of his dear prodigal son. "He is well, I hope?" said he, striving to speak with such sternness and dignity as self-respect taught in opposition to natural feeling.

"Well and happy; and I trust you will see him in a day or two, when we shall have chastised our rebels; justice, mingled with mercy, must first have its day."

"Where is he now?"

"With the main body of the army; in fact, he is my right hand. It is my fault, not his, that he is not here now; but we could not both leave, and he preferred that I should come and proffer my filial duty first, and perhaps that I should assure you of his love and duty, however appearances may have seemed against him."

Then the eye of Edwy caught Alfred. It must be remembered that Elfric had kept the secret of his brother's supposed death, even from the king.

"And of Alfred, too, I have ever been reminded by his brother; your name has seldom been long absent from our conversation."

Alfred reddened.

"I trust now," he continued, "that I may profitably renew an acquaintance suspended for three years. I am but young, only in my eighteenth year, and I have no father; let me find one in the wisest of the Mercians."

So bewitching was the grace of the fair speaker that he seemed to carry all before him. Ella began to think he must have misjudged the king. Alfred alone, who knew much more of the relations between the king and the Church than his father, still suspended his belief in these most gracious words.

Leaning upon the still powerful arm of Ella, his young agile form contrasting strongly with the powerful build of the old thane—powerful even in decay—they came in front of the hall, where the serfs and vassals all received them with joyful acclamations, and amidst the general homage, the king entered the hall.

There he reverentially saluted the lady Edith.

" The mother of my friend, my brother, Elfric, is my mother also," said he.

Then he was conducted to his chamber, where the bath was provided for him, and unguents for anointing himself, after which, accepting the loan of a change of clothing more suitable than his travelling apparel, he received the visit of Ella, who came to conduct him to the banquet.

All this while his followers had been received according to their several degrees; and a board was spread, of necessity, in a barn, for the due feasting of the soldiers of Edwy and the vassals of Æscendune; while the officers and the chief tenants of the family met at the royal table in the great hall once before introduced to our readers.

It boots not to repeat an oft-told tale, to describe the banquet in all its prodigal luxury, to tell how light the casks in the cellars of Æscendune seemed afterwards, how empty the larder; suffice it to say that in due course the banquet was ended, the toasts were drunk, and, with an occasional interlude in the gleeman's song and the harper's wild music, the conversation was at its height. Wine and wassail unloose men's tongues.

Redwald sat near the king, who had introduced him to Ella as a dear friend both to him and his son—" a very *Mentor*," he said, " who, since the unhappy quarrel into which my counsellors forced me—yes, *forced* me—with Dunstan, has done more to keep Elfric and me straight in our morals than at one time I should have thought possible for any man to do. Redwald, you need not blush; it is true, and your king is proud to own it."

Redwald was not exactly blushing; he had spent the interval before the banquet in looking eagerly and wistfully all round the house, and now his countenance had a cold composure, which made it seem as if he had never known emotion; still he answered fittingly to the king's humour—

"Alack, my lord, such credit is due only to the blessed saints, especially S. Wilfred, whom you first learned to love at Æscendune, as you have often told me."

"Yes," said Edwy; "you remember, Ella, how I used to steal away even from the chase, and visit his chapel at the priory which your worthy father founded; truly, I mused upon the saint so much that I marvel he appeared not to me; I think he did once."

"Indeed!" exclaimed his auditors.

"Yes; I had been musing upon my condition as a poor orphan boy, deprived of my brave father—he was your friend, Ella!—when methought a figure, in the dress of a very ancient bishop, stood beside me, yet immaterial as the breeze of evening. 'Thy prayer is heard,' said he to me; 'thou hast brought many gifts to S. Wilfred; he shall send thee one, even a friend.' It was fulfilled in Elfric."

"Truly, it was marvellous," said Father Cuthbert, who listened with open mouth. "I doubt not it was our sainted patron."

Alfred said nothing; his recollections of Edwy's days at Æscendune did not embrace many hours in the chapel of S. Wilfred.

The great wonderment of Ella may be conceived: he had always mourned over Edwy as a headstrong youth, dead to religion, and now he was called upon to contemplate him in so different a light. The reader may wonder at his credulity, but if he had listened to the sweet voice of the beautiful king, had gazed into that innocent-looking face—those eyes which always seemed to meet the gaze, and never lowered themselves or betrayed their owner—he would, perhaps, have been deceived too; yet Edwy was overdoing it, and a look from Redwald warned him of the fact. He took the other line.

"Alas!" he said, "I have been very very unworthy of S. Wilfred's fond interest in me, and may have done very rash things; but some day the saint may rejoice in mo again, and then he shall not find in me a rebellious son."

Further than this he was not disposed to go, for in truth he felt himself sickened by his very success in deceit, although half disposed to be proud of it at the same time. But Redwald had taken up the conversation.

"These halls of yours seem old, venerable thane; has your family long dwelt under this hospitable roof?"

"My remote ancestor fought by the side of Cynric in the victories which led to the foundation of Mercia."

"Ah! many a sad yet glorious tale and legend for the gleeman's harp, doubtless, adorns your annals."

"Not many; we have our traditions."

"For instance, is there one connected with the foundation of the priory hard by?"

"It is of recent date; my father built it."

"Strange, for generally these old places are reared up by repentant sinners, mourning over the sins they have committed, or the day of grace they have cast away; is there no tale attached to your foundation?"

"Alas! there is; but it is one whose stain is all too recent, one we cannot recount, or suffer gleeman's harp to set to music, lest we harrow the yet bleeding wound."

Redwald could not ask more; the answer was too plain and distinct, and so he was forced to repress his curiosity.

The conversation then became desultory, and, finally, when the gleemen began the well-known *pièce de resistance*, the battle of Brunanburgh, Edwy yawned and Redwald looked sleepy, while the old thane actually slept in his huge arm-chair, and was awakened only by the cessation of the music and singing.

Even in the presence of royalty itself Ella did not suffer the company to disperse before the chaplain had said the customary compline service, after which the guard was doubled at the door, and soon the whole household was buried in sweet and peaceful sleep.

Yet, although they knew it not, they nourished the deadliest foe of their race in the bosom of the family. There was one at least who could not sleep that night, who now paced his narrow chamber, now looked forth at the meadows, woods, and hills, sleeping in the summer twilight; now, unchecked, burst into the wildest excitement, and paced his chamber as a wild beast might pace the floor of his cage; now calmed down into a sarcastic smile.

"Yes!" he said in soliloquy, "and here I am at last; here in the halls which should have been *his* and mine, and shall be *mine* yet; here! and they know it not; here! and the reward of years of patient endurance is at hand; here! yes, here, in the halls of Æscendune—dreamed of, sighed after, prayed for at the shrine of such gods as promise vengeance; here, by Woden and Thor! here by Satan's help, if there be a Satan!—here! here! here!"

CHAPTER XVI.

"NAKED THOUGH LOCKED IN STEEL."

EARLY in the morning the whole household was astir, and the breakfast alone preceded the preparations for the departure of Edwy and his retinue. Redwald did not appear, and they became uneasy at his prolonged absence, until, sending to his room, they found him suffering from sudden, but severe illness; which, as the leech shortly decided, would absolutely prevent his travelling that day.

It was evident that Edwy was annoyed by this, but it was not until after a long conference with Redwald that he took Ella aside, and pointing out to him the exposed position of the hall, besought his permission to leave a garrison of fifty men under the command of this trusty officer, which would ensure their safety, in case of any sudden attack on the part of Edgar's troops.

"I can hardly feel that I need such protection, my royal master," replied Ella; "I dwell among my own people, and am perhaps safer when quite unprotected."

"In that case, may I press my own poor claims?" replied the king. "In case of the worst, I should have Æscendune to fall back upon, a retreat secured by chosen men behind me, where one might halt and turn to bay; again, Redwald's sudden illness necessitates my leaving him to your hospitality."

Thus pressed on every side, Ella felt he could but yield to a request which the speaker had not only the power but the right, as his feudal superior, to enforce; for Ella was not prepared to throw off his allegiance, as most

of his neighbours had done, and to make common cause
with Edgar. Again, the conversation of the previous
night had given him more confidence in Edwy, and more
hope of seeing Elfric again, like the returning prodigal,
than he had previously had. Edwy saw this, and continued—

"And it is but a few days hence, ere I propose to
return with Elfric—whom I could indeed put in command
of such forces as are necessary to secure you against our
mutual foes, when I return southward. Redwald and his
troops will hold the place in trust for Elfric, till he
arrives."

The last lingering feeling of reluctance was now forcibly
banished, and Ella consented to receive Redwald as his
guest, with a picked troop of fifty men.

"They shall be the best behaved warriors you have
ever seen, my own hus-carles—men who go to mass every
morning, and shrift every week," added the deceitful
prince; "at least," he added, as he saw the look of
incredulity Ella could not suppress, "some of them do, I
can't say how many."

In the course of an hour from this conversation, the
royal party took its departure, reduced to half its numbers.
Edwy left amidst the regret of all, so amiable had been
his manners, so winning his ways.

"I take a son's liberty," said he, as he saluted the
venerable cheek of the lady Edith; "but I will bring your
other son back with me in a few days."

The road leading over the hill and through the forest
had swallowed up the retreating force, when Ella personally superintended the distribution of quarters to the
guard of Redwald, many of whom afterwards volunteered
to follow him to the harvest field, and displayed uncommon
alacrity in carrying the wheat safely to its granaries, saying
the rebels should never have the reaping thereof.

There was, however, a kind of gloom over the whole
party through that day. The thought that deadly strife

impended close at hand weighed upon the spirits of Ella, but they brightened again at the renewed hope of meeting his prodigal, and he now hoped *repentant*, son in peace.

Meanwhile, very different scenes were on the point of being enacted only twice ten miles from the spot.

The main body of the army left its quarters on the right bank of the Avon, at the same hour in which Edwy left Æscendune to join them on their march ; and they proceeded in safety all through the morning. At mid-day they lay down to feed and to rest, and while thus resigning themselves to repose, with the guards posted carefully around, the sound of cavalry was heard in the distance, and shortly the royal party appeared. Elfric was alert to receive them, but could not conceal his surprise when he saw their diminished numbers, and perceived the absence of Redwald.

Edwy saw his look of embarrassment, and hastened to reply to the question it conveyed.

"They are left at Æscendune, fifty under the command of Redwald, to fortify the house until we return. You must go home this time, and you need not fear, for I have been a very saint at Æscendune, and they are expecting Dunstan will speedily return and canonise me. Elfric, I have used my sanctity for your advantage, since I have represented you as sharing it at least in some degree."

"I fear me, my father is too wise to be so easily deceived."

"Nothing of the kind ; he really seemed to believe in it ; at all events, I have promised you shall return with me."

"Did they really seem to wish to see me ?"

"They did *really*, especially your brother Alfred."

Elfric started as if an arrow had struck him. "Alfred, Alfred !" he said.

"Yes, why not Alfred ?"

"And you saw him alive and well ?"

"To be sure, why not ? Did you think he was dead."

Elfric became confused, and muttered some incoherent

answer, but he rejoiced in his very heart; he felt as if a
mountain were removed from him, and a sweet longing for
home, such as he had not felt since a certain Good Friday,
sprang up in his mind, so strongly that he would have gone
then and there, had circumstances permitted.   Alas, poor
boy! his wish was not thus easily to be gratified: he had
sinned very deeply—his penance had yet to be accomplished; well has the poet written—

> "Facilis descensus Averno . . . .
> Sed retrograre gradum, superasque evadere ad auras,
> Hoc opus—hic labor est." *

The midday halt concluded, the troops resumed their
march for Alcester, where they hoped to arrive about nightfall, and to surprise Edgar and his *few* followers.   All
that afternoon they proceeded through a dense woodland
country; and the evening was setting in upon them, when
suddenly the scouts in front came galloping back, and gave
the startling information that entrenchments were thrown
up across their path, and that a large force was evidently
entrenched behind.

At first Edwy could scarcely believe the report; but
Cynewulf, the experienced commander, upon whom, as we
have said, the real command of the force devolved, rode
forward, and soon returned, having previously ordered a
general halt, and that entrenchments sho uldbe thrown up
for their own protection during the night.

"Ealdorman," said Edwy, impatiently, "why throw
up entrenchments? can we not carry *theirs* by storm? we are
all ready, are we not, for a valiant charge?"

"Nay, my lord, we are but ill prepared," was the reply,
"for such desperate measures.   I am not certain they do
not outnumber us; even so, we probably excel them in

---

* The gate of hell stands open night and day;
  Smooth the descent, and easy is the way:
  But to return, and view the upper skies—
  In this the toil, in this the labour lies.—DRYDEN.

discipline and skill, and have every chance of victory to-morrow, which we should lose by fighting in the dark."

So Edwy, who did not lack personal courage, and would gladly have ended the short raid then and there, was forced to be governed by wiser heads; and accordingly the bivouacs were made, the fires lighted, and the royal tent pitched upon the slope of a gentle valley, which descended to a brook in the bottom, where the ground rose similarly on the other side, and was crowned by the hostile entrenchment, behind which rose the smoke of the enemy's fires. The heads of numerous soldiers, seen over the mound, showed how well they were prepared.

The entrenchment was dug, the mound thrown up, the sentinels posted, and all in so short a space of time, that, to the uninitiated in the art of war, it would have seemed little short of miraculous; but the discipline of the Danes, who owed their success generally to the skill with which they fortified their camps, had been partially inherited by their adversaries, and the hus-carles were not even all English; there were many Danes amongst them.

The suppers were soon cooked and eaten, the wine circulated freely, and patriotic songs began to be heard; but there was one who seemed to have no heart for them—Elfric. At the huge fire, which blazed near the royal tent, Edwy sat as master of the feast, and he was in a state of boisterous merriment. But all Elfric's efforts could not hide the depression of his spirits, and Edwy, who loved him sincerely—for the reader has seen that he was quite capable of love—tried to rouse him from it, anxious that no one should suspect the courage of his favourite.

Once or twice Elfric seemed to make great efforts to overcome this feeling of depression, and partially succeeded in veiling it from all but the observant young king.

At last the feast was over.

"My friends," said the king, "we must be stirring early in the morning, so we will now disperse for the night."

They drank a parting cup, then separated, while the king took Elfric's arm and led him aside.

"Elfric," said he, "did I not know my friend and most faithful follower, I should suspect that he feared the morrow's conflict."

"I cannot help it," said Elfric; "perhaps I *do* fear it; yet, had I but my father's forgiveness, could I but see him once more, I could laugh at the danger; it is not pain or death I fear, but I long to be where you have been. I would I had gone with you now."

"So do I."

"And now I have my forebodings that I shall never hear my father's forgiveness; and, Edwy, if I die without it, I believe my spirit cannot rest; I shall haunt the spot till the day of doom."

"This is all moonshine, Elfric. You have not been such a bad fellow after all; if you go wrong, what will happen to the greater part of those amongst us who may die to-morrow? When you once get into the fight, and your blood gets warm, you will be all right; it is only the first battle that gives one all these fancies."

"No; it is not that. I am of a race of warriors, and I do not suppose one of that race ever felt like this in his first battle. I have often looked forward to mine with joy, but now my mind is full of gloomy forebodings: I feel as if some terrible danger, not that of the fight, were hanging over me and mine, and as if I should never meet those I did love once, either in this world or the next."

"The next! all we know about that comes from the priestly pratings. I think, of the two heavens, Valhalla,* with its hunting or fighting by day, its feasting by night, would suit me best. I don't know why we should think ourselves wiser than our ancestors; they were most likely right about the matter, if there *be* another world at all."

"*I* cannot disbelieve, if you can," replied poor Elfric.

* See Note O.—Valhalla.

"I have tried to, but I can't. Well, I daresay I shall know all about it by this time to-morrow."

"Pshaw! let to-morrow take care of itself; 'tis our first fight, Elfric, and we will have no cowardly forebodings; we shall live to laugh at them all. What shall we do with Edgar, if we get him to-morrow? I suppose one must not shed a brother's blood, even if he be a rebel?"

"Certainly not; no, no."

"Perhaps it will be shed *for* me, and a lucky thrust with sword or lance may end all our trouble, and leave me sole king; but won't the holy fox Dunstan grieve if his pet, his favourite, gets hurt! Come, cheer up, Elfric, my boy; dismiss dull care, and be yourself again."

Elfric tried very hard to do so, and again partly succeeded. They had extended their walk all round the limits of the camp. It was a beautiful starlit night: there was a new moon, which was just going down, and an uncertain light hung about the field which was to be the scene of the conflict. It was one of those bright nights when the very aspect of nature suggests thoughts of the Eternal and the Infinite; when the most untutored being, gazing up into the deep blue void, finds his mind struggle vainly to grasp the hidden secrets those depths conceal; when the soul seems to claim her birthright, and dreams of an existence boundless, illimitable, as the starry wastes around. Such were, perhaps, the ideas which animated the philosophers of the old heathen world when they placed their departed heroes amongst the constellations; such, perhaps, the thoughts which led the dying apostate Julian to bid his followers weep no more for a prince about to be numbered with the stars.

Thoughts of peace would those radiant orbs have spoken, under any other circumstances, to the ardent youth as he gazed upon them; but now they oppressed him with the consciousness that he was at enmity with the mighty Unknown, that he was in danger, such danger as he could not comprehend; not *that* which comes from the lance-point or the sword-blade, but danger which fills the soul with the consciousness of its existence, yet is impalpable, not having revealed itself, only its presence.

" Good-night, Elfric," said Edwy, as they reached the camp on their return ; " good-night.   I hope you will be in better spirits in the morning."

Edwy retired within the folds which concealed the entrance to his own tent. Close by was the tent appointed for Elfric, who acted as his page ; and the latter entered also, and sat down on a camp-stool. His bed did not seem to invite him ; he sat on the seat, his face buried in his hands; then he suddenly rose, threw himself on his knees, only for a moment, rose up again—" I can't, I can't pray ; if my fate be death, then come death and welcome the worst. There will at least be nothing hidden then, nothing behind the scenes.   I will not be a coward."

The phrase was not yet written—" Conscience makes cowards of us all ; " yet how true the principle then as now—true before Troy's renown had birth, true in these days of modern civilisation.

He could not sleep peacefully, although he laid himself down ; his hands moved in the air, as if to drive off some unseen enemy, as if the danger whose presence was impalpable to the waking mind *revealed* itself in sleep. " No, no ! " he muttered ; " let the blow fall on me, on me, on me alone ! " then he rose as if he would defend some *third* person from the attack of an enemy, and the word " Father ! " once or twice escaped his lips ; yet he was only dreaming. " Father ! " again he cried, in the accents of warning, as if some imminent danger menaced the loved one.

He awoke, stared about, hardly recognising where he was.   " What can I have been dreaming about ? " he cried ; " what can it all mean ? I thought I was at Æscendune ;" and he strove vainly to recall the scenes of his dream.

The tread of the passing guard was the only sound which broke the stillness of the camp.   " I cannot sleep," said Elfric, and walked forth.

The night was waning, and in the east a red glow was creeping upwards ; the stars were, however, still brilliant. Opposite, at the distance of less than a mile, the reflection of the camp fires, now low, revealed the presence of the enemy ; before him the mist slowly arose in white thin smoke-like wreaths, from the grass whereon many should soon sleep their last sleep, now in unconsciousness of their fate. "I wonder where I shall lie?" thought Elfric, as if it were certain he would fall. He felt cooler now, as the hour drew near ; he watched the red light creeping upward, and saw the light clouds above catch the glow, until the birds began their songs, the glorious orb arose to gild the coming strife, and the shrill trumpet in the camp was answered by the distant notes in the camp of the foe, like an echo afar off.

CHAPTER XVII.

THE SLEEP OF PEACE.

THE first day after the departure of the king from Æscendune passed rapidly away. The soldiers who had remained behind with Redwald were quiet and orderly in their demeanour, and even, in obedience to secret orders, attended the evensong at the minster church, as if moved thereto by devotion, although the curious spectator might easily discover the unaccustomed character of their service, by the difficulty with which they followed the prayers, and the uneasy impatience with which they listened to a lengthened exposition of a portion of the Anglo-Saxon version of the Gospels from Father Cuthbert.

The old thane and all his family were very anxious, it may be readily believed, for the earliest news from the field of battle, for battle every one agreed was impending; and, to gratify their natural curiosity, Redwald sent out quick and alert members of his troop, to act as messengers, and bear speedy news from the scene of action.

The night set in clear and bright, as we have already seen; and while poor Elfric was wandering about uneasily beneath that brilliant sky, the same stars looked down peacefully upon his home, where all slept sweetly under the fostering care, as they would have said, of their guardian angels.

The morn broke brightly, and with every promise of a fine harvest day. The labourers were speedily again in the fields; the cattle wandered under the herdsman's care to their distant pastures; the subdued tinkling of the sheep-bells met the ear, and the other subdued sounds which soothe the air on a summer's day ; and so the hours fled by, and no one would have dreamed that, not twenty miles away, man met man in the fierce and deadly struggle of war.

When the reapers assembled for their midday meal, they discussed the merits of the quarrel, and nearly all those who had been brought under the eye of " Edwy the Fair " were eager in pleading his cause, and trying to find some extenuation of his misdeeds in the matter of the illegal marriage, for such it was, from the mildest point of view; and scarcely a voice was raised on the opposite side, until Ella drew near the scene of conversation, and observed that, " while God forbid they should judge the matter harshly, yet law was law, and right was right, and a beautiful face or winsome look could not change it."

Strolling near the field, seemingly absorbed in thought, walked Redwald, and seeing the reapers, he came towards them.

" A picture of peaceful enjoyment," he quietly said ; " how often have I wished I could but lay down sword and lance to take more innocent weapons in hand, and to spend my declining days 'mid scenes like these."

" Indeed ! " said Ella. " It is generally thought that men whose trade is war love their calling."

" Yes ; sometimes the fierce din of battle seems a pastime fit for the gods, but the banquet is apt to cloy."

" Have you followed your profession for many years ? "

" Since I was a mere child; even my boyhood was passed amid the din of arms."

There were very few *professional* soldiers in that day, and *they* were much dreaded. An Englishman was always ready to take up arms when lawfully called by his feudal superior, or when home or civil rights were in danger, but he generally laid them down and returned to his fields with joy ; hence the rustics looked upon a man like Redwald with much undisguised curiosity.

" Think you we shall soon hear from the contending parties ?" asked Alfred, who was, as usual, in attendance upon his father.

" Perhaps by nightfall ; one of my men has just returned to tell me that the king's progress was stopped by an entrenched camp of the rebels, and that they expected to fight at early dawn."

The news was unexpected, and every one felt his heart beat more quickly.

" I have a messenger already on the spot, and so soon as the royal forces have gained the victory he will speed hither as fast as four legs can bring him ; we shall probably hear by eventide."

It is needless to say how every one panted for the decisive news. Ella and Alfred soon returned to the castle, and Redwald took his horse, and rode out, as he said, to meet the messenger.

The hours seemed to pass more slowly ; the sun drew near the west, the shadows lengthened ; and Ella, with the lady Edith, Alfred, Edgitha, and all the members of the little society, could hardly bend their minds to any occupation, mental or physical. Elfric was ever in their thoughts.

" O Ella ! " said his wife, " this suspense is very hard to bear ; I long to hear about our boy."

The mother's heart was bound up in him, as if there were no other life in danger that day ; Edwy or Edgar, it was little to her in comparison with her longing for her first-born son.

" He is in God's Hands, dearest ! " returned her husband ; " and in better Hands than ours."

Well might the thoughts of the lady Edith be concentrated on the crisis before her. She had borne, with a mother's wounded heart, the separation of three years, and now it was a question of a few short hours whether she should ever see him again or not. Now fancy painted him wounded, nay dying, on the bloodstained field ; now it impelled her to sally forth towards the scene, as though her feeble strength could bear her to him. Now she sought the chapel, and found refuge in prayer, as she had found refuge many many hours of that eventful day, but especially since Redwald had borne the news of the imminent battle.

At length the long suspense was ended. Redwald was seen riding at full speed towards the castle, followed by the long-expected messenger.

"Victory! victory!" he cried; "the rebels are defeated; the king shall enjoy his own."

"But Elfric, my son! my son!"

"Is safe; and will be here in a day or two, perhaps to-morrow."

"Thank God!" and the overcharged heart found relief in tears—happy tears of joy.

The messenger who followed Redwald, brought detailed accounts of the event. According to his statements it appeared that the king had broken through the hostile entrenchment, and had scattered their forces in the first attack. The messenger particularly asserted that he had seen Elfric, and had been charged with the fondest messages for home, where the youth hoped to be in a few days at the latest, seeing there was no longer an enemy to fear.

The hearts of all present were filled with thankfulness and joy.

"Come, my beloved Edith," said the old thane, "let us go first to thank God;" and they went together to the chapel which had witnessed so many earnest prayers that day—now, they believed, so fully answered.

All gloom and despondency seemed removed, and Ella went forth to walk alone in the woods, to meditate in silence on the goodness of God. Nearly each evening this had been his habit. The woods, he said, were God's first temples, and when alone he best raised his heart from nature to nature's God.

His thoughts were happy that evening: his first-born boy would be restored to him, and, like the father in the

Gospels, he longed to embrace the prodigal, and to tell him that all was forgiven. But he schooled himself to patience, and many a fervent thanksgiving did he offer as he wandered amidst the grassy glades.

But he was more weary than usual with the toil and anxiety of the day, and shortly seated himself upon a mossy bank beneath an aged oak. The trees grew thickly behind and before him, on each side of the glade, which terminated at no great distance in the heart of the pathless forest, so that no occasional wayfarer would be likely to pass that way.

There he reposed, until a gentle slumber stole over him and buried all his senses in oblivion.

The day was nearly spent, the light clouds which still reflected the sun's ruddy glow were fast fading into a grey neutral tint, and darkness was approaching. Once a timid deer passed along the glade, and started as it beheld the sleeping form, then went on, but started yet more violently as it passed a thicket on the opposite side. The night breeze had arisen and was blowing freshly; but still the old man slept on, as though he slept that sleep from which none shall awaken until the archangel's trump.

Meanwhile they grew uneasy at the hall over his prolonged absence, and at length Alfred started to find his father, beginning to fear that the excitement of the day had been too great for him, and that he might need assistance. He knew the favourite glade wherein the aged thane was wont to walk, and the mossy bank whereon he frequently reposed, so he lost no time, but bent his steps directly for the spot.

As he drew near, he saw his father lying on the bank beneath the oak as still in sound sleep, and marvelled that the chilly air of the evening had not awoke him. He was not wont to sleep thus soundly. He approached closely, but his steps did not arouse the sleeper. He now bent over him, and put his hand on his shoulder affectionately and lovingly. "Father, awake," he said; "the night is coming on; you will take cold."

But there was no answering voice, and the sleeper stirred not. Alfred became seriously alarmed, but his alarm changed suddenly into dread certainty. The feathered shaft of an arrow met his eye, dimly seen in the darkness, as it stuck in the left side of the sleeping Ella. Sleeping, indeed. But the sleep was eternal.

Horrified at the sight, refusing to believe his eyes, the son first continued his vain attempts to awake his sire, then fell on his knees, and wrung his hands while he cried piteously, "O father, speak to me!" as if he could not accept the fact that those lips would never salute him more. The moonbeams fell on that calm face, calm as if in sleep, without a spasm of pain, without the contraction of a line of the countenance. The weapon had pierced through the heart; death had been instantaneous, and the sleeper had passed from the sleep of this earth to that which is sweetly called "sleep in the Lord," without a struggle or a pang. His heart full of joy and thanksgiving, he had gone to carry his tribute of praise to the very throne of God.

When the first paroxysm of pain and grief was over, the necessity of summoning some further aid, of bearing the sad news to his home, pressed itself upon the mind of Alfred, and he took his homeward road *alone,* as if he hardly knew what he was doing, but simply obeyed instinct. Arrived there, he could not tell his mother or sister; he only sought the chamberlain and the steward, and begged them to come forth with him, and said something had happened to his father. They went forth. "We must carry something to bear him home," he said, and they took a framework of wood upon which they threw some bearskins.

Alfred did not speak during the whole way, save that in answer to the anxious inquiries of his companions he replied, "You will see!" and they could but infer the worst from his manner, without giving him the pain of telling the fatal truth. At length they reached the glade where the dead body lay. The moon was bright, and in her light they saw the fatal truth at once. "Alas, my master! alas, my dear lord! Who has done this? Who could have done it?" was their cry. "Was there one who did not love and revere him?"

More demonstrative than Alfred had been were they in their lamentations, for the deepest grief is often the most silent.

At length they raised the body, the temple of so pure and holy a spirit, which had now returned to the God Who gave it, reverently as men would have handled the relics of some martyr saint, and placed it on the bier which they had prepared. Then they began their homeward route, and ere a long time had passed they stood before the great gate of the castle with their burden.

It now became a necessity for Alfred to announce the sad news to his widowed mother; and here the power of language fails us—the shock was so sudden, so unexpected. The half of her life was so suddenly torn from the bereaved one, that the pang was well-nigh insupportable. But God tempers the wind to the shorn lamb, and has promised that the strength of His beloved ones shall be even as their day. So He strengthened the sensitive frame to bear a shock which otherwise might have slain it.

The sounds of lamentation and woe were heard all over the castle as they slowly bore the body to the domestic chapel, while some drew near, impelled by an irresistible desire to gaze upon it, and then cried aloud in excess of woe. Amongst the others, Redwald approached, and gazed fixedly upon the corpse; and Eric the steward often declared, in later days, that he saw the wound bleed afresh under the glance of the ruthless warrior, but perhaps this was an afterthought.

Father Cuthbert, who had now been elected prior of the monastic house below, on the banks of the river, soon heard the sad news, and hastened up to tender the sweet consolations of religion—the only solace at such a time, for it is in seasons of suffering that we best comprehend the Cross. When he entered he saw the corpse in the chapel, where they had placed it before the altar, and he could only say, "Alas, my lord! alas, my dear friend!" until he knelt down to pray, and rose up somewhat calmed.

Then he sought the chamber where the lady Edith hid her woe, and there he showed her that God was love, hard though it was sometimes for the frail flesh to see it; and he bade her look to the Divine Sufferer of Whom it is said, "In all their afflictions He was afflicted;" and so by his gentle ministrations he brought calm to the troubled breast, and it seemed as if one had said to the waves of grief, "Peace, be still."

And then he gathered the household to prayer, and while they prayed many a "Requiescat" for the faithful soul, as they said the dirge commending to the Father's Hands a sheep of His fold, so they also prayed for strength to see the love which was hidden behind all this sad sad visitation, and to know the meaning of the words "Though He slay me, yet will I trust in Him."

And then he bade them rest—those, at least, who were able to do so—while he watched by the body, as was then the custom, all through the deep night.   And so the stars which had looked down from heaven so peacefully upon the house of Æscendune the night before, of which we wrote, now looked down as coldly bright as if no change had occurred, shining alike upon weal or woe, upon crime or holy deed of saint.   Yet as the kneeling friar saw them through the chapel window, he thought they were but the golden lights which lay about the confines of that happy region, where the faithful live in unspeakable felicity for ever with their Lord, and he found consolation in the thought of the Eternal and the Infinite.

CHAPTER XVIII.

THE BATTLE.

THE early morn, as we have already seen, broke upon the adverse hosts of Edwy and Edgar as the trumpet sounded to arouse them from their slumbers, in many instances from the last slumber they should ever enjoy.

Every soldier was on his legs in a moment, and, in the first place, preparations were made for breakfast; for it was a recognised fact amongst our ancestors that if you wanted a man to fight or do anything else *well*, you must feed him well first. So the care of the body was never neglected, however pressing the danger. Accordingly, Edwy called Elfric to sit by his side at the substantial meal which commenced the day, and saw, with much pleasure, that the cloud had partly passed from his friend's brow; for the hope of immediate action, of the excitement of battle, had done much to drive lowness and depression from the young warrior. So he strove to chat and laugh with the loudest, and when the moment came to marshal the host, and to put them in array, his spirits were as high as in old times.

The cavalry, which was their strongest arm, was under the command of Edwy himself, although a sturdy warrior, who had fought in many a battle, rode on his right hand to supply his lack of experience.

The main body of the infantry was under the command of Earl Cynewulf, while the reserve was under the command of Redwald's immediate subordinate, and consisted almost exclusively of the household guard.

The plan of attack, for it was quite decided that they

should take the initiative, was simple, and in accordance with the ordinary tactics of the times. The heavy-armed foot were bidden first to advance upon the entrenchments which crowned the opposite hill, and to break the infantry of the enemy, which was drawn up before them in formidable array; this done, the horse were immediately to avail themselves of the opening thus made, and the entrenchments to be assaulted by both cavalry and infantry.

Armed with huge axes, clad in mail, and bearing large shields, the foot advanced to the attack. They were a gallant company; and as the sun shone upon their glittering armour, or was reflected back from the bright steel of their axes, they might well inspire faint hearts with terror; but faint hearts were not amongst those opposed to them. The chosen men of the north-west, some of half-British blood, crowned the opposite hill, drawn up in front of their entrenchments, as if they scorned any other defence than that supplied by their living valour. They had borrowed their tactics from the Danes: deep and strong on all sides, they seemed to oppose an impenetrable wall to the foe; they had their shields to oppose to darts or arrows, their axes for the footmen, their spears to form a hedge of steel no horse could surmount.

Even *should* they yield to the pressure, still all would not be lost; their retreat was secured into the entrenchments, and there they might well hope to detain the enemy until the whole population should rise against the men of Wessex and their leader, and his cause become hopeless.

Steadily up the hill came the brave troops of Edwy, and from within their ranks, as they ascended the slope, a shower of arrows was discharged by the archers who accompanied them, under their protection; but no return was yet made by the foe, until they were close at hand, when a loud war-cry burst from the hostile ranks, and a perfect shower of darts and arrows rained upon the invaders.

Still they persevered, although they left a living, struggling line on the bloody grass behind them—persevered,

like men longing for the close hand-to-hand encounter,
longing to grasp their foes in deadly grip. The shock
arrived; and axe and sword were busy in reaping the
harvest of death. So great was the physical strength of the
combatants that arms and legs were mown off by a stroke,
and men were cloven in two, from the crown downwards,
by the sweeping blows of the deadly steel. It was a fearful
struggle, but it was a short one; the line was unshaken
in its strength; in vain Edwy's archers behind shot their
arrows so as to curve over the heads of their brethren and
fall amongst the foe; the men of Wessex recoiled and gave
way. Edwy seized what he thought the auspicious moment
when the ranks of the foe, although unbroken, were yet
weary and breathless, and ordered his cavalry to charge.
The Mercians beheld the coming storm at a distance; down
on their knees went the first line, their spears resting on
the ground; behind them the second bent over to strike
with their axes; while a third rank, the archers, drew their
bows, and prepared to welcome the rushing enemy with a
discharge of deadly arrows.

Every heart beat quickly as the fatal moment came
near; onward, with a sound like thunder, galloped the horse
of Edwy. He himself rode at their head, clad in light
armour, and by his side Elfric. All trace of fear was gone
now in the mad excitement of the charge; before them they
saw the wall of spear-points; nearer and nearer their
coursers bounded, until they seemed to fly. Every rider
leant forward, that his sword might smite as far as possible;
and, daring the points, trusting perhaps to the breast-plates
of their horses and their own ready blades, they rushed
madly upon the foe. In cold blood no one could, perhaps,
have ridden fearlessly against such an obstacle; but in the
excitement of the moment the warriors of Edwy seemed
capable of charging any imaginable barrier; and it became
almost a pure calculation, not of the respective bravery of
the troops, for none were cowards on either side, but of
mere physical laws of force and resistance.

M

Elfric scarcely looked where he was going. He saw a shining lance-point, about to impale him, he diverted it by his sword-blade, as he was hurried into the midst of axes, swords, lances, and beheld the warrior opposite to him in the second rank raise his axe to inflict a fearful blow, which would have severed his horse's neck, had not an arrow transfixed the foe.

The wedge seemed partly broken, and the king had begun to exult in the anticipation of speedy victory, when from behind each end of the entrenchment rushed two bodies of hostile cavalry ; they fell upon Edwy's forces in the rear, and in a few moments all was confusion.

The warriors of Edgar rallied, drove the horse out of their lines, advanced slowly, and the horsemen of the rival brothers, mingled together in deadly strife, in personal combat, where each man seemed to have sought and found his individual foe.

They moved slowly down the hill towards the brook, man after man falling and dotting the green sward of the hill with struggling, writhing bodies.

Meanwhile, Cynewulf was attempting to rally the flying foot, which had been cut almost in two by the charge of the Mercian cavalry : he succeeded, with great difficulty, in doing so at the brook which ran along the bottom of the valley, and, with the stream in their front, they prepared to afford a refuge to their *own*, and to resist the *hostile* horse.

Edwy saw the opportunity, and, raising himself in his stirrups, called upon his friends to follow him : he leapt the brook, and galloped round behind the foot, where nearly all the unwounded horsemen followed him. He had fought well, had slain more than one foe with his own royal hand, as became a descendant of Cerdic, and now he but retired to organise another and stouter resistance to the daring foe.

But he was forced to admit now that Cynewulf was right in his conjecture, and that they were utterly outnumbered, for the foe poured forth from their entrenchment and advanced in good order down the slope ; while the Mercian cavalry, forming in two detachments to the left and right, crossed the brook and charged along its banks upon the flanks of the Wessex infantry, at the same moment.

The warrior upon whose advice Edwy had been told to depend had fallen : he was left to his own resources. Alas ! he forgot he was a commander, and, waving his plumed cap as a signal for his brother knights to follow, charged upon the horsemen who were advancing up stream at like speed, forgetting that a similar body was advancing in the opposite direction, and that as all his force were following his lead, the opposite flank of the foot was unprotected.

In a single minute they were all engaged in the fiercest melée which imagination can well paint, fighting as furiously as men of the same blood *only* seem to fight when once the claims of kindred are cast aside. Swords ascended and descended with deadly violence ; horses raised themselves up on their hind legs, and, catching the deadly enthusiasm, seemed to engage their fellows ; riders fell, sternly repress-ing the groan which pain would extort, while their steeds, less self-controlled, uttered, when wounded, those ear-piercing cries only heard from the animals in deadly terror or pain. In the midst of this tumult Elfric engaged a Mercian of superior size and strength ; it was his second personal encounter ; in his first, he had seen his adversary fall with a warrior's stern joy, but now he was over-matched ; borne down by an arm twice as strong as his own, his guard was broken down, and a deadly blow laid open his shoulder, cutting the veins in the neck of his horse at the same fell sweep. The animal, blinded with blood, staggered, fell, and he was down amongst the horses' feet, confined by one leg, for his horse rolled partly upon him in its dying struggles ; while he felt the hoofs of other chargers in close proximity to his head.

A loud cry, "They fly ! they fly ! Victory ! Victory !" reached him even then. He well knew from which party the cries must proceed, and that he was left to the mercy of the victorious Mercians.

It was even so; the charge of the hostile cavalry on the left flank had broken down the ranks of the infantry on that side; the hostile foot had contrived to cross the brook in the confusion, and all was lost.

The reserve now came rapidly forward, but, seeing at a glance the state of things, retired to defend the entrenched camp, so as to give the king and his broken and routed followers time to escape, while they made good the defence with their lives. So they retired at once into the camp, whither Edwy and his few surviving companions galloped a moment after them.

Edwy was unhurt; he dismounted: his fair face flushed to a fiery red with heat and excitement, he leapt on the entrenchment and looked on the plain. He saw those of his own followers who had not yet made good their escape, ridden down, cut to pieces, slaughtered in the excitement of the moment without mercy; the sight stung him, he would have sallied out to their defence, but Cynewulf, who was yet living, met him in the gateway, and sternly seized the bridle of his steed.

"My lord and king," he said; "your life is precious to Wessex, you may not throw it away."

"I cannot see my followers slaughtered: loose my bridle, I command you;" and he raised his sword impetuously.

"You may cut me down, and so reward my faithful service; but, living, you shall not pass me on your road to destruction. My lord, I am old enough to be your father."

But there was one gay young noble present, who knew better than Cynewulf the key to Edwy's heart. He was one of the boon companions we have been before introduced to; but he had fought, poor young fellow, gallantly all that day, and now he could fight no longer: Edwy saw him reel and fall from his horse.

"Elfgar!" he said; as he strove to raise his friend and subject from the ground,—"not seriously wounded, I hope?"

"Dying, and for my king, as is my duty; let a dying voice reach you, my dear lord. Save yourself if you would save Elgiva, if you—if you—the words came broken and faint—are slain, she will be at the mercy of her deadly foes."

His head fell helplessly down upon his shoulder, and ere the king could make any reply, he saw that he was indeed past hope.

But his dying words had sunk deeply into the heart of Edwy. "Poor Elfgar! he was right. O Elgiva! Elgiva! this is a sad day for thee."

"Return then to her, my lord," said Cynewulf. "See, they are preparing now to assault the camp; I can hold it for hours, and if you are not here, I can make good terms with our foes; but, if you stay, you but embarrass us: ride out, my liege."

"And desert my subjects!"

"They will all acquit you: haste, my lord, haste, before they surround the camp, for your fair queen's sake, or you are lost."

"Come, my men, we must fly," said Edwy, sullenly; and he led the way reluctantly to the back of the camp. The road was partly encumbered with fugitives, but not wholly, as most of them sought the entrenched camp. Cynewulf accompanied him to the gate, where he stopped to give one last piece of advice. "Fly, my lord, for Wessex at once; lose no time; the best route will be the Foss-way; they will not suspect that you have taken that direction. Ride day and night; if you delay anywhere you are lost."

"Farewell, faithful and wise counsellor! Odin and Thor send that we may meet again;" and Edwy with only a dozen followers rode out at full speed. The Mercians had not yet reached that side of the camp, which was concealed by woods which were clear of all enemies, and he rode on rapidly.

"What has become of Elfric, my Leofric?" he said to one of his faithful train.

"I fear me he is dead: I saw him fall in the last struggle."

"Poor Elfric! poor Elfric! then his forebodings have come true; he will never see his father again."

"It is all fortune and fate, and none can resist his doom, my lord," said Leofric.

"But Elfric; yes, I loved Elfric. I would I had never left that fatal field."

"Think, my lord, of Elgiva."

"Yes, Elgiva—she is left to me; and left all is left. Ride faster, Leofric, I fancy I hear pursuers."

They had, at Cynewulf's suggestion, taken fresh horses from the reserve, and had little cause to fear pursuit; in an hour they reached the Foss-way, and rode along the route described in our former chapter, until, reaching the frontiers of the territory of the old Dobuni, they left the Foss, and rode by the Roman track-way which we have previously described, until they turned into a road which brought them deep into Oxfordshire. Here they were in a territory which had been a debateable land between Mercia and Wessex, where the sympathies of the people were not strongly enlisted on either side, and they were comparatively safe.

They passed Kirtlington; rested at Oxenford; then rode through Dorchester and Bensington to Reading, whence they struck southward for Winchester, where Edwy rested from his fatigue in the society of Elgiva.

So ended the ill-advised raid into Mercia.

CHAPTER XIX.

EARTH TO EARTH, AND DUST TO DUST.

ALTHOUGH Edwy and his little troop had been successful in
gaining the main road, and in escaping into Wessex, yet
few of his followers had been so fortunate, and his broken
forces were seeking safety and escape in all directions,
wanderers in a hostile country. A large number found a
refuge in the entrenched camp; but it was surrounded by
the foe in less than half-an-hour after the king's escape, and
all ingress or egress was thenceforth impossible.

While one large body fled eastward towards the Watling
Street, the soldiers who had accompanied the king to Æscendune naturally turned their thoughts in that direction. It
was, as they had seen, capable of a long defence—well pro-
visioned, and already partly garrisoned; nor could they doubt
the joy with which their old companions would receive them,
either to share in the defence of the post, or to accompany
them in an honourable retreat southward.

So, not only those who survived of the fifty who had
left Æscendune the previous morning, but all whom they
could persuade to join them, actuated separately by the same
considerations, made their way in small detachments through
the forest towards the hall. Redwald had thoroughly earned
the confidence of all his warriors, and they would follow him
to death or victory with equal devotion; *now*, in adversity,
they only sought to put themselves once more under the
rule of their talented and daring chieftain.

Therefore it was that while Father Cuthbert was yet
kneeling in the chapel, where the body of the departed

thane had been placed, the devotions of the good priest were disturbed by the blowing of horns and the loud shout whereby the first fugitives sought admittance into the castle.

Redwald had also been up nearly all night pacing his room, muttering incoherently to himself. Over and over again he regarded intently a locket containing a solitary tress of grey hair, and once or twice the word "Avenged!" rose to his lips.

" And they little know," said he, soliloquising, " who the avenger is, or what have been his wrongs ; little know they how the dead is represented in the halls of his sire!—blind! blind ! Whichever way the victory eventually turn, *he* is avenged."

While he thus soliloquised he was aroused by the same noise which had disturbed Father Cuthbert's devotions, and, recognising its source, betook himself to the gateway, where some of his own soldiers were on guard, who, true to discipline, awaited his permission to allow their comrades to enter : it is needless to say it was readily given.

Broken and dispirited was the little troop of ten or a dozen men, who first appeared in this manner after the fight : their garments torn and bloody, some of them wounded, they yet raised a shout of joy as they saw their trusted leader.

" Whence come ye, my comrades in arms ? " said he, " and what are your news ? you look like men who have fled from battle."

" We did not fly till all was lost."

The countenance of Redwald indicated some little emotion, though it was transient as the lightning's flash in the summer night.

" The king !—is it well with him ? "

" He has fled with a small troop to the south."

" Saw you aught of Elfric of Æscendune ? "

" He fell in the last charge of the cavalry."

" Dead ? "

" We think so."

"How is it that you have suffered yourselves to be beaten ?"

"Had you been there it might have ended differently. We became the aggressors, and attacked a superior force, while they had all the advantage of ground."

"Come in.   You must first have some food and wine ; then you shall tell me all. We may need your help here, and shall be glad of every able-bodied man."

"More are on the road."

And so it proved, for party after party continued to fall in.   The solemn quiet, which so well befitted the house of mourning, was banished by the presence of the soldiery in such large numbers, for early in the day nearly a hundred and fifty were gathered together, and accommodation threatened to fall short.

Under these circumstances the lady Edith became very anxious that either the departure of her unwelcome guests should be hastened, or that the loved remains should be removed at once to the priory church, where she could bemoan her grief in quiet solitude, and be alone with her beloved and God.   There seemed no rest or peace possible in the hall, and Redwald was apportioning all the accommodation to his followers as they came, preserving only the private apartments of the lady Edith from intrusion.

She was still expecting the arrival of Elfric, for Redwald had not communicated the news he had received, and she did not even know that King Edwy had been defeated ; so absorbed was she in her grief, that she did not note the thousand little circumstances which might have told her as much.

But before the hour of terce, Alfred came into the room where she was seated with her daughter, and she saw by his troubled countenance that he had something to communicate which pained him to tell.

"Elfric !" she said—"he is well ?"

"He has not come yet, my mother ; and I grieve to say that we were deceived yesterday—deceived about the battle."

" How so ? "

" The king was defeated ; he has fled southward, and there has been a great slaughter."

" But Elfric ? "

" No one can tell me anything about him," said Alfred, wringing his hands.   " Mother, you must leave this place."

" Leave our home—and *now ?* "

" They talk of defending it against the forces of the Etheling Edgar, who has been declared king ; and we should all be in great danger."

" But will they stay here against our will ? "

" Yes ; for they say their lives depend upon it, that the Mercians scour all the country round about, that all the roads are now occupied and guarded, so that they can only hope to defend this place until they can make terms with the King of Mercia, as they call Edgar, who is likely to be acknowledged by all north of the Thames.   The curse of the Church is, they say, upon Edwy."

" Father Cuthbert is still here, is he not ?—what does he advise ? where shall we go ? "

" He says we can have the old house in which he, and the mass-thanes* before him, lived while as yet the priory was incomplete or unbuilt.   It is very comfortable, and close to the church."

" But to take *him* so soon from his home ! "

" They will place him in God's house, before the altar ; there could not be a better place where they or we could wish his dear remains to await the last rites upon earth."

At that moment Father Cuthbert entered the room unannounced.

" Pardon me, my revered lady," he began ; " but I grieve to say that your safety demands instant action, and must excuse my intrusion ; your life and liberty are no longer safe here."

" Life and liberty ! "

" There is some foul plot to detain you all here, on pre-

* The parish priests were commonly called " Mass-Thanes."

tence your safety requires it. I have been this morning to
Redwald, and he refuses permission for any one to leave the
place, asserting that thus only can he assure your safety.
Now, it is plain that if the place comes to be besieged you
would be far safer in the priory or the old priests' house.
Our own countrymen would not injure us."

"He will not detain us by force?"

"I would not trust to that; but we must meet guile by
guile. I have pretended to be content on your behalf, and
he is just going to leave the hall, with the greater part of his
followers, to collect provisions and cattle. I have told him
that the Grange farm is well stocked; he has caught the
bait, and is going to superintend the work of spoliation in
person: far better, in the present need, that he should rob
the estate than that a hair of your head or of those of your
children should perish."

"But why do you suspect him of evil?"

"I cannot tell you now. I have overheard dark, dark
speeches. So soon as he has gone, Alfred and I must
summon all your own people who are in the hall. We
will then bring the body forth, and follow it ourselves; as
we shall outnumber those left behind I do not imagine they
will dare, in his absence, to interfere with our progress."

"I will go at once," said Alfred, "and summon the
household."

"No; you would be observed. I am older and perhaps a
little more discreet. Stay with your mother till all is ready."

Alfred reluctantly obeyed, and Father Cuthbert went
forth. So great was their anxiety that it almost banished
the power of prayer, save such mental shafts as could be sent
heavenward in each interval of thought. At last Alfred,
who was at the window, saw Redwald and his followers
—nearly a hundred in number—leave the castle and ride
across towards the forest in the direction of the farm in
question. Another moment and Father Cuthbert entered.

"Are you ready? If so, follow me."

He took them by a private passage into the chapel,

where four men already stood by the bier, ready to head the procession, and thirty or forty others were gathered in the chapel or about the door—their own vassals, good and true.   They all were armed.

Father Cuthbert ascended the wooden tower above the chapel, which served as a bell-cot.   He looked from its windows; the party of Redwald had disappeared behind the trees.

He came down and gave the signal.   The sad procession started; they descended the steps to the courtyard. Redwald had left some forty or fifty men behind—men who had grown old in arms, and who, if they had pleased, might perhaps have stopped the exit, but they were not sufficiently in the confidence of their leader to take the initiative; and the only man who was in his confidence, and whom he had charged to see that no one departed, was fortunately at that moment in another part of the building. The sentinel at the drawbridge was one of Redwald's troop. He menaced opposition, and refused to let the drawbridge be peaceably lowered.

"Art thou a Christian?" said Father Cuthbert, coming forward in his priestly attire, "and dost thou presume to interfere with a servant of the Lord and to delay a funeral?"

"I must obey my orders."

"Then I will excommunicate thee, and deliver thy soul to Satan."

And he began to utter some awful Latin imprecation, which so aroused the superstition of the sentinel that he made no further opposition, which perhaps saved his life, for the retainers of Æscendune were meditating instant violence, indignant at the delay and the outrage to their lady.

They themselves let the drawbridge down, and guarded the sad cortége over the plain.   Their numbers increased every moment, and before they reached the neighbourhood of the priory they had little cause to fear any attack, should Redwald have arrived and have been rash enough to attempt one.

The old parsonage-house, which had served for the residence of each successive parish priest, or mass-thane, was a large and commodious building, containing all such accommodation as the family absolutely required in the emergency, while furniture, provisions, and comforts of all kinds, were sent over from the priory; for the good fathers did not forget at this hour of need that they owed their own home to the liberality of Ella and his father.

So when they had deposited the loved remains before the altar of the church, and had knelt a brief season in prayer, the exiled family took possession of their temporary home. It was hard—very hard—to give up their loved dwelling at such a season of affliction, but the dread which Redwald had somehow inspired made it a great relief to be removed from his immediate presence.

Yet they could give no reason for the feeling they all shared. Father Cuthbert evidently suspected, or knew, things which he as yet concealed from them.

"Who could have slain the husband and father?" This was the unanswered question. Their suspicions could only turn to Redwald or some of his crew: no marauders were known to lurk in the forest; there was, they felt assured, not one of his own people who would not have died in his defence. Again, it was not the lust of gold which had suggested the deed, for they had found the gold chain he wore untouched. What then could have been the motive of the murderer?

Father Cuthbert had found a solution, which was based upon sad experience of the traditional feuds so frequently handed down from father to son. Still he would not suggest further cause of disquietude, and added no further words. The utter uncertainty about Elfric was another cause of uneasiness. Whether he had gone southward with the king, or had fallen on the battle-field, they knew not; or whether he had surrendered with the prisoners taken in the entrenched camp, and who had been all admitted to mercy.

In the course of the morning they saw Redwald return, laden with the spoils of the Grange farm—oxen and sheep, waggons containing corn, driven before him. What passed within on his entrance they could not tell; how narrow their escape they knew not—were not even certain it had been an escape at all.

It was now determined that the interment should take place on the morrow, and the intelligence was communicated rapidly to all the tenantry.

Hourly they expected the forces of Mercia to appear, and exact a heavy account from Redwald for his offences. He was supposed to be the instigator of the expedition which had failed so utterly; it was not likely that he would be allowed to retain Æscendune a long time. The only surprise people felt was that he should have dared to remain at the post when all hope of successful resistance had ceased. He had his own reasons, which they knew not.

Under these circumstances it seemed desirable to hurry forward the interment, lest it should be interfered with from without, in the confusion of hostile operations against the hall.

The priory church was a noble but irregular structure, of great size for those days. The cunning architect from the Continent, who had designed it, had far surpassed the builders of ordinary churches in the grandeur of his conception. The lofty roof, the long choir beyond the transept, gave the idea of magnitude most forcibly, and added dignity to the design. In the south transept was a chapel dedicated especially to S. Cuthbert, where the aged Offa reposed, and the mother of Ella. There they had removed the body to await the last solemn rites. Six large wax tapers burned around it, and watchers were there day and night—mourners who had loved him well, and felt that in him they had lost a dear friend. The wife, the son, or the daughter, were ever there, but seldom alone. For when the monks in the choir were not saying the canonical hours, or the low mass was not being said at one of the

side altars, still the voice of intercession arose, with its
burden—

> " Eternal rest give unto him, O Lord,
>   And let perpetual light shine upon him."

At length the morning came, the second only after
death. The neighbouring thanes whom the troubled times
did not detain at home, the churls of the estate, the thralls,
crowded the precincts of the minster, as the solemn bell
tolled the deep funeral knell. At length the monks poured
into the church, while the solemn " Domine refugium "
arose from their lips—the same grand words which for these
thousand years past have told of the eternity of God and
the destiny of the creature; speaking as deeply to the heart
then as in these days of civilisation.

The mourners entered, Alfred supporting his widowed
mother, who had summoned all her fortitude to render
the last sad offices to her dear lord ; her daughter, a few
distant relations — there were none nearer of kin. The
bier, with its precious burden, was placed in the centre
before the high altar. Six monks, bearing torches, knelt
around it. A pall, beautifully embroidered, covered the
coffin, a wreath of flowers surmounting a cross was placed
upon it.

The solemn requiem mass commenced, and the great
Sacrifice once offered upon Calvary was pleaded for the soul
of the deceased thane. When the last prayer had been said,
the coffin was sprinkled with hallowed water, and perfumed
with sweet incense, after which it was removed to its last
resting-place. The grave was already prepared. Again
the earthly cavern was sprinkled with the hallowed water,
emblematical of the blood of sprinkling which speaketh
better things than that of Abel, and the body—the sacred
dust for which Christ had died, in which God had dwelt
as in a temple—was lowered, to be sown in corruption, that
hereafter it might be raised in incorruption and joy unspeakable.

All crowded to take the last sad look.   Alfred felt his dear mother's arm tremble as she leant on him, yet gazed firmly into that last resting-place, while the solemn strain arose—"Ego sum resurrectio et vita.   Qui credit in Me, etiam si mortuus fuerit vivet; et omnis qui vivit, et credit in Me, non morietur in æternum."*

* "I am the resurrection and the life, saith the Lord.   He that believeth in Me, though he were dead, yet shall he live; and whosoever liveth, and believeth in Me, shall never die."

See Note P.—Anglo-Saxon Burials.

CHAPTER XX.

"AND THE DOOR WAS SHUT."

THE reader is, we trust, somewhat impatient to learn what had really been the fate of the unhappy Elfric of Æscendune—whether he had indeed been cut off with the work of repentance incomplete, or whether he yet survived to realise the calamity which had fallen upon his household.

He lived. When the blow of his adversary, as we have seen, crushed him to the earth, and he lay there with his head on the ground, prostrate, amidst kicking and plunging hoofs, and the roar and confusion of deadly strife, Providence, without which not one sparrow falleth to the ground, watched over him, and averted the iron hoofs from his forehead. Could one have concentrated his gaze upon that little spot of earth, and have seen the furious hoofs graze, without injuring, that tender forehead, could he have beheld the gallop of the retreating steeds over and around that senseless form, for it now lay senseless, he would have realised that there is *One* Whose Eye is observant of each minute detail which concerns the life of His beloved ones—nay, Who knows the movements of the tiniest insect, while His Hand directs the rolling spheres. And his care preserved Elfric for His Own wise ends, until the fight receded, leaving its traces behind it, as when the tide of ocean recedes after a storm, and the beach is strewn with wreck—bodies of men, of horses, mutilated, dismembered, dead or dying, disabled or desperately wounded.

Hours had passed, during which the sounds of the combat still maintained at the entrenched camp came freshly on the ear, and then died away, until the solemn night fell upon the scene, and the only sounds which smote the ear were faint, faint moans; cries of " Water! water! " incessantly repeated from hundreds of feeble lips.

It was then that Elfric awoke from the insensibility which had resulted from exhaustion and the stunning blow he had received in his fall. Every limb seemed in pain, for the loss of blood had not left the vital powers strength for the maintenance of the due circulation through the body, and the cold night air chilled the frame. He did not at first comprehend where he was, but as his senses returned he perceived all too well that he was left for dead.

His first impulse was to see whether he had strength to arise : he raised himself partially, first on one elbow, and then he strove to stand up, but fell back feebly and helplessly, like an infant who first essays to escape its mother's arms and to trust its feeble limbs. Then he looked around him, thus raising his head, and gazed upon the sad and shocking scene. Close by him, with the head cleft literally in two. by a battle-axe, lay a horseman, and his blood reddened all the ground around Elfric's feet, and had deeply dyed the youth's lower garments ; a horse, his own, lay dead, the jugular vein cut through, with all the surrounding muscles and sinews ; hard by, a rider had fallen with such impetus, that his helmet had fixed itself deeply in the ground, and the body seemed as if it had quivered for the moment in the air ; a dart had trans- fixed another through belt and stomach, and he lay with the weapon appearing on either side the body. Near these lay another, whose thigh had been pierced to the great artery, and who had bled to death, as the deadly paleness of the face showed ; here and there one yet lived, as faint moan and broken utterance testified ; but

Elfric could bear no more, his head sank upon the ground, and he hid his face.

It was bright starlight, and the gleam of the heavenly host seemed to mock the wounded youth as he thought of the previous night, when, sound in body, he had wandered beneath the glittering canopy of the heavens; and thus reminded, all the thoughts of that previous night came back upon him, especially the remembrance of his sin, of his desertion of his father, of his vicious life at court, of his neglect for three years and more of all the obligations of religion, and he groaned aloud in the anguish of his spirit. "Oh! spare me, my God!" he cried, "for I am not fit to die! spare me, that I may at least receive my father's forgiveness." For he felt as if he could not ask God to forgive him until he had been forgiven by his father. Little did he think, poor boy, that that father lay cold in death; that never could he hear the blessed words of forgiveness from his tongue; neither had he the consolation of knowing how completely he *had* been forgiven, and how lovingly he had been remembered in his father's last hours upon earth. "I cannot die! I cannot die!" thus he cried; and he strove again to raise himself from the ground, but in vain; strove again, as if he would have dragged his feeble body through pain and anguish all the way to Æscendune, but could not. The story of the prodigal son, often told him by Father Cuthbert, came back to him, not so much in its spiritual as in its literal aspect: he would fain arise and go to *his* father; but he could not. "O happy prodigal!" he cried; "thou couldst at least go from that far off country, and the husks which the swine did eat; but I cannot, I cannot!"

While thus grieving in bitterness of spirit, he saw a light flitting about amongst the dead bodies, and stopping every now and then; once he saw it pause, and heard a cry of expostulation, then a faint scream, and all was still; and he comprehended that this was no ministering angel, but one of those villanous beings who haunt the battle-field to prey upon the slain, and to despatch with short mercy those who offer resistance.

He lay very, very quiet, hoping that the light would not come near him, and he trembled every time it bent its course that way; but at length his fears seemed about to be realised—it drew near, and he saw the face of a hideous looking hag, dressed in coarse and vile garments, who held a bloody dagger in the right hand, and kept the left in a kind of bag, tied to her person, in which she had evidently accumulated great store. Her eyes were roaming about, until the light suddenly was reflected from the poor lad's brilliant accoutrements, and she advanced towards him.

He groaned, and sank backwards, and her hand was upon the dagger, while she cast such a look as the fabled vampire might cast upon her destined victim, loving gold much, but perhaps blood most, when all at once she turned and fled.

Elfric knew not what had saved him; when voices fell upon his ear, and the baying of a dog.

"Which way has that hag fled? pursue her, she murders the wounded."

The sound of rushing feet was heard, and Elfric felt that help was near, yet leaving him, and he cried aloud, "Help! help! for the love of God."

One delayed in his course, and came and stood over the prostrate form. It was a monk, for the boy recognised the Benedictine habit, and his heart sank within him as he remembered how pitilessly he had helped to drive that habit from Glastonbury.

"Art thou grievously wounded, my son?"

"I feel faint, even unto death, with loss of blood. Oh! remove me, and bear me home; if thou art a man of God leave me not here to perish in my sins."

The piteous appeal went to the heart of the monk, and he knelt down, and by the aid of a small lamp, examined the wounds of the sufferer.

"Thou mayst yet live, my son," he said; "tell me where is thy home; is it in Mercia?"

"It is! it is! My home is Æscendune; it is not far from here."

"Æscendune—knowest thou Father Cuthbert?"

"I do indeed; he was my tutor, once my spiritual father."

"Thy name?"

"Elfric, son of the thane Ella."

The monk started, then raised a loud cry, which speedily brought two or three men in the dress of thralls (theows) to his side.

"She will murder no more, father; the dog overtook her, and held her till we came; she was red with blood, and we knocked her down; Oswy here brained her with his club."

"It is well—she deserved her fate; but, Oswy, look at this face."

"S. Wilfred preserve us!" cried the man; "it is the young lord. He is not dying, is he? She hadn't hurt him—the she-wolf?"

"No, we were just in time, and only just in time; we must carry him home to his father."

The monk had started for the expected scene of battle, intent on doing good, with a small party of the thralls of Æscendune, just after Edwy had left the hall; consequently, he knew nothing of the death of the thane or the subsequent events. Oh, how sweetly his words fell upon Elfric's ears, "Carry him home to his father."

A litter was speedily made; one of the thralls jumped into a willow tree which overhung the stream, and cut down some of the stoutest boughs. The others wove them with withs into a kind of litter, threw their own upper garments thereon in their love, placed the poor wounded form as tenderly upon it as a mother would have done, and bore him from the field, ever and anon stopping to relieve some other poor wounded sufferer, and to comfort him with the intelligence that similar aid was at hand for all, as the various lights now appearing testified. For themselves, they felt all other obligations fade before their duty to their young lord. He was the object of their solicitude.

So they bore him easily along, until they reached a stream; there they paused and washed the heated brow, and allowed the parched lips to imbibe, but only slightly, the pure fresh beverage, sweeter far than the stimulant the good monk had poured down his throat on the field. Then they arranged his dress—bound up his wounds, for the Benedictine was an accomplished surgeon for the times; after which, having satisfied himself that his patient was able to bear the transit, he departed, with a cheerful benediction, to render the like aid to others.

So comforted was Elfric, and so relieved from pain, that he slept all through the following hours, as they bore him along through woodland paths; and he dreamt that he had met his father and was clasped lovingly in his forgiving arms.

At daybreak they were six or seven miles from the camp, and they rested, for the continued effort had wearied the bearers. They made a fire, cooked their breakfast, and tried to persuade Elfric to eat, which he did, sparingly.

Then they resumed their journey; they kept as much in the shade as possible, for it was a bright day; rested again at noon-tide, with only five or six miles before them; started when the heat was a little overpast, and just after sunset came in sight of the halls of Æscendune, from the opening in the forest whence Elfric had beheld them that night when he first brought Prince Edwy home in company with his brother Alfred.

The wounded youth raised himself up, looked with intense affection at the home of his youth, and sank back contented on his couch, thinking only of father and mother, brother and sister, and the sweet forgiveness he felt sure awaited him. Poor boy!

It was almost dark when they reached the gate of the castle, and the drawbridge was up. One of the bearers blew his horn loudly, and the summons brought the warder to the little window over the postern gate.

"Who are you, and what do you seek?" was the cry.

"We are bringing my young lord, Elfric of Æscendune, home from the battle-field wounded."

"Wait a while."

A few minutes passed; then the drawbridge was lowered, and the bearers bore their burden into the court-yard. Every moment Elfric expected to see the beloved faces bending over him; but all seemed strange, till he remembered that Redwald had remained behind at the hall; the four bearers spoke uneasily to one another, and Oswy disappeared in the dusky twilight.

At length three or four men, in the military costume so familiar to Elfric, approached the litter; and raising him, bore him into the interior of the building, up the stairs, into the gallery, which partly ran round at the height of the first floor. The door of a room was opened, a familiar room; it had been his father's bedroom, and Elfric was placed on the bed.

"Ask them to come to me," he said; "father, mother, Alfred, Edgitha!—where are they?"

But minute after minute passed by, and no one came near; there was no light in the room, and it was soon very dark. Elfric became very uncomfortable; it was not the kind of reception he had promised himself.

"Why does not my father come," he muttered impatiently, "to see his wounded boy?" and he felt at one moment his pride revive, then a sickening feeling of anxiety filled his heart.

But it was not until an hour had passed that he heard a heavy step on the stairs, and soon the door opened, and Redwald appeared.

Elfric gazed upon him with surprise; especially when

he noted the stern cold look which sat on his features.
As Redwald did not speak, Elfric took the initiative.

"Why is not my father here? I want to see him,
Redwald; do send him to me; say I must see him, I must,
—I cannot endure this longer; it is more than I can bear."

"Calm yourself and listen to me, for I have a strange
story to unfold to you."

"Not now; some other time; do send *them* to me."

"It must be heard now; and perhaps, when you have
heard it, you will comprehend why they do not come."

"But they *will* come?"

"Elfric, there was, two generations back, a man who
had two sons; he was a noble thane of high descent, his
eldest son was worthy of his father, high-souled, impetuous,
brave, fiery, and in short, all a warrior's son should be;
the younger son had the heart of a monk, and was learned
in all pious tricks; he stole the father's heart from his
elder brother."

Elfric began to listen at this point.

"At last, mis-judgment and unkindness drove the elder
brother from home, and he sought food and shelter from
men who had the souls of conquerors. With them he lived;
for his father disinherited him; he had no father, he had
no country."

Elfric began to draw his breath quickly.

"At length war arose between those who had sheltered
and protected him, and the people who should have been
his own people; say what side was the exile to be
found on?"

"He should have fought with his own people."

"His own people were those who had really adopted
him when his father and family disowned him, and with
them he fought for victory; but the fates were unpropitious,
the people with whom his father and brother fought were
successful; the son was taken prisoner, and adjudged to
die a traitor's death, his own father and brother consenting."

Elfric began to comprehend all.

" They put him on board an open boat, and sent him out to sea, at the mercy of winds and waves; but not alone; he had married amongst the people who had adopted him, and his boy would not forsake his sire, for he had *one* boy—the mother was dead. This boy besought the hard-hearted executioners of a tyrant's will to let him share the fate of his sire, so earnestly, that at last they consented."

"The boat, as it pleased fate, was driven by wind and tide on the shore of Denmark, and there the unhappy exile landed; but he had been wounded in the battle, and his subsequent exposure caused his early death; before he died he bequeathed one legacy, and only one, to his son—*" vengeance."*

Elfric was pale as death, and trembled visibly.

" Then you are "——

"Elfric, I am your cousin, and the deadly foe of you and yours!"

" Then my poor father; but if you must find a victim, seek it in me; spare him! oh, spare him!"

Redwald smiled; but such a smile.

"At least let me see him now, and obtain his forgiveness. Redwald, he is my father; you were faithful to your father; let me atone for my unfaithfulness to mine."

" You believe there is another world, perhaps?"

Elfric only answered by a look of piteous alarm.

"Because, in that case, you must seek your father there; although I fear Dunstan would say there is likely to be a gulf between you."

Elfric comprehended him, and with a cry which might have melted a heart of stone, fell back upon the bed. For a moment he lay like one stunned, then began to utter incoherent ravings, and gazed vacantly around, as one who is delirious.

Redwald seemed for one moment like a man contending with himself; like one who felt pity struggling with sterner emotions; yet the contest was very short.

"It is of no use—he must die; if hearts break, I hope his will break, and save me the task of shedding his blood, or causing it to be shed; there must be no weakness now; he has been sadly wounded; if he is left alone, he will die; better so—I would spare him if I were not bound by an oath so dread that I shudder to think of it. The others have escaped: he must die."

Still he walked to and fro, as if pity yet contended with the thirst for vengeance in his hardened breast: perhaps it was his day of grace, and the Spirit of Him, Who has said "Vengeance is Mine, I will repay," pleaded hard with the sinner. Yet the gentle Voice pleaded in vain; still he walked to and fro, until his resolution seemed firmly made; and he left the chamber, fastening it on the outside.

CHAPTER XXI.

"UNDER WHICH KING?"

IT will be remembered that one of the theows who had borne Elfric home from the field of battle had become alarmed by the suspicious aspect of things at the hall, and had escaped, by prompt evasion, the confinement which awaited his companions. Oswy, for it was he, thus showed his natural astuteness, while he also conferred the greatest possible obligation upon Elfric, since he bore the news of his ill-timed arrival at once to the priory.

Here his worst suspicions were confirmed; and the faithful thrall heard for the first time of the death of his late lord, and that he had given his young master into the hands of his bitter foes. Alfred was at once summoned; and a conference was held, in which Father Cuthbert, his brethren, and the chamberlain and steward of the hall, took part.

"It is now generally believed," said Father Cuthbert, "that Redwald is the bitter enemy, for some reason, of the house of Æscendune. Has any one here suspected that reason?"

No one could give any reply.

"I fear what I am about to say," he continued, "will startle you all. Redwald is a member of the family himself."

"A member of the family!"

"Yes. Is there any one present who remembers the unhappy brother of our late lamented lord—Oswald, the son of Offa?"

"Yes," said the old chamberlain, "I remember him well; and I see now what you mean."

"Is not the expression of the face identical? Are they not the same features, as one might say?"

"Yet Redwald is much darker."

"Because his mother was Danish, and he has inherited some of her peculiarities, that is all."

"Still," said the steward, "every one supposed that the unhappy Oswald perished at sea with his son. Never shall I forget the grief of the old thane Offa, when, inquiring for the son, he learned that he had gone with the father to his death. He would have adopted him."

"And do we not," added a Benedictine, "say a mass daily at S. Wilfred's altar for the souls of Oswald and his son Ragnar?"

"Oswald may be dead; Ragnar yet lives in Redwald. The name alone is changed."

"But where are the proofs? We cannot wholly trust an imaginary resemblance."

"It is not imaginary; and these are the proofs in question. The night after the murder (all looked at each other as if a sudden inspiration struck them), as I was going to the chapel from the lady Edith's apartments, I passed through a passage little used, but leading past the chamber allotted to Redwald, and only separated by a thin wainscoting. I was startled as I passed it by the sound of a pacing to and fro; an incessant pacing; and I heard the inmate of the room soliloquising with himself, as in a state of frenzied feeling. I caught only broken words, but again and again I heard 'Avenged;' and once 'Father, you are avenged;' and once 'Little do they know who is their guest;' once 'It is a good beginning,' and such like ejaculations. I remained a long time, because, as you will all see, the murderer stood revealed."

"Then why did you not tell us before?" exclaimed all, almost in a breath.

"Because it would have been of no avail. Had there

been the least chance of calling him to account, I should,
you may be sure, have proclaimed his guilt. But early in
the morning fresh forces began to arrive to his aid. My
only endeavour was to get the lady Edith and her remaining children safe from the castle; and it was only by dis-
sembling my feelings, by talking face to face with the man
of blood, by pretending to trust him, that I could succeed.
Had he not thought us all perfectly satisfied, he would never
have left the hall to go foraging in person; and now all
would be well, but for this sad, sad chance, which has placed
the poor lad Elfric in his power."

"But," said Alfred, "this makes the case worse than
ever. Poor Elfric! they will kill him. Oh, can this be
Ragnar?"

The Benedictines expressed themselves convinced, because the supposition explained the present circumstances
so clearly, and accounted for that hitherto unaccountable
circumstance—the murder. The steward and chamberlain
both fancied they recognised the family likeness; and so the
solution at which Father Cuthbert had arrived was accepted
by all.

The question was now what course to adopt, for the
night was fast wearing away.

"Two things are to be done," said Father Cuthbert.
"The first is to secure the safety of the lady Edith and her
children from any sudden attack from the castle, to which
effect I propose holding all the vassals in arms; and, in
case of any force leaving the hall, I purpose giving the lady
Edith and her daughter instant sanctuary in the priory,
while the vassals gather round its precincts; for, I fear me,
this Ragnar is a heathen, and would but little respect the
house of God."

"Could we not attack the hall and release Elfric?
Think of Elfric," said Alfred.

"It would be madness; Redwald has more than a
hundred and fifty men of war within it. The place is full;
we could not attack with the least chance of success. No; the

second thing I meant to propose was this, that we should send an instant message to King Edgar, who is near at hand, and explain the whole circumstances to him.   He has many causes of enmity against Redwald, and would probably come to our aid at once, as the safety of his realm would require him to do eventually."

"Let me be the messenger; he will surely listen to the pleadings of a brother for a brother."

"I had so designed," said Father Cuthbert; "and in order that no chance may be thrown away, I will adventure myself in the lion's den, and threaten with the penalties of excommunication this vindictive Redwald or Ragnar."

"No, father; you will never come out alive.   No, no," said they all.

The last proposal was universally discouraged.   Redwald had already special cause of enmity against Father Cuthbert, who had robbed him of part of his destined prey; and it was ultimately settled that Father Swithin, another of the order, should be charged with the mission, with the power to make conciliatory offers, or to act on the other course as he should see fit; in short, to use all his wit for Elfric.

Alfred did not delay a moment unnecessarily, but in the dawning light set forward to seek Edgar, of whom he had no definite information, but who was believed to linger in the neighbourhood of the battle-field, holding council with earls and thanes as to the further steps to be taken, and receiving the submission of the whole Mercian, East Anglian, and Northumbrian nobility.

Therefore, mounted upon a good steed, and accompanied by Oswy, he rapidly traversed the country over which his brother had been so painfully borne; slowly, however, in places, for here and there large tracts of swamp obstructed the way, and in other places the thickets were dense and impervious; even where the country was cultivated the unpaved roads were rough and hazardous for riders.

It was past the hour of nones, the ninth hour of the

day, when the riders reached the battle-field, which still bore
frightful traces of the recent combat; reddened with blood,
which had left its dark traces on large patches of the
ground, and encumbered with the bodies of horses and
men which had not yet found sepulture, although bands of
theows from the neighbouring estates were busily engaged
in the necessary toil, excavating huge pits, and placing the
dead—no longer rivals—reverently and decently in their
last long home.   Several wolves could be discerned, hanging
about under the skirts of the forest, but not daring to come
out into the plain while the day lasted and the men were
about; whole flocks of ravenous birds flew about the scene,
now settling down on the spots where the strife had been
hottest, now soaring away when disturbed in their sickening feast.

It was the first time Alfred had ever gazed upon a
battle-field ; and now he saw it stripped of all the romance
and glamour which bards had thrown over it, and the sight
appalled him.

He drew near a large pit into which the thralls were
casting the dead.   Many of the bodies presented, as we
have already seen, a most ghastly spectacle; and nearly all
had begun to decompose.   Mentally he thanked God that
Elfric, at least, was not there; and he turned aside his head
in horror at the sight.   He now inquired of the foreman of
the labourers whether he knew where the Etheling Edgar
would be.

" You mean King Edgar, for the Mercians will acknowledge no other king.   The people of Wessex may keep the
enemy of the saints, if they like."

"King Edgar, I mean.   Where is he now ? "

" He has been holding a council at Tamworth town, in
the old palace of King Offa ; and they say all the tributary
kings have come there to be his men, and all the great
earls."

" Can you tell me the nearest road to Tamworth ? "

" Why, it lies through the forest there, where you see

those wolves lurking about. They will begin to be dangerous when the sun goes down, and perhaps some of them would not mind a snap at a horse or even a man, now.

"We must take our chance;" said Alfred; "life and death hang on our speed," and he and Oswy rode on.

The wolves were no longer seen. In the summer they generally avoided men, at least during the day, and they were gradually becoming more uncommon at that date. Alfred entertained little fear as he proceeded, until the darkening shadows showed that night was near, and they were still in the heart of the forest, when he began to feel alarmed. The road before them was a good wide woodland path, and easy to follow even in the gathering darkness. Suddenly their horses started violently, as a loud howl was heard behind, and repeated immediately from different quarters of the forest.

Alfred felt that it was the gathering of the ferocious beasts, which had been attracted from distant forests by the scent of the battle-field, and had thus happened to lie in increased numbers around their path. The howling continued to increase, and their horses sped onward as if mad with fear—it was all they could do to guide them safely.

Nearer and nearer drew the fearful sound ; and looking back they beheld the fiery eyes swarming along the road after them. They had begun to abandon hope, when all at once they heard the sound of advancing horsemen in front of them, accompanied by the clank of arms. The wolves heard it too, and with all the cunning cowardice of their race scampered away from their intended prey, just as Alfred and Oswy avoided impaling themselves upon the lances of the coming deliverers.

"Whom have we here, riding at this pace through the woods ?" cried out a rough, manly voice.

"The wolves were after the poor fellows," said another.

"They may speak for themselves," said the leader, confronting Alfred. "Art thou a Mercian and a friend of King Edgar ? Under which king ? Speak, or die !"

"I seek King Edgar. My name is Alfred, son of Ella of Æscendune."

"Who sheltered the men of Wessex, and entertained the impious Edwy in his castle."

"We had no power to resist had we wished to do so."

"Which you evidently did not. May a plain soldier ask you now why you seek King Edgar?"

"Because," said Alfred, "my father has been murdered, and my brother made a prisoner by Redwald, the captain of King Edwy's hus-carles, who holds our house, and has driven us all out."

"Your father murdered! Your family expelled! Your brother a prisoner! These are strange news."

"Why this delay?" cried another speaker, riding up from behind. "The king is impatient to get on. Ride faster."

"The king!" cried Alfred. "Oh, lead me to him."

"Who is this," demanded the second officer, "who demands speech of the royal Edgar?"

"Alfred of Æscendune. He tells us that the infamous Redwald holds the fortified house there, has murdered the thane Ella, and expelled the family, save the brother, whom he holds to ransom."

"No, not to ransom," cried Alfred. "It is his life that is threatened. Oh, take me to Edgar!"

"He is close behind, in company with the Ealdorman of Mercia and Siward of Northumbria."

"Stay behind with him, Biorn, and let us continue our route. You may introduce him to the king, if he will see him."

The first party—the advance guard—now passed on, and was succeeded almost immediately by the main body, foremost amongst whom rode Prince or rather King Edgar, then only a youth of fifteen years of age. We last beheld him a boy of twelve, at the date of Elfric's arrival at the court of Edred. By his side rode Siward, Ealdorman of Northumbria.

" Who is this ? " cried the latter, as he saw Alfred and his attendant waiting to receive him.

" Alfred of Æscendune, with a petition for aid against Redwald, who has seized his father's castle."

" Alfred of Æscendune!" cried Edgar. " Halt, my friends, one moment. Alfred of Æscendune, tell me your story ; to me, Edgar, your king."

Alfred hastened to pour his tale of sorrows into an ear evidently not unsympathising, and when he had concluded Edgar asked—

" And tell me what is your request ? It shall be granted even to the uttermost."

" Only that you, my lord, would hasten to our aid, and deliver my brother for his poor widowed mother's sake."

" We should send a troop against Redwald in any case; but even had our plans been otherwise, know this, Alfred of Æscendune, that he who by his devoted service saved the life, or at least the liberty, of Dunstan, the light of our realm of England, and the favourite of heaven, has a claim to ask any favour Edgar can grant. Siward, my father, bid the advanced guard bend its course towards Æscendune at once."

" My lord, the men are too weary to travel all night. We had purposed halting when we reached the battle-field on our march southward. There is a cross-country road thence to Æscendune, almost impassable in the night."

" Then we will travel early in the morning; and doubt not, Alfred, we shall arrive in time to chastise this insolent aggressor. Redwald has been my poor brother's evil spirit in all things ; he shall die, I swear it," said the precocious Edgar, a man before his time.

" But, my lord," said Alfred, " may I ask but one favour, that you will permit *me* to proceed and relieve the anxiety of my people with the tidings of your approach ?"

" If you *must* leave our side, such an errand would seem to justify you. Poor Elfric! I remember him well. I should not have thought him in any danger from Redwald."

" Redwald is his, is *our* bitterest foe."

" Indeed," said Edgar, and proceeded to elicit the whole history of the case from Alfred. The sad tale was not complete till they reached the battle-field, and encamped in the entrenchments the young prince had occupied the night before the combat.

" We had intended," said Edgar, " to march at once for London, owing to news we have received from the south, but we will tarry at Æscendune until the work is completed there, even if it cost us our crown. Nay, Siward, I may have my way this once. I am soldier enough to know I may not leave an enemy behind me on my march."

" But a small detachment might accomplish the work."

" Then I will go with it myself; my heart is in it. But, Alfred, you look very ill; you cannot proceed to-night. When did you sleep last ?"

" Three nights ago."

" Then it would be madness to proceed; you must sleep, and at early dawn you shall precede us on my own charger —which has been led all the way—if your own is too wearied, and with an attendant or two in case of danger from man or beast. Nay, it must be so."

Alfred, who could scarcely stand for very fatigue, was forced to yield, and that night he slept soundly in the camp of Edgar. At the first dawn they aroused him from sleep, and he found a splendid war-horse awaiting him—a gift, they told him, from Edgar. Two attendants, well mounted, awaited him in company with Oswy. He would willingly have dispensed with their company; but he was told that the king, anxious for his safety, had insisted upon their attending him, and that they were answerable for his safe return to Æscendune, the country being considered dangerous for travellers in its present disturbed state. So he yielded; and before the king had arisen he left the camp, after a hasty meal, and rode as rapidly as the roads would permit towards his desolated home.

CHAPTER XXII.

LOVE STRONG AS DEATH.

MEANWHILE Father Swithin had gone alone and unprotected, save by his sacred character, into the very jaws of the lion; or rather, would have gone, had he been suffered to do so; for when he approached the hall he found the drawbridge up, and the whole place guarded as in a state of siege.

He advanced, nothing daunted, in front of the yawning gap where the bridge should have been, and cried aloud—

"What ho! porter; I demand speech of my lord Redwald."

"You may demand speech—swine may demand pearls—but I don't think you will get it. Deliver me your message."

"Tell your lord, rude churl, that I, Father Swithin, of the holy Order of S. Benedict, have come, in the name of the rightful owners of this house, and in the power of the Church, to demand that he deliver up Elfric of Æscendune to the safe keeping of his friends."

"I will send your message; but keep a civil tongue in your mouth, Sir Monk, and don't begin muttering any of your accursed Latin, or I will see whether the Benedictine frock is proof against an arrow."

In a short time Redwald appeared on the roof, above the gateway.

"What dost thou require, Sir Monk?" said he; "thy words sound strange in my ears."

"I am come, false traitor," said Father Swithin, waxing wroth, "to demand the person of Elfric of Æscendune, whom thou detainest contrary to God's law and the king's."

" Elfric of Æscendune ! right glad am I to hear that he is alive ; my followers have brought me word that they saw him fall in battle."

" Nay, spare thy deceit, thou son of perdition, for well do we know that he was brought home wounded last night. One of his bearers escaped thy toils, even as a bird the snare of the fowler, and is now with us."

" Assuredly the loon has lied unto you. Rejoiced should I be to see the unhappy youth, and to know that he yet lived. I but hold this place, faithful to his lord and mine, Edwy, King of all England."

" Then why hast thou expelled the rightful dwellers therein from their house and home ? We know Elfric is with thee, and that thou art a traitor, wherefore, deliver him up, or we will even excommunicate thee."

" Thou hadst better not begin in the hearing of the men who sit upon the wall ; for myself, excommunication cannot hurt a man who never goes to church, and does not company over much with those who do."

" Infidel! heretic! pagan! misbeliever! accursed *Ragnar!*" began the irate monk, when an arrow, perhaps only meant to frighten him (for they could hardly have missed so fair a mark), glanced by him. He retreated, but still continued his maledictions. " Excommunicabo te, et omnes tibi adhærentes ; thou art an accursed parricide, who hast raised thine hand against thy father's house. Vade retro, Sathanas, I will shake off the dust of my feet against thee,"—another arrow stuck in his frock—"thou shalt share the fate of Sodom, yea of Gomorrha ; in manus inimici trado te ;" by this time his words were inaudible ; and he departed, not having accomplished much good, but having nevertheless informed Redwald of two great facts—the first, that Elfric's return was blazed abroad ; the second, that his own identity was more than suspected.

" Ragnar ! " said he, " what fiend has told them *that?* how came they to suspect ? Confusion ! it will foil all my plans, and my vengeance will be incomplete ; at least this one victim must not escape, and yet I had sooner he should escape than any other member of the house. Poor boy ! the sins of the fathers are heavy upon the children, as these Christians have it ; but my oath, my oath, taken before a dying father ! no ; he *must* die !"

So spake the avenger of blood, a man whose heart was evidently not all of iron ; yet from childhood had he striven to restrain every tender impulse, and had bound himself to vengeance.   Long years of peace in England had come between him and the execution of his projects, and he had prepared himself for the task he never lost sight of, by acquiring all the accomplishments of a knight and warrior, and even of a man of letters, at that court of Rouen, now rapidly becoming the focus of European chivalry, where the fierce barbarian Northmen were becoming the refined but ruthless Normans.   Then, in England, he had wormed himself into the confidence of the future king with singular astuteness, and at length had found the occasion he had long sought, in a manner the most unforeseen save as a possible contingency.

And now he turned from the battlements to his own chamber, but on the way he paused, for he passed the door of the late thane's room, where poor Elfric lay.   He passed the sentinel and entered.   The unhappy boy was extended on the bed, in a raging fever ; ever and anon he called piteously upon his father, then he cried out that Dunstan was pursuing him, driving him into the pit ; then he cried— " Father, I did not murder thee ; not I, thy son ! nay, I always loved thee in my heart.   Who is laughing ? it is not Dunstan ; break his chamber open, slay him : is a monk's blood redder than a peasant's ?   O Elgiva ! hast thou slain my father ? see, I am all on fire ; it is thy doing.   Edwy, my king, Dunstan is burning me : save me !"

Then there was a long pause, and Redwald, or Ragnar as we may now call him, stood over his unhappy cousin. The fair head lay back on the pillow, with its profusion of golden locks ; the face was red and fiery, the eyes weak and bloodshot. "Water! water! I burn!" he said. There was no cooling medicine to alleviate the burning throat, no gentle hand to smooth the pillow, no mother to render the sweet offices of maternal love, no father to whisper forgiveness to the dying boy.

"Better he should die thus," said Ragnar, "since I cannot spare him without breaking my oath to the dead."

Then he left the room hastily, as if he feared his own resolution. The sentinel looked imploringly at him, as the cries of the revellers came from below. "Go!" said Ragnar, "join thy companions; no sentinel is required here. Go and feast; I will come and join you."

So he tried to drown his new-born pity in wine.

At a late hour of the day, Alfred and his attendants arrived, bringing news of the coming succour to Father Cuthbert and the other friends who awaited him with much anxiety. They had contrived to account for his absence to the lady Edith, from whom they thought it necessary to hide the true state of affairs.

But everything tended to increase Alfred's feverish anxiety about his brother. The relieving force could not arrive for hours; meanwhile he knew not what to do. No tidings were heard: Father Swithin had failed; and Elfric might perhaps even now be dead.

So Alfred, taking counsel only of his own brave, loving heart, left the priory in the dusk, attended by the faithful Oswy, and walked towards his former home. The night was dark and cloudy, the moon had not yet arisen, and they were close upon the hall ere they saw its form looming through the darkness. Neither spoke, but they paused before the drawbridge and listened.

Sounds of uproarious mirth arose from within; Danish war-songs, shouting and cheering; the whole body of the invaders were evidently feasting and revelling with that excess, of which in their leisure moments they were so capable.

"It is well!" said Alfred; and they walked round the

exterior of the moat, marking the brightly lighted.hall and the unguarded look of the place; yet not wholly unguarded, for they saw the figure of a man outlined against a bright patch of sky, pacing the leaded roof, evidently on guard.

And now they had reached that portion of their circuit which led them opposite the chamber window of the lamented Ella, and Alfred gazed sadly upon it, when both he and Oswy started as they heard cries and moans, and sometimes articulate words, proceeding therefrom. They listened eagerly, and caught the name "Dunstan," as if uttered in vehement fear, then the cry, "Water! I burn!" and cry after cry, as if from one in delirium.

"It is Elfric! it is Elfric!" said Alfred.

"It is my young lord's voice," said the thrall; "he is in a fever from his wound."

"What *can* we do?" and Alfred walked impatiently to and fro; at last he stopped.

"Oswy! if it costs me my life I will enter the castle!"

"It shall cost my life too then. I will live and die with my lord!"

"Come here, Oswy; they do not know the little postern door hidden behind those bushes; the passage leads up to the chapel, and to the gallery leading to my father's chamber, where Elfric lies dying. I remember that that door was left unlocked, and perhaps I can save him. They are all feasting like hogs; they will not know, and if Ragnar meet me, why, he or I must die;" and he put his hand convulsively upon the sword which was dependent from his girdle.

"Lead on, my lord; you will find your thrall ready to live or die with you!" said Oswy.

At the extreme angle of the building there was a large quantity of holly bushes which grew out of the soil between the moat and the wall, which itself was clothed with the thickest ivy; the roof above was slanting—an ordinary timber roof covering the chapel—so that no sentinel could be overhead.

Standing on the further side of the moat, all this and no more could be observed.

The first difficulty was how to cross the moat in the absence of either bridge or boat. It was true they might swim over; but in the event of their succeeding in the rescue of Elfric, how were they to bear him back? The difficulty had to be overcome, and they reflected a moment.

"There is a small boat down at the ferry," whispered Oswy.

It was all Alfred needed, and he and Oswy at once started for the river. They returned in a few minutes, bearing a light boat, almost like a British coracle, on which they instantly embarked, and a push or two with the pole sent them noiselessly across the moat.

They landed, made fast the boat, and searched in the darkness for the door; it was an old portal, almost disused, for it was only built that there might be a retreat in any such pressing emergency as might easily arise in those unsettled times; the holly bushes in front, and the thick branches of dependent ivy, concealed its existence from any person beyond the moat, and it had not even been seen by the watchful eye of Ragnar.

Alfred, however, had but recently made use of the door, when seeking bunches of holly wherewith to deck the board on the occasion of the feast given to King Edwy, and he had omitted to relock it on his return, an omission which now seemed to him of providential arrangement. He had, therefore, only to turn the rusty latch as noiselessly as might be, and the door slowly opened. The key was in the lock, on the inside.

Entering cautiously, taking off their heavy shoes and leaving them in the doorway, they ascended a flight of steps which terminated in front of a door which entered the chapel underneath the bell-cot, while another flight led upwards to the gallery, from which all the principal chambers on the first floor opened.

Arriving at this upper floor, Alfred listened intently for

one moment, and hearing only the sounds of revelry from beneath, he opened the door gently, and saw the passage lie vacant before him.

He passed along it until he came to the door of his father's chamber, feeling the whole time that his life hung on a mere thread, upon the chance that Ragnar and his warriors might remain out of the way, and that no one might be near to raise the alarm. With nearly two hundred inmates this was but a poor chance, but Alfred could dare all for his brother. He committed himself, therefore, to God's protection, and went firmly on till he reached the door.

He opened it with trembling eagerness, and the whole scene as we have already described it was before him. Elfric sat up in the bed, uttering the cries which had pierced the outer air. When Alfred entered he did not seem to know him, but saluted him as "Dunstan." His cries had become too familiar to the present inmates of the hall for this to attract attention. Alfred closed the door.

"It is I, Elfric !—I, your brother Alfred !"

Elfric stared vacantly, then fell back on the pillow: a moment only passed, and then it was evident that an interval of silence had begun, during which the patient only moaned. The noise from those who were feasting in the hall beneath, which communicated with the gallery by a large staircase, was loud and boisterous as ever.

A step was heard approaching.

Alfred took Oswy by the arm, and they both retired behind the tapestry, which concealed a small recess, where garments were usually suspended.

The heavy step entered the room, and its owner was evidently standing beside the bed gazing upon the couch. There he remained stationary for some minutes, and again left the room. It was not till the last sound had died away that Alfred and Oswy ventured to leave their concealment.

The silence still continued, save that it was sometimes broken by the patient's moans.

"Take and wrap these clothes round him; we must preserve him from the night air:" and they wrapped the blankets around him; then Oswy, who was very strongly built, took the light frame of Elfric in his arms, and they left the room.

One moment of dread suspense—the passage was clear—a minute more would have placed them in safety, when the paroxysm returned upon the unfortunate Elfric.

"Help, Edwy! Redwald, help! Dunstan has seized me, and is bearing me to the fire! I burn! help, I burn!"

Alfred groaned in his agony; the shrieking voice had been uttered just as they passed the staircase leading down to the hall. Up rushed Ragnar, followed by several of his men, and started back in amazement as he beheld Alfred and Oswy with their burden. Alfred drew his sword to dispute the passage, but was overpowered in a moment; Ragnar himself attacked Oswy, who was forced to relinquish his burden. All was lost.

Another moment and Ragnar confronted his prisoners. Elfric had been carried back to his bed. Alfred and Oswy stood before him, their arms bound behind them, in the great hall, while the soldiers retired at a signal a short distance from them.

"What has brought you here?"

"To deliver my brother."

"To share his fate, you mean. Know you into whose hands you have fallen?"

"Yes; into those of my cousin Ragnar."

"Then you know what mercy to expect."

"I came prepared to share my brother's fate."

"And you shall share it. It must be the hand of fate which has placed you both in my power, in *mine*, the representative of the rightful lord of Æscendune, dispossessed by your father, and being myself the legitimate heir."

"We do not dispute your title; give my brother his life and liberty, and take all; we have never injured you."

"All would be *nothing* without vengeance; you appeal

in vain to me.   Did I *wish* to spare you I could not ; an oath, a fearful oath, binds me, taken to one from whom I derived life, one whose death was far more agonising and lingering than yours shall be."

"Let us at least die together."

"Do you scorn the company of your thrall in death ?"

"God forbid !   Oswy, you have given your life for us ; we die in company.   God protect my poor mother, my poor childless mother !   She will be alone ! "

"You shall die together as you desire."   He addressed a few words in an unknown tongue to his men ; his face was now pale as death, his lips compressed as of one who has taken a desperate resolution.

"Retire to your brother's chamber again.   You will not compel me to use force ?"

They retired up the stairs ; Ragnar followed, two or three of his men at a respectful distance from him.

They re-entered the chamber ; Ragnar followed and stood before them.

"I will grant you all that is in my power ; you shall all die together, and you may tend your brother to the last."

"What shall be the manner of our death ?" asked Alfred, who was very calm, fearfully calm.

"You will soon discover ; my hand shall not be upon you, or red with your blood.   Believe me, I am, like you, the victim of stern necessity, although I am the avenger, you the victims."

"You cannot thus deceive yourself, or shake off the guilt of murder ; our father's blood is upon you.   You will answer for this, for him and for us, at the judgment-seat."

"I am willing to do so, if there be a judgment-seat whereat to answer.   I had a father too, who was condemned to a lingering death, by thirst, hunger, and madness ; I witnessed his agonies ; I swore to avenge them : you appeal to the memory of your father, who has perished a victim to avenging justice ; I appeal to that of mine.   If there be a

God, let Him deliver you, and perhaps I will believe in Him. Farewell for ever!"

He closed the door, and, with the aid of his men, securely fastened it on the outside, so that no strength from within could open it; he descended to the hall.

"Warriors," he said, "the moment I predicted has come; I have received a warning that the usurper Edgar already marches against us; to-morrow, at the latest, he will be here; before he arrives we shall be half-way to Wessex. Let every one secure his baggage and his plunder, and let the horses be all got ready for a forced march. We have eaten the last feast that shall ever be eaten in these halls."

A few moments of bustle and confusion followed, and before half-an-hour had expired all was ready, and the men-at-arms from without announced that every horse— their own and those of the thane, to carry their booty, the plunder of the castle—awaited them without.

"Then," said he, "listen, my men, to the final orders. *Fire the castle, every portion of it; fire the stables, the barns, the outbuildings.* We will leave a pile of blackened embers for Edgar when he comes; the halls where the princely Edwy has feasted shall never be his, or entertain him as a guest."

A loud shout signified the alacrity with which his followers bent themselves to the task; torches flashed in all directions, and in a few moments the flames began to do their destroying work. An officer addressed Ragnar—

"There are three thralls locked up in an outbuilding, shall we leave them to burn?"

"Nay; why should we grudge them their miserable lives; they have done us no harm."

At that moment a loud cry of dire alarm was heard, the trampling of an immense body of horse followed,—a rush into the hall already filled with smoke,—loud outcries and shrieks from without.

"What is the matter?" cried Ragnar.

"The Mercians are upon us! the Mercians are upon us!"

Ragnar rushed to the gateway, and a sight met his startled eyes he was little prepared to behold.

The clouds had been driven away by a fierce wind, the moon was shining brightly, and revealed a mighty host surrounding the hall on every side. Every horse before the gateway was driven away or seized, every man who had not saved himself by instant retreat had been slain by the advancing host ; without orders the majority of his men had repassed the moat, and had already raised the drawbridge against the foe, not without the greatest difficulty.

"Extinguish the fires which you have raised ; let each man fight fire—then we will fight the Mercians."

It was high time to fight fire, rather it was too late.

CHAPTER XXIII.

"VENGEANCE IS MINE, I WILL REPAY."

WHEN the door was finally closed upon the brothers and
their faithful thrall, Alfred did not give way to despair.
The words of Ragnar, "If there be a God, let Him
deliver you," had sunk deeply into his heart, and had produced precisely the opposite effect to that which his cousin
had intended; it seemed as if his cause were thus committed to the great Being in Whose Hand was the disposal
of all things; as if *His* Honour were at stake, Whom the
murderer had so impiously defied.

"'If there be a God, let Him deliver you,'" repeated
Alfred, and it seemed to him as if a Voice replied, "Is My
Arm shortened, that It cannot save?"

But how salvation was to come, and even in what
mode danger was to be expected, was unknown to them;
nay, was even unguessed. They heard the bustle below,
which followed Ragnar's announcement of his intended
departure from Æscendune. They heard the mustering of
the horses,—and at last the conviction forced itself upon
them that the foe were about to evacuate the hall. But
in that case, *how* would he inflict his sentence upon his
victims?

The dread truth, the suspicion of his real intention,
crept upon the minds of both Alfred and Oswy. Elfric
yet lay insensible, or seemingly so, upon the bed, lost to
all perception of his danger. Alfred sat at the head of
the bed, looking with brotherly love at the prostrate form

of him for whom he was giving his life; but feeling secretly grateful that there was no painful struggle imminent in his case; that death itself would come unperceived, without torturing forebodings.

It was at this moment that Oswy, who stood by the window, which was strongly barred, but which he had opened, for the night was oppressively warm, caught the faint and distant sound of a mighty host advancing through the forest; at first it was very faint, and he only heard it through the pauses in the storm of sound which attended Ragnar's preparations for departure, but it soon became more distinct, and he turned to Alfred.

"Listen, my lord, they come to our aid; listen, I hear the army of Edgar."

Alfred rushed to the window, the hope of life strong within him; at first he could hear nothing for the noise below, but at length there was a lull in the confusion, and then he heard distinctly the sound of the coming deliverers. Another minute, and he saw the dark lines leaving the shadow of the forest, and descending the hill in serried array, then deploying, as if to surround a foe in stealthy silence; he looked around for the object, and beheld Ragnar's forces all unconscious of their danger, not having heard the approach in their own hasty preparations for departure. Another moment of dread suspense, like that with which the gazer watches the dark thunder-cloud before the lightning's flash. A moment of dread silence— during which some orders, given loudly below, forced themselves upon him—

"*Fire the castle, every portion of it; fire the stables, the barns, the outbuildings;* we will leave a pile of blackened ruins for Edgar when he comes; the halls where the princely Edwy has feasted shall never be his, or entertain *him* as guest."

Meanwhile, the dark forces, unseen by the destroyers, were still surrounding the castle, deploying on all sides to surround it as in a net; for they saw the intention of their victims, and meant to cut off all chance of escape.

But the position of the brothers seemed as perilous as ever — for how could Edgar's troops rescue them if the place were once on fire? Alfred gazed with pallid face upon Oswy, but met only a resigned helpless glance in return. Yet, even at this moment of awful suspense, a voice seemed to whisper in his ear, " Stand still, and see the salvation of God."

"Oswy," he exclaimed, "we shall not die; I feel sure that God will save us."

"It must be *soon* then," replied Oswy; "*soon*, my lord, for they have already set the place on fire, just beneath us; can you not smell the smoke?"

Just at that moment came the war-cry of the Mercians, and the charge we have already described.

It was during the following few minutes, while Ragnar and all his men were vainly striving to extinguish the conflagration they had raised—for the dry timber of which the hall was chiefly built had taken fire like match-wood— it was while the friends without were preparing to attack, that a sudden change came over the patient.

" Alfred, my brother ! "

Alfred looked round in surprise; consciousness had returned, and the face was calm and possessed as his own.

" Elfric, my dear Elfric ! "——

"What does all this mean? how came I here? what makes this smoke?"

"We are in danger, great danger; prisoners in our own house, which they have set on fire."

" I remember now—is not this our dear father's room?"

" Yes; we are prisoners in it, they have barred the door upon us."

"But they cannot bar us in: there is another door, Alfred; one my father once pointed out to me, but told me to keep its existence a secret, as it always had been kept. Who are without?"

"The Mercians, Edgar's army, come to deliver us; if we can reach them, we are safe."

"I thought *they* were our foes, but all seems strange now. Alfred, lift up the tapestry which conceals the recess where dear father's armour hung."

Alfred complied.

"Now, just where the breastplate hung you will find a round knob of wood like a peg."

"Yes, it is here."

"Push it hard—*no*, harder."

Alfred did so, and a concealed door flew open; he stepped through it with a cry of joy, and found himself on the staircase leading up from the postern gate by which he had entered, just below the closed door which led into the gallery above.

"God be thanked! we are saved—saved, Elfric; Oswy, take him in your arms, quick! quick! I lead the way, and will get the boat ready—door open and boat ready."

It was all the work of a moment; they were on the private staircase, carrying Elfric, carefully wrapt up. The smoke had entered even here; the next moment they were at the entrance. Happily the whole attention of Ragnar was concentrated on self-preservation.

One more minute, and Elfric was placed in the coracle. The Mercians on the further bank now observed them, and at first, not knowing them, seemed disposed to treat them as foes; when Oswy cried aloud, "Spare your arrows; it is Elfric of Æscendune;" and they crowded to the bank joyfully, for the purpose of the attack was known to all, and now they saw its object placed beyond the reach of further risk of failure. The coracle touched the further bank; a dozen willing hands assisted them up the slope. And amidst shouts of vociferous joy and triumph they were conducted to King Edgar, who hastened towards the scene with Siward.

"Now, let the castle burn, let it burn," said Oswy.

"Alfred, is it you?" exclaimed the young king; "just

escaped from the flames ?   How came you there ? and this is
Elfric ; you have saved him."

"God has delivered us."

"But you have been the instrument ; you must tell me
all another time, get him into shelter quickly.   Here, men,
bear him to the priory, while we stay to do our duty here.
Alfred, you must not linger."

"One favour, my lord and king ; show mercy to Ragnar,
to Redwald, you know not how sad his story has been."

"Leave that to me ; he shall have all he deserves ;" and
Alfred was forced to be content.

At this moment, aroused by the shouts of joy, Ragnar,
forgetting even his danger, rushed to the roof.   There he
saw a crowd surrounding some object of their joy ; in the
darkness of the night he could not distinguish more, but
the cry, "Long live Alfred of Æscendune !" arose spontane-
ously from the crowd, just as the brothers departed.
Faint with toil as he was, his heart beating wildly with
apprehension, he rushed to the chamber through smoke
and flame, for the tongues of fire were already licking the
staircase.   He withdrew the bars, he rushed in, the room
was empty.

"It is magic, sorcery, witchcraft," he groaned.   But
the remembrance of his last words, of his scornful defiance
of God, came back to him, and with it a conviction that he
had indeed lifted up his arm against the Holy One.   He
felt a sickening feeling of horror and despair rush upon
him, when loud cries calling him from beneath aroused him.

"We must charge through them ; we cannot burn here ;
we must die fighting sword in hand, it is all that is left."

Not one voice spoke of surrender amongst those fierce
warriors, or of seeking mercy.

It was indeed high time, for all efforts to extinguish the
flames had proved vain; every part of the castle was on
fire ; the fiery element streamed from the lower windows,
and curled upwards around the towers ; it crackled and
hissed in its fury, and the atmosphere became unfit to

breathe ; it was like inhaling flame; sparks flew about in all directions, dense stifling smoke filled every room.   Not a man remained in the hall, when Redwald rushed down the gallery, holding his breath, for the hot air scorched the lungs, when, just as he arrived, the staircase fell with a huge crash, and the flames shot up in his face, igniting hair and beard, and scorching his flesh.   He rushed back to the opposite end of the passage, only to meet another blast of fire and smoke—for they had ignited the hall in twenty places at once ; they had done their work all too well.   He rushed to the room he had left, shut the door for a moment's respite from flame and smoke, and then, springing at the window, strove to tear the bars down, but all in vain.

"There must be some egress.   How did they escape ? How could they escape ?" he cried ; and he sought in vain for the exit, for they had closed the door again, and he knew not where to look ; in vain he lifted the tapestry, he could not discover the secret ; and at last, overpowered by the heat, he sprang again to the window, and drank in deep draughts of fresh cool air to appease the burning feeling in his throat.   Crash ! crash ! part of the roof had given way, and the whole chamber trembled ; then a single tongue of flame shot up through the floor, then another ; the door had caught outside.   Even in that moment he beheld his men, his faithful followers, madly seeking death from the swords of the foe ; they had lowered the drawbridge, and dashed out without a leader.

"Would I were with them !" he cried.   "Oh, to die like this !"

"Behold," cried a voice without, "he hath digged and graven a pit, and is fallen himself into the destruction he made for others."   It was Father Swithin, who had observed the face at the window, and who raised the cry which now drew all the enemy to gaze upon him, for they had no longer a foe to destroy.

The flames now filled the room, but still he clung to the window, and thus protracted his torments ; his foes,

even the stern monk, could but pity him now, so marred
and blackened was his visage, so agonised his lineaments;
like, as they said, the rude pictures of the lost, where the
last judgment was painted on the walls of the churches.
Yet he uttered no cry, he had resolved to die bravely; all
was lost now.   Another moment, and those who watched
saw the huge beams which supported the building bend
and quiver; then the whole framework collapsed, and
with a sound like thunder the roof tumbled in, and the
unhappy Ragnar was buried in the ruin; while the flames
from his funeral pyre rose to the very heavens, and the
smoke blotted the stars from view.

"Even so," said the monk, solemnly; "let Thine
enemies perish, O Lord, but let them that love Thee be
as the sun, when he goeth forth in his might."   But those
were not wanting who could not sympathise with the stern
sentiment, remembering better and gentler lessons from the
lips of the great Teacher and Master of souls.

"He has passed into the Hands of his God : there let
us leave him," said Father Cuthbert, who had just arrived
at the moment.   "It is not for us to judge a soul which
has passed to the judgment-seat, and is beyond the
sentence of men."

Meanwhile, they had borne Elfric first to the priory;
for they judged it not well that he should yet be brought
to his mother; they feared the sudden shock. Many of
the good monks had studied medicine, for they were in fact
the healers both of soul and body throughout the district,
and they attended him with assiduous care. They put
him to bed, they gave him cordials which soon produced
quiet sleep, and watched by him for many hours. It was
not till the day had far advanced that he awoke, greatly
refreshed, and saw Father Cuthbert and Alfred standing
by him. They had allayed the fever, bound up the wound,
which was not in itself dangerous, and he looked more like
himself than one could have imagined possible.

And now they thought they might venture to summon

the lady Edith; and Alfred broke the intelligence to her, for she knew not the events of the night.

"Mother," he said; "we have news of Elfric, both bad and good, to tell you."

"He lives then," she said; "he lives?"

"Yes, lives, and is near; but he was wounded badly in the battle."

"I must go to him," she said; and arose, forgetting all possible obstacles in a mother's love.

"He is near at hand, in the priory; you will find him much changed, but they say he will do well."

She shook like an aspen leaf, and threw her garments around her with nervous earnestness.

"Come, mother, take my arm."

"O Alfred, may I not come too?" said little Edgitha.

"Yes, you may come too;" and they left the house.

Elfric heard them approach, and sat up in his bed, Father Cuthbert supporting him with his arm; while another visitor, Edgar himself, stood at the head of the bed, but retired to give place to the mother, as if he felt no stranger could then intrude, when the widow clasped her prodigal to her loving breast.

CHAPTER XXIV.

SOW THE WIND, AND REAP THE WHIRLWIND.

WHEN Alfred rebuilt the city of Winchester, after it had been burned by the Danes, he erected a royal palace, which became a favourite retreat of his successors.

Here the unhappy Edwy retired after his defeat, to find consolation in the company of Elgiva. Indeed he needed it. Northumbria had followed the example of Mercia, and acknowledged Edgar, and he had no dominions left north of the Thames, while it was rumoured that worse news might follow. In an inner chamber of the palace, and remote from intrusion, sat the king and his chosen advisers. It was early in the year 958, a spring day when the sun shone brightly and all things spoke of the coming summer—the songs of the birds, the opening buds, the blossoming orchards.

But peace was banished from those who sat in that council-chamber. Edwy was strangely disturbed, his face was flushed, and he bore evidence of the most violent agitation.

"It must come to that at last, my king," exclaimed Cynewulf, "or Wessex will follow the example of Mercia."

"Better lose my crown then and become a subject, with a subject's liberty to love."

"A subject could never marry within the prohibited degree," said a greyheaded counsellor.

"We have messengers from all parts of Wessex, from Kent, from Essex, from Sussex, and they all unite in their demand that you should submit to the Church, and put away (forgive me for repeating their words) your concubine."

"Concubine!" said Edwy, and his cheek flushed, "she is my wife and your queen."

"Pardon me, my liege, I did not make the word my own."

"You should not have dared to repeat it."

"If I dare, my lord, it is for your sake, and for our country, which is dear to us all. Not an Englishman will acknowledge that your connection is lawful; from Exeter to Canterbury the cry is the same—'Let him renounce Elgiva, and we will obey him; but we will not serve a king who does not obey the voice of the Church or the laws of the land.'"

"Laws of the land! The king is above the laws."

"Nay, my lord, he is bound to set the first example of obedience, chief in that as in all things; an example to his people. Remember, my lord, your coronation oath taken at Kingston three years ago."

Edwy flushed. "Is this a subject's language?"

"It is the language of one who loves his king too well to flatter him."

At this moment an usher of the court knocked at the door, and obtaining permission to enter, stated that Archbishop Odo had arrived, and demanded admission to the council.

"I will not see him," said the king.

"My liege," exclaimed Athelwold, the old greyheaded counsellor we have mentioned, "permit one who loves you, as he loved your revered father, to entreat you to cease from this hopeless resistance. If you refuse to see him you are no longer a king."

"Then I will gladly abdicate."

"And become the scorn of Dunstan, and receive a retiring pension from Edgar, and put your hand between his, kneeling humbly and saying 'I am your man.'"

"No, no. Anything rather than that. Death first."

"All this may be averted with timely submission. Elgiva herself would not counsel you to sacrifice all for her.

" O Athelwold, my father, the only one of my father's counsellors who has been faithful to his firstborn, what can I do? She is dearer to me than life."

" But not than honour. You have both erred, both disobeyed the law of the Church, both forgotten the example due from those in high places."

" Tell Odo to enter," exclaimed Edwy.

The archbishop was close at hand, patiently awaiting the answer to his demand, yet determined, in case of a refusal, to take his pastoral staff in his hand and enter the council-room, announced or not. A more determined priest had never occupied the primacy, yet he was benevolent as determined, and, as we have mentioned, was known as Odo the Good amongst the poor. Stern and unyielding to the vices of the rich, he was gentle as a parent to the repentant sinner.

He had pronounced, as we have seen, the lesser excommunication,* in consequence of Edwy's refusal to put away Elgiva, immediately after the coronation; since which the guilty pair had never communicated at the altar, or even attended mass. Their lives had been practically irreligious, nay idolatrous, for they had been gods to each other.

And now, in the full pomp of the archiepiscopal attire, with the mitre of S. Augustine on his head and the crozier in his hand, Odo advanced, like one who felt his divine mission, to the centre of the room. His cross-bearer and other attendants remained in the ante-chamber.

" What dost thou seek, rude priest?" said Edwy.

" I am come in the Name of Him Whose laws thou hast broken, and speak to thee as the Baptist to Herod. Put away this woman, for it is not lawful for thee to have her."

" And would I could reply to thee as the holy fox Dunstan once informed me Herod replied to the insolent Baptist, and send thine head on a charger to Elgiva."

" My lord! my liege! my king! Remember his sacred office," remonstrated the counsellors.

* See Note Q.—The greater and lesser excommunications.

" Peace, my lords.   His threats or his blandishments would alike fail to move me.   The blood of Englishmen slain in civil war—if indeed any are found to fight for an excommunicate king—is that which I seek to avert.   In the Name of my Master, Whom thou hast defied, O king, I offer thee thy choice.   Thou must put away thy concubine, or thou shalt sustain the *greater* excommunication, when it will become unlawful for Christian people even to speak with thee, or wish thee God speed, lest they be partakers of thy evil deeds."

" My lord, you must yield," whispered Cynewulf.

" Son of the noble Edmund, thou must save thy father's name from disgrace."

" I cannot, will not, do Elgiva this foul wrong.   I tell thee, priest, that if thy benediction has never been pronounced upon our union, we are man and wife before heaven."

" I await your answer," said Odo.   " Am I to understand you choose the fearful penalty of excommunication ? "

" Nay ! nay ! he does not ; he cannot," cried the counsellors.   " Your   holiness !—father !—in   the   king's name we yield ! "

" You are all cowards and traitors ! let him do what he will, I cannot yield."

" Then, my lord king, I must proceed," said Odo. " You have not only acted wickedly in this matter, but you have misgoverned the people committed to your charge, and broken every clause of your coronation oath.   *First*, you have not given the Church of God peace, or preserved her from molestation, but have yourself ravaged her lands, and even slain her servants with the sword; one, specially honoured of God, you sought to slay, sending that wicked man, who has been called by fire to his judgment, to execute your impious will."

" That holy fox Dunstan ! would Redwald *had* slain him ! " muttered Edwy.

" *Secondly*," continued Odo, not heeding the interruption, "so far from preventing thefts and fraud in all manner of men, you have maintained notorious oppressors amongst your officers, and in your own person you have broken the oath; for did you not even rob your aged grandmother, and consume her substance in riotous living?"

"What could the old woman do with it all?"

"*Thirdly*, you have not maintained justice in your judicial proceedings, but have spent all your time, like Rehoboam of old, with the young and giddy, and in chastising your people with scorpions."

"Would I had a scorpion to chastise you! this is unbearable. My lords and counsellors, have you not a word to say for me?"

"Alas!" said Athelwold, "it is all too true; but give up Elgiva now, and all will be well!"

"It will be at least the beginning of reformation," said Odo.

"And the end, I suppose," said Edwy, "will be that I shall shave my head like a monk, banquet sumptuously upon herbs and water, spend three-fourths of the day singing psalms through my nose, wear a hair shirt, look as starved as a weasel, and at last, after sundry combats with the devil, pinch his nose, and go off to heaven in all the odour of sanctity. Go and preach all this to Edgar; I am not fool enough to listen to it. You have got him to be your obedient slave and vassal; you have bought him, body and soul, and the price has been Mercia, and now you want to add Wessex. Well, I wish you joy of him, and him of you all; for my part, if I could do it, I would restore the worship of Odin and Thor, and offer you priests as bloody sacrifices to him: I would!"

"Peace, my lord and king! peace! this is horrible." said Athelwold.

"Horrible!" said another. "He is possessed. My lord Odo, you had better exorcise him."

But Edwy had given way—he was young—and burst into a passionate fit of weeping, his royal dignity all forgotten.

"Give him time! give him time, father!" said they all.

"One day; he must then submit, or I must do my duty; I have no choice—none," replied the archbishop.

And the council sadly broke up; but Athelwold sought a private interview with Elgiva.

It was the evening of the same day, and the fair Elgiva sat alone in her apartment, into which the westering sun was casting his last beams of liquid light; tears had stained her cheeks and reddened her eyes, but she looked beautiful as ever, like the poet's or painter's conception of the goddess of love. Around her were numerous evidences of a woman's delicate tastes, of tastes too in advance of her day. The harp, which Edwy had given her the day of their inauspicious union, stood in one corner of the apartment; richly ornamented manuscripts lay scattered about—not, as usual, legends of the saints, and breviaries, but the writings of the heathen poets, especially those who sang most of love: for she was learned in such lore.

At last the well-known step was heard approaching, and her heart beat violently. Edwy entered, his face bearing the traces of his mental struggle; he threw himself down upon a couch, and did not speak for some few moments. She arose and stood beside him.

"Edwy, my lord, you are ill at ease."

"I am indeed, Elgiva; oh! if you knew what I have had to endure this day!"

"I know it all, my Edwy; you cannot sacrifice your Elgiva, but she can sacrifice herself."

"Elgiva! what do you mean?"

"You have to choose between your country and your wife; she has made the choice for you." Here she strove violently to repress her emotion.

"Elgiva! you shall never go—never, never! it will break my heart."

"It will break mine; but better hearts should break than that civil war should desolate our country, or that you should be dethroned."

"No more of this, Elgiva; you shall not go! I swear it! come weal or woe. Are we not man and wife? have we not ever been faithful to each other?"

"But this dreadful Church, my Edwy, which crushes men's affections and rules their intellects with a giant's strength more fearful than the fabled hammer of Thor. It crushed the sweet mythology of old, with all that ministered to love, and substituted the shaveling, the nun, the monk; it has no sympathy with poor hearts like ours; it is remorseless, as though it never knew pity or fear. You must yield, my Edwy! we must yield!"

"I cannot," he said; "we will fly the throne together."

"But where would you go? this Church is everywhere; who would receive an excommunicate man?"

"I cannot help it, Elgiva; say no more, it maddens me. Talk of our early days, before this dark shadow fell upon us."

She took up her harp, as if, like David, she could thereby soothe the perturbed spirit; but its sweet sounds woke no answer in his breast, and so the night came upon them—night upon the earth, night upon their souls.

Early in the morning she rose, strong in a woman's affection, while Edwy yet slept, and hastily arrayed herself; she looked around at her poor household gods, at the harp, at the many tokens of his love. "It is for him!" she said: she imprinted her last kiss on his sleeping forehead, she gazed upon him with fond, fond love; love had been her all, her heaven: and then she opened the door noiselessly.

Athelwold waited without.

"Well done, noble girl!" he said; "thou keepest thy word right faithfully."

She strove to speak, but could not; her pale bloodless lips would not frame the words. Silently they descended the stairs; the dawn reddened the sky; a horse with a lady's equipments waited without, and a guide.

The old thane slipped a purse of gold into her hands.

" You will need it," he said.   " Where are you going ? you have not told us."

" It is better none should know," she said ; " I will decide my route when without the city."   They never heard of her again.*

When Edwy awoke and found her gone he was at first frantic, and sent messengers in all directions to bring her back ; but when one after another came back unsuccessful, he accepted the heroic sacrifice and submitted.

Wessex, therefore, remained faithful to him, at least for a time, but Mercia was utterly lost ; and Edgar was recognised as the lawful king north of the Thames, by all parties, friends and foes, even by Edwy himself.

* See Note R.—Disappearance of Elgiva.

CHAPTER XXV.

"FOR EVER WITH THE LORD."

MANY months had passed away since the destruction of the
hall of Æscendune and the death of the unhappy Ragnar,
and the spring of 958 had well-nigh ended.   During the
interval, a long and hard winter had grievously tried the
shattered constitution of Elfric.   He had recovered from
the fever and the effects of his wound in a few weeks, yet
only partially recovered, for the severe shock had perma-
nently injured his once strong health, and ominous symptoms showed themselves early in the winter.   His breathing
became oppressed, he complained of pains in the chest, and
seemed to suffer after any exertion.

These symptoms continued to increase in gravity, until
his friends were reluctantly compelled to recognise the
symptoms of that insidious disease, so often fatal in our
English climate, which we now call consumption.

It was long before they would admit as much; but when
they saw how acutely he suffered in the cold frosts; how he,
who had once been foremost in every manly exercise, was
compelled to forego the hunt, and to allow his brother to
traverse the woods and enjoy the pleasures of the chase
without him ; how he sought the fireside and shivered at
the least draught; how a dry painful cough continually
shook his frame, they could no longer disguise the fact that
his days on earth might be very soon ended.

There was one fact which astonished them.   Although
he had returned with avidity to all the devotional habits
in which he had been trained, yet he always expressed himself unfit to receive the Holy Communion, and delayed to

make that formal confession of his sins, which the religious habits of the age imposed on every penitent.

Once or twice his fond mother, anxious for his spiritual welfare, pressed this duty upon him; and Alfred, whom he loved, as well he might, most dearly, urged the same thing, yet he always evaded the subject, or, when pressed, replied that he fully meant to do so; in short, it was a matter of daily preparation, but he could not come to be shriven yet.

When the winter at last yielded, and the bright spring sun spoke of the resurrection, when Lent was over, they hoped at least to see him make his Easter communion, and their evident anxiety upon the subject at last brought from him the avowal of the motives which actuated his conduct.

It was Easter Eve, and Alfred had enticed him out to enjoy the balmy air of a bright April afternoon. Close by the path they took, the hall was rapidly rising to more than its former beauty, for not only had the theows and ceorls all shown great alacrity in the work, but all the neighbouring thanes had lent their aid.

"It will be more beautiful than ever," said Alfred, "but not quite so home-like. Still, when you come of age, Elfric, it will be a happy home for you."

"It will never be my home, Alfred."

"You must not speak so despondently. The bright spring-tide will soon restore all your former health and vigour."

"No, Alfred, no; the only home I look for is one where my poor shattered frame will indeed recover its vigour, but it will not be the vigour or beauty of this world. Do you remember the lines Father Cuthbert taught us the other night?—

> "' Oh, how glorious and resplendent,
>   Fragile body, shalt thou be,
>   When endued with so much beauty,
>   Full of health, and strong and free,
>   Full of vigour, full of pleasure,
>   That shall last eternally.'

It will not be on earth though, my brother."

Alfred was silent; his emotions threatened to overcome him. He could not bear to think that he should lose Elfric, although the conviction was gradually forcing itself upon them all.

"Alfred," continued the patient, "it is of no use deceiving ourselves. I have often thought it hard to leave this beautiful world, for it is beautiful after all, and to leave you who have almost given your life for me, and dear mother, little Edgitha, and Father Cuthbert; but God's Will must be done, and what He wills must be best for us. No; this bright Easter tide is the last I shall see on earth; but did not Father Cuthbert say that heaven is an eternal Easter?"

So the repentant prodigal spoke, according to the lessons the Church had taught him. Superstitious in many points that Church of our forefathers may have been, yet how much living faith had its home therein will never be fully known till the judgment.

"And when I look at that castle," Elfric continued, "our own hall of Æscendune, rising from its ashes, I picture to myself how you will marry some day and be happy there; how our dear mother will see your children growing up around her knee, and teach them as she taught you and me; how, perhaps, you will name one after me, and there shall be another Elfric, gay and happy as the old one, but, I hope, ten times as good; and you will not let him go to court, I am sure, Alfred."

Alfred did not answer; he could not command his composure.

"And when you all come to the priory church on Sundays, and Father Cuthbert, or whoever shall come after him, sings the mass, you will remember me and breathe my name in your prayers when they say the memento for the faithful dead; and again, there shall be little children learning their paters and their sweet little prayers, as you and I learned them at our mother's knee; and you will show

Q

them my tomb, where I shall rest with dear father, and perhaps my story may be a warning to them. But you must never forget to show them how brotherly love was stronger than death when the old hall was burnt."

"After all," he continued, "our separation won't be long, the longest day comes to an end, and a thousand years are with Him as one day. We shall all be united at last— father, mother, Alfred, Edgitha, Elfric. Do you not hear the Easter bells ?"

They retraced their steps to the priory church for the services of Easter Eve.

"And one thing more, dear Alfred; you think me a strange penitent, that I am long, very long, before I make my confession. You do not know how I sigh for Communion; it is three years since I communicated, nearly four. But, Alfred, there is one who tried to stop me when I began going downward, downward, and I feel as if I must have his forgiveness before I can communicate, and it is to him I want to make my last confession. You know whom I mean ; he is in England now and near."

"I do indeed."

"Now you know my secret, let us go into church."

Oh, how sweetly those Easter psalms and lessons spoke to Alfred and Elfric that night ; how sweetly the tidings of a risen Saviour sounded in their ears. Easter joy was joy indeed. The very heavens seemed brighter that night, the moon—the Paschal moon—seemed to gladden the earth and render it a Paradise, like that happy Eden of old times, before sin entered its holy seclusion.

Eastertide was over, and Ascension drew near, but the sweet month of May had done little to restore health to poor Elfric. He had scarcely ever had a day free from pain. His eye was brighter than ever, but his attenuated face told a sad tale of the decay of the vital power.

From the time that Alfred knew how his brother yearned for Dunstan's forgiveness, and that he would be shriven by none but him, he had sought to accomplish his wish.   He heard that Dunstan had returned from abroad, and was about to be consecrated Bishop of Worcester, and to be their own diocesan, and he sought an early opportunity of seeing him.   At last, but not until after Dunstan's consecration, he gained the opportunity, not without much delay; for Dunstan was sometimes in Worcester, sometimes in London, which had thrown off Edwy's authority, and submitted, with all Essex, to Edgar; sometimes ordaining, sometimes confirming, sometimes assisting Edgar in the government; and he was, like all other great men, very inaccessible.   At last Alfred learned that he would be in Worcester by a certain day, and he started at once for that city.   He arrived there after a tedious journey; the roads were very difficult, and when he reached the city he heard the cathedral bells, and went at once to the high mass, for it was a festival.   There he saw Dunstan as he had seen him before at Glastonbury, at the altar, amidst all the solemn pomp in which our ancestors robed the sacred office.

Immediately after the service he repaired to the palace, and sent in his name.   Numbers, like himself, were awaiting an audience, but only a few minutes had passed ere an usher came into the ante-chamber and informed him that Dunstan requested his immediate presence.

He followed the usher amidst the envy of many who had the prospect of a long detention ere they could obtain the same favour, and soon he had clasped Dunstan's hand and knelt for his blessing.

" Nay! rise up, my son, it is thine : Deus benedicat et custodiat te, in omnibus viis tuis.   Thinkest thou, my son, thy name has been forgotten in my poor prayers ?   God made thee His instrument, but thou wast a very very willing one; and now, my son, wherein can I serve thee ? thou hast but to speak."

Thus encouraged, Alfred told all his tale, and Dunstan listened with much emotion.

" Yet two days and I will be with you at Æscendune.

Go back and comfort thy brother; he shall indeed have my forgiveness, and happy shall I be as an ambassador of Christ to fulfil the blessed office of restoring the lost sheep to the fold, the prodigal to his Heavenly Father."

When Alfred returned to Æscendune he found Elfric eagerly awaiting him; he had not been so well in the absence of his brother, and every one saw symptoms of the coming end.

Still he seemed so happy when Alfred delivered his message that every one remarked it, and that evening he sat up later than usual, listening as Father Cuthbert read for the hundredth time his favourite story from King Alfred's Anglo-Saxon version of the Gospels, the parable of the prodigal son, which had filled his mind on the night after the battle; then he spoke to his mother about past days, before a cloud came between him and his home; and talked of his father, and of the little incidents of early youth. Always loving, he was more so than usual that night, as if he felt time was short in which to show a son's love.

That night his mother came, as she always came, when he was asleep, to his chamber to gaze upon him, when she was struck by the difficulty of his breathing; she felt alarmed when she saw the struggles he seemed to make for breath, and saw the damp sweat upon his brow, so she called Alfred.

Alfred saw at once that his brother was seriously worse, and summoned Father Cuthbert, who no sooner gazed upon him than he exclaimed that the end was near.

During all that night he breathed heavily and with difficulty, as if each breath would be the last. Towards morning, however, he rallied, and immediate danger seemed gone, although only for a short time.

He sat up for the last time that day: it was a lovely day in May, and in the heat of the day he seemed to drink in the sweet atmosphere, as it came gently through the open window, laden with the scents of a hundred flowers. Often his lips moved as if in prayer, and sometimes he spoke to his brother, and asked when Dunstan would come ; but he was not equal to prolonged conversation.

At length one of the ceorls came riding in to say that the Bishop, with his retinue, was approaching the village, and Father Cuthbert went out to meet him. The impatient anxiety of poor Elfric became painful to witness. " He is coming, Elfric ! he is coming !" said Alfred from the window. " I see him near ; see ! he stops to salute Father Cuthbert, whom he knew years ago ; I must go down to receive him. Mother ! you stay with Elfric !"

A sound as of many feet ; another moment, a firm step was heard upon the stairs, and Dunstan entered the room.

He advanced to the bed, while all present stood in reverent silence, and gazed upon the patient with a look of such affection as a father might bestow upon a dying son as he took the weak nerveless hand.

Elfric looked round with a mute appeal which they all comprehended, and left him alone with Dunstan. " Father, pardon me !" he said.

" Thou askest pardon of me, my son—of me, a sinner like thyself; I cannot tell thee how freely I give it thee ; and now, my son, unburden thyself before thy God, for never was it known that one pleaded to Him and was cast out."

When, after an interval, Dunstan summoned the lady Edith and Alfred back into the room, a look of such calm, placid composure, such satisfied happiness, sat upon his worn face, that they never forgot it ; " surely," thought they, " such is the expression the blessed will wear in heaven."

And then, in their presence, Dunstan administered the Blessed Sacrament of the Body and Blood of Christ to the happy penitent ; it was the first Communion which he had willingly made since he first left home, a bright happy boy of fifteen ; and words would fail to describe the deep faith and loving penitence with which he gathered his dying strength to receive the Holy Mysteries.

And then Dunstan administered the last of all earthly rites—the holy anointing;* while amidst their tears the mourners yet thought of Him Who vouchsafed to be anointed before He sanctified the grave to be a bed of hope to His people.

"Art thou happy now, my son?" said Dunstan, when all was over.

"Happy indeed! happy! yes, so happy!"

They were almost the last words he said, until an hour had passed and the sun had set, leaving the bright clouds suffused in rich purple, when he sat up in the bed.

"Mother! Alfred!" he said, "do you hear that music? many are singing; surely that was father's voice; oh! how bright!"   He fell back, and Dunstan began the solemn commendatory prayer, for he saw the last moment was come.

"Go forth, O Christian soul, from this world, in the name of God the Father Who hath created thee, of God the Son Who hath redeemed thee, of God the Holy Ghost Who hath been poured out upon thee; and may thy abode be this day in peace, in the heavenly Sion, through Jesus Christ thy Lord!"

It was over! over that brief but eventful life! over all the bright hopes which had centred on him in this world; but the battle was won, and the eternal victory gained.

We have little more to add to our tale; the remainder is matter of history. The real fate of the unhappy Elgiva is not known, for the legend which represents her as suffering a violent death at the hands of the partisans of Edgar or Odo rests upon no solid foundation, but is repugnant to actual facts of history. Let us hope that she found the only real consolation in that religion she had hitherto, unhappily, despised, but which may perhaps have come to her aid in adversity.

The unhappy Edwy sank from bad to worse. When

* See Note S.—The last anointing.

Elgiva was gone he seemed to have nothing to live for; he yielded himself up to riotous living to drown care, while his government became worse and worse. Alas! he never repented, so far as we can learn, and the following year he died at Gloucester—some said of a broken heart, others of a broken constitution—in the twentieth year only of his age.

Poor unhappy Edwy the Fair! yet he had been his own worst enemy. Well has it been written:—"Rejoice, O young man, in thy youth, and walk in the ways of thine heart, and in the sight of thine eyes; but know thou that for all these things God will bring thee into judgment!"

Edgar succeeded to the throne, and all England acknowledged him as lord; while under Dunstan's wise administration the land enjoyed peace and plenty unexampled in Anglo-Saxon annals. Such was Edgar's power, that more than three thousand vessels kept the coast in safety, and eight tributary kings did him homage.

Alfred became in due course Thane of Æscendune, and his widowed mother lived to rejoice in his filial care many a long year, while the dependants and serfs blessed his name as they had once blessed that of his father. "The boy is the father of the man" it has been well said, and it was not less true than usual in this case: a bright pure boyhood ushered in a manhood of healthful vigour and bright intellect.

Children grew up around him after his happy marriage with Alftrude, the daughter of the thane of Rollrich. The eldest boy was named Elfric, and was bright and brave as the Elfric of old. Need we say he never went to court, although Edgar would willingly have numbered him in the royal household. Truly, indeed, were fulfilled the words which the Elfric of old had spoken on that Easter eve. To his namesake, and to all that younger generation, the memory of the uncle they had never seen was surrounded by a mysterious halo of light and love; and when they said their prayers around his tomb, it seemed as if he were still one of themselves—sharing their earthly joys and sorrows.

And here we must leave them—time passing sweetly on, the current of their lives flowing softly and gently to the mighty ocean of eternity—

> " Where the faded flower shall freshen,
>   Freshen never more to fade ;
> Where the shaded sky shall brighten,
>   Brighten never more to shade."
>
> *Bonar.*

NOTES.

Note A, p. 2.—*Homilies in the Anglo-Saxon Church.*

" The mass priest, on Sundays and mass days, shall speak the sense of the Gospel to the people in English, and of the Paternoster, and of the Creed, as often as he can, for the inciting of the people to know their belief, and to retain their Christianity. Let the teacher take heed of what the prophet says, ' They are dumb dogs, and cannot bark.' We ought to bark and preach to laymen, lest they should be lost through ignorance. Christ in His gospel says of unlearned teachers, ' If the blind lead the blind, they both fall into the ditch.' The teacher is blind that hath no book-learning, and he misleads the laity through his ignorance. Thus are you to be aware of this, as your duty requires."—23d Canon of Elfric, *about* A.D. 957. Elfric was then only a private monk in the abbey of Abingdon, and perhaps composed these canons for the use of Wulfstan, Bishop of Dorchester, with the assistance of the abbot, Ethelwold. They commence " Ælfricus, humilis frater, venerabili Episcopo Wulfsino, salutem in Domino." Others think this " Wulfsinus " was the Bishop of Sherborne of that name. Elfric became eventually Archbishop of Canterbury, A.D. 995-1005, dying at an advanced age. No other English name before the Conquest is so famous in literature.

Note B, p. 7.—*Services of the Church.*

It concerns mass-priests, and all God's servants, to keep their churches employed with God's service. Let them sing therein the seven tide songs that are appointed them, as the Synod earnestly requires—that is, the uht song (matins) ; the prime song (seven A.M.) ; the undern song (terce, nine A.M.) ; the midday song (sext) ; the noon-song (*nones*, three P.M.) ; the even-song (six P.M.) ; the seventh or night song (compline, nine P.M.)——19th Canon of Elfric. It is not to be supposed that the laity either were expected to attend, or could attend, all these services, which were strictly kept in monastic bodies ; but it would appear that mass, and sometimes matins and evensong, or else compline, were generally frequented. And these latter would be, as represented in the text, the ordinary services in private chapels.

Note C, p. 9.—*Battle of Brunanburoh.*

In this famous battle, the English, under their warlike king, defeated a most threatening combination of foes ; Anlaf, the Danish prince, having united his forces to those of Constantine, King of the Scots, and the Britons, or Welsh of Strathclyde and Cumbria. So proud were the English of the victory, that their writers break into poetry when they come to that portion of their annals. Such is the case with the writer of the Anglo-Saxon Chronicle, from whom the following verses are abridged. They have been already partially quoted in the text.

Here Athelstane king,	The candle of God,
Of earls the lord,	Ran her course through the heavens ;
To warriors the ring-giver,	Till red in the west
Glory world-long	She sank to her rest.
Had won in the strife,	Through the live-long day
By edge of the sword,	Fought the people of Weasex,
At Brunanburgh.	Unshrinking from toil,
The offspring of Edward,	While Mercian men,
The departed king,	Hurled darts by their side.
Cleaving the shields,	Fated to die
Struck down the brave.	Their ships brought the Danes ;
Such was their valour,	Five kings and seven earls,
Worthy of their sires,	All men of renown,
That oft in the strife	And Scots without number
They shielded the land	Lay dead on the field.
'Gainst every foe.	Constantine, hoary warrior,
The Scottish chieftains,	Had small cause to boast,
The warriors of the Danes,	Young in the fight,
Pierced through their mail,	Mangled and torn,
Lay dead on the field.	Lay his son on the plain.
The field was red	Nor Anlaf the Dane
With warriors' blood,	With wreck of his troops,
What time the sun,	Could vaunt of the war
Uprising at morn,	

Of the clashing of spears,	The King and the Etheling,
Or the crossing of swords,	To Wessex returned,
With the offspring of Edward.	Leaving behind
The Northmen departed	The corpses of foes
In their mailed barks,	To the beak of the raven,
Sorrowing much ;	The eagle and kite,
While the two brothers,	And the wolf of the wood.

The Chronicle simply adds, "A.D. 937.—This year King Athelstan, and the Etheling Edmund, his brother, led a force to Brunanburgh, and there fought against Anlaf, and, Christ helping them, they slew five kings and seven earls."

Note D, p. 15.—*Murder of Edmund.*

A certain robber named Leofa, whom Edmund had banished for his crimes, returning after six years' absence, totally unexpected, was sitting, on the feast of S. Augustine, the apostle of the English, and first Archbishop of Canterbury, among the royal guests at Pucklechurch, for on this day the English were wont to regale, in commemoration of their first preacher ; by chance, too, he was placed near a nobleman, whom the king had condescended to make his guest. This, while the others were eagerly carousing, was perceived by the king alone ; when, hurried with indignation, and impelled by fate, he leaped from the table, caught the robber by the hair, and dragged him to the floor ; but he, secretly drawing a dagger from its sheath, plunged it with all his force into the breast of the king as he lay upon him. Dying of the wound, he gave rise over the whole kingdom to many fictions concerning his decease. The robber was shortly torn limb from limb by the attendants who rushed in, though he wounded some of them ere they could accomplish their purpose. S. Dunstan, at that time Abbot of Glastonbury, had foreseen his ignoble end, being fully persuaded of it from the gesticulations and insolent mockery of a devil dancing before him. Wherefore, hastening to court at full speed, he received intelligence of the transaction on the road. By common consent, then, it was determined that his body should be brought to Glastonbury, and there magnificently buried in the northern part of the tower. That such had been his intention, through his singular regard for the abbot, was evident from particular circumstances. The village, also, where he was murdered, was made an offering for the dead, that the spot, which had witnessed his fall, might ever after minister aid to his soul.—William of Malmesbury, B. ii. c. 7, Bohn's Edition.

Note E, p. 26.—*Wulfstan, and the See of Dorchester.*

When Athelstane was dead, the Danes, both in Northumberland and Mercia, revolted against the English rule, and made Anlaf their king. Archbishop Wulfstan, then of York, sided with them, perhaps being himself of Danish blood. The kingdom was eventually divided between Edmund and Anlaf, until the death of the latter. When Edred ascended the throne—after the murder of Edmund, who had, before his death, repossessed himself of the whole sovereignty—the wise men of Northumberland, with Wulfstan at their head, swore submission to him, but in 948 rebelled, and chose for their king Eric of Denmark. Edred marched at once against them, and subdued the rebellion with great vigour, not to say *rigour.* He threw the archbishop into prison at Jedburgh in Bernicia. After a time he was released, but only upon the condition of banishment from Northumbria, and he was made Bishop of Dorchester, a place familiar to the tourist on the Thames, famed for the noble abbey church which still exists, and has been grandly restored.

Although Dorchester is now only a village, it derives its origin from a period so remote that it is lost in the mist of ages. It was probably a British village under the name Cair Dauri, the camp on the waters ; and coins of Cunobelin, or Cassivellaunus, have been found in good preservation. Bede mentions it as a Roman station, and Richard of Cirencester marks it as such in the xviii. Iter, under the name Durocina.

Its bishopric was founded by Birinus, the apostle of the West Saxons ; and the present bishoprics of Winchester, Salisbury, Exeter, Bath and Wells, Worcester and Hereford, were successively taken from it, after which it still extended from the Thames to the Humber.

Suffering grievously from the ravages of the Danes, it became a small town, and it suffered again grievously at the Conquest, when the inhabited houses were reduced by the Norman ravages from 172 to 100, and perhaps the inhabitants were reduced in proportion. In consequence, Remigius, the first Norman bishop, removed the see to Lincoln, because Dorchester, on account of its size and small population, did not suit his ideas, as John of Brompton observes. From this period its decline was rapid, in spite of its famous abbey, which Remigius partially erected with the stones from the bishop's palace.

Note F, p. 30.—*Anglo-Saxon Literature.*

In the age of Bede, the eighth century, Britain was distinguished for its learning ; but the Danish invasions caused the rapid decline of its renown.

The churches and monasteries, where alone learning flourished, and which were the only libraries and schools, were the first objects of the hatred of the ferocious pagans ; and, in consequence, when Alfred came to the throne, as he tells us in his own words—"South of the Humber there were few priests who could understand the meaning of their common prayers, or translate a line of Latin into English ; so few, that in Wessex there was not one." Alfred set himself diligently to work to correct this evil. Nearly all the books in existence in England were in Latin, and it was a "great" library which contained fifty copies of these. There was a great objection to the use of the vernacular in the Holy Scriptures, as tending to degrade them by its uncouth jargon ; but the Venerable Bede had rendered the Gospel of S. John into the Anglo-Saxon, together with other extracts from holy Scripture ; and there were versions of the Psalter in the vulgar tongue, very rude and uncouth ; for ancient translators generally imagined a translation could only be faithful which placed all the words of the vulgar tongue in the same relative positions as the corresponding words in the original. An Anglo-Saxon translation upon this plan is extant.

Alfred had taught himself Latin by translating : there were few vocabularies, and only the crabbed grammar of old Priscian. Shaking himself free from the trammels we have enumerated, he invited learned men from abroad, such as his biographer, Asser, and together they attempted a complete version of the Bible. Some writers suppose the project was nearly completed, others, that it was interrupted by his early death. Still, translations were multiplied of the sacred writings, and the rubrics show that they were read, as described in the text, upon the Sundays and festivals. From that time down to the days of Wickliffe, England can boast of such versions of the sacred Word as can hardly be paralleled in Europe.

The other works we have mentioned were also translated *by* or *for* Alfred. "The Chronicle of Orosius," a history of the world by a Spaniard of Seville ; " The History of the Venerable Bede ;" "The Consolations of Philosophy," by Boethius ; "Narratives from Ancient Mythology ;" "The Confessions of S. Augustine ;" "The Pastoral Instructions of S. Gregory ;" and his "Dialogue," form portions of the works of this greatest of kings, and true father of his people. His "Apologues," imitated from Æsop, are unfortunately lost.

Note G, p. 36.—*The Court of Edred.*

All the early chroniclers appear to take a similar view of the character and court of Edred. William of Malmesbury says— " The king devoted his life to God, and to S. Dunstan, by whose admonition he bore with patience his frequent bodily pains, prolonged his prayers, and made his palace altogether the school of virtue." But although pious, he was by no means wanting in manly energy, as was shown by his vigorous and successful campaign in Northumbria, on the occasion of the attempt to set Eric, son of Harold, on the throne of Northumbria. The angelic apparition to S. Dunstan, mentioned on page 59, is told by nearly all the early historians, but with varying details. According to many, it occurred while Dunstan was hastening to the aid of Edred. The exigencies of the tale required a slightly different treatment of the legend.

Note H, p. 46.—*Confession in the Anglo-Saxon Church.*

On the week next before holy night shall every one go to his shrift (*i.e.* confessor), and his shrift shall shrive him in such a manner as his deeds which he hath done require ; and he shall charge all that belong to his district that if any of them have

discord with any, he make peace with him ; if any one will not
be brought to this, then he shall not shrive him ; [but] then he
shall inform the bishop, that he may convert him to what is right,
if he be willing to belong to God: then all contentions and disputes
shall cease, and if there be any one of them that hath taken
offence at another, then shall they be reconciled, that they may
the more freely say in the Lord's Prayer, " Forgive us our tres-
passes, as we forgive them that trespass against us," etc.   And
having thus purified their minds, let them enter upon the holy
fast-tide, and cleanse themselves by satisfaction against holy
Easter, for this satisfaction is as it were a second baptism.   As
in Baptism the sins before committed are forgiven, so, by satisfaction, are the sins committed after Baptism.—Theodulf's
Canons, A.D. 994 (Canon 36).   It is evident, says Johnson, that
" holy night " means " lenten night," as the context shows.

NOTE I, p. 61.—*Incense in the Anglo-Saxon Church.*

Dr. Rock, in his " Hierurgia Anglicana," states that incense
was used at the Gospel.   In vol. i., quoting from Ven. Bede,
he writes—" Conveniunt omnes in ecclesiam B. Petri ipse
(Ceolfridas Abbas) thure incenso, et dicto oratione, ad altare
pacem dat omnibus, stans in gradibus, thuribulum habens in
manu."   In Leofric's Missal is a form for the blessing of incense.
Theodore's Penitential also affixes a penance to its wilful or careless destruction.   Ven. Bede on his deathbed gave away incense
amongst his little parting presents, as his disciple, Cuthbert,
relates.   Amongst the furniture of the larger Anglo-Saxon
churches was a huge censer hanging from the roof, which emitted
fumes throughout the mass.

> " Hic quoque thuribulum, capitellis undique cinctum,
> Pendet de summo, fumosa foramina pandens :
> De quibus ambrosia spirabunt thura Sabæa,
> Quando sacerdotes missas offerre jubentur."
> ALCUINI *Opera*, B. ii., p. 550.

NOTE J, p. 77.—*Legends about S. Dunstan.*

" It is a great pity," says Mr. Freeman, in his valuable " Old
English History," " that so many strange stories are told about him

[Dunstan], because people are apt to think of those stories and not of his real actions." This has indeed been the case to such an extent that his talents, as a statesman and as an ecclesiastical legislator, are almost unknown to many who are very familiar with the story of his seizing the devil by the nose with a pair of tongs. Sir Francis Palgrave supposes that S. Dunstan's seclusion at the time had led him to believe, like so many solitaries, that he was attacked in person by the fiend, and that he related his visions, which were accepted as absolute facts by his credulous hearers. Hence the author has assumed the currency of some of these marvellous legends in his tale, and has introduced a later one into the text of the present chapter, p. 105. But the whole life of the saint, as related by his monkish biographers, is literally full of such legends, some terrible, some ludicrous. One of the most remarkable deserves mention, bearing, as it does, upon our tale. It is said that he learned that Edwy was dead, and that the devils were about to carry off his soul in triumph, when, falling to fervent prayer, he obtained his release. A most curious colloquy between the abbot and the devils on this subject may be found in Osberne's " Life of Dunstan."

Note K, p. 77.—*The Benedictine Rule.*

S. Benedict, the founder of the great Benedictine Order, was born in the neighbourhood of Nursia, a city of Italy, about A.D. 480. Sent to study at Rome, he was shocked at the vices of his fellow-students, ran away from the city, and shut himself up in a hermitage, where he resigned himself to a life of the strictest austerity. Three years he spent in a cave near Subiaco, about forty miles from Rome, where he was so removed from society that he lost all account of time. He did not, however, lead an idle life of self-contemplation ; he instructed the shepherds of the neighbourhood, and such were the results of his instruction that his fame spread widely, until, the abbot of a neighbouring monastery dying, the brethren almost compelled him to become their superior, but, not liking the reforms he introduced, subsequently endeavoured to poison him, whereupon he returned to his cave, where, as S. Gregory says, " he dwelt with himself," and became more celebrated than ever. After this the number of his disciples increased so greatly, that, emerging from his solitude, he built twelve monasteries, in each of which he placed twelve monks under a superior, finally laying the foundation of the great monastery of Monte Cassino, which has ever since been regarded as the central institution of the order.

Here was drawn up the famous Benedictine rule, which was far more adapted than any other code to prevent the cloister from becoming the abode of idleness or lascivious ease. To the three vows of poverty, chastity, and obedience, was added the obligation of manual labour, the brethren being required to work with their hands at least seven hours daily. The profession for life was preceded by a novitiate of one year, during which the rule was deeply studied by the novice, that the life vow might not be taken without due consideration. The colour of the habit was usually dark, hence the brethren were called the Black Monks.

S. Benedict died of a fever, which he caught in ministering to the poor, on the eve of Passion Sunday, A.D. 543. Before his death, the houses of the order were to be found in all parts of Europe, and by the ninth century it had become general throughout the Church, almost superseding all other orders.

Note L, p. 80.—*The Roman Roads.*

Roman roads were thus constructed :—Two shallow trenches were dug parallel to each other, marking the breadth of the proposed road ; the loose earth was removed till a solid foundation was reached, and above this were laid four distinct strata—the first of small broken stones, the second of rubble, the third of fragments of bricks or pottery, and the fourth the pavement, composed of large blocks of solid stone, so joined as to present a perfectly even surface. Regular footpaths were raised on each side, and covered with gravel. Milestones divided them accurately. Mountains were pierced by cuttings or tunnels, and arches thrown over valleys or streams. Upon these roads, posting houses existed at intervals of six miles, each provided with forty horses, so that journeys of more than 150 miles were sometimes accomplished in one day.

From the arrival of our uncivilised ancestors, these magnificent roads were left to ruin and decay, and sometimes became the quarry whence the thane or baron drew stones for his castle ; but they still formed the channels of communication for centuries. Henry of Huntingdon (*circa* 1154) mentions the Icknield Street, from east to west ; the Erninge, or Ermine Street, from south to north ; the Watling Street, from south-east to north-west ; and the Foss-way, from north-east to south-west, as the four principal highways of Britain in his day. Once ruined, no communications so perfect existed until these days of railroads.

Note M, p. 87.—*The Rollright Stones.*

These stones are still to be seen in the parish of Great Roll-right near Chipping Norton, Oxon, anciently Rollrich or Rholdrwygg. They lie on the edge of an old Roman trackway, well defined, which extends along the watershed between Thames and Avon. The writer has himself heard from the rustics of the neighbourhood the explanation given by Oswy ; while that put in the mouth of Father Cuthbert is the opinion of the learned.

Note N, p. 111.—*Ruined British Cities.*

The resistance of the Britons (or Welsh) to their Saxon (or English) foes was so determined, that, as in all similar cases, it increased the miseries of the conquered. In Gaul the conquered Celts united with the Franks to make one people ; in Spain they united with the Goths ; but the conquerors of Britain came from that portion of Germany which had been untouched by Roman valour or civilisation, and consequently there was no disposition to unite with their unhappy victims, but the war became one of extermination. Long and bravely did the unhappy Welsh struggle. After a hundred years of warfare they still possessed the whole extent of the western coast, from the wall of Antoninus to the extreme promontory of Cornwall ; and the principal cities of the inland territory still maintained the resistance. The fields of battle, says Gibbon, might be traced in almost every district by the monuments of bones ; the fragments of falling towers were stained by blood ; the Britons were mas sacred ruthlessly to the last man in the conquered towns, without distinction of age or sex, as in Anderida. Whole territories returned to desolation ; the district between the Tyne and Tees, for example, to the state of a savage and solitary forest. The wolves, which Roman authorities describe as non-existent in England, again peopled those dreary wastes ; and from the soft civilisation of Rome the inhabitants of the land fell back to the barbarous manners and customs of the shepherds and hunters of the German forests. Nor did the independent Britons, who had taken refuge finally in Wales, or Devon and Cornwall, fare much better. Separated by their foes from the rest of mankind, they returned to that state of barbarism from which they had emerged, and became a scandal at last to the growing civilisation of their English foes.

Under these circumstances the Saxons or English* cared little to inhabit the cities they conquered ; they left them to utter desolation, as in the case described in the text, until a period came when, as in the case of the first English assaults upon Exeter and the west country, they no longer destroyed, but appropriated, while they spared the conquered.

Note O, p. 147.—*Valhalla.*

Valhalla or Walhalla was the mythical Scandinavian Olympus, the celestial locality where Odin and Edris dwelt with the happy dead who had fallen in battle, and who had been conducted thither by the fair Valkyries. Here they passed the days in fighting and hunting alternately, being restored sound in body for the banquet each night, where they drank mead from the skulls of the foes they had vanquished in battle. Such was the heaven which commended itself to those fierce warriors.

Note P, p. 176.—*Anglo-Saxon Burials.*

It was not the usual English custom, in those days, to bury the dead in coffins, still it was often done, in the case of the great, from

---

* The Saxons founded the kingdoms of Wessex and Essex ; the Jutes, Kent ; the Angles all the others. The predominance of the latter caused the term English to become the general appellation.

the earliest days of Christianity. For instance, a stone coffin, supposed to contain the dust of the fierce Offa, who died A.D. 796, was dug up, when more than a thousand years had passed away, in the year 1836, at Hemel-Hempstead, with the name Offa rudely carved upon it. The earliest mention of churchyards in English antiquities is in the canons called the " Excerptions of Ecgbriht," A.D. 740, when Cuthbert was Archbishop of Canterbury ; and here the word, " atria " is used, which may refer to the outbuildings or porticoes of a church.

NOTE Q, p. 217—*The Greater and Lesser Excommunications.*

The lesser excommunication excluded men from the participation of the Eucharist and the prayers of the faithful, but did not necessarily expel them from the Church. The greater excommunication was far more dreadful in its operation. It was not lawful to pray, speak, or eat, with the excommunicate (Canons of Ecgbriht). No meat might be given into their hands even in charity, although it might be laid before them on the ground. Those who sheltered them incurred a heavy " were-gild," and endangered the loss of their estates ; and finally, in case of obstinacy, outlawry and banishment followed. —King Canute's *Laws Ecclesiastical.*

NOTE R, p. 222.—*Disappearance of Elgiva.*

The writer has already in the preface stated his reasons for rejecting the usual sad story about the fate of the hapless Elgiva. The other story, that she was seized by Archbishop Odo, branded on the face, and sent to Ireland, as Mr. Freeman observes, rests on no good authority ; all that is certainly known is that *she disappeared.*

At the time commonly assigned to these events, Dunstan was still in Flanders ; yet he is generally credited with the atrocities by modern writers, even as if he had been proved guilty after a formal trial. His return probably took place about the time occupied by the action of the last chapter, when the partition of the kingdom had already occurred.

Note S, p. 230.—*The last Anointing.*

The priest shall also have oil hallowed, separately, for children, and for sick men ; and solemnly anoint the sick in their beds. Some sick men are full of vain fears, so as not to consent to the being anointed. Now we will tell you how God's Apostle Jacob hath instructed us in this point; he thus speaks to the faithful : " If any of you be afflicted, let him pray for himself with an even mind, and praise his Lord. If any be sick among you, let him fetch the mass-priests of the congregation, and let them sing over him, and pray for him, and anoint him with oil in the Name of the Lord. And the prayer of faith shall heal the sick ; and the Lord shall raise him up : and if he be in sins they shall be forgiven him. Confess your sins among yourselves, pray for yourselves among yourselves, that ye be healed." Thus spake Jacob the Apostle concerning the unction of the sick. But the sick man, before his anointing, shall with inward heart confess his sins to the priest, if he hath any for which he hath not made satisfaction, according to what the Apostle before taught : and he must not be anointed, unless he request it, and make his confession. If he were before sinful and careless, let him then confess, and repent, and do alms before his death, that he may not be adjudged to hell, but obtain the Divine mercy.

Such is Johnson's version of the 32d canon of Elfric, in which he has preserved closely Elfric's translation, or rather paraphrase, of the passage in St. James. The name James was not then in use, the Latin Jacobus was rendered Jacob.—Johnson's *English Canons*, A.D. 957, 32.

THE END.

January, 1880.

A CLASSIFIED CATALOGUE OF BOOKS

Selected from the Publications of

Messrs. RIVINGTON

WATERLOO PLACE, LONDON

MAGDALEN STREET, OXFORD; TRINITY STREET, CAMBRIDGE

Contents.

1. The Prayer Book and the Church Service.

The Compendious Edition of the

Annotated Book of Common Prayer, forming a concise Commentary on the Devotional System of the Church of England. Edited by the Rev. John Henry Blunt, M.A., F.S.A., Editor of the "Dictionary of Sects and Heresies," &c. &c. Crown 8vo. 10*s.* 6*d.* ; in half-morocco, 16*s.* ; or in morocco limp, 17*s.* 6*d.*

The Annotated Book of Common

Prayer; being an Historical, Ritual, and Theological Commentary on the Devotional System of the Church of England. Edited by the Rev. JOHN HENRY BLUNT, M.A., F.S.A., Editor of the "Dictionary of Sects and Heresies," &c., &c. Seventh Edition. Imperial 8vo. 36*s.*; or in half-morocco, 48*s.*

[This large edition contains the Latin and Greek originals, together with technical Ritual Annotations, Marginal References, &c., which are necessarily omitted for want of room in the "Compendious Edition."]

" Whether as, historically, shewing how the Prayer Book came to be what it is, or, ritually, how it designs itself to be rendered from word into act, or, theologically, as exhibiting the relation between doctrine and worship on which it is framed, the book amasses a world of information carefully digested, and errs commonly, if at all, on the side of excess."—GUARDIAN.

" The most complete and compendious Commentary on the English Prayer Book ever yet published. Almost everything that has been written by all the best liturgical and historical authorities ancient and modern (of which a formidable list is prefixed to the work) is quoted, or referred to, or compressed into the notes illustrative of the several subjects."*—JOHN BULL.

" The book is a mine of information and research—able to give an answer almost on anything we wish to know about our present Prayer Book, its antecedents and originals—and ought to be in the library of every intelligent Churchman. Nothing like it has as yet been seen."—CHURCH REVIEW.

Liber Precum Publicarum Ecclesiæ

Anglicanæ. A GULIELMO BRIGHT, S.T.P., Ædis Christi apud Oxon. Canonico, et PETRO GOLDSMITH MEDD, A.M., Collegii Universitatis apud Oxon. Socio Seniore, Latine redditus. Editio tertia, cum Appendice. [In hac editione continentur Versiones Latinæ—1. Libri Precum Publicarum Ecclesiæ Anglicanæ; 2. Liturgiæ Primæ Reformatæ; 3. Liturgiæ Scoticanæ; 4. Liturgiæ Americanæ.] With Rubrics in Red. Small 8vo. 7*s.* 6*d.*

The First Book of Common Prayer of

Edward VI. and the Ordinal of 1549. Together with the Order of the Communion, 1548. Reprinted entire. Edited by the Rev. HENRY BASKERVILLE WALTON, M.A., late Fellow and Tutor of Merton College; with Introduction by the Rev. PETER GOLDSMITH MEDD, M.A., Rector of North Cerney; Hon. Canon of St. Albans; late Senior Fellow of University College, Oxford; and Rector of Barnes. Small 8vo. 6*s.*

The Prayer Book Interleaved; with
Historical Illustrations and Explanatory Notes arranged parallel to the Text. By W. M. CAMPION, D.D., and W. J. BEAMONT, M.A. With a Preface by the LORD BISHOP OF WINCHESTER. Tenth Edition. Small 8vo. 7s. 6d.

"An excellent publication, combining a portable Prayer Book with the history of the text and explanatory notes."—SPECTATOR.

"This book is of the greatest use for spreading an intelligent knowledge of the English Prayer Book, and we heartily wish it a large and continuous circulation."—CHURCH REVIEW.

"The work may be commended as a very convenient manual for all who are interested to some extent in liturgical studies, but who have not time or the means for original research. It would also be most useful to examining chaplains."—CHURCH TIMES.

The Book of Common Prayer, and
Administration of the Sacraments and other Rites and Ceremonies of the Church, according to the use of THE PROTESTANT EPISCOPAL CHURCH in the UNITED STATES of AMERICA, together with the Psalter, or Psalms of David. Royal 32mo. French roan limp, 2s. 6d.

An Illuminated Edition of the Book
of Common Prayer, printed in Red and Black, on fine toned paper; with Borders and Titles designed after the manner of the 14th Century. By R. R. HOLMES, F.S.A., and engraved by O. JEWITT. Crown 8vo. 16s.

A Book of Litanies, Metrical and Prose.
With an Evening Service. Edited by the Compiler of "The Treasury of Devotion." And accompanying Music arranged under the Musical Editorship of W. S. HOYTE, Organist and Director of the Choir at All Saints', Margaret Street, London. Crown 4to. 7s. 6d.

Also may be had, an Edition of the Words, 18mo., 6d.; or in paper cover, 4d. With Hymns (A. and M.) in one vol., cloth, 1s. 10d. Separately: Metrical Litanies, 18mo., 5d.; or in paper cover, 3d. Prose Litanies, with an Evening Service, in paper cover, 3d. An Evening Service, 1d.

A Key to the Knowledge and Use of

the Book of Common Prayer. By the Rev. JOHN HENRY BLUNT, M.A., F.S.A., Editor of the "Annotated Book of Common Prayer," &c. New Edition. Small 8vo. 2s. 6d. Also a Cheap Edition, 1s. 6d.

Forming a Volume of "Keys to Christian Knowledge."

" Impossible to praise too highly. It is the best short explanation of our offices that we know of, and would be invaluable for the use of candidates for confirmation in the higher classes."— JOHN BULL.

" To us it appears that Mr. Blunt has succeeded very well. All necessary *information seems to be included, and the arrangement is excellent."—*LITERARY CHURCHMAN.

*" A very valuable and practical manual, full of information. It deserves high commendation."—*CHURCHMAN.

Sacraments and Sacramental Ordi-

nances of the Church; being a Plain Exposition of their History, Meaning, and Effects. By the Rev. JOHN HENRY BLUNT, M.A., F.S.A., Editor of the "Annotated Book of Common Prayer," &c. Small 8vo. 4s. 6d.

A Commentary, Expository and De-

votional, on the Order of the Administration of the Lord's Supper, according to the Use of the Church of England; to which is added, an Appendix on Fasting Communion, Noncommunicating Attendance, Auricular Confession, the Doctrine of Sacrifice, and the Eucharistic Sacrifice. By EDWARD MEYRICK GOULBURN, D.D., Dean of Norwich. Sixth Edition. Small 8vo. 6s.

Also a Cheap Edition, uniform with "Thoughts on Personal Religion," and "The Pursuit of Holiness." 3s. 6d.

Comment upon the Collects appointed

to be used in the Church of England on Sundays and Holy Days throughout the Year. By JOHN JAMES, D.D., sometime Canon of Peterborough. New Edition. Small 8vo. 3s. 6d. Also a Fine Edition, on Toned Paper. Crown 8vo. 5s.

The Priest to the Altar; or, Aids to
the Devout Celebration of Holy Communion, chiefly after the
Ancient English Use of Sarum. Third Edition, revised and
enlarged. Royal 8vo. 12s.

Notitia Eucharistica; a Commentary,
Explanatory, Doctrinal, and Historical, on the Order for the
Administration of the Lord's Supper, or Holy Communion,
according to the use of the Church of England. With an
Appendix on the Office for the Communion of the Sick. By
the Rev. W. E. SCUDAMORE, M.A., Rector of Ditchingham,
and formerly Fellow of St. John's College, Cambridge. Second
Edition, revised and enlarged. 8vo. 32s.

The Athanasian Origin of the Athan-
asian Creed. By J. S. BREWER, M.A., Preacher at the
Rolls, and Honorary Fellow of Queen's College, Oxford.
Crown 8vo. 3s. 6d.

The "Damnatory Clauses" of the
Athanasian Creed rationally explained in a Letter to the Right
Hon. W. E. GLADSTONE, M.P. By the Rev. MALCOLM
MACCOLL, M.A., Rector of St. George, Botolph Lane.
Crown 8vo. 6s.

The Athanasian Creed: an Examina-
tion of Recent Theories respecting its Date and Origin.
With a Postscript referring to Professor Swainson's Account of
its Growth and Reception, which is contained in his Work
entitled "The Nicene and Apostles' Creeds, their Literary
History." By G. D. W. OMMANNEY, M.A., Vicar of Dray-
cot, Somerset. Crown 8vo. 8s. 6d.

The New Mitre Hymnal, containing New

Music by Sir JOHN GOSS, Sir GEORGE ELVEY, Dr. STAINER, HENRY GADSBY, Esq., J. BAPTISTE CALKIN, Esq., BERTHOLD TOURS, Esq., JAMES LANGRAN, Esq., and other eminent Composers; together with Scandinavian Tunes now first introduced into this Country. Royal 8vo. 5*s.*

An Edition of the Words without the Music may also be had. 18mo., cloth limp, 1*s.*; or in cloth boards, extra gilt, 1*s.* 6*d.*

[A large reduction to purchasers of quantities.]

Psalms and Hymns adapted to the

Services of the Church of England; with a Supplement of additional Hymns, and Indices. By the Rev. W. J. HALL, M.A. 8vo., 5*s.* 6*d.*; 18mo., 3*s.*; 24mo., 1*s.* 6*d.*; cloth limp, 1*s.* 3*d.*; 32mo., 1*s.*; cloth limp, 8*d.*

Selection of Psalms and Hymns; with

Accompanying Tunes selected and arranged by JOHN FOSTER, of Her Majesty's Chapels Royal. By the Rev. W. J. HALL, M.A. Crown 8vo. 2*s.* 6*d.* The Tunes only, 1*s.*

A Commentary, Practical and Exegeti-

cal, on the Lord's Prayer. By the Rev. W. DENTON, M.A. Small 8vo. 5*s.*

The Psalter, or Psalms of David. (The

Prayer Book Version.) Printed in red and black. Small 8vo. 2*s.* 6*d.*

2. The Holy Scriptures.

The Greek Testament. With a Critically

Revised Text; a Digest of Various Readings; Marginal References to Verbal and Idiomatic Usage; Prolegomena; and a Critical and Exegetical Commentary. For the use of Theological Students and Ministers. By HENRY ALFORD, D.D., late Dean of Canterbury. New Edition. 4 Volumes. 8vo. 102s.

The Volumes are sold separately, as follows :—

Vol.   I.—The Four Gospels. 28s.
Vol. II.—Acts to 2 Corinthians. 24s.
Vol. III.—Galatians to Philemon. 18s.
Vol. IV.—Hebrews to Revelation. 32s.

The New Testament for English

Readers : containing the Authorized Version, with a revised English Text ; Marginal References ; and a Critical and Explanatory Commentary. By HENRY ALFORD, D.D., late Dean of Canterbury. New Edition. 2 Volumes, or 4 Parts. 8vo. 54s. 6d.

The Volumes are sold separately, as follows :—

Vol. 1, Part I.—The Three first Gospels. 12s.
Vol. 1, Part II.—St. John and the Acts. 10s. 6d.
Vol. 2, Part I.—The Epistles of St. Paul. 16s.
Vol. 2, Part II.—Hebrews to Revelation. 16s.

The Holy Bible; with Notes and Introductions.

By CHR. WORDSWORTH, D.D., Bishop of Lincoln. New Edition. 6 Vols. Imperial 8vo. 120*s*.

The Volumes are sold separately, as follows :—

Vol. I.—The Pentateuch. 25*s*.
Vol. II.—Joshua to Samuel. 15*s*.
Vol. III.—Kings to Esther. 15*s*.
Vol. IV.—Job to Song of Solomon. 25*s*.
Vol. V.—Isaiah to Ezekiel. 25*s*.
Vol. VI.—Daniel, Minor Prophets, and Index. 15*s*.

The New Testament of our Lord and

Saviour JESUS CHRIST, in the original Greek ; with Notes, Introductions, and Indices. By CHR. WORDSWORTH, D.D., Bishop of Lincoln. New Edition. 2 Vols. Imperial 8vo. 60*s*.

The Volumes are sold separately, as follows :—

Vol. I.—Gospels and Acts. 23*s*.
Vol. II.—Epistles, Apocalypse, and Index. 37*s*.

Notes on the Greek Testament. The

Gospel according to S. Luke. By the Rev. ARTHUR CARR, M.A., Assistant-Master at Wellington College, late Fellow of Oriel College, Oxford. Crown 8vo. 6*s*.

"It is a most useful and scholarly work, well adapted to the higher classes of public schools and the students at our colleges."—STANDARD.

"The notes are brief, scholarly, and based on the best authorities. . . . The introduction will be found to be of especial value to the young student, informing him, as it does, of the Greek manuscripts which form the basis of the Greek text, and giving a most thorough and comprehensive account of S. Luke's life and the style of his writing."—SCHOOL BOARD CHRONICLE.

"Grammatical peculiarities are brought into the foreground, and contrasted with classical usages ; questions of various reading are carefully noted ;

historical and archæological information is supplied plentifully when needful to illustrate a passage ; the drift of a narrative or discourse and the sequence of the thoughts is traced out and carefully analysed ; in short, the Gospel is treated as we treat a classical author, and the student is here supplied with an apparatus criticus superior in kind and completeness to any we have ever seen afforded to him for the purpose elsewhere. A very clever and taking book."—LITERARY CHURCHMAN.

"Admirably adapted for the use of those who begin the study of the New Testament in the original after having acquired a fair acquaintance with classical Greek."—SCOTSMAN.

The Annotated Bible, being a House-

hold Commentary upon the Holy Scriptures, comprehending the Results of Modern Discovery and Criticism. By the Rev. JOHN HENRY BLUNT, M.A., F.S.A., Editor of "The Annotated Book of Common Prayer," "The Dictionary of Theology," etc. etc. Three Vols. Demy 4to, with Maps, etc.

Vol. I. (668 pages.)—Containing the GENERAL INTRODUCTION, with Text and Annotations on the Books from GENESIS to ESTHER. 31s. 6d.

Vol. II. (720 pages.)—Completing the OLD TESTAMENT and APOCRYPHA. 31s. 6d.

This Work has been written with the object of providing for educated readers a compact intellectual exposition of the Holy Bible, in which they may find such explanations and illustrations of the Sacred Books as will meet the necessities of the ordinary, as distinguished from the laboriously learned, inquirer of the present day. Great care has been taken to compress as much information as possible into the Annotations by condensed language, by giving the results of inquiry without adding the detailed reasonings by which those results have been arrived at, by occupying scarcely any space with controversy, and by casting much matter into a tabular form.

Every book has an Introduction prefixed to it, which gives some account of its authorship, date, contents, object, and such other particulars as will put the reader in possession of the best modern conclusions on these subjects. The Annotations are also illustrated by text maps and other engravings when necessary, and full-page coloured maps are added for the general illustration of Biblical Geography from the best authorities.

The Commentary is preceded by a General Introduction, which contains chapters on the Literary History of the Bible (illustrated by engraved facsimiles, and by specimens of English Bibles from the tenth to the seventeenth centuries), on the trustworthiness of the Bible in its existing form, the revelation and inspiration of Holy Scripture, the interpretation of Holy Scripture, and the liturgical use of the Bible. There are also special Introductions to the New Testament and the Apocrypha.

"*We do not know any one publication in which the great mass of facts relating to the language, the transcription, the versions, and the extant copies of the Bible is contained in a form at once so comprehensive, so brief and succinct, and so pleasant to peruse. . . . The annotation all through is just what it should be, brief, suggestive, and clear.*"—CHURCH QUARTERLY REVIEW.

"*Only those who have made a regular study of the subject can even guess what a quantity of reading has been necessary to put before the reader the results here set down.*"—CHURCH TIMES.

"*Alike in the critical introduction of eighty pages, in the introduction to each book, and in the notes, which are more extensive than the sacred text, the Bible is treated as a literary book on its human side, and as a completely inspired authority on its Divine side. Criticism, exegetics, and dogmatics, meet in a more harmonious unity than we have yet seen in the work of any one author on Scripture.*"—EDINBURGH DAILY REVIEW.

"*The work, to which the Editor must have devoted immense zeal and labour, promises to be, when completed, a valuable addition to Biblical literature.*"—MANCHESTER EXAMINER.

"*We are sure this 'Annotated Bible' will be rapidly recognised as a very important and valuable aid for Bible readers.*"—CHURCH REVIEW.

An Introduction to the Devotional

Study of the Holy Scriptures: with a Prefatory Essay on their Inspiration, and specimens of Meditations on various passages of them. By EDWARD MEYRICK GOULBURN, D.D., Dean of Norwich. Tenth Edition, revised and enlarged. Small 8vo. 6s. 6d.

" The value of this work is too well known to need any notice on our part. The sale of nine large editions is sufficient evidence of its appreciation. In this, the tenth edition, the author has added an essay on the Inspiration of Scripture, and appended some meditations originally printed in a detached form. By so doing he has added to the completeness, and therefore to the value of the volume. It is strictly of a devotional character, though in saying this we would not imply that the intellectual element was at all wanted. In its present form it will be welcomed by the devout members of the Church, and will assist in the devotional study of the Word of God."—JOHN BULL.

" When a book has reached its tenth edition little can be said in favour of its usefulness. It has proved its value by its popularity. This is the case with this volume of Dean Goulburn's. Still there will be many who have not yet made personal use of it, and to such we can heartily recommend this new edition. Previous to this issue, the whole work has been thoroughly reconsidered and revised, the essay on Inspiration re-written, and a series of Meditations added. The whole forms a most desirable companion for all who seek to attain to a greater knowledge of the inner and spiritual teaching of Holy Writ."—NATIONAL CHURCH.

The Microscope of the New Testament.

By the late Rev. WILLIAM SEWELL, D.D., formerly Fellow of Exeter College, sometime Professor of Moral Philosophy in the University of Oxford, and Whitehall Preacher. Edited by the Rev. W. J. CRICHTON, M.A. 8vo. 14s.

" The style of the book, in which the results of the most scholarly investigations are set forth in comparatively popular language, ought to recommend it not only to the systematic Biblical student, but to the general reader whose mind is capable of being attracted by an earnest treatment of the grandest subject to which the human intellect can lead itself." — MANCHESTER COURIER.

" Will be a work of deep interest to reverent investigators of the Greek of the sacred canon. . . . Much light is thrown on various controverted passages of the New Testament, many difficulties *are removed, and many obscure passages fully elucidated. We may instance as truly valuable additions to Biblical criticism the essays on " The Accounts of the Resurrection," and " The Last Scenes of our Lord's Life." Indeed, all earnest Biblical scholars will do well to procure this volume, and make it for a time their constant companion. We venture to think that when it has been so used, it will for the future be kept within easy reach for constant reference. It takes a laborious lifetime to produce such results as these."*—NATIONAL CHURCH.

Analytical Notes on Obadiah and

Habakuk, for the use of Hebrew Students. By the Rev. WILLIAM RANDOLPH, M.A., of St. John's College, Cambridge. 8vo. 5s. 6d.

"*Show a thoughtful study of the original, without the advantage of many modern appliances.*"—ACADEMY.

"*Mr. Randolph is filling up a serious gap in exegetical literature, and has attempted to do for individual parts of the Hebrew Testament what Ellicott, Lightfoot, and others are doing for portions of the Greek Testament. We are glad to see he promises, if encouraged, to follow this volume up 'by others of a similar character.' Mr. Randolph's accurate distinctions of Hebrew words, and the pains he is at to convey the true meaning of the* original, show him to be a laborious and conscientious worker.*"—IRISH ECCLESIASTICAL GAZETTE.

"*This is intended for the use of Hebrew students, who will find here valuable help in mastering the subtle niceties of diction, the emphatic forms, and the artificial arrangement of sentences, so characteristic of the original. The accuracy of its Hebrew scholarship, and its clear insight into the most abstruse difficulties of the language made use of by this prophetical writer, render the work invaluable even to the scholar.*"—NATIONAL CHURCH.

The Psalms. Translated from the Hebrew.

With Notes, chiefly Exegetical. By WILLIAM KAY, D.D., Rector of Great Leghs, late Principal of Bishop's College, Calcutta. Third Edition. 8vo. 12s. 6d.

"*Like a sound Churchman, he reverences Scripture, upholding its authority against sceptics; and he does not denounce such as differ from him in opinion with a dogmatism unhappily too common at the present day. Hence, readers will be disposed to consider his conclusions worthy of attention; or perhaps to adopt them without inquiry. It is superfluous to say that the translation is better and more accurate on the whole than our received one, or that it often reproduces the sense of the original happily.*"—ATHENÆUM.

"*Dr. Kay has profound reverence for Divine truth, and exhibits considerable reading, with the power to* make use of it.*"—BRITISH QUARTERLY REVIEW.

"*The execution of the work is careful and scholarly.*"—UNION REVIEW.

"*To mention the name of Dr. Kay is enough to secure respectful attention to his new translation of the Psalms. It is enriched with exegetical notes containing a wealth of sound learning, closely occasionally, perhaps too closely condensed. Good care is taken of the student not learned in Hebrew; we hope the Doctor's example will prevent any abuse of this consideration, and stimulate those who profit by it to follow him into the very text of the ancient Revelation.*"—JOHN BULL.

Ecclesiastes: the Authorized Version, with

a running Commentary and Paraphrase. By the Rev. THOS. PELHAM DALE, M.A., Rector of St. Vedast with St. Michael City of London, and late Fellow of Sidney Sussex College, Cambridge. 8vo. 7s. 6d.

Ruling Ideas in Early Ages and their

Relation to Old Testament Faith. Lectures delivered to Graduates of the University of Oxford. By J. B. MOZLEY, D.D., late Canon of Christ Church, and Regius Professor of Divinity in the University of Oxford. Second Edition. 8vo. 10s. 6d.

"*Has all the same marks of a powerful and original mind which we observed in the volume of University Sermons. Indeed, as a continuous study of the rudimentary conditions of human thought, even as developed under the immediate guidance of a Divine Teacher, this volume has a higher intellectual interest than the last.*"—SPECTATOR.

"*Canon Mozley's volume must undeniably, we think, stand in the very front rank for its combination of philosophic breadth and depth of insight, with a thoroughly reverent treatment of its subject. . . . Treated with great ability, and with much richness of illustration. . . . They are entirely worthy of those on which we have commented.*"—GUARDIAN.

"*One of the most remarkable books in the department of theology that has appeared in the present generation. Dr. Mozley has won a place in the foremost rank of religious philosophers. . . . It is a bold but successful attempt to explain the peculiar morality recognised in certain transactions of the Old Testament upon rational grounds. For the first time in our experience we have met with a satisfactory solution of what all students of the Bible have felt to be a most difficult problem. . . . We commend Dr Mozley's work as one which will accomplish in our day what Bishop Butler's did in his. It is one which should be read and studied by everybody.*" — CHURCHMAN (New York).

A Companion to the Old Testament;

being a Plain Commentary on Scripture History, down to the Birth of our Lord. Small 8vo. 3s. 6d.

"*A very compact summary of the Old Testament narrative, put together so as to explain the connection and bearing of its contents, and written in a very good tone; with a final chapter on the history of the Jews between the Old and New Testaments. It will be found very useful for its purpose. It does not confine itself to merely chronological difficulties, but comments briefly upon the religious bearing of the text also.*"—GUARDIAN.

"*A most admirable Companion to the Old Testament, being far the most concise yet complete commentary on Old Testament history with which we have met. Here are combined orthodoxy and learning, an intelligent and at the same time interesting summary of the leading facts of the sacred story. It should be a text-book in every school, and its value is immensely enhanced by the copious and complete index.*"—JOHN BULL.

"*This will be found a very valuable aid to the right understanding of the Bible. It throws the whole Scripture narrative into one from the creation downwards, the author thus condensing Prideaux, Shuckford, and Russell, and in the most reverential manner bringing to his aid the writings of all modern annotators and chronologists. The book is one that should have a wide circulation amongst teachers and students of all denominations.*"—BOOKSELLER.

"*The handbook before us is so full and satisfactory, considering its compass, and sets forth the history of the old covenant with such conscientious minuteness, that it cannot fail to prove a godsend to candidates for examination in the Rudimenta Religionis as well as in the corresponding school at Cambridge.*"—ENGLISH CHURCHMAN.

A Key to the Narrative of the Four

Gospels. By the Rev. JOHN PILKINGTON NORRIS, B.D., Canon of Bristol, Vicar of St. Mary Redcliffe, and Examining Chaplain to the Bishop of Manchester. New Edition. Small 8vo. 2s. 6d. Also a Cheap Edition, 1s. 6d.

Forming a Volume of "Keys to Christian Knowledge."

*"This is very much the best book of its kind we have seen. The only fault is its shortness, which prevents its going into the details which would support and illustrate its statements. It is, however, a great improvement upon any book of its kind we know. It bears all the marks of being the condensed work of a real scholar, and of a divine too. The bulk of the book is taken up with a 'Life of Christ,' compiled from the Four Gospels, so as to exhibit its steps and stages and salient points."—*LITERARY CHURCHMAN.

*"This book is no ordinary compendium, no mere 'cram-book;' still less is it an ordinary reading-book for schools; but the schoolmaster, the Sunday-school teacher, and the seeker after a comprehensive knowledge of Divine truth will find it worthy of its name. Canon Norris writes simply, reverently, without great display of learning, giving the result of much careful study in a short compass, and adorning the subject by the tenderness and honesty with which he treats it. We hope that this little book will have a very wide circulation, and that it will be studied; and we can promise that those who take it up will not readily put it down again."—*RECORD.

"This is a golden little volume. . . . Its design is exceedingly modest. Canon Norris writes primarily to help 'younger students' in studying the Gospels. But this unpretending volume is one which all students may study with advantage. It is an admirable manual for those who take Bible Classes through the Gospels. Closely sifted in style, so that all is clear and weighty; full of unostentatious learning, and pregnant with suggestion; deeply reverent and altogether Evangelical in spirit; Canon Norris's book supplies a real want, and ought to be welcomed by all earnest and devout students of the Holy Gospels."—LONDON QUARTERLY REVIEW.

A Key to the Narrative of the Acts of

the Apostles. By the Rev. JOHN PILKINGTON NORRIS, B.D., Canon of Bristol, Vicar of St. Mary Redcliffe, and Examining Chaplain to the Bishop of Manchester. New Edition. Small 8vo. 2s. 6d. Also a Cheap Edition, 1s. 6d.

Forming a Volume of "Keys to Christian Knowledge."

*"The book is one which we can heartily recommend."—*SPECTATOR.

*"Few books have ever given us more unmixed pleasure than this."—*LITERARY CHURCHMAN.

*"This is a sequel to Canon Norris's 'Key to the Gospels,' which was published two years ago, and which has become a general favourite. The sketch of the Acts of the Apostles is done in the same style; there is the same reverent spirit and quiet enthusiasm running through it, and the same instinct for seizing the leading points in the narrative."—*RECORD.

A Devotional Commentary on the

Gospel Narrative. By the Rev. ISAAC WILLIAMS, B.D., formerly Fellow of Trinity College, Oxford. New Edition. 8 Vols. Crown 8vo. 5*s.* each. Sold separately. Or the Eight Volumes may be had in a Box, 45*s.*

THOUGHTS ON THE STUDY OF THE HOLY GOSPELS.

Characteristic Differences in the Four Gospels—Our Lord's Manifestations of Himself—The Rule of Scriptural Interpretation furnished by our Lord—Analogies of the Gospel—Mention of Angels in the Gospels—Places of our Lord's Abode and Ministry—Our Lord's mode of dealing with His Apostles—Conclusion.

A HARMONY OF THE FOUR EVANGELISTS.

Our Lord's Nativity—Our Lord's Ministry (second year)—Our Lord's Ministry (third year)—The Holy Week—Our Lord's Passion—Our Lord's Resurrection.

OUR LORD'S NATIVITY.

The Birth at Bethlehem—The Baptism in Jordan—The First Passover.

OUR LORD'S MINISTRY (Second Year).

The Second Passover—Christ with the Twelve—The Twelve sent forth.

OUR LORD'S MINISTRY (Third Year).

Teaching in Galilee—Teaching at Jerusalem—Last Journey from Galilee to Jerusalem.

THE HOLY WEEK.

The Approach to Jerusalem—The Teaching in the Temple—The Discourse on the Mount of Olives—The Last Supper.

OUR LORD'S PASSION.

The Hour of Darkness—The Agony—The Apprehension—The Condemnation—The Day of Sorrows—The Hall of Judgment—The Crucifixion—The Sepulture.

OUR LORD'S RESURRECTION.

The Day of Days—The Grave Visited—Christ appearing—The going to Emmaus—The Forty Days—The Apostles assembled—The Lake of Galilee—The Mountain in Galilee—The Return from Galilee.

" There is not a better companion to be found for the season than the beautiful ' Devotional Commentary on the Gospel Narrative,' by the Rev. Isaac Williams. A rich mine for devotional and theological study."—GUARDIAN.

" So infinite are the depths and so innumerable the beauties of Scripture, and more particularly of the Gospels, that there is some difficulty in describing the manifold excellences of Williams' exquisite Commentary. Deriving its profound appreciation of Scripture from the writings of the early Fathers, it is only what every student knows must be true to say, that it extracts a whole wealth of meaning from each sentence, each apparently faint allusion, each word in the text."—CHURCH REVIEW.

" Stands absolutely alone in our English literature; there is, we should say, no chance of its being superseded by any better book of its kind; and its merits are of the very highest order."—LITERARY CHURCHMAN.

Waterloo Place, London

WILLIAMS' DEVOTIONAL COMMENTARY—*Continued.*

" This is, in the truest sense of the word, a ' Devotional Commentary' on the Gospel narrative, opening out everywhere, as it does, the spiritual beauties and blessedness of the Divine message; but it is something more than this, it meets difficulties almost by anticipation, and throws the light of learning over some of the very darkest passages in the New Testament."—ROCK.

"It would be difficult to select a more useful present, at a small cost, than this series would be to a young man on his first entering into Holy Orders, and many, no doubt, will avail themselves of the republication of these useful volumes for this purpose. There is an abundance of sermon material to be drawn from any one of them." — CHURCH TIMES.

Female Characters of Holy Scripture.

A Series of Sermons. By the Rev. ISAAC WILLIAMS, B.D., formerly Fellow of Trinity College, Oxford. New Edition. Crown 8vo. 5*s*.

CONTENTS.

Eve—Sarah—Lot's Wife—Rebekah—Leah and Rachel—Miriam—Rahab—Deborah—Ruth—Hannah—The Witch of Endor—Bathsheba—Rizpah—The Queen of Sheba—The Widow of Zarephath—Jezebel—The Shunammite—Esther—Elizabeth—Anna—The Woman of Samaria—Joanna—The Woman with the Issue of Blood—The Woman of Canaan—Martha—Mary—Salome—The Wife of Pilate—Dorcas—The Blessed Virgin.

The Characters of the Old Testament.

A Series of Sermons. By the Rev. ISAAC WILLIAMS, B.D., formerly Fellow of Trinity College, Oxford. New Edition. Crown 8vo. 5*s*.

CONTENTS.

Adam—Abel and Cain—Noah—Abraham—Lot—Jacob and Esau—Joseph—Moses—Aaron—Pharaoh—Korah, Dathan, and Abiram—Balaam—Joshua—Samson—Samuel—Saul—David—Solomon—Elijah—Ahab—Elisha—Hezekiah—Josiah—Jeremiah—Ezekiel—Daniel—Joel—Job—Isaiah—The Antichrist.

The Apocalypse. With Notes and Reflections.

By the Rev ISAAC WILLIAMS, B.D., formerly Fellow of Trinity College, Oxford. New Edition. Crown 8vo. 5*s*.

Beginning of the Book of Genesis,

with Notes and Reflections. By the Rev. ISAAC WILLIAMS, B.D., formerly Fellow of Trinity College, Oxford. Small 8vo. 7*s*. 6*d*.

Short Notes on the Greek Text of

the Acts of the Apostles. By J. HAMBLIN SMITH, M.A., of Gonville and Caius College, late Lecturer in Classics at S. Peter's College, Cambridge.   Crown 8vo.   4s. 6d.

" This reprint of notes drawn up by the editor for the use of his own pupils twelve years ago, will be found most useful by all young students of the original text of the Book of the Acts. Believing that its author, in connection with his visit to Syracuse, studied the account of the Sicilian Expedition, Mr. Smith makes many references to Thucydides, whose sixth book has a large number of words and phrases in common with the Acts of the Apostles." —EDINBURGH DAILY REVIEW.

" These notes are the product of a careful study of the most recent and the most successful commentators. The classical and non-classical idioms are carefully explained, the historical allusions fully illustrated, and especial attention is given to derivation and technical scholarship, especially respecting the Greek synonyms, tenses, and particles. The geography and Church history of the Acts have considerable attention given to them, and in no other work on the subject intended for the young is this department of annotation wrought out so fully and serviceably for the young.' —SCHOOL BOARD CHRONICLE.

Ecclesiastes for English Readers.   The

Book called by the Jews Koheleth.   Newly translated, with Introduction, Analysis, and Notes.   By the Rev. W. H. B. PROBY, M.A., formerly Tyrwhitt Hebrew Scholar in the University of Cambridge.   8vo.   4s. 6d.

The Ten Canticles of the Old Testa-

ment Canon, namely, the Songs of Moses (First and Second), Deborah, Hannah, Isaiah (First, Second, and Third), Hezekiah, Jonah, and Habakkuk.   Newly translated, with Notes and Remarks on their Drift and Use.   By the Rev. W. H. B. PROBY, M.A., formerly Tyrwhitt Hebrew Scholar in the University of Cambridge.   8vo.   5s.

Genesis.   With Notes.   [The Hebrew Text,

with Literal Translation.]   By the Rev. G. V. GARLAND, M.A., late Vicar of Aslacton, Norfolk.   8vo.   21s.

The Acts of the Deacons; being a

Commentary, Critical and Practical, upon the Notices of St. Stephen and St. Philip the Evangelist, contained in the Acts of the Apostles.   By EDWARD MEYRICK GOULBURN, D.D., Dean of Norwich.   Second Edition.   Small 8vo.   6s.

A Key to the Knowledge and Use of

the Holy Bible. By the Rev. JOHN HENRY BLUNT, M.A., F.S.A., Editor of the "Dictionary of Theology," &c. &c. New Edition. Small 8vo. 2s. 6d. Also a Cheap Edition, 1s. 6d. Forming a Volume of "Keys to Christian Knowledge."

" Another of Mr. Blunt's useful and workmanlike compilations, which will be most acceptable as a household book, or in schools and colleges. It is a capital book too for schoolmasters and pupil teachers. Its subject is arranged under the heads of—I. The Literary History of the Bible. II. Old Testament Writers and Writings. III. New Testament ditto. IV. Revelation and Inspiration. V. Objects of the Bible. VI. Interpretation of ditto. VII. The Bible a guide to Faith. VIII. The Apocrypha. IX. The Apocryphal Books associated with the New Testament. Lastly, there is a serviceable appendix of peculiar Bible words and their meanings."—LITERARY CHURCHMAN.

" We have much pleasure in recommending a capital handbook by the learned Editor of ' The Annotated Book of Common Prayer.'"—CHURCH TIMES.

" Merits commendation, for the lucid and orderly arrangement in which it presents a considerable amount of valuable and interesting matter."—RECORD.

Daniel the Prophet: Nine Lectures

delivered in the Divinity School of the University of Oxford. With copious Notes. By the Rev. E. B. PUSEY, D.D., Regius Professor of Hebrew, Canon of Christ Church, Oxford. Third Edition. 8vo. 10s. 6d.

Commentary on the Minor Prophets;

with Introductions to the several Books. By the Rev. E. B. PUSEY, D.D., Regius Professor of Hebrew, Canon of Christ Church, Oxford. 4to. 31s. 6d.

Parts I., II., III., IV., V., 5s. each. Part VI., 6s.

The Mystery of Christ: being an Exa-

mination of the Doctrine contained in the First Three Chapters of the Epistle of Paul the Apostle to the Ephesians. By GEORGE STAUNTON BARROW, M.A., Vicar of Stowmarket. Crown 8vo. 7s. 6d.

Bible Readings for Family Prayer.
By the Rev. W. H. RIDLEY, M.A., Rector of Hambleden.
Crown 8vo.

Old Testament—Genesis and Exodus.   2s.
The Four Gospels, 3s. 6d.
St. Matthew and St. Mark. 2s.
St. Luke and St. John. 2s.
The Acts of the Apostles, 2s.

A Complete Concordance to the Old
and the New Testament; or, a Dictionary, and Alphabetical Index to the Bible, in two Parts.   To which is added, a Concordance to the Apocrypha.   By ALEXANDER CRUDEN, M.A.   With a Life of the Author, by ALEXANDER CHALMERS, F.S.A., and a Portrait.   Sixteenth Edition.   4to.   21s.

The Inspiration of Holy Scripture, its
Nature and Proof.   Eight Discourses preached before the University of Dublin.   By WILLIAM LEE, D.D., Archdeacon of Dublin.   Fourth Edition.   8vo.   15s.

On the Inspiration of the Bible.   Five
Lectures delivered at Westminster Abbey.   By CHR. WORDSWORTH, D.D., Bishop of Lincoln.   Eighth Edition.   Small 8vo.   1s. 6d., or in paper cover, 1s.

Syntax and Synonyms of the Greek
Testament.   By the Rev. WILLIAM WEBSTER, M.A., late Fellow of Queen's College, Cambridge.   8vo.   9s.

3. Devotional Works

Library of Spiritual Works for English Catholics.

Elegantly printed with red borders, on extra superfine toned paper. Small 8vo. 5*s.* each.

OF THE IMITATION OF CHRIST. In 4 Books. By THOMAS À KEMPIS. A New Translation.

THE CHRISTIAN YEAR: Thoughts in Verse for the Sundays and Holydays throughout the Year.

THE SPIRITUAL COMBAT; together with the Supplement and the Path of Paradise. By LAURENCE SCUPOLI. A New Translation.

THE DEVOUT LIFE. By S. FRANCIS DE SALES, Bishop and Prince of Geneva. A New Translation.

THE LOVE OF GOD. By S. FRANCIS DE SALES, Bishop and Prince of Geneva. A New Translation.

THE CONFESSIONS OF S. AUGUSTINE. In 10 Books. A New Translation.

The Volumes can also be had in Morocco and other extra bindings.

Cheap Editions, 32*mo, cloth limp,* 6*d. each, or cloth extra, red edges,* 1*s. each.*

Of the Imitation of Christ.	The Hidden Life of the Soul.
The Spiritual Combat.	Spiritual Letters of S. Francis de
The Christian Year.	Sales.

These Five Volumes, cloth extra, may be had in a Box, price 7*s.*

[Other Volumes are in preparation.]

The Child Samuel. A Practical and
Devotional Commentary on the Birth and Childhood of the
Prophet Samuel, as recorded in 1 Sam. i., ii. 1-27, iii. De-
signed as a Help to Meditation on the Holy Scriptures for
Children and Young Persons. By EDWARD MEYRICK GOUL-
BURN, D.D., Dean of Norwich. Small 8vo. 5*s*.

The Gospel of the Childhood: a Practi-
cal and Devotional Commentary on the Single Incident of our
Blessed Lord's Childhood (St. Luke ii. 41 to the end) ; designed
as a Help to Meditation on the Holy Scriptures, for Children
and Young Persons. By EDWARD MEYRICK GOULBURN,
D.D., Dean of Norwich. Second Edition. Square crown 8vo.
5*s*.

Thoughts on Personal Religion ; being
a Treatise on the Christian Life in its Two Chief Elements,
Devotion and Practice. By EDWARD MEYRICK GOULBURN,
D.D., Dean of Norwich. New Edition. Small 8vo. 6*s*. 6*d*.
Also a Cheap Edition, 3*s*. 6*d*. Presentation Edition, elegantly
printed on Toned Paper. Two vols. Small 8vo. 10*s*. 6*d*.

The Pursuit of Holiness: a Sequel to
"Thoughts on Personal Religion," intended to carry the
Reader somewhat farther onward in the Spiritual Life. By
EDWARD MEYRICK GOULBURN, D.D. Sixth Edition.
Small 8vo. 5*s*. Also a Cheap Edition, 3*s*. 6*d*.

Short Devotional Forms, for Morn-
ing, Night, and Midnight, and for the Third, Sixth, Ninth
Hours and Eventide of each Day of the Week. Arranged to
meet the Exigencies of a Busy Life. By EDWARD MEYRICK
GOULBURN, D.D. Fourth Edition. 32mo. 1*s*. 6*d*.

The Star of Childhood: a First Book of
Prayers and Instruction for Children. Compiled by a Priest.
Edited by the Rev. T. T. CARTER, M.A., Rector of Clewer.
With Illustrations. Fourth Edition. Square 16mo. 2s. 6d.

The Way of Life: a Book of Prayers and
Instruction for the Young at School, with a Preparation for
Confirmation. Compiled by a Priest. Edited by the Rev.
T. T. CARTER, M.A. Second Edition. 18mo. 1s. 6d.

The Path of Holiness: a First Book of
Prayers, with the Service of the Holy Communion, for the
Young. Compiled by a Priest. Edited by the Rev. T. T.
CARTER, M.A. With Illustrations. Third Edition. Crown
16mo. 1s. 6d.; cloth limp, 1s.

The Treasury of Devotion: a Manual of
Prayer for General and Daily Use. Compiled by a Priest.
Edited by the Rev. T. T. CARTER, M.A. New Edition, in
Large Type. Crown 8vo. 5s.
    Smaller Edition. 18mo. 2s. 6d.; cloth limp, 2s., or
bound with the Book of Common Prayer, 3s. 6d.

The Guide to Heaven: a Book of Prayers
for every Want. (For the Working Classes.) Compiled by
a Priest. Edited by the Rev. T. T. CARTER, M.A. Seventh
Edition. 18mo. 1s. 6d.; cloth limp, 1s.
    Large-Type Edition. Crown 8vo. 1s. 6d.; cloth limp, 1s.

Meditations on the Life and Mysteries
of Our Lord and Saviour Jesus Christ. From the French.
By the Compiler of "The Treasury of Devotion." Edited by
the Rev. T. T. CARTER, M.A. Crown 8vo.
    Vol. I.—The Hidden Life of Our Lord. 3s. 6d.
    Vol. II.—The Public Life of Our Lord. 2 Parts. 5s. each.
    Vol. III.—The Suffering Life and the Glorified Life of Our
    Lord. 3s. 6d.

Prayers and Meditations for the Holy

Communion. By JOSEPHINE FLETCHER. With a Preface by C. J. ELLICOTT, D.D., Lord Bishop of Gloucester and Bristol. With red rubrics and borders. New Edition. Royal 32mo. 2s. 6d. An Edition without the red rubrics. 32mo. Cloth limp. 1s.

" Devout beauty is the special character of this new manual, and it ought to be a favourite. Rarely has it happened to us to meet with so remarkable a combination of thorough practicalness with that almost poetic warmth which is the highest flower of genuine devotion."—LITERARY CHURCHMAN.

" The Bishop recommends it to the newly confirmed, to the tender-hearted and the devout, as having been compiled by a youthful person, and as being marked by a peculiar ' freshness.' We have pleasure in seconding the recommendations of the good Bishop. We know of no more suitable manual for the newly confirmed, and nothing more likely to engage the sympathies of youthful hearts. There is a union of the deepest spirit of devotion, a rich expression of experimental life, with a due recognition of the *objects of faith, such as is not always to be found, but which characterises this manual in an eminent degree."*—CHURCH REVIEW.

" Among the supply of Eucharistic Manuals, one deserves special attention and commendation. ' Prayers and Meditations' merits the Bishop of Gloucester's epithets of ' warm, devout, and fresh.' And it is thoroughly English Church besides."—GUARDIAN.

" We are by no means surprised that Bishop Ellicott should have been so much struck with this little work, on accidentally seeing it in manuscript, as to urge its publication, and to preface it with his commendation. The devotion which it breathes is truly fervent, and the language attractive, and as proceeding from a young person the work is altogether not a little striking."—RECORD.

Words to Take with Us. A Manual of

Daily and Occasional Prayers, for Private and Common Use. With Plain Instructions and Counsels on Prayer. By W. E. SCUDAMORE, M.A., Rector of Ditchingham, and formerly Fellow of S. John's College, Cambridge. Fifth Edition, revised. Small 8vo. 2s. 6d.

Sunday Evenings in the Family.

Being Expositions of the Gospels and Articles of the Church of England. Small 8vo. 3s.

Private Devotions for School-boys;

with Rules of Conduct. By WILLIAM HENRY, Third Lord Lyttelton. New Edition. 32mo. 6d.

For Days and Years. A Book contain-

ing a Text, Short Reading, and Hymn for every Day in the Church's Year. Selected by H. L. SIDNEY LEAR. 16mo. 2s. 6d.

" Here are no platitudes, no mere 'goody' talk; there is in each day's portion sound and healthful food for the mind and soul, and also for the imagination, whose need of support and guidance is too often forgotten. Text and comment and hymn are chosen with a pure and cultured taste, and by the religious earnestness which they show, tend to develop it in the reader. The book is, in fact, the best of its kind we have ever seen, and for the use of church people ought to supersede all others."—LITERARY CHURCHMAN.

" Will be found exceedingly useful to those who thoughtfully read its con- *tents. The readings have been carefully selected from the writings of some of the most eminent divines of ancient and modern times with whose names the majority of our readers will be familiar. The compiler has displayed considerable tact and judgment in making judicious selections, and in the general arrangement of the contents. This volume commends itself to the consideration of all devoted members of the Church."*—COURT CIRCULAR.

" We heartily commend both the plan and the execution. . . . The author has proved that good may be got from men of the most diverse minds."—ENGLISH CHURCHMAN.

A Selection from Pascal's Thoughts.

Translated by H. L. SIDNEY LEAR. Square 16mo. Printed on Dutch hand-made paper. 3s. 6d.

" We should think highly of the spirituality and intellectual tastes of the man or woman who turned to this little book whenever the soul was weary, or the mind dull, or the heart careworn, or the spirit was aspiring.'—EDINBURGH DAILY REVIEW.

" Makes a charming little volume. Pascal is always of interest. . . . The Selection has been made with taste."—EXAMINER.

" Will be welcome as a gift-book, and will enrich and purify the mind of its readers, and suggests thoughts especially valuable in time of perplexity and doubt, as indeed all times *are on this troublous earth. The simple-hearted, the learned, the witty, and the devout, all may learn something from these thoughts, and will certainly be the better for the learning."*—JOHN BULL.

" An unusually excellent specimen of translation. [The translator] has a delicate sense for style, both French and English; and has the still rarer gift of perceiving and preserving in the latter the literary equivalents of the former language . . . . These selections really put Pascal's thought before us."—NATION (New York).

Faith and Life: Readings for the greater

Holy Days, and the Sundays from Advent to Trinity. Compiled from Ancient Writers. By WILLIAM BRIGHT, D.D., Canon of Christ Church, and Regius Professor of Ecclesiastical History in the University of Oxford. Second Edition. Small 8vo. 5s.

Daily Gleanings of the Saintly Life.

Compiled by C. M. S., with an Introduction by the Rev. M. F. SADLER, M.A., Prebendary of Wells, and Rector of Honiton, Devon.   Small 8vo.   3s. 6d.

"The meditations are entirely taken from the works of 'the leading divines of the Great Catholic Revival in the Church of England in our own day.' The passages chosen are full of chastened beauty and wise instruction, and will bear comparison with the best of the manuals compiled from ancient sources. There is a wholesome Church of England tone about this volume not always to be found in manuals of this description."—NATIONAL CHURCH.

Self-Renunciation.   From the French.

With an Introduction by the Rev. T. T. CARTER, M.A., Rector of Clewer, Berks.   Crown 8vo.   6s.

Also a Cheap Edition.   Small 8vo.   3s. 6d.

"It is excessively difficult to review or criticise, in detail, a book of this kind, and yet its abounding merits, its practicalness, its searching good sense and thoroughness, and its frequent beauty, too, make us wish to do something more than announce its publication. . . . . The style is eminently clear, free from redundance and prolixity."—LITERARY CHURCHMAN.

"Few save Religious and those brought into immediate contact with them are, in all probability, acquainted with the French treatise of Guilloré, a portion of which is now, for the first time we believe, done into English. . . . . Hence the suitableness of such a book as this for those who, in the midst of their families, are endeavouring to advance in the spiritual life. Hundreds of devout souls living in the world have been encouraged and helped by such books as Dr. Neale's 'Sermons preached in a Religious House.' For such the present work will be found appropriate, while for Religious themselves it will be invaluable."—CHURCH TIMES.

Spiritual Guidance.   With an Introduc-

tion by the Rev. T. T. CARTER, M.A., Rector of Clewer, Berks.   Crown 8vo.   6s.

EXTRACT FROM PREFACE.

["The special object of the volume is to supply practical advice in matters of conscience, such as may be generally applicable. While it offers, as it is hoped, much valuable help to Directors, it is full of suggestions, which may be useful to any one in private. It thus fulfils a double purpose, which is not, as far as I am aware, otherwise provided for, at least, not in so full and direct a manner."]

"As a work intended for general use, it will be found to contain much valuable help, and may be profitably studied by any one who is desiring to make progress in spiritual life. Much of the contents of this little book will be found more or less applicable to all persons amid the ordinary difficulties and trials of life, and a help to the training of the mind in habits of self-discipline."—CHURCH TIMES.

Voices of Comfort. Edited by the Rev.

THOMAS VINCENT FOSBERY, M.A., sometime Vicar of St. Giles's, Reading. · Fourth Edition. Crown 8vo. 7s. 6d.

[This Volume, of prose and poetry, original and selected, aims at revealing the fountains of hope and joy which underlie the griefs and sorrows of life.

It is so divided as to afford readings for a month. The key-note of each day is given by the title prefixed to it, such as: 'The Power of the Cross of Christ, Day 6. Conflicts of the Soul, Day 17. The Communion of Saints, Day 20. The Comforter, Day 22. The Light of Hope, Day 25. The Coming of Christ, Day 28.' Each day begins with passages of Holy Scripture. These are followed by articles in prose, which are succeeded by one or more short prayers. After these are Poems or passages of poetry, and then very brief extracts in prose or verse close the section. The book is meant to meet, not merely cases of bereavement or physical suffering, but 'to minister specially to the hidden troubles of the heart, as they are silently weaving their dark threads into the web of the seemingly brightest life.']

Hymns and Poems for the Sick and

Suffering. In connexion with the Service for the Visitation of the Sick. Selected from various Authors. Edited by the Rev. THOMAS VINCENT FOSBERY, M.A., sometime Vicar of St. Giles's, Reading. New Edition. Small 8vo. 3s. 6d.

[This Volume contains 233 separate pieces; of which about 90 are by writers who lived prior to the eighteenth century; the rest are modern, and some of these original. Amongst the names of the writers (between 70 and 80 in number) occur those of Sir J. Beaumont; Sir T. Brown; F. Davison; Elizabeth of Bohemia; P. Fletcher; G. Herbert; Dean Hickes; Bishop Ken; Norris; Quarles; Sandys; Bishop J. Taylor; Henry Vaughan; and Sir H. Wotton. And of modern writers :—Mrs. Barrett Browning; Bishop Wilberforce; S. T. Coleridge; Sir R. Grant; Miss E. Taylor; W. Wordsworth; Archbishop Trench; Rev. Messrs. Chandler, Keble, Lyte, Monsell, and Moultrie.]

The Christian Year : Thoughts in Verse

for the Sundays and Holydays throughout the Year. New Edition, printed in large type. Crown 8vo. 3s. 6d.

Elegantly printed with red borders. 16mo. 2s. 6d. Cheap Edition, without the red borders, cloth limp, 1s. ; or in paper cover, 6d.

Forming a Volume of "Rivington's Devotional Series."

Also New Editions, forming Volumes of the "Library of Spiritual Works for English Catholics." Small 8vo. 5s. 32mo, cloth limp, 6d. ; cloth extra, 1s. [See page 19.]

Spiritual Letters to Men. By ARCHBISHOP FÉNELON. By the Author of "Life of Fénelon," "Life of S. Francis de Sales," &c. &c. Crown 8vo. 6s.

"*Clergy and laity alike will welcome this volume. Fénelon's religious counsels have always seemed to us to present the most remarkable combination of high principle and practical common-sense, and now in this English dress it is really wonderful how little of the aroma of their original expression has evaporated. Elder clergy will delight in comparing their own experiences with Fénelon's ways of-treating the several classes of cases here taken in hand. To younger clergy it will be quite a series of specimen examples how to deal with that which is daily becoming a larger and larger department of the practical work of any really efficient clergyman, and laymen will find it so straightforward and intelligible, so utterly free from technicality, and so entirely sympathetic with a layman's position, that we hope it will be largely bought and read among them. A more useful work has* rarely been done than giving these letters to English readers."—CHURCH QUARTERLY REVIEW.

"*This volume should take a place amongst the most precious of the Christian classics.*"—NONCONFORMIST.

"*One of those renderings which by faithfulness to their original, and the idiomatic beauty of their style, are real works of art in their way. It is not too much to say that these Letters read as if they had been first written in English, and that by some master-hand. . . . Of the whole book it would be difficult to speak too highly.*"—LITERARY CHURCHMAN.

"*Those who have the 'Life of Fénelon' by this author will not omit to add his 'Spiritual Letters.' They are unique for their delicacy and tenderness of sentiment, their subtle analysis of character, and deep insight into the human heart.*"—CHURCH ECLECTIC (New York).

Spiritual Letters to Women. By ARCHBISHOP FÉNELON. By the Author of "Life of Fénelon," "Life of S. Francis de Sales," &c. &c. Crown 8vo. 6s.

"*As for the 'Spiritual Letters,' they cannot be read too often, and each time we take them up we see new beauties in them. The time to read them is in the early morning, when they seem to breathe the very atmosphere of heaven, and have all the fragrance of fresh spiritual thought about them, as the flowers carry on their bosom the early dew. A stillness of devotion and wrapt contemplation of God and of heavenly things characterizes every page.*"—IRISH ECCLESIASTICAL GAZETTE.

"*Writing such as this will do more to commend religion than all the vain dogmatic thunder in which so many of its professors indulge; whilst the sweet and tender piety which runs* through every page will impress the reader with the highest conceivable respect for the character of the author.*"—MORNING ADVERTISER.

"*This is an exceedingly well-got-up edition, admirably translated, of Fénelon's celebrated 'Spiritual Letters.' The translation is by the author of the valuable Lives of Fénelon and Bossuet, and forms a very suitable companion to the previous work. Of the Letters themselves, there is no need to speak. The judgment to be formed of them depends so much on the point of view from which they are regarded; but any one will be ready to admit the beauty of their thoughts, the grace of their tone, and the nobility of their sentiments.*"—EXAMINER.

A Selection from the Spiritual Letters

of S. Francis de Sales, Bishop and Prince of Geneva. Translated by the Author of "Life of S. Francis de Sales," "A Dominican Artist," &c. &c. Crown 8vo. 6s.

*"It is a collection of epistolary correspondence of rare interest and excellence. With those who have read the Life, there cannot but have been a strong desire to know more of so beautiful a character."—*CHURCH HERALD.

"A few months back we had the pleasure of welcoming the Life of S. Francis de Sales. Here is the promised sequel:—the 'Selection from his Spiritual Letters' then announced:—

*and a great boon it will be to many. The Letters are addressed to people of all sorts:—to men and to women:—to laity and to ecclesiastics, to people living in the world, or at court, and to the inmates of Religious Houses. We hope that with our readers it may be totally needless to urge such a volume on their notice."—*LITERARY CHURCHMAN.

Also a Cheap Edition, forming a Volume of the "Library of Spiritual Works for English Catholics." 32mo, cloth limp, 6d.; cloth extra, 1s. [See page 19.]

A Manual for the Sick; with other

Devotions. By LANCELOT ANDREWES, D.D., sometime Lord Bishop of Winchester. Edited with a Preface by H. P. LIDDON, D.D., Canon of St. Paul's. With Portrait. Third Edition. Large type. 24mo. 2s. 6d.

Our Work for Christ among His

Suffering People. A Book for Hospital Nurses. By M. A. MORRELL. Small 8vo. 2s. 6d.

*" The thoroughly sensible advice contained in this book cannot fail to be of the highest possible use; indeed, the whole work is so eminently practical, and deserves such hearty recognition, that we cordially recommend it, with the hope that it may find its way into the hands of all who minister to the sick within our hospital wards. The prayers at the end of the book seem exactly suited to their purpose, dealing as they do with the trials and necessities of a nurse's daily life."—*JOHN BULL.

" It should be in the hands of every sick-nurse who desires to fulfil her

*duties from the highest and holiest motives."—*CHURCH BELLS.

*"Contains excellent advice on the subject of nursing, with the aim of raising its lowliest duties to a standard of high and holy motives."—*GRAPHIC.

*"This excellent little book is intended for a limited class of readers, but the practical lessons it teaches on how to sanctify the labour of nursing, and how to overcome its difficulties, may be read with profit by those who are called on to nurse as amateurs in private homes, as well as by those who have adopted the occupation as a profession."—*AUNT JUDY'S MAGAZINE.

The English Poems of George Herbert,

together with his Collection of Proverbs, entitled JACULA PRUDENTUM. With red borders. 16mo. 2s. 6d.

Forming a Volume of "Rivington's Devotional Series.

" This beautiful little volume will be found specially convenient as a pocket manual. The 'Jacula Prudentum,' or proverbs, deserve to be more widely known than they are at present. In many copies of George Herbert's writings these quaint sayings have been unfortunately omitted."—ROCK.

" George Herbert is too much a household name to require any introduction. It will be sufficient to say that Messrs. Rivington have published a most compact and convenient edition of the poems and proverbs of this illustrious English divine."—ENGLISH CHURCHMAN.

" An exceedingly pretty edition, the most attractive form we have yet seen from this delightful author, as a gift-book."—UNION REVIEW.

" A very beautiful edition of the quaint old English bard. All lovers of the ' Holy' Herbert will be grateful to Messrs. Rivington for the care and pains they have bestowed in supplying them with this and withal convenient copy of poems so well known and so deservedly prized."—LONDON QUARTERLY REVIEW.

" A very tasteful little book, and will doubtless be acceptable to many."—RECORD.

" We commend this little book heartily to our readers. It contains Herbert's English poems and the ' Jacula Prudentum,' in a very neat volume, which does much credit to the publishers; it will, we hope, meet with extensive circulation as a choice gift-book at a moderate price."—CHRISTIAN OBSERVER.

A Short and Plain Instruction for the

better Understanding of the Lord's Supper; to which is annexed the Office of the Holy Communion, with proper Helps and Directions. By the Right Rev. THOMAS WILSON, D.D., sometime Lord Bishop of Sodor and Man. Complete Edition, in large type, with rubrics and borders in red. 16mo. 2s. 6d.

Also a Cheap Edition, without the red borders, 1s.; or in paper cover, 6d.

Forming a Volume of " Rivington's Devotional Series."

" The Messrs. Rivington have published a new and unabridged edition of that deservedly popular work, Bishop Wilson on the Lord's Supper. The edition is here presented in three forms, suited to the various members of the household."—PUBLIC OPINION.

" We cannot withhold the expression of our admiration of the style and elegance in which this work is got up.—PRESS AND ST. JAMES' CHRONICLE.

" A departed Author being dead yet speaketh in a way which will never be out of date; Bishop Wilson on the Lord's Supper, published by Messrs. Rivington, in bindings to suit all tastes and pockets."—CHURCH REVIEW.

Of the Imitation of Christ. By

Thomas à Kempis. With Red borders. 16mo. 2*s.* 6*d.*

Also a Cheap Edition, without the red borders, 1*s.* ; or in paper cover, 6*d.*

Forming a Volume of " Rivington's Devotional Series."

Also a New Translation, forming a Volume of the "Library of Spiritual Works for English Catholics." Small 8vo. 5*s.* 32mo, cloth limp, 6*d.* ; cloth extra, 1*s.* [See page 19.]

Introduction to the Devout Life.

From the French of S. Francis de Sales, Bishop and Prince of Geneva. A New Translation. With red borders. 16mo. 2*s.* 6*d.*

Forming a Volume of " Rivington's Devotional Series."

Also a New Translation, forming a Volume of the "Library of Spiritual Works for English Catholics." Small 8vo. 5*s.* [See page 19.]

The Love of God. By S. FRANCIS DE

SALES, Bishop and Prince of Geneva. Small 8vo. 5s.

Forming a Volume of the "Library of Spiritual Works for English Catholics." [See page 19.]

The Rule and Exercises of Holy Liv-

ing. By the Right Rev. JEREMY TAYLOR, D.D., sometime Bishop of Down and Connor, and Dromore. With red borders. 16mo. 2*s.* 6*d.*

Also a Cheap Edition, without the red borders, 1*s.*
Forming a Volume of " Rivington's Devotional Series."

The Confessions of S. Augustine. In

10 Books. A New Translation. Small 8vo. 5s.

Forming a Volume of the " Library of Spiritual Works for English Catholics. [See page 19.]

The Spirit of S. Francis de Sales, Bishop

and Prince of Geneva. Translated from the French by the Author of "The Life of S. Francis de Sales," "A Dominican Artist," &c. &c. Crown 8vo. 6s.

" S. Francis de Sales, as shown to us by the Bishop of Belley, was clearly as bright and lively a companion as many a sinner of witty reputation. He was a student of human nature on the highest grounds, but he used his knowledge for amusement as well as edification. Naturally we learn this from one of his male friends rather than from his female adorers. This friend is Jean-Pierre Camus, Bishop of Belley, author, we are told, of two hundred books—one only however still known to fame, the Spirit of S. Francis de Sales, which has fairly earned him the title of the ecclesiastical Boswell." —Saturday Review.

" An admirable translation of Bishop Camus' well-known collection of sayings and opinions. As a whole, we can imagine no more delightful companion than ' The Spirit of S. Francis de Sales,' nor, we may add, a more useful one." —People's Magazine.

The Hidden Life of the Soul. By the

Author of "A Dominican Artist," "Life of Bossuet," &c. &c. New Edition. Small 8vo. 2s. 6d.

Also a Cheap Edition, forming a Volume of the "Library of Spiritual Works for English Catholics." 32mo. Cloth limp, 6d. ; cloth extra, 1s. [See page 19.]

" It well deserves the character given it of being ' earnest and sober,' and not ' sensational.'" —Guardian.

" From the French of Jean Nicolas Grou, a pious Priest, whose works teach resignation to the Divine will. He loved, we are told, to inculcate simplicity, freedom from all affectation and unreality, the patience and humility which are too surely grounded in self-knowledge to be surprised at a fall, but withal so allied to confidence in God as to make recovery easy and sure." —Public Opinion.

" There is a wonderful charm about these readings—so calm, so true, so thoroughly Christian. We do not know where they would come amiss. As materials for a consecutive series of meditations for the faithful at a series of early celebrations they would be excellent, or for private reading during Advent or Lent." —Literary Churchman.

A Practical Treatise concerning Evil

Thoughts : wherein their Nature, Origin, and Effect are distinctly considered and explained, with many Useful Rules for restraining and suppressing such Thoughts ; suited to the various conditions of Life, and the several tempers of Mankind, more especially of melancholy Persons. By William Chilcot, M.A. New Edition. With red borders. 16mo. 2s. 6d.

Forming a Volume of " Rivington's Devotional Series."

The Devotional Birthday Book. [In-
tended to record the Birth of Relations and Friends. The
Birthdays of celebrated people are printed in the Diary, with
Devotional Extracts in Verse and Prose suitable to the season
of the year.] With red borders. 16mo. 2s. 6d.

Forming a Volume of "Rivington's Devotional Series."

The Rule and Exercises of Holy
Dying. By the Right Rev. JEREMY TAYLOR, D.D., sometime
Bishop of Down and Connor, and Dromore. With red borders.
16mo. 2s. 6d.

Also a Cheap Edition, without the red borders, 1s.

The 'HOLY LIVING' and the 'HOLY DYING' may be had
bound together in one Volume, 5s. ; or without the red
borders, 2s. 6d.

Forming a Volume of "Rivington's Devotional Series."

Ancient Hymns. From the Roman
Breviary. For Domestic Use every Morning and Evening of
the Week, and on the Holy Days of the Church. To which
are added, Original Hymns, principally of Commemoration and
Thanksgiving for Christ's Holy Ordinances. By RICHARD
MANT, D.D., sometime Lord Bishop of Down and Connor.
New Edition. Small 8vo. 5s.

" Real poetry wedded to words that breathe the purest and the sweetest spirit of Christian devotion. The translations from the old Latin Hymnal are close and faithful renderings." —STANDARD.

" As a Hymn writer Bishop Mant deservedly occupies a prominent place in the esteem of Churchmen, and we doubt not that many will be the readers who will welcome this new edition of his translations and original composisions." —ENGLISH CHURCHMAN.

" A new edition of Bishop Mant's 'Ancient Hymns from the Roman Breviary' forms a handsome little volume, and it is interesting to compare some of these translations with the more modern ones of our own day. While we have no hesitation in awarding the palm to the latter, the former are an evidence of the earliest germs of that yearning of the devout mind for something better than Tate and Brady, and which is now so richly supplied." —CHURCH TIMES.

" The translations are graceful, clear, and forcible, and the original hymns deserve the highest praise. Bishop Mant has caught the very spirit of true psalmody, and there is a tuneful ring in his verses which especially adapts them for congregational singing." —ROCK.

Consoling Thoughts in Sickness.

Edited by HENRY BAILEY, B.D. Small 8vo. 1*s.* 6*d.*; or in paper cover, 1*s.*

Consolatio; or, Comfort for the

Afflicted. Edited by the Rev. C. E. KENNAWAY. With a Preface by SAMUEL WILBERFORCE, D.D., late Lord Bishop of Winchester. New Edition. Small 8vo. 3*s.* 6*d.*

The Armoury of Prayer. A Book of

Devotion. Compiled by BERDMORE COMPTON, Vicar of All Saints', Margaret Street. 18mo. 3*s.* 6*d.*

" It has a marked individuality of its own, and will no doubt meet with a certain number of persons—chiefly men, it is probable—to whose spiritual wants it is fitted above others. Those —and their number is far larger than is generally borne in mind—will find here a manual rich and abundant in its material for devotion, but remarkably modern in its tone—fitted to express the feelings and to interpret the aspirations of a cultured dweller in towns; and it is emphatically a book of and for the times." — LITERARY CHURCHMAN.

" The great characteristic of the book is its thorough reality. It puts into the mouth of the worshipper words which express, without exaggeration, what an earnest English Christian would feel and desire. The language is neither a reproduction of foreign or mediæval sentiment nor an affected reproduction of archaic forms, but good English of the Bible and Prayer Book type. . . . We could not wish the book to be different, and on the whole we heartily recommend it as one of the best we know." — CHURCH BELLS.

The Light of the Conscience. By

the Author of "The Hidden Life of the Soul," &c. With an Introduction by the Rev. T. T. CARTER, M.A., Rector of Clewer, Berks. Crown 8vo. 5*s.*

" It is a book of counsels for those who wish to lead a pious and godly life, and may fill up a gap that has been felt since the external devotional habits of the advanced portion of the present generation have so much altered from those of the last, that the books of counsel previously in use are not deemed applicable to those who follow the full teachings of the extreme ritualistic party, for this book deals with the most 'advanced' customs." — GUARDIAN.

" It consists of four-and-thirty short chapters or readings, every one of them full of quiet, sensible, practical advice, and directions upon some one point of Christian living or Christian feeling. It is a very beautiful little book, and it is a most thoroughly Christian little book, and it is, moreover, what many good books fall short of being, namely, a very wise little book. Its calm, gentle sagacity is most striking." — LITERARY CHURCHMAN.

A Manual of Devotion, chiefly for the
use of Schoolboys. By the Rev. WILLIAM BAKER, D.D.,
Head Master of Merchant Taylors' School. With Preface by
J. R. WOODFORD, D.D., Lord Bishop of Ely. Crown 16mo.
Cloth limp. 1s. 6d.

Family Prayers. Compiled from various
Sources (chiefly from Bishop Hamilton's Manual), and arranged
on the Liturgical Principle. By EDWARD MEYRICK GOUL-
BURN, D.D., Dean of Norwich. New Edition. Large type.
Crown 8vo. 3s. 6d. Cheap Edition. 16mo. 1s.

Morning Notes of Praise. A Series of
Meditations upon the Morning Psalms. Dedicated to the
Countess of Cottenham. By LADY CHARLOTTE-MARIA
PEPYS. New Edition. Small 8vo. 2s. 6d.

Quiet Moments; a Four Weeks' Course
of Thoughts and Meditations' before Evening Prayer and at
Sunset. By LADY CHARLOTTE-MARIA PEPYS. New Edition. Small 8vo. 2s. 6d.

A Book of Family Prayer. Compiled
by WALTER FARQUHAR HOOK, D.D., F.R.S., late Dean of
Chichester. Eighth Edition, with Rubrics in Red. 18mo. 2s.

Aids to Prayer; or, Thoughts on the
Practice of Devotion. With Forms of Prayer for Private Use.
By DANIEL MOORE, M.A., Chaplain in Ordinary to the Queen,
and Vicar of Holy Trinity, Paddington. Second Edition.
Square 32mo. 2s. 6d.

The Words of the Son of God, taken

from the Four Gospels, and arranged for Daily Meditation throughout the Year.   By ELEANOR PLUMPTRE.   Crown 8vo. 7*s*. 6*d*.

" The quotations have been made judiciously, and contain much that is valuable and practically useful. . . . We sincerely unite with the compiler in her desire that the plan adopted in this volume may prove useful to its readers."—RECORD.

" The authoress of this volume has woven together with loving care and reverent hand the sayings of the Son of God, and it will perhaps surprise some of those who have not viewed our Lord's words from this aspect to find how complete a manual they make of doctrine and practice. . . . We can most cordially recommend this volume to our readers, not only for personal use, but for reading at morning and evening prayer; while to the clergy it will, we believe, be found to be a thesaurus of golden sayings which will be both suggestive and useful."--CHURCHMAN'S SHILLING MAGAZINE.

The Good Shepherd; or, Meditations

for the Clergy upon the Example and Teaching of Christ. By the Rev. W. E. HEYGATE, M.A., Rector of Brighstone. Second Edition, revised.   Small 8vo.   3*s*.

CONTENTS.

Thoughts on Meditation—Devotions Preparatory to Ordination—Early Life—Temptation—Fasting—Prayer—Divine Scripture—Retirement—Frequent Communion— Faith — Hope — Love — Preaching — Catechizing—Private Explanation—Intercession—Bringing Christians to Holy Communion—Preparation of those about to Communicate—Jesus absolving Sinners—Jesus celebrating the Eucharist—Care of Children—Care of the Sick and Afflicted—The Healing of Schism—Treatment of the Worldly—Treatment of Penitents—Care of God's House—Fear and Fearlessness of Offence—Bearing Reproach—Bearing Praise—Seeking out Sinners—Sorrow over Sinners—Consoling the Sorrowful—Rebuke—Silence—Disappointment—Compassion—Refusing those who suppose Godliness to be Gain—Peace-giving—Poverty—Opportunities of Speech—With Christ or Without—Watchfulness—In what to Glory—The Salt which has lost its Savour—Hard Cases—Weariness—Falling Back—Consideration for Others—Love of Pre-eminence—The Cross my Strength—The Will of God—The Fruit of Humiliation—The Praise of the World the Condemnation of God—Jesus rejoicing—Work while it is Day—Meeting again—The Reward. Further Prayers suitable to the Clergy—Prayer for the Flock—A General Prayer—Celebration of the Holy Eucharist—Preaching—Visitation.

The Virgin's Lamp: Prayers and Devout

Exercises for English Sisters.   By the Rev. J. M. NEALE, D.D., late Warden of Sackville College, East Grinsted. Small 8vo.   3*s*. 6*d*.

Waterloo Place, London

The Guide of Life : a Manual of

Prayers for Women ; with the Office of the Holy Communion, and Devotions. By C. E. SKINNER. Edited by the Rev. JOHN HEWETT, M.A., Vicar of Babbacombe, Devon. Crown 16mo. 2*s*. 6*d*.

" Clergymen will be glad to know of this little manual as one which they may most safely put into the hands of intelligent women of the better class of those who have to work for their living. It is very complete in its scope, and it is not only a manual of devotions, but is really what it is entitled,'a Guide of Life,' and is evidently the work of one who thoroughly understands the needs and the trials of the important class for which it is in-tended."—CHURCH QUARTERLY RE-VIEW.

" A very excellent manual for single young women. The prayers are marked with a strong common-sense tone which is especially commendable." —CHURCH TIMES.

" Well-selected prayers and hymns for all estates and conditions of woman-kind. It is earnest, devout, and withal, sober and loyal in its tone."—JOHN BULL.

Sickness; its Trials and Blessings.

Fine Edition. Small 8vo. 3*s*. 6*d*. Cheap Edition, 1*s*. 6*d*. ; or in paper cover, 1*s*.

Help and Comfort for the Sick Poor.

By the same Author. New Edition. Small 8vo. 1*s*.

Prayers for the Sick and Dying. By

the same Author. Fourth Edition. Small 8vo. 1*s*. 6*d*.

From Morning to Evening : a Book for

Invalids. From the French of M. l'Abbé Henri Perreyve. Translated and adapted by an Associate of the Sisterhood of S. John Baptist, Clewer. New Edition. Crown 8vo. 5*s*.

Vita et Doctrina Jesu Christi; or,

Meditations on the Life of our Lord. By AVANCINI. In the Original Latin. Adapted to the use of the Church of England by a CLERGYMAN. 18mo. 2*s*. 6*d*.

The Mysteries of Mount Calvary.
Translated from the Latin of Antonio de Guevara. Edited by the Rev. ORBY SHIPLEY, M.A. Square crown 8vo. 3*s*. 6*d*.

Counsels on Holiness of Life. Translated from the Spanish of "The Sinner's Guide" by Luis de Granada. Edited by the Rev. ORBY SHIPLEY, M.A. Square crown 8vo. 5*s*.

Preparation for Death. Translated from the Italian of Alfonso, Bishop of S. Agatha. Edited by the Rev. ORBY SHIPLEY, M.A. Square crown 8vo. 5*s*.

Examination of Conscience upon Special Subjects. Translated and abridged from the French of Tronson. Edited by the Rev. ORBY SHIPLEY, M.A. Square crown 8vo. 5*s*.

Christian Watchfulness, in the Prospect of Sickness, Mourning, and Death. By JOHN JAMES, D.D., sometime Canon of Peterborough. New Edition. 12mo. 3*s*.

4. Parish Work.

The Book of Church Law. Being an Exposition of the Legal Rights and Duties of the Clergy and Laity of the Church of England. By the Rev. JOHN HENRY BLUNT, M.A., F.S.A. Revised by WALTER G. F. PHILLIMORE, D.C.L., Barrister-at-Law, and Chancellor of the Diocese of Lincoln. Second Edition, revised. Crown 8vo. 7s. 6d.

CONTENTS.

"*We have tested this work on various points of a crucial character, and have found it very accurate and full in its information. It embodies the results of the most recent Acts of the Legislature on the clerical profession and the rights of the laity.*"—STANDARD.

"*Already in our leading columns we have directed attention to Messrs. Blunt and Phillimore's 'Book of Church Law,' as an excellent manual for ordinary use. It is a book which should stand on every clergyman's shelves ready for use when any legal matter arises about which its possessor is in doubt. . . . It is to be hoped that the authorities at our Theological Colleges sufficiently recognise the value of a little legal knowledge on the part of the clergy to recommend this book to their students. It would serve admirably as the text-book for a set of lectures.*"—CHURCH TIMES.

---

and at Oxford and Cambridge

Flowers and Festivals; or, Directions

for the Floral Decoration of Churches. By W. A BARRETT,
Mus. Bac., Oxon., of St. Paul's Cathedral. With Coloured
Illustrations. Second Edition. Square crown 8vo. 5s.

The Chorister's Guide. By W. A. BAR-

RETT, Mus. Bac., Oxon., of St. Paul's Cathedral. Second
Edition. Crown 8vo. 2s. 6d.

"... One of the most useful books of instructions for choristers—and, we may add, choral singers generally—that has ever emanated from the musical press. . . . Mr. Barrett's teaching is not only conveyed to his readers with the consciousness of being master of his subject, but he employs words terse and clear, so that his meaning may be promptly caught by the neophyte. . . ."—ATHENÆUM.

"A nicely graduated, clear, and excellent introduction to the duties of a chorister."—STANDARD.

"It seems clear and precise enough to serve its end."—EXAMINER.

"A useful manual for giving boys such a practical and technical knowledge of music as shall enable them to sing both with confidence and precision."—CHURCH HERALD.

"In this little volume we have a manual long called for by the requirements of church music. In a series of thirty-two lessons it gives, with an admirable conciseness, and an equally observable completeness, all that is necessary a chorister should be taught out of a book, and a great deal calculated to have a value as bearing indirectly upon his actual practice in singing."—MUSICAL STANDARD.

"We can highly recommend the present able manual."—EDUCATIONAL TIMES.

"A very useful manual, not only for choristers, or rather those who may aim at becoming choristers, but for others, who wish to enter upon the study of music."—ROCK.

"The work will be found of singular utility by those who have to instruct choirs."—CHURCH TIMES.

"A most grateful contribution to the agencies for improving our Services. It is characterised by all that clearness in combination with conciseness of style which has made 'Flowers and Festivals' so universally admired."—TORONTO HERALD.

Priest and Parish. By the Rev. HARRY

JONES, M.A., Rector of St. George's-in-the-East, London.
Square crown 8vo. 6s. 6d.

Notes on Church Organs: their Position

and the Materials used in their Construction. By C. K. K.
BISHOP. With Illustrations. Small 4to. 6s.

Stones of the Temple; or, Lessons

from the Fabric and Furniture of the Church. By WALTER FIELD, M.A., F.S.A., late Vicar of Godmersham. With numerous Illustrations. New Edition. Crown 8vo. 7s. 6d.

" Any one who wishes for simple information on the subjects of Church architecture and furniture, cannot do better than consult 'Stones of the Temple.' Mr. Field modestly disclaims any intention of supplanting the existing regular treatises, but his book shows an amount of research, and a knowledge of what he is talking about, which make it practically useful as well as pleasant. The woodcuts are numerous, and some of them very pretty."—GRAPHIC.

"A very charming book, by the Rev. Walter Field, who was for years Secretary of one of the leading Church Societies. Mr. Field has a loving reverence for the beauty of the domus mansionalis Dei, as the old law books called the Parish Church. . . . . Thoroughly sound in Church feeling, Mr. Field has chosen the medium of a tale to embody real incidents illustrative of the various portions of his subject. There is no attempt at elaboration of the narrative, which, indeed, is rather a string of anecdotes than a story, but each chapter brings home to the mind its own lesson, and each is illustrated with some very interesting engravings. . . . . The work will properly command a hearty reception from Churchmen. The footnotes are occasionally most valuable, and are always pertinent, and the text is sure to be popular with young folks for Sunday reading."—STANDARD.

" Mr. Field's chapters on brasses, chancel screens, crosses, encaustic tiles, mural paintings, porches and pavements, are agreeably written, and people with a turn for Ritualism will no doubt find them edifying. The illustrations of Church architecture and Church ornaments are very attractive."—PALL MALL GAZETTE.

" 'Stones of the Temple' is a grave book, the result of antiquarian, or rather ecclesiological, tastes and of devotional feelings. We can recommend it to young people of both sexes, and it will not disappoint the most learned among them. . . . Mr. Field has brought together, from well-known authorities, a considerable mass of archæological information, which will interest the readers he especially addresses."—ATHENÆUM.

" Very appropriate as a Christmas present, is an elegant and instructive book. . . . A full and clear account of the meaning and history of the several parts of the fabric and of the furniture of the Church. It is illustrated with a number of carefully drawn pictures, sometimes of entire churches, sometimes of remarkable monuments, windows, or wall paintings. We may add that the style of the commentary, which is cast in the form of a dialogue between a parson and some of his parishioners, and hangs together by a slight thread of story, is quiet and sensible, and free from exaggeration or intolerance."—GUARDIAN.

A Handy Book on the Ecclesiastical

Dilapidations Act, 1871. With the Amendment Act, 1872. By EDWARD G. BRUTON, F.R.I.B.A., Diocesan Surveyor, Oxford. With Analytical Index and Precedent Forms. Second Edition. Crown 8vo. 5s.

The Bishopric of Souls.   By ROBERT

WILSON EVANS, B.D., late Vicar of Heversham and Archdeacon of Westmoreland. With an Introductory Memoir by EDWARD BICKERSTETH, D.D., Dean of Lichfield. With Portrait. Fifth Edition. Small 8vo. 5s. 6d.

Twenty-One Years in S. George's

Mission. An account of its Origin, Progress, and Work of Charity. With an Appendix. By C. F. LOWDER, M.A., Vicar of S. Peter's, London Docks. Crown 8vo. 6s.

Directorium Pastorale.   The Principles

and Practice of Pastoral Work in the Church of England. By the Rev. JOHN HENRY BLUNT, M.A., F.S.A., Editor of " The Annotated Book of Common Prayer," &c. &c.   New Edition, revised. Crown 8vo. 7s. 6d.

" This is the third edition of a work which has become deservedly popular as the best extant exposition of the principles and practice of the pastoral work in the Church of England. Its hints and suggestions are based on practical experience, and it is further recommended by the majority of our Bishops at the ordination of priests and deacons."—STANDARD.

" Its practical usefulness to the paro-chial clergy is proved by the acceptance it has already received at their hands, and no faithful parish priest, who is working in real earnest for the extension of spiritual instruction amongst all classes of his flock, will rise from the perusal of its pages without having obtained some valuable hints as to the best mode of bringing home our Church's system to the hearts of his people."—NATIONAL CHURCH.

Ars Pastoria.   By FRANK PARNELL, M.A.,

Rector of Oxtead, near Godstone. Second Edition. Small 8vo. 2s.

Instructions for the Use of Candidates

for Holy Orders, and of the Parochial Clergy; with Acts of Parliament relating to the same, and Forms proposed to be used. By CHRISTOPHER HODGSON, M.A., Secretary to the Governors of Queen Anne's Bounty. Ninth Edition. 8vo. 16s.

The Church Builder : a Quarterly Journal

of Church Extension in England and Wales. Published in connexion with "The Incorporated Church Building Society." 14 Annual Volumes. With Illustrations. Crown 8vo. 1*s*. 6*d*. New Series. Enlarged. Volumes for 1876, 1877, 1878, and 1879. 3*s*. each.

List of Charities, General and Diocesan,

for the Relief of the Clergy, their Widows and Families. New Edition. Small 8vo. 3*s*.

5. The Church and Doctrine.

The Holy Catholic Church; its Divine

Ideal, Ministry, and Institutions. A short Treatise. With a Catechism on each Chapter, forming a Course of Methodical Instruction on the subject. By EDWARD MEYRICK GOULBURN, D.D., Dean of Norwich. Second Edition. Crown 8vo. 6s. 6d.

CONTENTS.

What the Church is, and when and how it was founded—Duty of the Church towards those who hold to the Apostles' doctrine, in separation from the Apostles' fellowship—The Unity of the Church, and its Disruption—The Survey of Zion's towers, bulwarks, and palaces—The Institution of the Ministry, and its relation to the Church—The Holy Eucharist at its successive stages—On the powers of the Church in Council—The Church presenting, exhibiting, and defending the Truth—The Church guiding into and illustrating the Truth—On the Prayer-Book as a Commentary on the Bible—Index.

"Dr. Goulburn has conferred a great boon on the Church of England by the treatise before us, which vindicates her claim as a branch of the Catholic Church on the allegiance of her children, setting forth as he does, with singular precision and power, the grounds of her title-deeds, and the Christian character of her doctrine and discipline."—STANDARD.

"His present book would have been used for an educational book even if he had not invited men to make that use of it by appending a catechism to each particular chapter, and thus founding a course of methodical instruction upon his text. We have not yet come across any better book for giving to Dissenters or to such inquirers as hold fast to Holy Scripture. It is, we need scarcely say, steeped in Scripturalness, and full of bright and suggestive interpretations of particular texts."—ENGLISH CHURCHMAN.

"Must prove highly useful, not only to young persons, but to the very large class, both Churchmen and Dissenters, who are painfully ignorant of what the Catholic Church really is, and of the peculiar and fixed character of her institutions."—ROCK.

"The catechetical questions and answers at the end of each chapter will be useful both for teachers and learners, and the side-notes at the head of the paragraphs are very handy."—CHURCH TIMES.

"It contains a great deal of instructive matter, especially in the catechisms—or, as they might be called, dialogues—and is instinct with a spirit at once temperate and uncompromising. It is a good book for all who wish to understand, neither blindly asserting it nor being half ashamed of it, the position of a loyal member of the English Church."—GUARDIAN.

Waterloo Place, London

Dictionary of Sects, Heresies, Ecclesias-

tical Parties and Schools of Religious Thought. By Various
Writers. Edited by the Rev. JOHN HENRY BLUNT, M.A.,
F.S.A., Editor of the "Dictionary of Doctrinal and Historical
Theology," the "Annotated Book of Common Prayer," &c.
&c. Imperial 8vo. 36s. ; or in half-morocco, 48s.

*" We doubt not that the Dictionary
will prove a useful work of reference ; and it may claim to give in
reasonable compass a mass of information respecting many religious
schools knowledge of which could previously only be acquired from amid a
host of literature. The articles are
written with great fairness, and in
many cases display careful scholarly
work."*—ATHENÆUM.

*" A very comprehensive and bold
undertaking, and is certainly executed
with a sufficient amount of ability
and knowledge to entitle the book to
rank very high in point of utility."*—
GUARDIAN.

*" That this is a work of some learn-
ing and research is a fact which
soon becomes obvious to the reader."*—
SPECTATOR.

*" A whole library is condensed into
this admirable volume. All authorities
are named, and an invaluable index
is supplied."* — NOTES AND QUERIES.

*" We have tested it rigidly, and in
almost every instance we have been
satisfied with the account given under
the name of sects, heresy, or ecclesiastical party."*—JOHN BULL.

*" It is the fullest and most trust-
worthy book of the kind that we
possess. The quantity of information
it presents in a convenient and accessible form is enormous, and having
once appeared, it becomes indispensable
to the theological student."*—CHURCH
TIMES.

*" It has considerable value as a
copious work of reference, more especially since a list of authorities is in
most cases supplied."*—EXAMINER.

The Doctrine of the Church of England,

as stated in Ecclesiastical Documents set forth by Authority
of Church and State, in the Reformation Period between 1536
and 1662. Edited by the Rev. JOHN HENRY BLUNT, M.A.,
F.S.A., Editor of the "Dictionary of Doctrinal and Historical
Theology," the "Annotated Book of Common Prayer," &c.
&c. 8vo. 7s. 6d.

The Orthodox Doctrine of the Church

of England explained in a Commentary on the Thirty-Nine
Articles. By the Rev. T. I. BALL. With an Introduc
tion by the Rev. W. J. E. BENNETT, M.A., Vicar of Frome-
Selwood. Crown 8vo. 7s. 6d.

Dictionary of Doctrinal and Historical

Theology. By Various Writers. Edited by the Rev. JOHN HENRY BLUNT, M.A., F.S.A., Editor of the "Annotated Book of Common Prayer," &c. &c. Second Edition. Imperial 8vo. 42*s.* ; or in half-morocco, 52*s.* 6*d.*

"*We know no book of its size and bulk which supplies the information here given at all; far less which supplies it in an arrangement so accessible, with a completeness of information so thorough, and with an ability in the treatment of profound subjects so great. Dr. Hook's most useful volume is a work of high calibre, but it is the work of a single mind. We have here a wider range of thought from a greater variety of sides. We have here also the work of men who evidently know what they write about, and are somewhat more profound (to say the least) than the writers of the current Dictionaries of Sects and Heresies.*"—GUARDIAN.

"*Thus it will be obvious that it takes a very much wider range than any undertaking of the same kind in our language ; and that to those of our clergy who have not the fortune to spend in books, and would not have the leisure to use them if they possessed them, it will be the most serviceable and reliable substitute for a large library we can think of. And in many cases, while keeping strictly within its province as a Dictionary, it contrives to be marvellously suggestive of thought and reflections, which a serious-minded man will take with him and ponder over for his own elaboration and future use. We trust most sincerely that the book may be largely used. For a present to a Clergyman on his ordination, or from a parishioner to his pastor, it would be most appropriate. It may indeed be called 'a box of tools for a working clergyman.'*"—LITERARY CHURCHMAN.

"*Seldom has an English work of equal magnitude been so permeated with Catholic instincts, and at the same time seldom has a work on theology been kept so free from the drift of rhetorical incrustation. Of course,* it is not meant that all these remarks apply in their full extent to every article. In a great Dictionary there are compositions, as in a great house there are vessels, of various kinds. Some of these at a future day may be replaced by others more substantial in their build, more proportionate in their outline, and more elaborate in their detail. But admitting all this, the whole remains a home to which the student will constantly recur, sure to find spacious chambers, substantial furniture, and (which is most important) no stinted light.*"—CHURCH REVIEW.

"*Within the sphere it has marked out for itself, no equally useful book of reference exists in English for the elucidation of theological problems. . . . Entries which display much care, research, and judgment in compilation, and which will make the task of the parish priest who is brought face to face with any of the practical questions which they involve far easier than has been hitherto. The very fact that the utterances are here and there somewhat more guarded and hesitating than quite accords with our judgment, is a gain in so far as it protects the work from the charge of inculcating extreme views, and will thus secure its admission in many places where moderation is accounted the crowning grace.*"—CHURCH TIMES.

"*It will be found of admirable service to all students of theology, as advancing and maintaining the Church's views on all subjects as fall within the range of fair argument and inquiry. It is not often that a work of so comprehensive and so profound a nature is marked to the very end by so many signs of wide and careful research, sound criticism, and well-founded and well-expressed belief.*"—STANDARD.

An Eirenicon of the Eighteenth Cen-

tury. Proposal for Catholic Communion. By a Minister of the Church of England. Edited by HENRY NUTCOMBE OXENHAM, M.A. New Edition. With Introduction, Appendices, and Notes. 8vo. 10*s*. 6*d*.

"His especial merit is that of putting it in a form sufficiently simple and telling to come home to the understandings of all fairly educated persons, however unversed in the technicalities of controversial divinity."—CHURCH QUARTERLY REVIEW.

"Mr. Oxenham has disinterred, and here presents to the public, an historical curiosity. . . . To this treatise he has prefixed a highly-interesting sketch of the various attempts which have been made from time to time to re-establish communion between the Churches."—LITERARY CHURCHMAN.

"All interested in Reunion will welcome the reprint of an important book on this great subject. . . . It certainly is the most important contribution to the Reunion movement since the celebrated 'Essays,' and deserves to be read and preserved by all peacemakers."—REUNION MAGAZINE.

Apostolical Succession in the Church

of England. By the Rev. ARTHUR W. HADDAN, B.D., late Rector of Barton-on-the-Heath. New Edition. 8vo. 12*s*.

"Thoroughly well written, clear and forcible in style, and fair in tone. It cannot but render valuable service in placing the claims of the Church in their true light before the English public."—GUARDIAN.

"Among the many standard theological works devoted to this important subject Mr. Haddan's will hold a high place."—STANDARD.

"We should be glad to see the volume widely circulated and generally read."—JOHN BULL.

"A weighty and valuable treatise, and we hope that the study of its sound and well-reasoned pages will do much to fix the importance, and the full meaning of the doctrine in question, in the minds of Church people. . . . We hope that our extracts will lead our readers to study Mr. Haddan for themselves."—LITERARY CHURCHMAN.

"This is not only a very able and carefully written treatise upon the doctrine of Apostolical Succession, but it is also a calm yet noble vindication of the validity of the Anglican Orders: it well sustains the brilliant reputation which Mr. Haddan left behind him at Oxford, and it supplements his other profound historical researches in ecclesiastical matters. This book will remain for a long time the classic work upon English Orders."—CHURCH REVIEW.

"A very temperate and well-reasoned book."—WESTMINSTER REVIEW.

The Civil Power in its Relations to the

Church; considered with Special Reference to the Court of Final Ecclesiastical Appeal in England. By the Rev. JAMES WAYLAND JOYCE, M.A., Prebendary of Hereford, and Examining Chaplain to the Bishop of Hereford. 8vo. 10*s*. 6*d*.

The Theory of Development.   A Criticism of Dr. Newman's Essay on the Development of Christian Doctrine, reprinted from "The Christian Remembrancer," January 1847.   By J. B. MOZLEY, D.D., late Canon of Christ Church, and Regius Professor of Divinity in the University of Oxford.   Crown 8vo.   5s.

Miscellanies, Literary and Religious. By CHR. WORDSWORTH, D.D., Bishop of Lincoln.   3 Vols. 8vo.   36s.

The Holy Angels : Their Nature and Employments, as recorded in the Word of God.   Small 8vo. 6s.

The Principal Ecclesiastical Judgments delivered in the Court of Arches, 1867-1875.   By the Right Hon. Sir ROBERT PHILLIMORE, D.C.L.   8vo.   12s.

Our Mother Church : being Simple Talk on High Topics.   By ANNE MERCIER.   New Edition. Small 8vo.   3s. 6d.

" We have rarely come across a book dealing with an old subject in a healthier and, as far as may be, more original manner, while yet thoroughly practical.   It is intended for and admirably adapted to the use of girls.   Thoroughly reverent in its tone, and bearing in every page marks of learned research, it is yet easy of comprehension, and explains ecclesiastical terms with the accuracy of a lexicon without the accompanying dulness.   It is to be hoped that the book will attain to the large circulation it justly merits."—JOHN BULL.

" We have never seen a book for girls of its class which commends itself to us more particularly.   The author calls her work 'simple talk on great subjects,' and calls it by a name that describes it almost as completely as we could do in a longer notice than we can spare the volume.   No one can fail to comprehend the beautifully simple, devout, and appropriate language in which Mrs. Mercier embodies what she has to say; and for the facts with which she deals she has taken good care to have their accuracy assured."*—STANDARD.

" The plan of this pleasant-looking book is excellent.   It is a kind of Mrs. Markham on the Church of England, written especially for girls, and we shall not be surprised to find it become a favourite in schools.   It is really a conversational hand-book to the English Church's history, doctrine, and ritual, compiled by a very diligent reader from some of the best modern Anglican sources."—ENGLISH CHURCHMAN.

Waterloo Place, London

After Death. An Examination of Primi-

tive Times respecting the State of the Faithful Dead, and their Relationship to the Living. In Two Parts. By HERBERT MORTIMER LUCKOCK, D.D., Canon of Ely, Principal of the Theological College, Examining Chaplain to the Bishop, and sometime Fellow of Jesus College, Cambridge. Crown 8vo. 6s.

CONTENTS.

PART I.—*The State of the Faithful Dead and the Good Offices of the Living in their Behalf*: Vincentian Canon—Value of the Testimony of the Primitive Fathers—The Intermediate State—Change in the Intermediate State—Prayers for the Dead: Reasons for our Lord's Silence on the Subject—Testimony of Holy Scripture—Testimony of the Catacombs—Testimony of the Early Fathers—Testimony of the Primitive Liturgies—Prayers for the Pardon of Sins of Infirmity and the Effacement of Sinful Stains—Inefficacy of Prayer for those who died in wilful unrepented Sin.

PART II.—*The Good Offices of the Faithful Dead in Behalf of the Living*: Primitive Testimony to the Intercession of the Saint—Primitive Testimony to the Invocation of the Saints—Trustworthiness of the Patristic Evidence for Invocation tested—The Primitive Liturgies and the Roman Catacombs—Patristic Opinion on the extent of the Knowledge possessed by the Saints—Testimony of Holy Scripture upon the same Subject—Beatific Vision not yet attained by any of the Saints—Conclusions drawn from the foregoing Testimony.

Out of the Body. A Scriptural Inquiry.

By the Rev. JAMES S. POLLOCK, M.A., Incumbent of S. Alban's, Birmingham. Crown 8vo. 5s.

CONTENTS.

Introduction—Scope of the Inquiry—The Presentiment—The Anticipation—The Departure—The Life of the Body—The Life of the Spirit—Dream-Life—The Spirit-World—Spirit-Groups—Helping one another—Limits of Communication—Spiritual Manifestations.

Prophecies and the Prophetic Spirit

in the Christian Era: an Historical Essay. By JOHN J. IGN. VON DÖLLINGER, D.D., D.C.L. Translated, with Introduction, Notes, and Appendices, by the Rev. ALFRED PLUMMER, M.A., Master of University College, Durham, late Fellow of Trinity College, Oxford. 8vo. 10s. 6d.

Lectures on the Reunion of the

Churches. By JOHN J. IGN. VON DÖLLINGER, D.D., D.C.L. Authorized Translation, with Preface by HENRY NUTCOMBE OXENHAM, M.A., late Scholar of Balliol College, Oxford. Crown 8vo. 5s.

Eight Lectures on the Miracles; being

the Bampton Lectures for 1865. By J. B. MOZLEY, D.D.,
late Canon of Christ Church, and Regius Professor of Divinity
Oxford. Fourth Edition. Crown 8vo. 7s. 6d.

*"There is great brightness and beauty in many of the images in which the author condenses the issues of his arguments. And many passages are marked by that peculiar kind of eloquence which comes with the force of close and vigorous thinking; passages which slime-like steal through their very temper, and which are instinct with a controlled energy, that melts away all ruggedness of language. There can be no question that, in the deeper qualities of a scientific theology, the book is thoroughly worthy of the highest reputation which had been gained by Mr. Mozley's previous writings."—*CONTEMPORARY REVIEW.

*" Mr. Mozley's Bampton Lectures are an example, and a very fine one, of a mode of theological writing which is characteristic of the Church of England, and almost peculiar to it. The distinguishing features, a combination of intense seriousness with a self-restrained, severe calmness, and of very vigorous and wide-ranging reasoning on the realities of the case. . . . . . Mr. Mozley's book belongs to that class of writings of which Butler may be taken as the type. It is strong, genuine argument about difficult matters fairly facing what is difficult, fairly trying to grapple, not with what appears the gist and strong point of a question, but with what really and at bottom is the knot of it."—*TIMES.

The Happiness of the Blessed con-

sidered as to the Particulars of their State : their Recognition
of each other in that State : and its Differences of Degrees.
To which are added Musings on the Church and her Services.
By RICHARD MANT, D.D., sometime Lord Bishop of Down
and Connor. New Edition. Small 8vo. 3s. 6d.

*"A welcome republication of a treatise once highly valued, and which can never lose its value. Many of our readers already know the fulness and discrimination with which the author treats his subject, which must be one of the most delightful topics of meditation to all whose hearts are where the only true treasure is, and particularly to those who are entering upon the evening of life."—*CHURCH REVIEW.

*"All recognise the authority of the command to set the affections on things above, and such works as the one now before us will be found helpful towards this good end. We are, therefore, sincerely glad that Messrs. Rivington have brought out a new edition of Bishop Mant's valuable treatise."—*RECORD.

St. John Chrysostom's Liturgy. Trans-

lated by H. C. ROMANOFF, Author of " Sketches of the Rites
and Customs of the Greco-Russian Church," &c. With Illustrations. Square crown 8vo. 4s. 6d.

Dogmatic Faith: an Inquiry into the

Relation subsisting between Revelation and Dogma. Being the Bampton Lectures for 1867. By EDWARD GARBETT, M.A., Incumbent of Christ Church, Surbiton. New Edition. Crown 8vo. 5*s*.

Thirty-two Years of the Church of

England, 1842-1875: The Charges of Archdeacon SINCLAIR. Edited by WILLIAM SINCLAIR, M.A., Prebendary of Chichester, Rector of Pulborough, late Vicar of S. George's, Leeds. With a Preface by ARCHIBALD CAMPBELL TAIT, D.D., Archbishop of Canterbury, and a Historical Introduction by ROBERT CHARLES JENKINS, M.A., Hon. Canon of Canterbury, Rector and Vicar of Lyminge. 8vo. 12*s*. 6*d*.

The Thirty-nine Articles of the Church

of England explained in a Series of Lectures. By the Rev. R. W. JELF, D.D., late Canon of Christ Church, Oxford, and sometime Principal of King's College, London. Edited by the Rev. J. R. KING, M.A., Vicar of St. Peter's-in-the-East, Oxford, and formerly Fellow and Tutor of Merton College. 8vo. 15*s*.

Letters from Rome on the Council.

By QUIRINUS. Reprinted from the "Allgemeine Zeitung." Authorized Translation. Crown 8vo. 12*s*.

The Pope and the Council. By JANUS.

Authorized Translation from the German. Fourth Edition. Crown 8vo. 7*s*. 6*d*.

6. Sermons.

Sermons Preached before the University

sity of Oxford. (Second Series, 1860-1879.) By HENRY PARRY LIDDON, D.D., D.C.L., Canon of St. Paul's, and Ireland Professor of Exegesis in the University of Oxford. Crown 8vo. 5s.

CONTENTS.

Prejudice and Experience—Humility and Truth—Import of Faith in a Creator —Worth of Faith in a Life to Come—Influences of the Holy Spirit— Growth in the Apprehension of Truth—The Life of Faith and the Athanasian Creed—Christ's Service and Public Opinion—Christ in the Storm—Sacerdotalism—The Prophecy of the Magnificat—The Fall of Jericho—The Courage of Faith—The Curse on Meroz—The Gospel and the Poor—Christ and Human Law.

Sermons Preached before the University

sity of Oxford. (First Series, 1859-1868.) By HENRY PARRY LIDDON, D.D., D.C.L., Canon of St. Paul's, and Ireland Professor of Exegesis in the University of Oxford. Sixth Edition. Crown 8vo. 5s.

CONTENTS.

God and the Soul—The Law of Progress—The Honour of Humanity—The Freedom of the Spirit—Immortality—Humility and Action—The Conflict of Faith with undue Exaltation of Intellect—Lessons of the Holy Manger —The Divine Victim—The Risen Life—Our Lord's Ascension, the Church's Gain—Faith in a Holy Ghost—The Divine Indwelling a motive to Holiness.

Some Elements of Religion. Lent

Lectures. By HENRY PARRY LIDDON, D.D., D.C.L., Canon of St. Paul's, and Ireland Professor of Exegesis in the University of Oxford. Second Edition. Crown 8vo. 5s.

CONTENTS.

The Idea of Religion—God, the Object of Religion—The Subject of Religion, the Soul—The Obstacle to Religion, Sin—Prayer, the Characteristic action of Religion—The Mediator, the Guarantee of Religious Life.

Waterloo Place, London

The Divinity of our Lord and Saviour

Jesus Christ. Being the Bampton Lectures for 1866. By HENRY PARRY LIDDON, D.D., D.C.L., Canon of St. Paul's, and Ireland Professor of Exegesis in the University of Oxford. Eighth Edition. Crown 8vo. 5*s*.

Church Doctrine and Spiritual Life.

Sermons preached in the Chapel of Lincoln's Inn. By F. C. COOK, M.A., Chaplain in Ordinary to the Queen, Canon of Exeter, Preacher to the Honourable Society of Lincoln's Inn. Crown 8vo. 7*s*. 6*d*.

CONTENTS.

The Law given by Moses—Grace and Truth in Jesus Christ—Baptismal Fire—Baptism in One Body—Hidden Life—The Manifested Life—Sabbatic Rest—The Dignity of Prayer—The Efficacy of Prayer—Unity of the Church—Christ Draweth all Men—Spiritual Resurrection—The Past Required—The Intermediate State—Ministering Spirits—The Holy Spirit as Reprover—The Holy Trinity—Testimony of the Church in the Athanasian Creed—First Meeting of St. Peter and St. Paul at Jerusalem—Clement of Rome, Witness to the Faith of the Early Church—Justin Martyr, Witness to the Power of Life in the Early Church—Justin Martyr, Witness to the Gospels and to Eucharistic Worship—Justin Martyr, Witness to Eucharistic Doctrine—St. Athanasius, Witness to the Permanency of Eucharistic Doctrine—Hilary of Poictiers, Witness to the Unity of Doctrine and of Spiritual Life in the Early Church.

Pleadings for Christ. Being Sermons,

Doctrinal and Practical, preached in St. Andrew's Church, Liverpool. By WILLIAM LEFROY, M.A., Incumbent. Crown 8vo. 6*s*.

Warnings of the Holy Week, &c. Being

a Course of Parochial Lectures for the Week before Easter and the Easter Festivals. By the Rev. W. ADAMS, M.A., Author of "Sacred Allegories," &c. Seventh Edition. Small 8vo. 4*s*. 6*d*.

CONTENTS.

The Warning given at Bethany—The Warning of the Day of Excitement—The Warning of the Day of Chastisement—The Warning of the Fig Tree—The Warning of Judas—The Warning of Pilate—The Warning of the Day of Rest—The Signs of Our Lord's Presence—The Remedy for Anxious Thoughts—Comfort under Despondency.

Sermons on the Epistles and Gospels

for the Sundays and Holy Days throughout the Year. By the Rev. ISAAC WILLIAMS, B.D., Author of a " Devotional Commentary on the Gospel Narrative." New Edition. 2 Vols. Crown 8vo. 5*s.* each. Sold separately.

CONTENTS OF VOL. I.

The King of Salem—The Scriptures bearing Witness—The Church bearing Witness—The Spirit bearing Witness—The Adoption of Sons—Love strong as Death—The Love which passeth Knowledge—Of|such is the Kingdom of Heaven—The Spirit of Adoption—The Old and the New Man—The Day Star in the Heart—Obedience the best Sacrifice—The Meekness and Gentleness of Christ — The Faith that overcometh the World—Our Refuge in Public Troubles—Light and Safety in Love—The Great Manifestation—Perseverance found in Humility— Bringing forth Fruit with Patience—The most excellent Gift—The Call to Repentance—The accepted Time—Perseverance in Prayer—The Unclean Spirit returning—The Penitent refreshed—Our Life in the Knowledge of God—The Mind of Christ—The Triumph of the Cross—The Man of Sorrows—The Great Sacrifice—The Memorial of the Great Sacrifice—The Fulfilment—Buried with Christ—The Power of Christ risen—Walking in Newness of Life—Belief in the Resurrection of Christ—The Faith that overcometh the World—Following the Lamb of God—A little while—The Giver of all Good—Requisites of effectual Prayer—Ascending with Christ—The Days of Expectation—They shall walk with Me in White—The Holy Spirit and Baptism—Let all Things be done in order.

CONTENTS OF VOL. II.

The Door opened in Heaven—Love the mark of God's Children—The Gospel a Feast of Love—The Lost Sheep—Mercy the best preparation for Judgment—The peaceable ordering of the World—Brotherly Love and the Life in Christ—The Bread which God giveth—By their Fruits ye shall know them—Looking forward, or Divine Covetousness—The Day of Visitation—The Prayer of the Penitent—Weakness of Faith—Love the fulfilling of the Law—Thankfulness the Life of the Regenerate—My Beloved is Mine and I am His—The Knowledge which is Life Eternal—The Sabbath of Christ found in Meekness—Christ is on the Right Hand of God—The Forgiveness of Sins—Love and Joy in the Spirit—The Warfare and the Armour of Saints—The Love of Christians—The Earthly and Heavenly Citizenship—Mutual Intercessions—Gleanings after Harvest—Bringing unto Christ—Slowness in believing—Grace not given in Vain—The Refiner's Fire—The Lost Crown—Faith in the Incarnation—Value of an Inspired Gospel—The severe and social Virtues—Go and do thou likewise—Joy at hearing the Bridegroom's Voice—The Strength of God in Man's Weakness—Hidden with Christ in God—Do good, hoping for nothing again—The good exchange—War in Heaven—Healing and Peace—The Sacrament of Union—They which shall be accounted Worthy.

Selection, adapted to the Seasons of

the Ecclesiastical Year, from the "Parochial and Plain Sermons" of JOHN HENRY NEWMAN, B.D., sometime Vicar of St. Mary's, Oxford. Edited by the Rev. W. J. COPELAND, B.D., Rector of Farnham, Essex. Crown 8vo. 5*s.*

CONTENTS.

Advent:—Self-denial the Test of Religious Earnestness—Divine Calls—The Ventures of Faith—Watching. *Christmas Day*:—Religious Joy. *New Year's Sunday*:—The Lapse of Time. *Epiphany*:—Remembrance of Past Mercies—Equanimity—The Immortality of the Soul—Christian Manhood—Sincerity and Hypocrisy—Christian Sympathy. *Septuagesima*:—Present Blessings. *Sexagesima*:—Endurance the Christian's Portion. *Quinquagesima*:—Love the One Thing Needful. *Lent*:—The Individuality of the Soul—Life the Season of Repentance—Bodily Suffering—Tears of Christ at the Grave of Lazarus—Christ's Privations a Meditation for Christians—The Cross of Christ the Measure of the World. *Good Friday*:—The Crucifixion. *Easter Day*:—Keeping Fast and Festival. *Easter-Tide*:—Witnesses of the Resurrection—A Particular Providence as Revealed in the Gospel—Christ Manifested in Remembrance—The Invisible World—Waiting for Christ. *Ascension*:—Warfare the Condition of Victory. *Sunday after Ascension*:—Rising with Christ. *Whitsunday*:—The Weapons of Saints. *Trinity Sunday*:—The Mysteriousness of our Present Being. *Sundays after Trinity*:—Holiness Necessary for Future Blessedness—The Religious Use of Excited Feelings—The Self-wise Inquirer—Scripture a Record of Human Sorrow—The Danger of Riches—Obedience without Love, as instanced in the Character of Balaam—Moral Consequences of Single Sins—The Greatness and Littleness of Human Life—Moral Effects of Communion with God—The Thought of God the Stay of the Soul—The Power of the Will—The Gospel Palaces—Religion a Weariness to the Natural Man—The World our Enemy—The Praise of Man—Religion Pleasant to the Religious—Mental Prayer—Curiosity a Temptation to Sin—Miracles no Remedy for Unbelief—Jeremiah: a Lesson for the Disappointed—The Shepherd of our Souls—Doing Glory of God in Pursuits of the World.

"The selection has been made with great judgment, and the volume, which is daintily printed, has thus a very special value."—CHURCH TIMES.

"The publishers of the present volume have gathered together in a cheap and convenient form a series of Dr. Newman's earliest sermons, preached before he entered the Latin Church. These sermons are, of course, masterly, and, as they are not doctrinal, can be read with profit and pleasure by those who belong to the past as well as to the present creed of the learned doctor. The selection consists, with few exceptions, of sermons for the most important Church Festivals of the Year, and will be found admirably adapted for reading in the various seasons as they pass. To praise the noble language of Dr. Newman, an acknowledged master of English, would be superfluous; and these sermons, composed in the vigour of his years, are marked with the rarest grandeur and breadth of thought, and can be read with profit and pleasure by all, the religious for their profound piety, and by the student of English for their purity of diction."—MORNING POST.

"Those who, like ourselves, have long used and valued the eight volumes of Dr. Newman's Parochial Sermons, will be first to rejoice that a 'Selection' of about fifty sermons has been made, and issued in a handsome volume."—LITERARY CHURCHMAN.

"Most of the subjects treated of are practical, and it is not necessary to say how they are treated by such a master as John Henry Newman. It is but fair to add that the selection seems to keep steadily clear of matter suggestive of polemics."—FREEMAN'S JOURNAL.

Parochial and Plain Sermons. By JOHN HENRY NEWMAN, B.D., formerly Vicar of St. Mary's, Oxford. Edited by the Rev. W. J. COPELAND, B.D., Rector of Farnham, Essex. New Edition. 8 Vols. Crown 8vo. 5s. each. Sold separately.

CONTENTS OF VOL. I.

Holiness necessary for Future Blessedness—The Immortality of the Soul—Knowledge of God's Will without Obedience—Secret Truths—Self-denial the Test of Religious Earnestness—The Spiritual Mind—Sins of Ignorance and Weakness—God's Commandments not grievous—The Religious use of exalted Feelings—Profession without Practice—Profession without Hypocrisy—Profession without Ostentation—Promising without Doing—Religious Emotion—Religious Faith Rational—The Christian Mysteries—The Self-wise Inquirer—Obedience the Remedy for Religious Perplexity—Times of Private Prayer—Forms of Private Prayer—The Resurrection of the Body—Witnesses of the Resurrection—Christian Reverence—The Religion of the Day—Scripture a Record of Human Sorrow—Christian Manhood.

CONTENTS OF VOL. II.

The World's Benefactors—Faith without Sight—The Incarnation—Martyrdom—Love of Relations and Friends—The Mind of Little Children—Ceremonies of the Church—The Glory of the Christian Church—His Conversion viewed in Reference to His Office—Secrecy and Suddenness of Divine Visitations—Divine Decrees—The Reverence due to Her—Christ, a Quickening Spirit—Saving Knowledge—Self-contemplation—Religious Cowardice—The Gospel Witnesses—Mysteries in Religion—The Indwelling Spirit—The Kingdom of the Saints—The Gospel, a Trust committed to us—Tolerance of Religious Error—Rebuking Sin—The Christian Ministry—Human Responsibility—Guilelessness—The Danger of Riches—The Powers of Nature—The Danger of Accomplishments—Christian Zeal—Use of Saints' Days.

CONTENTS OF VOL. III.

Abraham and Lot—Wilfulness of Israel in rejecting Samuel—Saul—Early years of David—Jeroboam—Faith and Obedience—Christian Repentance—Contracted Views in Religion—A particular Providence as revealed in the Gospel—Tears of Christ at the Grave of Lazarus—Bodily Suffering—The Humiliation of the Eternal Son—Jewish Zeal a Pattern to Christians—Submission to Church Authority—Contest between Truth and Falsehood in the Church—The Church Visible and Invisible—The Visible Church an Encouragement to Faith—The Gift of the Spirit—Regenerating Baptism—Infant Baptism—The Daily Service—The Good Part of Mary—Religious Worship a Remedy for Excitements—Intercession—The Intermediate State.

CONTENTS OF VOL. IV.

The Strictness of the Law of Christ—Obedience without Love, as instanced in the Character of Balaam—Moral Consequences of Single Sins—Acceptance of Religious Privileges compulsory—Reliance on Religious Observances—The Individuality of the Soul—Chastisement amid Mercy—Peace and Joy amid Chastisement—The State of Grace—The Visible Church for the sake of the Elect—The Communion of Saints—The Church a

NEWMAN'S PAROCHIAL AND PLAIN SERMONS—
Continued.

Home for the Lonely—The Invisible World—The Greatness and Little-ness of Human Life—Moral Effects of Communion with God—Christ Hidden from the World—Christ Manifested in Remembrance—The Gain-saying of Korah—The Mysteriousness of our Present Being—The Ventures of Faith—Faith and Love—Watching—Keeping Fast and Festival.

CONTENTS OF VOL. V.

Worship, a Preparation for Christ's Coming—Reverence, a Belief in God's Presence—Unreal Words—Shrinking from Christ's Coming—Equanimity—Remembrance of past Mercies—The Mystery of Godliness—The State of Innocence—Christian Sympathy—Righteousness not of us, but in us—The Law of the Spirit—The New Works of the Gospel—The State of Salva-tion—Transgressions and Infirmities—Sins of Infirmity—Sincerity and Hypocrisy—The Testimony of Conscience—Many called, few chosen—Present Blessings—Endurance, the Christian's portion—Affliction a School of Comfort—The thought of God, the stay of the Soul—Love the one thing needful—The Power of the Will.

CONTENTS OF VOL. VI.

Fasting, a Source of Trial—Life, the Season of Repentance—Apostolic Absti-nence, a Pattern for Christians—Christ's Privations, a Meditation for Christians—Christ the Son of God made Man—The Incarnate Son, a Sufferer and Sacrifice—The Cross of Christ the Measure of the World—Difficulty of realizing Sacred Privileges—The Gospel Sign addressed to Faith—The Spiritual Presence of Christ in the Church—The Eucharistic Presence—Faith the Title for Justification—Judaism of the present day—The Fellowship of the Apostles—Rising with Christ—Warfare the Condi-tion of Victory—Waiting for Christ—Subjection of the Reason and Feel-ings to the Revealed Word—The Gospel Palaces—The Visible Temple—Offerings for the Sanctuary—The Weapons of Saints—Faith without Demonstration—The Mystery of the Holy Trinity—Peace in Believing.

CONTENTS OF VOL. VII.

The Lapse of Time—Religion, a Weariness to the Natural Man—The World our Enemy—The Praise of Men—Temporal Advantages—The Season of Epiphany—The Duty of Self-denial—The Yoke of Christ—Moses the Type of Christ—The Crucifixion—Attendance on Holy Communion—The Gospel Feast—Love of Religion, a new Nature—Religion pleasant to the Religious—Mental Prayer—Infant Baptism—The Unity of the Church—Steadfastness in the Old Paths.

CONTENTS OF VOL. VIII.

Reverence in Worship—Divine Calls—The Trial of Saul—The Call of David—Curiosity a Temptation to Sin—Miracles no remedy for Unbelief—Josiah, a Pattern for the Ignorant—Inward Witness to the Truth of the Gospel—Jeremiah, a Lesson for the Disappointed—Endurance of the World's Cen-sure—Doing Glory to God in Pursuits of the World—Vanity of Human Glory—Truth hidden when not sought after—Obedience to God the Way to Faith in Christ—Sudden Conversions—The Shepherd of our Souls—Religious Joy—Ignorance of Evil.

Lectures on the Doctrine of Justifica-

tion. By JOHN HENRY NEWMAN, B.D., sometime Fellow of Oriel College, Oxford. New Edition. Crown 8vo. 5*s.*

CONTENTS.

Faith considered as the Instrument of Justification—Love considered as the Formal Cause of Justification—Primary Sense of the term Justification—Secondary Senses of the term Justification—Misuse of the term Just or Righteous—On the Gift of Righteousness—The Characteristics of the Gift of Righteousness—Righteousness viewed as a Gift and as a Quality—Righteousness the Fruit of our Lord's Resurrection—The Office of Justifying Faith—The Nature of Justifying Faith—Faith viewed relatively to Rites and Works—On preaching the Gospel—Appendix.

Sermons Bearing upon Subjects of the

Day. By JOHN HENRY NEWMAN, B.D., sometime Fellow of Oriel College, Oxford. Edited by the Rev. W. J. COPELAND, B.D., Rector of Farnham, Essex. New Edition. Crown 8vo. 5*s.*

CONTENTS.

The Work of the Christian—Saintliness not forfeited by the Penitent—Our Lord's Last Supper and His First—Dangers to the Penitent—The Three Offices of Christ—Faith and Experience—Faith and the World—The Church and the World—Indulgence in Religious Privileges—Connection between Personal and Public Improvement—Christian Nobleness—Joshua, a Type of Christ and His Followers—Elisha, a Type of Christ and His Followers—The Christian Church a continuation of the Jewish—The Principle of continuity between the Jewish and Christian Churches—The Christian Church an Imperial Power—Sanctity the Token of the Christian Empire—Condition of the Members of the Christian Empire—The Apostolical Christian—Wisdom and Innocence—Invisible Presence of Christ—Outward and Inward Notes of the Church—Grounds for Steadfastness in our Religious Profession—Elijah the Prophet of the Latter Days—Feasting in Captivity—The Parting of Friends.

Fifteen Sermons preached before the

University of Oxford, between A.D. 1826 and 1843. By JOHN HENRY NEWMAN, B.D., sometime Fellow of Oriel College, Oxford. New Edition. Crown 8vo. 5*s.*

CONTENTS.

The Philosophical Temper first enjoined by the Gospel—The Influence of Natural and Revealed Religion respectively—Evangelical Sanctity the Perfection of Natural Virtue—The Usurpations of Reason—Personal Influence, the means of Propagating the Truth—Our Justice, as a Principle of Divine Governance—Contest between Faith and Light—Human Responsibility, as Independent of Circumstances—Wilfulness the Sin of Saul—Faith and Reason, contrasted as Habits of Mind—The Nature of Faith in Relation to Reason—Love the Safeguard of Faith against Superstition—Implicit and Explicit Reason—Wisdom, as contrasted with Faith and with Bigotry—The Theory of Developments in Religious Doctrine.

The Catholic Sacrifice. Sermons Preached

at All Saints, Margaret Street. By the Rev. BERDMORE COMPTON, M.A., Vicar of All Saints, Margaret Street. Crown 8vo. 5*s.*

CONTENTS.

The Eucharistic Life—The Sacrifice of Sweet Savour—The Pure Offering—The Catholic Oblation—The Sacrificial Feast—The Preparation for the Eucharist—The Introductory Office—The Canon—Degrees of Apprehension—The Fascination of Christ Crucified—The Shewbread—Consecration of Worship and Work—Water, Blood, Wine—The Blood of Sprinkling—The Mystery of Sacraments—The Oblation of Gethsemane—Offertory and Tribute Money.

The Sayings of the Great Forty Days,

between the Resurrection and Ascension, regarded as the Outlines of the Kingdom of God. In Five Discourses. With an Examination of Dr. Newman's Theory of Development. By GEORGE MOBERLY, D.C.L., Bishop of Salisbury. Fifth Edition. Crown 8vo. 5*s.*

Plain Sermons, preached at Brighstone.

By GEORGE MOBERLY, D.C.L., Bishop of Salisbury. Third Edition. Crown 8vo. 5*s.*

CONTENTS.

Except a Man be Born again—The Lord with the Doctors—The Draw-Net—will lay me down in Peace—Ye have not so learned Christ—Trinity Sunday—My Flesh is Meat indeed—The Corn of Wheat dying and multiplied—The Seed Corn springing to new Life—I am the Way, the Truth, and the Life—The Ruler of the Sea—Stewards of the Mysteries of God—Ephphatha—The Widow of Nain—Josiah's Discovery of the Law—The Invisible World : Angels—Prayers, especially Daily Prayers—They all with one consent began to make excuse—Ascension Day—The Comforter—The Tokens of the Spirit—Elijah's Warning, Fathers and Children—Thou shalt see them no more for ever—Baskets full of Fragments—Harvest—The Marriage Supper of the Lamb—The Last Judgment.

Sermons preached at Winchester College.

By GEORGE MOBERLY, D.C.L., Bishop of Salisbury. 2 Vols. Small 8vo. 6*s.* 6*d.* each. Sold separately.

Sermons, Parochial and Occasional.

By J. B. MOZLEY, D.D., late Canon of Christ Church, and Regius Professor of Divinity in the University of Oxford. Crown 8vo.   7s. 6d.

CONTENTS.

The Right Eye and the Right Hand—Temptation treated as Opportunity—The Influences of Habit on Devotion—Thought for the Morrow—The Relief of Utterance—Seeking a Sign—David Numbering the People—The Heroism of Faith—Proverbs—The Teaching of Events—Growing Worse—Our Lord the Sacrifice for Sin—The Parable of the Sower—The Religious Enjoyment of Nature—The Threefold Office of the Holy Spirit—Wisdom and Folly Tested by Experience—Moses, a Leader—The Unjust Steward —Sowing to the Spirit—True Religion a Manifestation—St. Paul's Exaltation of Labour—Jeremiah's Witness against Idolatry—Isaiah's Estimate of Worldly Greatness—The Shortness of Life—The Endless State of Being —The Witness of the Apostles—Life a Probation—Christian Mysteries the Common Heritage—Our Lord's Hour—Fear—The Educating Power of Strong Impressions—The Secret Justice of Temporal Providence— Jacob as a Prince Prevailing with God.

"His sermons are the solemn and piercing reflections of a man who intently scrutinizes the world and God's dealings with it for the spiritual benefit of himself and others. The poetry of his sermons is unsought for, and results, where it exists, from a desire to give adequate expression to an intense appreciation of what is in itself elevated and astonishing; and if he is thus lifted into simile or metaphor, it is because he is at a loss to convey in any other way the height or depth or breadth of what he sees."— GUARDIAN.

"All who have read the 'University Sermons,' or the volume entitled the 'Ruling Ideas as in the Early Ages,' of the late Dr. Mozley, are aware with what unusual profundity and originality of thought they are marked; and

by all such this further instalment of Dr. Mozley's sermons will be welcomed. They will be of great use to the clergy in the preparation of their own discourses; they will be of still greater use to them if read and studied privately by way of mental discipline." —LITERARY CHURCHMAN.

"We may say at once, and after reading nearly every page of it, that there is not one sermon here devoid of interest, and there is not one which does not bear the same stamp which was impressed upon the great University Series. . . . . . No man can read these sermons without feeling his conscience stirred and cleared, and if he has any good in him, without feeling his will braced for fresh efforts."— CHURCH BELLS.

Seven Addresses delivered at S.

Paul's Cathedral at the Mid-Day Service, Good Friday, 1879. By V. S. S. COLES, M.A., Rector of Shepton Beauchamp. Small 8vo.   1s.

CONTENTS.

Forgiveness of Sin, the First Great Need—True Prayer, the Means of Forgiveness—Privilege of Forgiven Souls—Suffering of the Human Soul—Suffering of the Human Body—Perseverance in Effort—Trust in God.

Sermons preached before the University

of Oxford, and on various occasions. By J. B. MOZLEY, D.D., late Canon of Christ Church, and Regius Professor of Divinity, Oxford. Fourth Edition. Crown 8vo. 7s. 6d.

CONTENTS.

The Roman Council—The Pharisees—Eternal Life—The Reversal of Human Judgment—War—Nature—The Work of the Spirit on the Natural Man—The Atonement—Our Duty to Equals—The Peaceful Temper—The Strength of Wishes—The unspoken Judgment of Mankind—The true test of Spiritual Birth—Ascension Day—Gratitude—The Principle of Emulation—Religion the First Choice—The Influence of Dogmatic Teaching on Education.

*" There are sermons in it which, for penetrating insight into the mysteries and anomalies of human character, its power of holding together strange opposites, its capacity for combination, for disguise, and unconscious transformation, are as wonderful, it may almost be said as terrible, in their revelations and suggestions as are to be found anywhere. There are four sermons, one on the ' Pharisees,' one on ' Eternal Life,' one on the ' Reversal of Human Judgment,' the fourth on the ' Unspoken Judgment of Mankind,' which must almost make an epoch in the thought and history of any one who reads them and really takes in what they say. There is in them a kind of Shakspearian mixture of subtlety of remark with boldness and directness of phrase, and with a grave, pathetic irony, which is not often characteristic of such compositions."—*TIMES.

" These are unusually remarkable sermons. They are addressed to educated, reflective, and, in some cases, philosophical readers, and they exhibit, by turns or in combination, high philosophical power, a piercing appreciation of human motives, vivid conceptions, and a great power of clothing those conceptions in the language of trenchant aphorism, or lofty, earnest poetry."—GUARDIAN.

" A new gleam of religious genius. . . . Keen simplicity and reality in the way of putting things is characteristic of these sermons of Dr. Mozley's, but not less characteristic of them—and this is what shows that the Christian faith has in him appealed to a certain original faculty of the kind which we call ' genius '—is the instinctive sympathy which he seems to have with the subtler shades of Christ's teaching, so as to make it suddenly seem new to us, as well as more wonderful than ever."—SPECTATOR.

*" The volume possesses intrinsic merits so remarkable as to be almost unique. . . . There is scarcely a sermon in it which does not possess eloquence, in a very true sense, of a high order. But it is the eloquence not so much of language as of thought. It is the eloquence of concentration, of vigorous grasp, of delicate irony, of deep but subdued pathos, of subtle delicacy of touch, of broad strong sense; it impresses the mind rather than strikes the ear. We cannot help feeling, as we read, not only that the preacher means what he says, but that he has taken pains to think out his meaning, and has applied to the process the whole energy and resources of no common intellect." —*SATURDAY REVIEW.

Sermons.   By HENRY MELVILL, B.D., late

Canon of St. Paul's, and Chaplain in Ordinary to the Queen. New Edition. 2 Vols. Crown 8vo. 5*s.* each. Sold separately.

CONTENTS OF VOL. I.

The First Prophecy—Christ the Minister of the Church—The Impossibility of Creature-Merit—The Humiliation of the Man Christ Jesus—The Doctrine of the Resurrection viewed in connection with that of the Soul's Immortality—The Power of Wickedness and Righteousness to reproduce themselves—The Power of Religion to strengthen the Human Intellect—The Provision made by God for the Poor—St. Paul, a Tent-Maker—The Advantages of a state of Expectation—Truth as it is in Jesus—The Difficulties of Scripture.

CONTENTS OF VOL. II.

Jacob's Vision and Vow—The continued Agency of the Father and the Son—The Resurrection of Dry Bones—Protestantism and Popery—Christianity a Sword—The Death of Moses—The Ascension of Christ—The Spirit upon the Waters—The Proportion of Grace to Trial—Pleading before the Mountains—Heaven—God's Way in the Sanctuary.

*"Every one who can remember the days when Canon Melvill was the preacher of the day, will be glad to see these four-and-twenty of his sermons so nicely reproduced. His Sermons were all the result of real study and genuine reading, with far more theology in them than those of many who make much more profession of theology. There are sermons here which we can personally remember; it has been a pleasure to us to be reminded of them, and we are glad to see them brought before the present generation. We hope that they may be studied, for they deserve it thoroughly."—*LITERARY CHURCHMAN.

"The Sermons of Canon Melvill, now republished in two handy volumes, need only to be mentioned to be sure of a hearty welcome. Sound learning, well-weighed words, calm and keen logic, and solemn devoutness, mark the whole series of masterly discourses, which embrace some of the chief doctrines of the Church, and set them forth in clear and Scriptural strength."—*STANDARD.

*"The Sermons abound in thought, and the thoughts are couched in English which is at once elegant in construction and easy to read."—*CHURCH TIMES.

*"Henry Melvill's intellect was large, his imagination brilliant, his ardour intense, and his style strong, fervid, and picturesque. Often he seemed to glow with the inspiration of a prophet."—*AMERICAN QUARTERLY CHURCH REVIEW.

Lectures delivered at St. Margaret's,

Lothbury. By HENRY MELVILL, B.D., late Canon of St. Paul's, and Chaplain in Ordinary to the Queen. New Edition. Crown 8vo. 5*s.*

CONTENTS.

The Return of the Dispossessed Spirit—Honey from the Rock—Easter—The Witness in Oneself—The Apocrypha—A Man a Hiding-place—The

MELVILL'S LOTHBURY LECTURES—*Continued.*

Hundredfold Recompense—The Life more than Meat—Isaiah's Vision—St. John the Baptist—Building the Tombs of the Prophets—Manifestation of the Sons of God—St. Paul's Determination—The Song of Moses and the Lamb—The Divine Longsuffering—Sowing the Seed—The Great Multitude—The Kinsman Redeemer—St. Barnabas—Spiritual Decline.

Sermons on Certain of the Less

Prominent Facts and References in Sacred Story. By HENRY MELVILL, B.D., late Canon of St. Paul's, and Chaplain in Ordinary to the Queen. New Edition. 2 Vols. Crown 8vo. 5s. each. Sold separately.

CONTENTS OF VOL. I.

The Faith of Joseph on his Death-bed—Angels as Remembrancers—The Burning of the Magical Books—The Parting Hymn—Cæsar's Household—The Sleepless Night—The Well of Bethlehem—The Thirst of Christ—The second Delivery of the Lord's Prayer—Peculiarities in the Miracle in the Coasts of Decapolis—The Latter Rain—The Lowly Errand—Nehemiah before Artaxerxes—Jabez.

CONTENTS OF VOL. II.

The Young Man in the Linen Cloth—The Fire on the Shore—The Finding the Guest-Chamber—The Spectre's Sermon a truism—Various Opinions—The Misrepresentations of Eve—Seeking, after Finding—The Bird's Nest—Angels our Guardians in trifles—The appearance of failure—Simon the Cyrenian—The power of the Eye—Pilate's Wife—Examination of Cain.

" We are glad to see this new edition of what we have always considered to be Melvill's best sermons, because in them we have his best thoughts. . . . Many of these sermons are the strongest arguments yet adduced for internal evidence of the veracity of the Scriptural narratives."—STANDARD.

" Unusually interesting. . . . . No one can read these sermons without deriving instruction from them, without being compelled to acknowledge that new light has been cast for him on numerous passages of Scripture, which he must henceforth read with greater intelligence and greater interest than before." — EDINBURGH COURANT.

" For skill in developing the significance of the less prominent facts of Holy Scripture' no one could compete with the late Canon Melvill, four volumes of whose discourses—two of them occupied entirely with his sermons on subjects of this class—are before us. His preaching was unique. He selected for the most part texts that are not frequently treated, and when he chose those of a more ordinary character, he generally presented them in a new light, and elicited from them some truth which would not have suggested itself to any other preacher. He was singularly ingenious in some of his conceptions, and wonderfully forcible and impressive in his mode of developing and applying them."—NONCONFORMIST.

" The publishers of these well-known, almost classic sermons, have conferred a boon on all lovers of our pulpit literature by this beautiful, portable eaition of some of the most brilliant and original discourses that have been delivered to this generation."—BRITISH QUARTERLY REVIEW.

Selection from the Sermons preached

during the Latter Years of his Life, in the Parish Church of Barnes, and in the Cathedral of St. Paul's. By HENRY MELVILL, B.D., late Canon of St. Paul's, and Chaplain in Ordinary to the Queen. New Edition. 2 Vols. Crown 8vo. 5s. each. Sold separately.

CONTENTS OF VOL. I.

The Parity of the consequences of Adam's Transgression and Christ's Death—The Song of Simeon—The Days of Old—Omissions of Scripture—The Madman in Sport—Peace, Peace, when there is no Peace—A very lovely Song—This is that King Ahaz—Ariel—New Wine and Old Bottles—Demas—Michael and the Devil—The Folly of Excessive Labour—St. Paul at Philippi—Believing a Lie—The Prodigal Son—The Foolishness of Preaching—Knowledge and Sorrow—The Unjust Steward—The Man born blind.

CONTENTS OF VOL. II.

Rejoicing as in Spoil — Satan a Copyist — The binding the Tares into Bundles — Two walking together—Agreeing with the Adversary—God speaking to Moses—Hoping in Mercy—Faith as a Grain of Mustard Seed—Mary's Recompense—War in Heaven—Glory into Shame—The Last Judgment—Man like to Vanity—God so Loved the World—Saul—And what shall this Man do?—The Sickness and Death of Elisha—Abiding in our Callings—Trinity Sunday.

" The main characteristics of Canon Melvill's sermons are these—they are not polemical; the odium theologicum is nowhere to be found in them, and nowhere is the spirit of true Christian charity and love absent from them. This will widen their usefulness, for they will on this account make a ready way amongst all sects and creeds of professing Christians. Again, these sermons are eminently practical and devotional in their tone and aim. The truths here proclaimed pierce the heart to its very core, so true is the preacher's aim, so vigorous is the force with which he shoots the convictions of his own heart into the hearts of his hearers." —STANDARD.

" There are in the sermons before us all Melvill's wonted grace of diction, strength of reasoning, and aptness of illustration."—WEEKLY REVIEW.

" Two other volumes of the late Canon Melvill's sermons contain forty discourses preached by him in his later years, and they are prefaced by a short memoir of one of the worthiest and most impressive preachers of recent times."—EXAMINER.

" Many years have now elapsed since we first heard Henry Melvill. But we can still recall the text, the sermon, the deep impression made upon us by the impassioned eloquence of the great preacher. It was our first, and very profitable experience of what influence there resides in the faithful preaching of the Gospel of the Lord Jesus Christ. For while it was impossible to be indifferent to the messenger, yet the message was brought home by him to the heart and to the conscience. It is pleasant in these, the latest sermons delivered by Mr. Melvill, to find the same faithful utterance."—CHRISTIAN OBSERVER.

The Life of Justification. A Series of

Lectures delivered in Substance at All Saints', Margaret Street. By the Rev. GEORGE BODY, B.A., Rector of Kirkby Misperton. Fifth Edition. Crown 8vo. 4s. 6d.

CONTENTS.

Justification the Want of Humility—Christ our Justification—Union with Christ the Condition of Justification—Conversion and Justification—The Life of Justification—The Progress and End of Justification.

"On the whole we have rarely met with a more clear, intelligible and persuasive statement of the truth as regards the important topics on which the volume treats. Sermon II. in particular, will strike every one by its eloquence and beauty, but we scarcely like to specify it, lest in praising it we should seem to disparage the other portions of this admirable little work."—CHURCH TIMES.

"These discourses show that their author's position is due to something more and higher than mere fluency, gesticulation, and flexibility of voice. He appears as having drunk deeply at the fountain of St. Augustine, and as understanding how to translate the burning words of that mighty genius into the current language of to-day."—UNION REVIEW.

"There is real power in these sermons:—power, real power, and plenty of it. . . . There is such a moral veraciousness about him, such a profound and over-mastering belief that Christ has proved a bonâ-fide cure for unholiness, and such an intensity of eagerness to lead others to seek and profit by that means of attaining the true sanctity which alone can enter Heaven—that we wonder not at the crowds which hang upon his preaching, nor at the success of his fervid appeals to the human conscience. If any one doubts our verdict, let him buy this volume. No one will regret its perusal."—LITERARY CHURCHMAN.

The Life of Temptation. A Course of

Lectures delivered in Substance at St. Peter's, Eaton Square ; also at All Saints', Margaret Street. By the Rev. GEORGE BODY, B.A., Rector of Kirkby Misperton. Fourth Edition. Crown 8vo. 4s. 6d.

CONTENTS.

The Leading into Temptation—The Rationale of Temptation—Why we are Tempted—Safety in Temptation—With Jesus in Temptation—The End of Temptation.

"Regeneration and conversion seem here to occupy their proper places in the Christian economy, and the general subject of temptation is worked out with considerable ability."—CHURCH TIMES.

"This is another volume of simple, earnest, soul-stirring words, dealing with the mysteries of Christian experience."—LONDON QUARTERLY REVIEW.

"A collection of sermons, pious, earnest, and eloquent."—ENGLISH CHURCHMAN.

Sermons on Special Occasions. By

DANIEL MOORE, M.A., Chaplain in Ordinary to the Queen, and Vicar of Holy Trinity, Paddington. Crown 8vo. 7s. 6d.

CONTENTS.

The Words of Christ imperishable—The Gospel Welcome—The Conversion of St. Paul—The Christian's Mission—Business and Godliness—Soberness and Watchfulness—The Joy of the Disciples at the Resurrection—The Saviour's Ascension—Jesus in the Midst—The Moral Attractions of the Cross—The Gospel Workmen—The Work of the Holy Spirit—The Doctrine of the Holy Trinity—The Law of Moral Recompenses—The Goodness of King Joash—The Tenderness of Christ—Christ our Example in Youth—Jacob in Life and in Death—The Spiritual Mind—Britain's Obligations to the Gospel—The Throne in Mourning—Prayer and Providence—The Unsearchableness of God.

The Age and the Gospel; Four Sermons preached before the University of Cambridge, at the Hulsean Lecture, 1864. With a Discourse on Final Retribution. By DANIEL MOORE, M.A., Chaplain in Ordinary to the Queen, and Vicar of Holy Trinity, Paddington. Crown 8vo. 5s.

The Mystery of the Temptation: a Course of Lectures. By the Rev. W. H. HUTCHINGS, M.A., Sub-Warden of the House of Mercy, Clewer. Crown 8vo. 4s. 6d.

CONTENTS.

The Entrance into the Temptation—The Fast—The Personality of Satan—The First Temptation—The Second Temptation—The Third Temptation—The End of the Temptation.

" *We can mention with unmixed praise a series of lectures on ' The Mystery of the Temptation,' by Mr. Hutchings of Clewer. They are deeply thoughtful, full, and well written, in a style which, from its calmness and dignity, befits the subject.*"—GUARDIAN.

" *This book is one of the refreshing proofs still occasionally met with that the traditional culture and refinement of the Anglican clergy is not quite exhausted, nor its exhaustion implied, by the endless and vulgar controversies that fill the columns of religious newspapers. The sober earnestness that* has always been a characteristically Anglican virtue has not failed in a preacher like Mr. Hutchings.*"—ACADEMY.

" *Students of Scripture will find in ' The Mystery of the Temptation' sound reasoning, the evidences of close study, and the spirit of reverence and fervent faith.*"—MORNING POST.

" *This is a volume of lectures which will repay serious study. They are earnest to the last degree.*"—LITERARY CHURCHMAN,

" *Very good indeed.*"—NEW YORK CHURCH JOURNAL.

The Religion of the Christ: its His-
toric and Literary Development considered as an Evidence of
its Origin. Being the Bampton Lectures for 1874. By the
Rev. STANLEY LEATHES, M.A., Minister of St. Philip's,
Regent Street, and Professor of Hebrew, King's College,
London. Second Edition. Crown 8vo. 7s. 6d.

The Witness of the Old Testament to
Christ. Being the Boyle Lectures for the year 1868. By the
Rev. STANLEY LEATHES, M.A., Minister of St. Philip's,
Regent Street, and Professor of Hebrew, King's College,
London. 8vo. 9s.

The Witness of St. Paul to Christ.
Being the Boyle Lectures for 1869. With an Appendix on
the Credibility of the Acts, in Reply to the Recent Strictures
of Dr. Davidson. By the Rev. STANLEY LEATHES, M.A.,
Minister of St. Philip's, Regent Street, and Professor of
Hebrew, King's College, London. 8vo. 10s. 6d.

The Witness of St. John to Christ.
Being the Boyle Lectures for 1870. With an Appendix on
the Authorship and Integrity of St. John's Gospel, and the
Unity of the Johannine Writings. By the Rev. STANLEY
LEATHES, M.A., Minister of St. Philip's, Regent Street, and
Professor of Hebrew, King's College, London. 8vo. 10s. 6d.

Short Sermons on the Psalms in their
Order. Preached in a Village Church. By W. J. STRACEY,
M.A., Rector of Oxnead, and Vicar of Buxton, Norfolk, for-
merly Fellow of Magdalen College, Cambridge. Crown 8vo.

Vol. I.—Psalms I—XXV. 5s.
Vol. II.—Psalms XXVI—LI. 5s.

Sermons Preached in the Temporary

Chapel of Keble College, Oxford, 1870—1876. Second Edition. Crown 8vo. 6*s*.

CONTENTS.

The Service of God the Principle of Daily Life—The Costliness of Acceptable Offerings—The Hearing of Sermons—The Missionary Character of all Christian Lives—The Revelation of the Son as well in Nature as in the Incarnation—The New Chapel—The Secret of Spiritual Strength—The Preparation of Lent—The Spirit of the Daily Services : I. The Spiritual Sacrifice of the Universal Priesthood. II. Offering to God of His Own—The Life of Love—The Resurrection—Redeeming the Time—The Devotional Study of Holy Scripture—Conversion—Conversation—Enthusiasm—Growth in the Knowledge of God—The Imitation of Christ—Manliness—Truth—Saints' Days—Eternity—Life.

Farewell Counsels of a Pastor to his

Flock, on Topics of the Day. By EDWARD MEYRICK GOULBURN, D.D., Dean of Norwich. Third Edition. Small 8vo. 4*s*.

CONTENTS.

Absolution—Ritualism—The Doctrine of the Eucharist—The Atonement—The Stability of an Orthodox Faith—The Stability of Personal Religion—On Preaching Christ Crucified—The Responsibility of Hearers.

The Doctrine of the Cross : specially

in its relation to the Troubles of Life. Sermons preached during Lent in the Parish Church of New Windsor by HENRY J. ELLISON, M.A. (sometime Vicar of Windsor), Honorary Chaplain to the Queen, Honorary Canon of Christ Church, and Rector of Haseley, Oxon. Small 8vo. 2*s*. 6*d*.

CONTENTS.

The Troubles of Life—The Doctrine of the Cross—The Christian Crucified with Christ—The Cross of Chastisement—The Cross of Trial—Voluntary Crosses—The Crown.

The Way of Holiness in Married Life.

A Course of Sermons preached in Lent. By the Rev. HENRY J. ELLISON, M.A., Hon. Canon of Christ Church, and Vicar of New Windsor, Berks. Second Edition. Small 8vo. 2*s*. 6*d*.

Waterloo Place, London

Sermons Preached in the Parish

Church of Barnes, 1871 to 1876. By PETER GOLDSMITH
MEDD, M.A., Rector of North Cerney, Hon. Canon of St.
Albans, and Examining Chaplain to the Bishop; late Senior
Fellow of University College, Oxford, and Rector of Barnes.
Crown 8vo. 7s. 6d.

CONTENTS.

Thankfulness for God's Mercies—Subjection to the Civil Power—Christ's Pro-
phecy of the End—God's Purpose of Love in Creation—The Introduction
of Evil into the Creation—Christian Love—Christianity a Religion of Self-
Denial—The Nature of Sin—The Consequences of Sin (No. 1)—The
Consequences of Sin (No. 2)—The Remedy of Sin (No. 1)—The Remedy
of Sin (No. 2)—With Christ in Paradise—The Remedy of Sin (No. 3)—
The Remedy of Sin (No. 4)—Christ the Resurrection and the Life—The
Hope of the Resurrection—The Three Resurrections—The Hope of the
Christian—The Publican's Prayer—The Conflict of Flesh and Spirit—
Christian Unity—The Duty of Forgiveness—Present Salvation—The
Marks of the Children of God—Against Religious Narrowness—The
Necessity of Meditation on Religious Subjects—The Need of Effort in the
Christian Life—Bodily Works of Mercy—The Athanasian Creed—Con-
scious Religion—The Comfort of the Christian Faith—Appendix.

*" The special merit of his volume is
its thoughtfulness; and as Mr. Medd
writes in a very condensed style, the
thirty-two sermons which he has given
us contain a great deal more of valuable matter than many books of much
larger bulk. . . . We believe that
many of our readers, among the
clergy as well as the laity, will thank
us for having drawn their attention
to the excellences of the volume before
us."—*GUARDIAN.

*" They range over a wide circle of
subjects, theological and practical;
but are always full, vigorous, and
energetic, yet with a sobriety of style
and an elegance of treatment that
must have charmed the hearer just
as they win upon the reader. We do*
*not often meet with a volume of dis-
courses of such uniform excellence.
Nothing hazardous is attempted; but
in all that he attempts Mr. Medd
entirely succeeds. The teaching is
plain, direct, and effective; while the
breadth of view and the liberality of
sentiment are most refreshing in these
days when the sermon is too often
made a party manifesto. Professor
Blackie would find in them both
'vigour' and 'grace.' And the reader
will also find in them a considerable
knowledge of the heart, an intelligent
comprehension of the Christian system,
much lucid exposition of Scriptural
truth, and a forcible application of it
to the human conscience."—*SCOTTISH
GUARDIAN.

The Permanence of Christianity. Con-

sidered in Eight Lectures preached before the University of
Oxford, in the year 1872, on the Foundation of the late Rev.
John Bampton, M.A. By JOHN RICHARD TURNER EATON,
M.A., late Fellow and Tutor of Merton College, Rector of
Lapworth, Warwickshire. 8vo. 12s.

The Christian Character; Six Sermons preached in Lent. By JOHN JACKSON, D.D., Bishop of London. Seventh Edition. Small 8vo. 3*s.* 6*d.*

The Reconciliation of Reason and Faith. Being Sermons on Faith, Evil, Sin and Suffering, Immortality, God, Science, Prayer, and other Subjects. By REGINALD E. MOLYNEUX, M.A. Crown 8vo. 4*s.*

The Soul in its Probation: Sermons Preached at the Church of S. Alban the Martyr, Holborn, on the Sundays in Lent, 1873. By the Rev. F. N. OXENHAM, M.A. 8vo. 5*s.*

The Last Three Sermons preached at Oxford by PHILIP N. SHUTTLEWORTH, D.D., sometime Lord Bishop of Chichester. Justification through Faith—The Merciful Character of the Gospel Covenant—The Sufficiency of Scripture a Rule of Faith. To which is added a Letter addressed in 1841 to a Young Clergyman, now a Priest in the Church of Rome. New Edition. Small 8vo. 2*s.* 6*d.*

Not Tradition but Scripture. By the late PHILIP NICHOLAS SHUTTLEWORTH, D.D., Warden of New College, Oxford, and Rector of Foxley, Wilts, afterwards Bishop of Chichester. Fourth Edition. Crown 8vo. 3*s.* 6*d.*

7. Religious Education.

A Key to Christian Doctrine and Prac-

tice, founded on the Church Catechism. By the Rev. JOHN HENRY BLUNT, M.A., F.S.A., Editor of "The Annotated Book of Common Prayer," &c. &c. Small 8vo. 2s. 6d. Forming a Volume of "Keys to Christian Knowledge."

" Of cheap and reliable text-books of this nature there has hitherto been a great want. We are often asked to recommend books for use in Church Sunday-schools, and we therefore take this opportunity of saying that we know of none more likely to be of service both to teachers and scholars than these 'Keys.'" — CHURCHMAN'S SHILLING MAGAZINE.

" This is another of Mr. Blunt's most useful manuals, with all the precision of a school book, yet diverging into matters of practical application so freely as to make it most serviceable, either as a teacher's suggestion book, or as an intelligent pupil's reading book." — LITERARY CHURCHMAN.

" Will be very useful for the higher classes in Sunday-schools, or rather for the fuller instruction of the Sunday-school teachers themselves, where the parish priest is wise enough to devote a certain time regularly to their preparation for their voluntary task." — UNION REVIEW.

Household Theology: a Handbook of

Religious Information respecting the Holy Bible, the Prayer Book, the Church, the Ministry, Divine Worship, the Creeds, &c. &c. By the Rev. JOHN HENRY BLUNT, M.A., F.S.A., Editor of "The Annotated Book of Common Prayer," &c. &c. New Edition. Small 8vo. 3s. 6d.

CONTENTS.

The Bible—The Prayer Book—The Church—Table of Dates—Ministerial Offices—Divine Worship—The Creeds—A Practical Summary of Christian Doctrine—The Great Christian Writers of Early Times—Ancient and Modern Heresies and Sects—The Church Calendar—A short explanation of Words used in Church History and Theology—Index.

---

and at Oxford and Cambridge

Manuals of Religious Instruction.

Edited by JOHN PILKINGTON NORRIS, B.D., Canon of Bristol, Vicar of St. Mary, Redcliffe, and Examining Chaplain to the Bishop of Manchester.

3 Volumes.   Small 8vo.   3*s*. 6*d*. each.   Sold separately.

The Old Testament.
The New Testament.
The Prayer Book.

Or each Volume in Five Parts.   1*s*. each Part.

[These Manuals are intended to supply a five years' course of instruction for young people between the ages of thirteen and eighteen.

It will be seen that fifteen small graduated text-books are provided :—

Five on the Old Testament ;
Five on the New Testament ;
Five on the Catechism and Liturgy.

In preparing the last, the Editor has thought it best to spread the study of the Catechism over several years, rather than compress it into one.

This may give rise to what may appear some needless repetition. But the Lessons of our Catechism are of such paramount importance, that it seems desirable to keep it continually in our Pupils' hands, as the best key to the study of the Prayer Book.

There has been a grievous want of *definiteness* in our young people's knowledge of Church doctrine. Especially have the Diocesan Inspectors noticed it in our Pupil Teachers. It has arisen, doubtless, from their Teachers assuming that they had clear elementary ideas about religion, in which really they had never been grounded. It is therefore thought not too much to ask them to give one-third of their time to the study of the Prayer Book.

In the Old Testament and New Testament Manuals the greatest pains have been taken to give them such a character as shall render it impossible for them to supersede the Sacred Text. Two main objects the writers of the Old and New Testament Manuals have proposed to themselves; first, to stimulate interest; second, to supply a sort of running commentary on the inspired page. Especial pains have been taken to draw the reader's attention to the *spiritual* teaching of Holy Scripture, and to subordinate to this the merely historical interest.

The writer of the Old Testament Manual has made it his endeavour to help the reader to see our Lord Christ in Law, in Psalms, in Prophets.

The New Testament Manual is confined to the Gospels and Acts. It was found impossible to include any of the Epistles. But the Fourth Part of the Prayer Book Manual will in some measure supply this deficiency.

Although they were originally prepared with special regard to Pupil Teachers, they will be found adapted also for all students of a like age (from thirteen to eighteen) who have not access to many books.]

Waterloo Place, London

Rudiments of Theology. A First Book

for Students. By JOHN PILKINGTON NORRIS, B.D., Canon of Bristol, Vicar of St. Mary, Redcliffe, and Examining Chaplain to the Bishop of Manchester. Second Edition, revised. Crown 8vo. 7s. 6d.

"It is altogether a remarkable book. We have seldom seen clear, incisive reasoning, orthodox teaching, and wide-mindedness in such happy combination."—LITERARY CHURCHMAN.

"A most useful book for theological students in the earlier part of their course. . . . The book is one for which the Church owes a debt of gratitude to Canon Norris, combining, as it does, orthodoxy and learning, and logical accuracy of definition with real charity. We heartily commend it."—JOHN BULL.

"We can recommend this book to theological students as a useful and compendious manual. It is clear and well arranged. . . . We venture to believe that, on the whole, he is a very fair exponent of the teaching of the English Church, and that his book may be profitably used by those for whom it is chiefly intended—that is, candidates for ordination."—SPECTATOR.

"This unpretending work supplies a real desideratum. *. . . It seeks to lead us from the shifting sands of human systems to the solid ground of Divine revelation, wisely recognising as its most trustworthy interpreters those who came nearest to its times,*

and directing the student's mind to 'what the early Fathers thought and wrote in the days when the Church's theologians had to hold their own against an adverse world.'"—GUARDIAN.

"This work was prepared as a handbook for theological students. But it is to reach a far wider field. It is capable of doing a most important service among all classes. We have seldom, if ever, met a more satisfactory or a clearer presentation of the fundamental facts of theology than those given in these pages. . . . The author has the rare faculty—it amounts really to genius—of saying just the thing that ought to be said, and of presenting any truth in such a shape that the reader can easily take hold of it and make it his own. . . . We commend this work to Churchmen generally as one from which all can derive profit. To the Clergy it will serve as a model method of dogmatic teaching, and to the laity it will be a rich storehouse of information concerning the things to be believed. . . . The whole thing is so admirable in tone, arrangement, and style that it will, no doubt, become universally popular."—CHURCHMAN (NEW YORK).

The Young Churchman's Companion

to the Prayer Book. By the Rev. J. W. GEDGE, M.A., Winchester Diocesan Inspector of Schools for West Surrey and the Channel Islands. (Recommended by the late and present Lord Bishops of Winchester.)

Part I.—Morning and Evening Prayer and Litany.
Part II.—Baptismal and Confirmation Services.
Part III.—Holy Communion.

18mo., 1s. each Part ; or in paper cover, 6d.

A Catechism on Gospel History, inculcating Church Doctrine.

By the Rev. SAMUEL KETTLEWELL, M.A., late Vicar of St. Mark's, Leeds. Third Edition. Small 8vo. 3s. 6d.

"This work has deservedly reached a third edition. Originally composed when its author was at Leeds, its usefulness was tested in the parish church schools there. It has since been enlarged and carefully revised, and will be found exceedingly well suited for the use of parents in giving religious instruction to their own children, as well as for teachers generally."—NATIONAL CHURCH.

"Sunday-school teachers and others engaged in the instruction of the young will find in its pages many useful suggestions."—ROCK.

A Help to Catechizing.

For the Use of Clergymen, Schools, and Private Families. By JAMES BEAVEN, D.D., formerly Professor of Divinity in the University of King's College, Toronto. New Edition. 18mo. 2s.

Catechetical Exercises on the Apostles'

Creed; chiefly from Bp. Pearson. By EDWARD BICKERSTETH, D.D., Dean of Lichfield. New Edition. 18mo. 2s.

Questions illustrating the Thirty-Nine

Articles of the Church of England, with Proofs from Holy Scripture, and the Primitive Church. By EDWARD BICKERSTETH, D.D., Dean of Lichfield. Sixth Edition. Small 8vo. 3s. 6d.

The Idle Word : Short Religious Essays

upon the Gift of Speech. By EDWARD MEYRICK GOULBURN, D.D., Dean of Norwich. Fourth Edition. Small 8vo. 3s.

CONTENTS.

The Connexion of Speech with Reason—The Connexion of Speech with Reason—The Heavenly Analogy of the Connexion of Speech with Reason—An Idle Word Defined from the Decalogue—An Idle Word defined from the Decalogue—What is an Idle Word?—Words of Business and innocent Recreation not Idle—Speech the Instrument of Prophecy and Sacrifice—Hints for the Guidance of Conversation—On Religious Conversation—Appendix.

A Manual of Confirmation, Comprising

—1. A General Account of the Ordinance. 2. The Baptismal Vow, and the English Order of Confirmation, with Short Notes, Critical and Devotional. 3. Meditations and Prayers on Passages of Holy Scripture, in connexion with the Ordinance. With a Pastoral Letter instructing Catechumens how to prepare themselves for their first Communion. By EDWARD MEYRICK GOULBURN, D.D., Dean of Norwich. Ninth Edition. Small 8vo. 1s. 6d.

Easy Lessons Addressed to Candidates

for Confirmation. By JOHN PILKINGTON NORRIS, B.D., Canon of Bristol, Vicar of St. Mary, Redcliffe, and Examining Chaplain to the Bishop of Manchester. Small 8vo. 1s. 6d.

"An admirable hand-book on confirmation. It is sound, scriptural, plain, and practical. It brings out only important points, and is not over-loaded with unessential things. Besides, it has the rare merit of being adapted to persons of varying ages."— CHURCHMAN (NEW YORK).

"Is so arranged as to convey the teaching of the Catechism to those who, from early disadvantages, are unable to commit it to memory. Earnest counsels are appended for the guidance of the confirmed in maturer years."— NATIONAL CHURCH.

"The Canon aims in the first nine lessons to transfuse the substance of the Catechism into a form which such persons could readily apprehend; and in this he has entirely succeeded. His little book, however, is equally well adapted for better educated candidates, whose interest in the time-honoured formula so often repeated will probably be stimulated afresh by the novelty of the arrangement. Canon Norris's explanations are thoroughly clear, and it is needless to say that his teaching is sound and moderate."— SCOTTISH GUARDIAN.

"A valuable little work, in which the principal points of the Church's teaching are clearly and fully set forth. The remarks on the Sacraments are exceedingly good, and although these 'Lessons' are primarily intended for those who are preparing for confirmation, they might with advantage be studied by those who, having passed this stage, are desirous of refreshing their memories respecting the doctrines they profess to believe."— ROCK.

Catechesis; or, Christian Instruction

preparatory to Confirmation and First Communion. By CHARLES WORDSWORTH, D.C.L., Bishop of St. Andrews. New Edition. Small 8vo. 2s.

8. Allegories and Tales.

Allegories and Tales. By the Rev. W. E. HEYGATE, M.A., Rector of Brighstone. Crown 8vo. 5s.

"It is eminently original, and every one of its sixty-three short allegories is a story that the dullest child will read and the intelligent child will understand and enjoy. Grave thought, kindly raillery, biting sarcasm, grim humour, sincere indignation, wise counsel, a broad charity, and other characteristics, run through the allegories, many of which are highly poetical and good models of that style of composition."—EDINBURGH COURANT.

"Mr. Heygate's volume contains about sixty short tales or allegories, all rife with good teaching, plainly set forth, and written in a very engaging and attractive style. As a present for children this book would be at once acceptable and beneficial. It can be highly commended."—CHURCH HERALD.

"There are both grace and precision about these 'Allegories and Tales,' which make them charming to read either for young or for old. The stories are some of them quaint, some of them picturesque, all of them pleasant; and the moral they inclose shines out soft and clear as through a crystal. This is a book that may be recommended for a present, not only for young people, but for those of larger growth."—ATHENÆUM.

"The Rector of Brighstone has the gift of writing moral and spiritual lessons for the young in the most attractive fashion. His 'Allegories and Tales' are excellent specimens of stories, with a moral, in which the moral is not obtrusive and yet is not lost."—ENGLISH INDEPENDENT.

"A book of very great beauty and power. Mr. Heygate is a thoughtful, earnest and able writer, on whom more than any one is fallen in a striking manner the mantle of the great author of 'Agathos.'"—JOHN BULL.

Sacred Allegories. The Shadow of the Cross—The Distant Hills—The Old Man's Home—The King's Messengers. By the Rev. WILLIAM ADAMS, M.A., late Fellow of Merton College, Oxford. New Edition. With numerous Illustrations. Crown 8vo. 5s.

The Four Allegories may be had separately, with Illustrations. 16mo. 1s. each.

The First Chronicle of Æscendune.

A Tale of the Days of Saint Dunstan. By the Rev. A. D. CRAKE, B.A., Author of the "History of the Church under the Roman Empire," &c. &c. Crown 8vo. 3*s.* 6*d.*

"*The volume will possess a strong interest, especially for the young, and be useful, too, for though in form a tale, it may be classed among ' the side-lights of history.'*"—STANDARD.

"*Altogether the book shows great thought and careful study of the manners and customs of those early Saxon times.*"—JOHN BULL.

"*We shall be glad when Mr. Crake takes up his pen once more, to give us a further instalment of the annals of the House of Æscendune.*"—CHURCH TIMES.

"*A very interesting and well-written story of Saxon times—the times of Dunstan and the hapless Edwy. The author has evidently taken great pains to examine into the real history of the period. We can scarcely imagine it possible that it should be anything else than a great favourite.*"—LITERARY CHURCHMAN.

"*It is one of the best historical tales for the young that has been published for a long time.*"—NONCONFORMIST.

"*Written with much spirit and a careful attention to the best authorities on the history of the period of which he treats.*"—NATIONAL CHURCH.

"*The facts upon which the Chronicle is based have been carefully brought together from a variety of sources, and great skill has been shown in the construction of the narrative. The aim of the author is certainly a good one, and his efforts have been attended with a considerable amount of success.*"—ROCK.

Alfgar the Dane, or the Second Chron-

icle of Æscendune. A Tale. By the Rev. A. D. CRAKE, B.A., Author of the "History of the Church under the Roman Empire," &c. &c. Crown 8vo. 3*s.* 6*d.*

"*Mr. Crake's 'Chronicles of Æscendune' have their second instalment in ' Alfgar the Dane,' a youth who is saved from the massacre on S. Brice's night to meet with many capital adventures.*"—GUARDIAN.

"*Sure to be excessively popular with boys, and we look forward with great interest to the Third Chronicle, which will tell of the Norman invasion.*"—CHURCH TIMES.

"*As in his former production, Mr. Crake seems to have taken great pains to be correct in his facts, and he has, we really believe, combined accuracy with liveliness. Schoolboys, not at Bloxham only, ought to be very grateful to him; though in thus speaking we by no means intend to imply that seniors will not find this little book both interesting and instructive. Its tone is as excellent as that of Mr. Crake's previous tale.*"—CHURCH QUARTERLY REVIEW.

"*Here, strung together with characters in harmony with the times, is a thoroughly well-written history of the later Danish invasions of England. . . . . As a tale his work is interesting; as a history it is of very considerable value.*"—NONCONFORMIST.

"*It is not often that a writer combines so completely the qualities which go to make up the historian and the novelist, but Mr. Crake has this happy conjunction of faculties in an eminent degree.*"—STANDARD.

Semele; or, The Spirit of Beauty: a
Venetian Tale. By the Rev. J. D. MEREWEATHER, B.A.
English Chaplain at Venice. Small 8vo. 3*s*. 6*d*.

The Hillford Confirmation.   A Tale.
By M. C. PHILLPOTTS. New Edition. 16mo. 1*s*.

9. History and Biography.

Bossuet and his Contemporaries.
By H. L. SIDNEY LEAR. Crown 8vo. 3*s*. 6*d*.

Forming a Volume of "Christian Biographies."

"It contains so many interesting facts that it may be profitably read even by those who already know the man and the period."—SPECTATOR.

"Here is a clear and good work, the product of thorough industry and of honest mind."—NONCONFORMIST.

"All biography is delightful, and this story of Bossuet is eminently so." —NOTES AND QUERIES.

"Bossuet's daily life, his style of preaching, his association with the stirring political, social, and ecclesiastical events of his time, are presented in a simple but picturesque way."— DAILY NEWS.

"We are always glad to welcome a fresh work from the graceful pen of the author of 'A Dominican Artist.'"— SATURDAY REVIEW.

Fénelon, Archbishop of Cambrai. A
Biographical Sketch. By H. L. SIDNEY LEAR. Crown 8vo. 3*s*. 6*d*.

Forming a Volume of "Christian Biographies."

"Those who know—and we may fairly ask, who does not?—the charming books which we have already had from the present writer, will need nothing more than the announcement of it to make them welcome this new account of the life of the saintly Fénelon." —CHURCH QUARTERLY REVIEW.

"The history of the Church offers few more attractive biographies than that of the great Archbishop, whom everybody appreciated save his king." —GUARDIAN.

"The delightful volume under notice will add much to the well-deserved reputation of its author."—CHURCH TIMES.

"The writer has found a subject which suits her genius, and she handles it with both skill and sympathy. . . . The account of his life at Cambrai is one of the most delightful narratives that we have ever read. It would be scarcely too much to extend the same praise to the whole book."—SPECTATOR.

"Fénelon is thoroughly readable, and is much more than a biographical sketch. There are nearly 500 pages, and there are very few which fail to give a reader something for glad or serious thought."—NOTES AND QUERIES.

"We doubt much whether the real man was ever so vividly portrayed or his portrait so elegantly framed as in this choice and readable book."— WATCHMAN.

"One of the great charms of this work consists in the letters scattered up and down its pages, some addressed to his royal pupil, and others to his friends. The sweet nature and singular fascination of the Archbishop shine forth conspicuously in these self-revelations, which breathe a truly religious spirit."—ENGLISH INDEPENDENT.

---

and at Oxford and Cambridge

A Christian Painter of the Nineteenth

Century; being the Life of Hippolyte Flandrin. By H. L.
SIDNEY LEAR. Crown 8vo. 3s. 6d.

Forming a Volume of "Christian Biographies."

"*This is a touching and instructive story of a life singularly full of nobility, affection, and grace, and it is worthily told.*"—SPECTATOR.

"*Sympathetic, popular, and free, almost to a fault, from technicalities. . . . The book is welcome as a not untimely memorial to a man who deserves to be held up as an example.*"—SATURDAY REVIEW.

"*The record of a life marked by exalted aims, and crowned by no small* amount of honour and success, cannot but be welcome to earnest students of all kinds. . . . There are many fine pieces of criticism in this book,—utterances of Flandrin's which show the clear wit of the man, his candour, and self-balanced judgment. . . . . We have written enough to show how interesting the book is.*"—ATHENÆUM.

"*This is a charming addition to biographical literature.*"—NOTES AND QUERIES.

A Dominican Artist: A Sketch of the

Life of the Rev. Père Besson, of the Order of St. Dominic.
By H. L. SIDNEY LEAR. Crown 8vo. 3s. 6d.

Forming a Volume of "Christian Biographies."

"*The author of the Life of Père Besson writes with a grace and refinement of devotional feeling peculiarly suited to a subject-matter which suffers beyond most others from any coarseness of touch. It would be difficult to find ' the simplicity and purity of a holy life' more exquisitely illustrated than in Father Besson's career, both before and after his joining the Dominican Order under the auspices of Lacordaire. . . . Certainly we have never come across what could more strictly be termed in the truest sense ' the life of a beautiful soul.' The author has done well in presenting to English readers this singularly graceful biography, in which all who can appreciate genuine simplicity and nobleness of Christian character will find much to admire and little or nothing to condemn.*"—SATURDAY REVIEW.

"*It would indeed have been a deplorable omission had so exquisite a biography been by any neglect lost to English readers, and had a character* so perfect in its simple and complete devotion been withheld from our admiration. . . . . But we have dwelt too long already on this fascinating book, and must now leave it to our readers.*"—LITERARY CHURCHMAN.

"*A beautiful and most interesting sketch of the late Père Besson, an artist who forsook the easel for the altar.*"—CHURCH TIMES.

"*Whatever a reader may think of Père Besson's profession as a monk, no one will doubt his goodness; no one can fail to profit who will patiently read his life, as here written by a friend, whose sole defect is in being slightly unctuous.*"—ATHENÆUM.

"*The story of Père Besson's life is one of much interest, and told with simplicity, candour, and good feeling.*"—SPECTATOR.

"*We strongly recommend it to our readers. It is a charming biography, that will delight and edify both old and young.*"—WESTMINSTER GAZETTE.

The Life of Madame Louise de France,

Daughter of Louis XV., also known as the Mother Térèse de S. Augustin. By H. L. SIDNEY LEAR. Crown 8vo. 3s. 6d.

Forming a Volume of "Christian Biographies."

*" Such a record of deep, earnest, self-sacrificing piety, beneath the surface of Parisian life, during what we all regard as the worst age of French godlessness, ought to teach us all a lesson of hope and faith, let appearances be what they may. Here, from out of the court and family of Louis XV. there issues this Madame Louise, whose life is set before us as a specimen of as calm and unworldly devotion—of a devotion, too, full of shrewd sense and practical administrative talent—as any we have ever met with."—*LITERARY CHURCHMAN.

The Revival of Priestly Life in the

Seventeenth Century in France. CHARLES DE CONDREN—S. PHILIP NERI and CARDINAL DE BERULLE—S. VINCENT DE PAUL — SAINT SULPICE and JEAN JACQUES OLIER. By H. L. SIDNEY LEAR. Crown 8vo. 3s. 6d.

Forming a Volume of "Christian Biographies."

*" A book the authorship of which will command the respect of all who can honour sterling worth. No Christian, to whatever denomination he may belong, can read without quick sympathy and emotion these touching sketches of the early Oratorians and the Lazarists."—*STANDARD.

Life of S. Francis de Sales. By H. L.

SIDNEY LEAR. Crown 8vo. 3s. 6d.

Forming a Volume of "Christian Biographies."

*" It is written with the delicacy, freshness, and absence of all affectation which characterized the former works by the same hand, and which render these books so very much more pleasant reading than are religious biographies in general. The character of S. Francis de Sales, Bishop of Geneva, is a charming one. His unaffected humility, his freedom from dogmatism in an age when dogma was placed above religion, his freedom from bigotry in an age of persecution, were alike admirable."—*STANDARD.

*" The author of ' A Dominican Artist,' in writing this new life of the wise and loving Bishop and Prince of Geneva, has aimed less at historical or ecclesiastical investigation than at a vivid and natural representation of the inner mind and life of the subject of his biography, as it can be traced in his own writings and in those of his most intimate and affectionate friends. The book is written with the grave and quiet grace which characterizes the productions of its author, and cannot fail to please those readers who can sympathize with all forms of goodness and devotion to noble purpose."—*WESTMINSTER REVIEW.

*" A book which contains the record of a life as sweet, pure, and noble, as any man by divine help, granted to devout sincerity of soul, has been permitted to live upon earth. The example of this gentle but resolute and energetic spirit, wholly dedicated to the highest conceivable good, offering itself, with all the temporal uses of mental existence, to the service of infinite and eternal beneficence, is extremely touching. It is a book worthy of acceptance."—*DAILY NEWS.

Henri Perreyve. By A. GRATRY, Prêtre

de l'Oratoire, Professeur de Morale Evangélique à la Sorbonne, et Membre de l'Académie Française. Translated by special permission. With Portrait. By H. L. SIDNEY LEAR. Crown 8vo. 3*s.* 6*d.*

Forming a Volume of "Christian Biographies."

"A most touching and powerful piece of biography, interspersed with profound reflections on personal religion, and on the prospects of Christianity."—CHURCH REVIEW.

"The works of the translator of Henri Perreyve form, for the most part, a series of saintly biographies which have obtained a larger share of popularity than is generally accorded to books of this description. . . . The description of his last days will probably be read with greater interest than any other part of the book; presenting as it does an example of fortitude under suffering, and resignation, when cut off so soon after entering upon a much-coveted and useful career, of rare occurrence in this age of self-assertion. This is, in fact, the essential teaching of the entire volume."—MORNING POST.

"Those who take a pleasure in reading a beautiful account of a beautiful character would do well to procure the Life of 'Henri Perreyve.' . . . . We would especially recommend the book for the perusal of English priests, who may learn many a holy lesson from the devoted spirit in which the subject of the memoir gave himself up to the duties of his sacred office, and to the cultivation of the graces with which he was endowed."—CHURCH TIMES.

"It is easy to see that Henri Perreyve, Professor of Moral Theology at the Sorbonne, was a Roman Catholic priest of no ordinary type. With comparatively little of what Protestants call superstition, with great courage and sincerity, with a nature singularly guileless and noble, his priestly vocation, although pursued, according to his biographer, with unbridled zeal, did not stifle his human sympathies and aspirations. He could not believe that his faith compelled him 'to renounce sense and reason,' or that a priest was not free to speak, act, and think like other men. Indeed, the Abbé Gratry makes a kind of apology for his friend's free-speaking in this respect, and endeavours to explain it. Perreyve was the beloved disciple of Lacordaire, who left him all his manuscripts, notes, and papers, and he himself attained the position of a great pulpit orator."—PALL MALL GAZETTE.

The Last Days of Père Gratry. By PÈRE

ADOLPHE PERRAUD, of the Oratory, and Professor of La Sorbonne. Translated by special permission. By the Author of "Life of S. Francis de Sales," &c. Crown 8vo. 3*s.* 6*d.*

Walter Kerr Hamilton, Bishop of Salis-

bury. A Sketch by HENRY PARRY LIDDON, D.D., Canon of St. Paul's, and Ireland Professor of Exegesis in the University of Oxford. Second Edition. 8vo. 2*s.* 6*d.*

Life of S. Vincent de Paul. With Introduction by the Rev. R. F. WILSON, M.A., Prebendary of Salisbury and Vicar of Rownhams, and Chaplain to the Bishop of Salisbury. Crown 8vo. 9s.

"*A most readable volume, illustrating plans and arrangements, which from the circumstances of the day are invested with peculiar interest.*"—ENGLISH CHURCHMAN.

"*All will be pleased at reading the present admirably written narrative, in which we do not know whether to admire more the candour and earnestness of the writer or his plain, sensible, and agreeable style.*"—WEEKLY REGISTER.

"*We trust that this deeply interesting and beautifully written biography will be extensively circulated in England.*"—CHURCH HERALD.

"*We heartily recommend the introduction to the study of all concerned with ordinations.*"—GUARDIAN.

"*We are glad that S. Vincent de Paul, one of the most remarkable men produced by the Gallican Church, has at last found a competent English biographer. The volume before us has evidently been written with conscientious care and scrupulous industry. It is based on the best authorities, which have been compared with praiseworthy diligence; its style is clear, elegant, and unambitious; and it shows a fine appreciation of the life and character of the man whom it commemorates.*"—SCOTTISH GUARDIAN.

"*Mr. Wilson has done his work admirably and evidently* con amore, *and he completely proves the thesis with which he starts, viz., that in the life of the Saint there is a homeliness and simplicity, and a general absence of the miraculous or the more ascetic type of saintliness.*"—JOHN BULL.

Life of Robert Gray, Bishop of Cape Town and Metropolitan of the Province of South Africa. Edited by his Son, the Rev. CHARLES GRAY, M.A., Vicar of Helmsley, York. With Portrait and Map. 2 Vols. 8vo. 32s.

"*This work is more than a biography; it is a valuable addition to the history of the nineteenth century. Mr. Keble more than once described Bishop Gray's struggles as 'like a bit out of the fourth century.'*"—GUARDIAN.

"*We welcome it as a worthy tribute to the memory of one who possessed the true apostolic spirit, was a faithful son of the Church, and a distinguished ornament of the Episcopate.*"—STANDARD.

"*Not only interesting as the record of a good man's life, but extremely valuable as materials for Church history.*"—CHURCH TIMES.

Life, Journals, and Letters of Henry ALFORD, D.D., late Dean of Canterbury. Edited by his WIDOW. With Portrait and Illustrations. New Edition. Crown 8vo. 9s.

History of the Church under the

Roman Empire, A.D. 30-476. By the Rev. A. D. CRAKE, B.A. New Edition. Crown 8vo. 7s. 6d.

*"A compendious history of the Christian Church under the Roman Empire will be hailed with pleasure by all readers of ecclesiastical lore. . . . The author is quite free from the spirit of controversialism; wherever he refers to a prevalent practice of ancient times he gives his authority. In his statement of facts or opinions he is always accurate and concise, and his manual is doubtless destined to a lengthened period of popularity."—*MORNING POST.

*"It is very well done. It gives a very comprehensive view of the progress of events, ecclesiastical and political, at the great centres of civilisation during the first five centuries of Christianity."—*DAILY NEWS.

*"In his well-planned and carefully written volume of 500 pages Mr. Crake has supplied a well-known and long-felt want. Relying on all the highest and best authorities for his main facts and conclusions, and wisely making use of all modern research, Mr. Crake has spared neither time nor labour to make his work accurate, trustworthy, and intelligent."—*STANDARD.

*"Really interesting, well suited to the needs of those for whom it was prepared, and its Church tone is unexceptionable."—*CHURCH TIMES.

*"As a volume for students and the higher forms of our public schools it is admirably adapted."—*CHURCH HERALD.

*"We cordially recommend it for schools for the young."—*ENGLISH CHURCHMAN.

*"Mr. Crake gives us in a clear and concise form a narrative of the Church history during the period with which it is most important that the young should first be made acquainted. The different events appear to be described with a judicious regard to their relative importance, and the manual may be safely recommended."—*JOHN BULL.

*"The facts are well marshalled, the literary style of the book is simple and good; while the principles enunciated throughout render it a volume which may be safely put into the hands of students. For the higher forms of grammar-schools it is exactly the book required. Never ponderous, and frequently very attractive and interesting, it is at once readable and edifying, and fills efficiently a vacant place in elementary historical literature. Furthermore its type is clear and bold, and it is well broken up into paragraphs."—*UNION REVIEW.

*"It retells an oft-told tale in a singularly fresh and perspicuous style, rendering the book neither above the comprehension of an intelligent boy or girl of fourteen or upwards, nor beneath the attention of an educated man. We can imagine no better book as an addition to a parochial library, as a prize, or as a reading book in the upper forms of middle-class schools."—*SCOTTISH GUARDIAN.

Church Memorials and Characteristics;

being a Church History of the six First Centuries. By the late WILLIAM ROBERTS, Esq., M.A., F.R.S. Edited by his Son, ARTHUR ROBERTS, M.A., Rector of Woodrising, Norfolk. 8vo. 7s. 6d.

Essays, Historical and Theological.

By J. B. MOZLEY, D.D., late Canon of Christ Church, and Regius Professor of Divinity in the University of Oxford. Two Vols. 8vo. 24*s*.

CONTENTS.

Volume I.—Introduction and Memoir of the Author—Lord Strafford—Archbishop Laud—Carlyle's Cromwell—Luther.

Volume II.—Dr. Arnold—Blancho White—Dr. Pusey's Sermon—The Book of Job—Maurice's Theological Essays—Indian Conversion—The Argument of Design—The Principle of Causation considered in Opposition to Atheistic Theories—In Memoriam—List of the Author's Articles and Works.

"*These volumes, we cannot doubt, will be eagerly welcomed and largely read. They contain specimens, well selected, and extending over a period of thirty years, of the work of a great mind; the real greatness of which was, indeed, well known to all students of theology. . . . We trace in every page the handwriting of a mind which, though it may look with keen interest on all the varying movements of thought, in days past and present, and though it can handle with the grasp of a master any form of thought with which it comes to deal, yet is evidently a mind of deep, quiet reflection, facing alone before God the great questions of Truth and Being, 'brooding' over them (to use his own expression) until they take definite shape, never suffering them to come forth in the shape of that crude suggestion and hazy speculation so fashionable in these days, which touch many truths without really grasping them, and raise many questions but thoroughly answer none. . . . We hope we have said enough to give our readers some idea of these remarkable volumes, and to induce them to study them as a whole. Many other features might fairly claim notice; but these may be left to speak for themselves. As we read, we grieve more and more that it has pleased God to call from us so able a champion of His truth, and one hardly more impressive by the strength of his argument than by 'the quietness and confidence' of his spirit.*"—GUARDIAN.

"*We have said enough, we trust, to induce our readers to study these volumes for themselves. They will find in them much that will bear, not one, but many perusals.*"—SATURDAY REVIEW

"*These essays will be welcome even beyond the circle of those who, during his lifetime, had any knowledge of, or acquaintance with, their author. They are the products of a lucid, comprehensive, and powerful mind; the mind of one who was a student and a thinker, but who, by his vivid grasps of ideas, his firm faith in the principles he had made his own, and his faculty of impressive illustration, had much of the facility which is usually acquired only in the actual experience of the world.*"—BRITISH QUARTERLY REVIEW.

"*Selected from the earliest as well as the latest of Dr. Mozley's writings, this collection represents not only the full extent of his mental powers, but also the course and ultimate issue of his intellectual career; for as it was by tenacity of purpose and determination of will that he obtained for his opinions recognition and esteem, so also, owing to his argumentative tenacity and intensity of aim, some of these essays, if the prophecy may be hazarded, will retain a lasting place in literature.*"—ATHENÆUM.

"*These Essays stand above the line of ephemeral literature. For the more experienced student of history it would be difficult to name a more positively refreshing book. Dr. Mozley was a hard hitter, and few writers have been able to strike so decisively on the weak points of an adversary's case.*"—CONTEMPORARY REVIEW.

---

and at Oxford and Cambridge

A Key to the Knowledge of Church

History (Ancient). Edited by the Rev. JOHN HENRY BLUNT, M.A., F.S.A., Editor of "The Annotated Book of Common Prayer," &c. &c. Small 8vo. 2*s.* 6*d.* Also a Cheap Edition, 1*s.* 6*d.*

Forming a Volume of "Keys to Christian Knowledge."

"It offers a short and condensed account of the origin, growth, and condition of the Church in all parts of the world, from A.D. 1 *down to the end of the fifteenth century. Mr. Blunt's first object has been conciseness, and this has been admirably carried out, and to students of Church history this feature will readily recommend itself. As an elementary work 'A Key' will be specially valuable, inasmuch as it points out certain definite lines of thought, by which those who enjoy the opportunity may be guided in reading the statements of more elaborate histories. At the same time it is but fair to Mr. Blunt to remark that, for general readers, the little volume contains everything that could be consistently expected in a volume of its character. There are many notes, theological, scriptural, and historical, and the 'get up' of the book is specially commendable. As a text-book for the higher forms of schools the work will be acceptable to numerous teachers."—* PUBLIC OPINION.

"It contains some concise notes on Church History, compressed into a small compass, and we think it is likely to be useful as a book of reference."— JOHN BULL.

"A very terse and reliable collection of the main facts and incidents connected with Church History."— ROCK.

A Key to the Knowledge of Church

History (Modern). Edited by the Rev. JOHN HENRY BLUNT, M.A., F.S.A., Editor of "The Annotated Book of Common Prayer," &c. &c. Small 8vo. 2*s.* 6*d.* Also a Cheap Edition, 1*s.* 6*d.*

Forming a Volume of "Keys to Christian Knowledge."

The Reformation of the Church of

England; its History, Principles, and Results. A.D. 1514-1547. By the Rev. JOHN HENRY BLUNT, M.A., F.S.A., Editor of "The Annotated Book of Common Prayer," &c. &c. Fourth Edition. 8vo. 16*s.*

Perranzabuloe, the Lost Church Found;

or, The Church of England not a New Church, but Ancient, Apostolical, and Independent, and a Protesting Church Nine Hundred Years before the Reformation. By the Rev. C. T. COLLINS TRELAWNY, M.A., late Rector of Timsbury, Somerset. New Edition. Crown 8vo. 3*s.* 6*d.*

The Principles of Catholic Reform;

or, The Harmony of Catholicism and Civilization. Conferences of 1878 in the Cirque d'Hiver, Paris. By HYACINTHE LOYSON, Priest. Translated by LADY DURAND. Crown 8vo, 3s. 6d.; or in paper cover, 3s.

The Life of Alexander Lycurgus,

Archbishop of the Cyclades. By F. M. F. SKENE. With an Introduction by the BISHOP OF LINCOLN. Crown 8vo. 3s. 6d.; or in paper cover, 3s.

Historical Narratives. From the Russian.

By H. C. ROMANOFF, Author of "Sketches of the Rites and Customs of the Greco-Russian Church," &c. Crown 8vo. 6s.

Sketches of the Rites and Customs of

the Greco-Russian Church. By H. C. ROMANOFF. With an Introductory Notice by the Author of "The Heir of Redclyffe." Second Edition. Crown 8vo. 7s. 6d.

"The volume before us is anything but a formal liturgical treatise. It might be more valuable to a few scholars if it were, but it would certainly fail to obtain perusal at the hands of the great majority of those whom the writer, not unreasonably, hopes to attract by the narrative style she has adopted. What she has set before us is a series of brief outlines, which, by their simple effort to clothe the information given us in a living garb, reminds us of a once-popular child's book which we remember a generation ago, called 'Sketches of Human Manners.'"—CHURCH TIMES.

"The twofold object of this work is 'to present the English with correct descriptions of the ceremonies of the Greco-Russian Church, and at the same time with pictures of domestic life in Russian homes, especially those of the clergy and the middle class of nobles;' and, beyond question, the author's labour has been so far successful that, whilst her Church scenes may be commended as a series of most dramatic and picturesque tableaux, her social sketches enable us to look at certain points beneath the surface of Russian life, and materially enlarge our knowledge of a country concerning which we have still a very great deal to learn."—ATHENÆUM.

Curious Myths of the Middle Ages.

By S. BARING-GOULD, M.A., Author of "Origin and Development of Religious Belief," &c. With Illustrations. New Edition. Crown 8vo. 6s.

Hellenica. A Collection of Essays on

Greek Poetry, Philosophy, History, and Religion. Edited by
EVELYN ABBOTT, M.A., LL.D., Fellow and Tutor of Balliol
College, Oxford. 8vo. 16*s*.

CONTENTS.

Aeschylus. E. Myers, M.A.—The Theology and Ethics of Sophocles. E.
Abbott, M.A., LL.D.—System of Education in Plato's Republics. R. L.
Nettleship, M.A.—Aristotle's Conception of the State. A. C. Bradley,
M.A.—Epicurus. W. L. Courtney, M.A.—The Speeches of Thucydides.
R. C. Jebb, M.A., LL.D.—Xenophon. H. G. Dakyns, M.A.—Polybius
J. L. S. Davidson, M.A.—Greek Oracles. F. W. H. Myers, M.A.

[See RIVINGTON'S EDUCATIONAL LIST.]

The Antiquities of Greece. Translated

from the German of G. F. SCHOEMANN. By E. G. HARDY,
M.A., Head-Master of the Grammar School, Grantham, and
late Fellow of Jesus College, Oxford ; and J. S. MANN, M.A.,
Fellow of Trinity College, Oxford. 8vo. 18*s*.

VOL. I.—THE STATE.

[See RIVINGTON'S EDUCATIONAL LIST.]

Historical Biographies. Edited by the

Rev. M. CREIGHTON, M.A., late Fellow of Merton College,
Oxford. With Maps. Small 8vo.

SIMON DE MONTFORT. 2*s*. 6*d*.

THE BLACK PRINCE. 2*s*. 6*d*.

SIR WALTER RALEGH. 3*s*.

THE DUKE OF WELLINGTON. 3*s*. 6*d*.

THE DUKE OF MARLBOROUGH. 3*s*. 6*d*.

[See RIVINGTON'S EDUCATIONAL LIST.]

A History of England.   By the Rev.

J. FRANCK BRIGHT, M.A., Fellow of University College, and Historical Lecturer in Balliol, New, and University Colleges, Oxford; late Master of the Modern School in Marlborough College. With Numerous Maps and Plans. New Editions, Crown 8vo.

> PERIOD I.—FEUDAL MONARCHY. The Departure of the Romans, to Richard III. A.D. 449-1485. 4*s*. 6*d*.
>
> PERIOD II.—PERSONAL MONARCHY. Henry VII. to James II. A.D. 1485-1688. 5*s*.
>
> PERIOD III.—CONSTITUTIONAL MONARCHY. William and Mary, to the present time. A.D. 1689-1837. 7*s*. 6*d*.
>
> [See RIVINGTON'S EDUCATIONAL LIST.]

A History of England for Children.

By GEORGE DAVYS, D.D., formerly Bishop of Peterborough. New Edition. 18mo. 1*s*. 6*d*.

Fables respecting the Popes of the

Middle Ages. A Contribution to Ecclesiastical History. By JOHN J. IGN. VON DÖLLINGER, D.D., D.C.L. Translated by the Rev. ALFRED PLUMMER, M.A., Master of University College, Durham, late Fellow of Trinity College, Oxford. 8vo. 14*s*.

The Annual Register: a Review of Public

Events at Home and Abroad, for the Years 1863 to 1879. New Series. 8vo. 18*s*. each.

10. Miscellaneous.

Lyra Apostolica. [Poems, by J. W.
Bowden, R. H. Froude, J. Keble, J. H. Newman, R. J. Wilberforce, and J. Williams; and a New Preface by Cardinal Newman.] New Edition. 16mo. Red borders. 2s. 6d.

Yesterday, To-Day, and for Ever: A
Poem in Twelve Books. By Edward Henry Bickersteth, M.A., Vicar of Christ Church, Hampstead. One Shilling Edition, 18mo; 16mo, with Red Borders, 2s. 6d.

Forming Volumes of "Rivington's Devotional Series."

The small 8vo Edition, 3s. 6d.; and small 4to Presentation Edition, with Red Borders, 10s. 6d., may still be had.

*"We should have noticed among its kind a very magnificent presentation edition of 'Yesterday, To-day, and for Ever,' by the Rev. E. H. Bickersteth. This blank-verse poem, in twelve books, has made its way into the religious world of England and America without much help from the critics. It is now made splendid for its admirers by morocco binding, broad margins, red lines, and beautiful photographs."—*Times.

*"The most simple, the richest, and the most perfect sacred poem which recent days have produced."—*Morning Advertiser.

*"A poem worth reading, worthy of attentive study; full of noble thoughts, beautiful diction, and high imagination."—*Standard.

*"In these light miscellany days there is a spiritual refreshment in the spectacle of a man girding up the loins of his mind to the task of producing a genuine epic. And it is true poetry. There is a definiteness, a crispness about it, which in these moist, viewy, hazy days is no less invigorating than novel."—*Edinburgh Daily Review.

*"Mr. Bickersteth writes like a man who cultivates at once reverence and earnestness of thought."—*Guardian.

The Two Brothers, and other Poems. By
Edward Henry Bickersteth, M.A., Vicar of Christ Church, Hampstead. Second Edition. Small 8vo. 6s.

Waterloo Place, London

The Knight of Intercession, and other

Poems. By the Rev. S. J. STONE, M.A., Pembroke College, Oxford. Fourth Edition. Crown 8vo. 6s.

An Introduction to the Study of

Painted Glass. By A. A. Crown 8vo. 2s. 6d.

" *This modest little book, by a very modest author, though little more than a compilation, is sensibly and simply arranged and very carefully written. To those who have not time or opportunity to make a thorough study of the larger works on the subject, and yet wish to be able to take an intelligent interest in the windows of the churches they may see on their travels, it will prove a very valuable* vade-mecum. *The characteristics of the different periods of glass-painting are clearly and shortly noted, and a sufficient account is given of the most remarkable examples of each style. . . . We are bound to say that the sound remarks scattered through the book on the principles of the art will be of much use to the student in forming a correct judgment as to the merit of any window he may see."—* ACADEMY.

" *A little volume not intended to supersede the larger works on the same subject in great art libraries, but as a brief historical introduction decidedly most valuable."—* GRAPHIC.

An Introduction to Form and Instru-

mentation, for the Use of Beginners in Composition. By W. A. BARRETT, Mus. Bac. Oxon., F.R.S.L., Vicar-Choral of St. Paul's Cathedral, Author of "Flowers and Festivals," "The Chorister's Guide," etc. Crown 8vo. 2s. 6d.

A Shadow of Dante. Being an Essay

towards studying Himself, his World, and his Pilgrimage. By MARIA FRANCESCA ROSSETTI. With Illustrations. Second Edition. Crown 8vo. 10s. 6d.

" *We find the volume furnished with useful diagrams of the Dantesque universe, of Hell, Purgatory, and the ' Rose of the Blessed,' and adorned with a beautiful group of the likenesses of the poet, and with symbolic figures (on the binding) in which the taste and execution of Mr. D. G. Rossetti will be recognised. The exposition appears to us remarkably well arranged and digested; the author's appreciation of Dante's religious sentiments and opinions is peculiarly hearty, and her style refreshingly independent and original."—* PALL MALL GAZETTE.

" *The result has been a book which is not only delightful in itself to read, but is admirably adapted as an encouragement to those students who wish to obtain a preliminary survey of the land before they attempt to follow Dante through his long and arduous pilgrimage. Of all poets Dante stands most in need of such assistance as this book offers."—* SATURDAY REVIEW.

Parish Musings; or, Devotional Poems.

By JOHN S. B. MONSELL, LL.D., late Vicar of S. Nicholas, Guildford, and Rural Dean. New Edition. Small 8vo. 5*s*.
Also a Cheap Edition. Cloth limp, 1*s*. 6*d*. ; or in paper cover, 1*s*.

A Reverie, and other Poems. By H.

A. FENTON, M.A. Imperial 16mo. 3*s*. 6*d*.

Miscellaneous Poems. By HENRY

FRANCIS LYTE, M.A. New Edition. Small 8vo. 5*s*.

A Dictionary of English Philosophical

Terms. By the Rev. FRANCIS GARDEN, M.A., Professor of Theology and Rhetoric at Queen's College, London, and Sub-Dean of Her Majesty's Chapels-Royal. Small 8vo. 4*s*. 6*d*.

At Home and Abroad; or, First Lessons

in Geography. By J. K. LAUGHTON, M.A., F.R.A.S., F.R.G.S., Mathematical Instructor and Lecturer in Meteorology at the Royal Naval College. Crown 8vo. 3*s*. 6*d*.

Mazzaroth; or, the Constellations. By

FRANCES ROLLESTON. Royal 8vo. 12*s*.

The Testimony of the Stars to Truths

revealed in the Bible. Abridged from the late Miss FRANCES ROLLESTON's "Mazzaroth; or, The Constellations." By CAROLINE DENT. Crown 8vo. 1*s*. 6*d*.

A Life Record; or, The Godparent's

Gift-Book. Printed on Dutch hand-made paper. Square 16mo. Cloth gilt, 3s. 6d. ; or in white cloth gilt, extra, 4s. 6d.

The Authorship of the "De Imita-

tione Christi." With many interesting particulars about the Book. By SAMUEL KETTLEWELL, M.A., late Vicar of St. Mark's, Leeds. Containing Photographic Engravings of the "De Imitatione" written by Thomas à Kempis, 1441, and of two other MSS. 8vo. 14s.

The Origin and Development of Reli-

gious Belief. By the Rev. S. BARING-GOULD, M.A., Author of "Curious Myths of the Middle Ages," &c. New Edition. Two Parts. Crown 8vo. 6s. each. Sold separately.

Part I. MONOTHEISM and POLYTHEISM.
Part II. CHRISTIANITY.

" The ability which Mr. Baring-Gould displays in the treatment of a topic which branches out in so many directions, and requires such precise handling, is apparent. His pages abound with the results of large reading and calm reflection. The man of culture, thought, philosophic cast, is mirrored in the entire argument. The book is sound and healthy in tone. It excites the reader's interest, and brightens the path of inquiry opened to his view. The language, too, is appropriate, neat, lucid, often happy, sometimes wonderfully terse and vigorous." —ATHENÆUM.

" Mr. Baring-Gould has undertaken a great and ambitious work. And no one can deny that he possesses some eminent qualifications for this great work. He has a wealth of erudition of the most varied description, especially in those particular regions of *mediæval legend and Teutonic mythology which are certain to make large contributions to the purpose he has in hand. It is a contribution of very high value."* —GUARDIAN.

" Mr. Baring-Gould's work, from the importance of its subject and the lucid force of its expositions, as well as from the closeness of argument and copiousness of illustration with which its comprehensive views are treated, is entitled to attentive study, and will repay the reader by amusement and instruction." —MORNING POST.

" Our space warns us that we are attempting in vain to compress into a few columns the contents of a work which has had few equals for brilliancy, learning, and point in this department of literature. We therefore conclude by recommending the volume itself to all students of mind and theology." —CHURCH TIMES.

Rivington's Devotional Series.

IN ELEGANT BINDINGS, SUITABLE FOR PRESENTS.

"TO many persons there is something repulsive in a devotional volume unbound, and Messrs. Rivington have now turned their attention to the binding of their Devotional Library in forms that, like the books themselves, are neat, handsome, good, and attractive."—*The Bookseller*.

The Christian Year.

16MO.   ELEGANTLY PRINTED WITH RED BORDERS.

	£	s.	d.
CALF *or* MOROCCO *limp, blind tooled*	0	5	0
THE SAME, ILLUSTRATED WITH STEEL ENGRAVINGS .	0	6	6
THE SAME, ILLUSTRATED WITH A CHOICE SELECTION OF PHOTOGRAPHS	0	9	0
MOROCCO *superior*	0	6	6
RUSSIA *limp, gilt cross*	0	8	6
RUSSIA *limp, gilt lines and gilt cross*, ILLUSTRATED WITH A CHOICE SELECTION OF PHOTOGRAPHS . . .	0	12	6
TURKEY MOROCCO, *limp circuit*	0	7	6
RUSSIA, *limp circuit*	0	9	0

The Christian Year.

CHEAP EDITION, WITHOUT THE RED BORDERS.

	£	s.	d.
FRENCH ROAN, *red inlaid or gilt outline cross* . .	0	1	6
THE SAME, ILLUSTRATED WITH STEEL ENGRAVINGS .	0	2	6
FRENCH MOROCCO, *gilt extra*	0	2	0

The Imitation of Christ is also kept in the above-mentioned styles at the same prices.

The other Volumes of "The Devotional Series," viz.:—

Chilcot's Evil Thoughts	**De Sales' Devout Life**
Devotional Birthday Book	**Taylor's Holy Living**
Herbert's English Poems	**Taylor's Holy Dying**
and Proverbs	**Wilson's Lord's Supper**

Yesterday, To-Day, and for Ever

Can also be had in a variety of elegant bindings.

Waterloo Place, London

Index.

www.ingramcontent.com/pod-product-compliance
Lightning Source LLC
Chambersburg PA
CBHW051126120726
47905CB00005B/1436